The Legends of Regia

LIGHTNING FLOWER

A NOVEL

Tenaya Jayne

COLD FIRE PUBLISHING LLC

Other titles by Tenaya Jayne

Noble Daughters

Forbidden Forest

Forest Fire

Verdant

Dark Soul

Burning Bridges

Blood Lock

ISBN-10:0-9986741-0-9

ISBN-13:978-0-9986741-0-0

Cover Art created by Erika Doucesse

Edited by Amanda Fiske & Valerie Hatfield

Proofread by Ally Robertson

COLD FIRE PUBLISHING, LLC

PROLOGUE

I am Tesla... but I cannot speak my name aloud. Technically, I am only two years old, but inside I am infinite, ageless. I have two loving parents, but I am alone. Like an island in the sea. There is no one else like me. I am totally, uncontested, and damnably unique. My body is the distilled perfection of pain. Even in my mother's womb, before I took my first breath, there was pain. Don't scoff, I remember it.

How can it be that I am the merging of two people, and be so different from them? The poison that entered my mother invaded me. Poison and magic became reactive agents that twisted me before I was born. So, I am screwed up, probably more than anyone else you've ever met. They tell me I'm beautiful, but when I look at my reflection, all I see is the chaos of the tempest of magic inside me. My skin is the paint. I am the portrait of agony.

No one sees what I see. Their eyes only perceive the surface. Even those who can see the layers and use them, my grandfather, my friend Merhl, even they cannot see past the second atmosphere. They don't know about the currents and moods of the dark elements. They have never felt the wind in the dangerous grey of the Everpath. I walk alone through maps of other worlds. Searching for the answer... Hunting the last puzzle piece to make my machine of safety impenetrable.

I carry Regia on my back. If I fail... we all die.

CHAPTER ONE

The ground under Tesla's feet was neither solid nor liquid, and she lost her balance as she ran. Crying out in pain, she went down on one knee as an arrow coated in foreign poison sank deep into her shoulder. The army behind rushed closer, more arrows flew around her. She had to get out. She had to find the door. The toxin on the arrow was already making her head swim. She grabbed a handful of the alien ground and shoved it into her pocket. *Focus, focus...* She took a deep breath. She didn't have time to find the door she snuck through into this world, more arrows whistled past her. She would be hit again if she didn't get out now. There was no choice; she would have to punch through the wall.

The bones of her fingers rattled as she shoved her hands through the atmosphere and tore it open. Blinding light stabbed her eyes as the wind of the Everpath wrapped around her and pulled her into its cold grey nothingness. Her heart thundered, sweat poured down her back, and she was on the verge of hyperventilating if she didn't ease her breathing.

She quickly looked down one side, and then the other, of the endless hallway in that dangerous place that was nowhere. She was alone. Nausea churned in her stomach as the poison continued to invade her blood. She reached around and grabbed the arrow, but it was at the worst possible angle. She let go of it, realizing what she would have to do.

Damn. This little mishap was going to blow her cover. At least partly.

She walked down the row of doors to the one she needed and opened it. Sickness, like she had never felt before, hit her hard as she landed in the *Rune-dy's* headquarters. The antechamber was empty. Rahaxeris was probably asleep, seeing as it was the middle of the night.

Tesla's vision doubled, and she fell forward, onto the table. She cried out in her odd way, unable to form actual words.

The cold, sharp hands of her grandfather on her back sent relief all through her. He spoke in an urgent tone, asking her no doubt what had happened, but she couldn't make out the words over the ringing in her ears. He lifted her up as she fell into unconsciousness.

Tesla woke abruptly on a jolt of adrenaline. She was in a bed. Whatever she'd been suffering from was gone. Her blood was clean, the wound closed. She sat up. Rahaxeris sat in a chair, looking at her and twisting the arrow he'd removed from her shoulder around and around in his fingers. He gave her a severe look. She swallowed. There was no doubt in her mind that he loved her, but he wasn't someone to trifle with. A half smirk lifted his cheek, barely, but she caught it.

"What have you been up to, naughty girl?"

Just jumping. She signed flippantly.

"Uh-huh." His voice was flat. He waved the arrow back and forth slowly. "Where in the hell did this come from? And why were you there?"

It was an accident. I didn't mean to end up there. Where ever it was.

He narrowed his ruby eyes at her. "Why are you lying to me, Tesla?"

She looked away from him.

"Fear? Is that your reason for lying?"

She contemplated. Should she tell him the truth? Was it time?

Would it help lift the terrible burden she'd been carrying around by herself, ever since the blood lock had been turned on?

He crossed his arms over his chest. "I'm waiting."

She looked back at him, her eyes wide and desperate. She flexed her aching fingers and took a deep breath. *Please, Grandfather... I'm sorry for lying.* Her hands trembled as she began to confess. *The blood lock doesn't work. I mean, it works, but not the way it should. Not the way we need it to. Every night, for the last year, I sneak out as soon as Mom and Dad are asleep. If I'm not jumping, then I'm at the Heart, shoring up the lock with temporary bandages. I jump all over...searching for something that will make the lock what everyone believes it to be. I look at the lock...it's an equation. There's a missing strand, particle, or protein to fill in the gap. In my mind, I take it apart and put it back together over and over but there's a gap, and I can't fill it! It's got an unusual shape and can only be filled with the right thing, and I've not yet found it!*

He leaned forward, put his head in his hands, and sighed. "I love you, Tesla. I need you to remember that right now, because I'm not sure I've ever been this angry in my entire life! Why didn't you tell me this? Are you really so arrogant that you believe you are the only one who might have something to offer?"

His words smacked at her. *Arrogant? Really? That's the pot calling the kettle! I wanted to tell you many times, but the Heart told me not to. You have no idea how heavy this secret has been! You have no idea what it feels like to carry the lives of everyone you know on your shoulders. The Heart told me I'm the only one who can do this. Is the Heart wrong? Does it lie? Because I'd be more than happy to pass this shit to you!*

He scowled and sat back in his chair but the tight lines around his eyes eased a little. "All right." He held up his hands. "I'm sorry for snapping at you, but you're not going to shut me out of this, now that I know about it. We can coordinate. I've been jumping a lot longer than you, my girl. We can go together. It would be safer, since you obviously go to some dangerous places…I'm glad you came to me tonight. That arrow was nasty. Is that the first time you've been wounded while jumping?"

No. It's not the first time, but it was the worst so far… Are you going to rat me out?

He snorted. "I don't know. I need to think about this."

Come on! She pleaded. *Do you know what Mom and Dad will do if they find out?*

"They are going to lose their shit first, then they will calm down."

She gave him a droll stare. *Yeah, well you aren't going to be the one to catch the shit when they lose it. Please just wait. I need to get home before they wake up. I know I can't keep it from them forever, but I don't think it's the right time.*

"I'll hold off while I mull it over. They have to know soon. So prepare yourself for the repercussions."

She signed a few swear words, with precise, emphatic movements. He laughed.

"Watch your mouth, I mean hands, young lady. How about this? I'll wait to decide how you and I will explain it to them after your birthday next week?"

She relaxed and nodded. *Thanks.*

"Go home, sneaker. Come back and see me this afternoon, so you can tell me everything you've been hiding."

But it's my day off from school. She whined.

8

"If you don't show by lunchtime, I *will* rat you out, as you put it."

Resigned, she nodded in agreement, stood up, pulled the strata open and slid through it to her bedroom. The room was dark. She held still, listening. Her parents were still asleep, but not for long. The dawn was on its way.

Tesla took the mushy alien soil she'd snatched, out of her pocket and poured it into the bottom of her glass jewelry box. She'd check it out later. She stripped out of her dirty, bloodied clothes, and with a shock from her hands, set them on fire. She tossed the ashes out the window.

She hesitated before closing her window again, inhaling the predawn air and glancing at the sky. A red wave of energy rolled through the clouds, rumbling long and low as it went. The blood color shimmered as the wizards attacked on the other side, trying again to get through. She wondered what the blood lock looked like to everyone else. Did they all feel caged? Even though it was for their protection? She would have felt like that, except she wasn't bound by it the way the rest of Regia was. She could go anywhere, anytime.

Her heart clenched in fear as it did every time the blood lock shuddered. Would they get through this time? Or the next? The rumble stopped. She exhaled, relaxing. The wizards had ceased for the moment. They would try again. Maybe in a few minutes, or a few days. Her white-hot hatred for the wizards burned her up inside.

Socially, she was isolated from anyone her age. Instead of going to the Academy, she spent the weekdays in Kyhael, being tutored by Rahaxeris. Occasionally, Merhl showed up and tried to teach her coping skills over the painful overflow of magic in her hands. He was the closest thing she had to a real friend. They made each other laugh, and usually, their lessons deteriorated into a free-for-all magical creation contest. He was the big brother she didn't have. Zeren also contributed to her education, coming once a week for a few hours to teach her history and Regian law theory.

9

Tesla yawned, realizing she wasn't going to get much rest. She closed her window and went to get some pajamas on, but as she crossed to her closet she passed her mirror and paused. She stood naked in front of herself and frowned. Her birthday was coming. She would be two years old. Shivers rose on her skin. Two years old, but she was also eighteen.

Her jaw clenched, and tears slicked her eyes as she gazed at the red flower shape that flashed over her heart with her pulse. *Freak.* She thought. *Why can't I be beautiful like Mom? No one is ever going to love me the way Dad loves her. No one will ever look at me the way he looks at her. Not because I'm unworthy, I'll just never find someone as screwed up as me. I'll never find my equal.*

The lightning flower flashed faster as her heart accelerated in response to her emotions. The edges of the flower reached up around the curve of her breast. She lifted her hands and covered the flower. If she wanted to, she could get older right then. Maybe when she'd fixed the blood lock and she was sure Regia was safe…she could just age until…until she died. It wouldn't take long. Just a moment, and she'd be gone. The pain would be over. She'd never again have to see the pity and the fear in everyone's eyes when they looked at her.

The lightning in her hands surged a little, trying to connect to the power in her heart. She closed her eyes and saw herself standing on the edge of a cliff overlooking the sea. Directly below her were knife-like rocks, stretching up like hands, ready to receive her, ready to drink up her blood. She gasped and lowered her hands, a chill running under her skin at her suicidal thoughts. It was the knowledge that she *could* kill herself. She was capable.

Noises came from the other side of the house. She shook herself, quickly pulled on her pajamas, and jumped into bed. She heard her parents' door open and her father's bare feet pad across the house to the kitchen. Tesla sighed and closed her eyes, soothed by the familiar sound of coffee brewing. A small smile curved her mouth. Dad didn't drink it, but every morning he got up first and made it for Mom. Her parents taught her what love was, just by her seeing the way they loved each other. It wasn't just the grand gestures, it was the quiet, everyday things, like him making her coffee.

He knocked softly on her door, waited a beat, and then opened it a crack. She pretended to be asleep. He came in, leaned over, and kissed her temple. She rolled over and buried her face in the pillow. He didn't leave. Tesla groaned and rolled to her back, looking up at him.

What? She signed.

"Just checking on you."

She gave him a halfhearted scowl. *Geez. Let me sleep. It's my day off.*

"Are you feeling okay? How are your hands?"

They hurt. They always hurt. You know that.

He nodded sadly. "What about your heart?"

Erratic, but not painful.

He touched her face, running his thumb under her eye. "You're not resting well. You always look so tired these days."

She shrugged.

He sat on the edge of the bed. "Give me your hands."

She did. His power ran over the top of her skin, connecting with hers. He didn't take the overflow like Rahaxeris did, instead it was an alignment. Her power, so wild, like electrical currents on frayed wires, organized under the gentle pressure of her father's hands.

Thanks, Dad.

11

He kissed her forehead. "I'm going to work early today. You still haven't told me what you want for your birthday."

I want...no, never mind.

"What? Tell me."

No. It's stupid. You decide what you want to give me.

"You know I'll get it wrong. If it were up to me, I'd give you things most two year olds would want. Like a dollhouse."

She gave him a dirty look. *Don't you dare!*

He chuckled. "Well, maybe you should tell me what you want then."

You're not going to like it. She warned.

He just blinked at her, waiting.

Fine. She caved. *I want combat training.*

His eyebrows rose, but after a second, he smiled, then shook his head and laughed. "You are just like your mother."

Yeah sure. She rolled her eyes. *We're twins.*

He stood up. "Go back to sleep, sweetheart. I'll see you this evening."

She yawned and pulled the blanket over her head as he closed the door behind him. Tesla exhaled and tumbled into a dream of scattered, blood-covered, unsolvable equations. Frustrated tears pushed from her closed eyes as she tossed and turned. The answer she sought danced away, laughing at her powerless attempts to grab hold of it.

She woke abruptly, feeling more tired than before she'd slept. Fear slid into her stomach as she heard voices coming under the door from the living room. She must have overslept and missed her agreed time to visit her grandfather, so now he was here. She listened to the tone of their voices and relaxed a bit. There was no anger or stress in the cadence of their conversation, so he must've decided to not rat her out. She got out of bed and dressed quickly. She didn't want to test his patience.

She opened the door and stalked past the living room to the kitchen, feigning sullen teenage indifference for her mother and grandfather.

Forest walked into the kitchen behind her. "Good afternoon, sleepyhead."

Tesla looked at her but didn't sign anything, pouring some juice into a glass instead. *Why is Grandfather here?* She asked after putting her glass down.

"He says you didn't finish your lessons yesterday. That's not like you. What happened?"

It was hard. The pain was bad. Couldn't focus.

Forest walked up to her and placed her hands on Tesla's cheeks. "Are you okay today? Is the pain too much for you to do your work? Rahaxeris will understand."

I'll be fine. Don't fuss.

Her heart ached at the sorrow in her mom's eyes. Their relationship always seemed off balance. Not bad, just strained and disconnected. It wasn't from lack of trying for either of them. They were both guilty of trying too hard.

Forest looked her over with a critical eye.

What? She signed.

"You look...pale. How long has it been since you've had blood?"

13

I don't know. I don't ever want it. It tastes bad.

She gave her small smile. "I know, honey. But you need it to stay healthy."

Tesla cursed her chin for trembling and her cheeks for heating. *I'm not healthy, and I never will be. Blood makes no difference.*

Forest's eyes narrowed in angry determination, and she turned and opened the fridge. She pulled out a stainless steel bottle and set it on the counter with a harsh clank. Tesla grimaced as she poured the blood into a glass and forced it into her hand. Forest crossed her arms over her chest and gave her the hawk-like mommy look.

Tesla brought the glass to her mouth and hesitated, steeling herself to take her medicine. What kind of half vampire was she?

"Just get it over with."

Tesla looked at her pleadingly. Forest's face softened.

"Would it be easier to drink from me? You can."

Tesla shook her head. *I don't want to hurt you.*

"It's okay. I'm tough."

She shook her head again and downed the blood in her glass. Gah, she hated it. Forest ran her hands through Tesla's hair.

"There. All over. You'll feel better."

I should go now. Don't want to keep Grandpa waiting.

"Work hard and be respectful," Forest said, tapping Tesla on the nose gently with her index finger.

She nodded. *I love you, Mom.*

"I love *you*, my baby."

Tesla rolled her eyes as she walked away. Forest smacked her on the butt as she went.

"Ready?" Rahaxeris asked blandly as she came into the living room.

She nodded. He struck the air, opening a portal, and they went to Kyhael. As soon as her feet hit the floor, she slumped into her usual chair at the grand table where the priests of the *Rune-dy* used to have their meetings. Now it was where she did her school work.

You lied to Mom.

He raised one eyebrow as he sat down across the table from her. "I did. Don't expect me to again."

I don't expect anything.

"Drop the attitude. It's time for you to explain the things you've been hiding from me."

She rubbed her hands together as she considered. *Send for Merhl. He needs to see this, too.*

He stood and left the room. In a few minutes he was back, Merhl in tow behind him. Merhl was usually laid back, but at the moment he looked apprehensive. She smiled at him. He looked at her closely and frowned.

"Are you all right?" he asked.

I'm fine, Merhl. But I'm afraid I have bad news.

Tesla sighed as she stood and placed both of her hands flat on the table. She closed her eyes as a flash shot out from her hands. A perfect image of Regia, in red light, rose off the table's surface like a 3-D digital map. She pulled at it, making the Heart bigger, so they could see the blood lock suspended inside it.

The blood lock is not what I led you to believe. It's not impenetrable. So far it has held our enemies back, but there will come a time when the force of them will breach it. I have added to it many times. Look...

She wiped the map away with a brush of her hand and showed them the equation inside the blood lock, the one she had created but still found it incomplete and inadequate.

This is the lock as it stands right now.

Merhl wasn't looking at it, he was looking at her. "What do you mean you've added to it many times? Added what?"

She pointed to the hole in the molecular code of the blood lock. *See this? There is nothing on Regia to fill this void. I don't even know what I'm looking for, but I'm sure I'll know it when I see it. So I jump. I search other worlds for the missing piece. So far, nothing has been as helpful as my discovery of the dark elements. I added a free radical into the chain here.* She pointed to the place. *And since then, when the wizards attack, those who get close to our defenses suffer burns that worsen over time. The frequency of their attempts lessened as soon as I put that in.*

Rahaxeris and Merhl leaned in to look closely at the intricate structure of the blood lock. There was no denying there was beauty to the living machine.

After a few minutes, Merhl sat down and rubbed his eyes. "I've got nothing. It's so different than what we originally worked on together. I don't even understand half of what you've created, Tesla. I'm sorry."

Rahaxeris took his time examining her work, but then he too sat down. "There are no mistakes in your work. The science and magic are perfect. I'm impressed with your creativity and improvisation. I've never seen the type of mixing you've done. The only idea I have is that the void you seek to fill in the code is not what you think it is, but I could be wrong."

What do you mean? She asked.

"What worlds have you jumped to?"

Her shoulders slumped. *There are too many, Grandfather. I don't know their names. I get in and get out as quickly as I can.*

Rahaxeris began going through a list of worlds he knew, describing them if the name didn't catch with her. Finally, he exhausted his own knowledge. "Is there anywhere else you've been?"

Lots of places.

"How is that possible?"

How is it possible you don't know there are infinitely more worlds than you've just listed? She looked desperately at Merhl. *You know them, don't you?*

He looked apologetic and shook his head. Then his eyes brightened. "Have you reached the Everpath?"

Tesla nodded.

"The what?" Rahaxeris demanded.

"I..." Merhl looked at her with total amazement. "I never knew if it was real or just a myth. When I was a boy, my father told me that one night he tried to push the boundaries of the strata to see if it would give more. He was just experimenting, thinking nothing would come of it. Then he said he broke through a level no one ever told him about and ended up in a strange grey place. An endless hallway of doors. Terrified, he quickly fled back through the hole he'd made. He said he feared losing himself there. And when he got home he just knew the place was called the Everpath, even though no one told him that. He tried to go back many times but was unsuccessful."

I go there all the time. It's the only way to go beyond the second atmosphere. She looked at Rahaxeris. *All the worlds you have jumped to are close to home. The Everpath is the in-between, the hub.*

"How did you discover it? What did you do to find a place so very far away?" Merhl asked.

The Everpath is tied to everything. It called to me. I could see the entrance to it every time I jumped.

Rahaxeris abruptly got to his feet. "Take me there."

I can't. There is no way to open a channel there. If you cannot see it, there is nothing I can do to show you.

His cheeks flushed, and he turned and left the room. Tesla sighed and looked at Merhl. *Why is he angry?*

"I don't know. I'm sure he'll tell us when he comes back. If every world is connected to the Everpath, then the blood lock is protecting the entrance to Regia there as well?"

Yes. I was terribly worried about that the first time I went there, but there is nothing to be concerned about with that. If the wizards can access the Everpath at all—I don't think they can—they could not get through...Is there anything, anything at all you can think of to help me, Merhl?

"When you jump, don't always go for the obvious. Chose to visit worlds that seem weak as well as the strong ones. Go places that have no magic, for you might be surprised at what you find...I wish I could do something more. Do you think perhaps you could show me how to see the Everpath? I would go with you. Protect you."

She smiled warmly at him. *If your father was able to discover it, perhaps you too have the ability locked inside you. But I don't know how to instruct you. I see it. I could always see it.* She wiped the red light

18

image of the blood lock away with her hand and sat back down, feeling more hopeless than ever.

"Maybe you're overthinking it, Tesla. Try to just go with your instincts. Turn your head off and let the magic in your heart lead you."

CHAPTER TWO

CONTARREN.
BARBARIC HUMAN WORLD.

The hungry flames surged through the dry wood and up, grabbing on to the hem of the old woman's dress. She looked down, the fire reflected on the surface of her eyes. Tied to the post, there was no way for her to evade the death now crawling up her clothes. Her craggy voice began to cry out as the smell of her legs cooking filled the air. The fire ate up her clothes until she was naked, and then it began peeling away her skin.

"Death to the witch! Death to the witch!" the crowd shouted over and over.

Alex hung back from the cluster of people pushing forward to see the tragedy better. He crossed his arms over his chest and scowled, trying his best to exude a nonchalant indifference. His friends, Paul, Marcus, Stephan, and Troy, followed his lead, like always, and stood next to him. He hoped none of them could see the conflict he was going through.

He wanted to leave. The old woman was no witch. She was just an aged spinster suffering from the beginning effects of dementia. But killing her would make everyone feel better and help them to sleep that night. His stomach turned partially from the smell, but also from the way the people acted. He knew them all. Most of them were mild, kind people. But on days like today, they transformed into monsters. Gathered together, they rode on each other's emotional waves, going temporarily insane with a lust for violence.

Determined to not lose face over what he was feeling, instead of watching the woman die, Alex focused his eyes on the flames at the base of the wood pile and tried to let his mind drift onto something else. It was hard with all the shouting from the people, the screams of pain from the woman, and the nasty smell filling his nostrils. The whole damn world was full of injustice, or at least it seemed that way to him. But what could he do? Nineteen years old, he was barely considered a man. And why would anyone listen to him anyway? He wasn't a politician, he was a blacksmith.

He wondered if there was a real witch. Was she here, in the crowd? Was she someone he'd known his whole life? Hiding in plain sight? Or did she live out in the dark forest? Everyone was so terrified of magic users, but he wasn't. He'd never seen the effects of magic. And he wasn't sure he believed the stories.

Troy elbowed him in the side. Alex looked at him questioningly. Troy smirked and nodded in the direction he wanted him to look. Alex turned his head, knowing the second his eyes hit the target of what his friend wanted him to see. Isolde.

She glanced his way from the side of her eye, and her pouty lips curved slightly. She filled her lungs, her cleavage rising higher over her bodice. She shook her long blond hair off her shoulders, giving him a better view. She licked her lips slowly, damn girl. She was killing him, and she knew it.

"Lucky bastard," Troy whispered in his ear.

Alex elbowed him roughly in the chest. "Stop looking at her."

Troy coughed once. "Bloody impossible, mate. She's so choice."

"Yeah, well, she's mine. You've got your own."

Troy rolled his eyes. "Don't remind me. I'm going to have to be shitfaced drunk to marry Joan, let alone the stuff after. Guess it's just your luck your parents would betroth you to the most beautiful girl."

Alex smiled. "Yep. Nothing can touch my luck. I had my doubts about Isolde a few years ago, wasn't sure she'd grow into her front teeth. Remember that?"

"I'd take her *with* her beaver teeth any day over Joan."

"At least Joan is sweet. Isolde can be..."

"What?"

"Nothing. Never mind."

Alex looked back at the old woman engulfed in flames, and his stomach turned again, this time with guilt. She was dead. He should have done something, spoken up when she was sentenced. Surely he wasn't the only person to know she hadn't really been a witch. Was he?

He looked away. It was all right for him to leave. No one would think anything of it now. He looked back over at Isolde, and then at his friends, who waited for him to tell them what they would do now. He glanced back at her, and all of them looked.

"I've got some important *business* to attend to now, boys."

"Yeah, you do," Troy said, and they all smirked and laughed.

He strode toward her, leaving his friends behind. She turned fully to face him, taunting heat in her eyes. He took her hand and pressed his lips against it, since it was contrary to social standards to kiss her mouth in public, betrothed or not.

"Alexander." She drew his name out slowly. "Care to escort me home?"

"Hmm." His voice rumbled in his throat. "Shall we go the long way?"

Her eyes flashed, but this time in anger, not desire. "Of course not!"

He scowled at her. She had no idea how flexing her newly found power over him was making him feel. Anger slammed hard into his stomach. "Tease," he accused coldly.

She pulled her hand from his and lifted her chin defiantly. "I am not."

"Why do you keep doing this to me? Hot then cold then hot. You know exactly what you're doing when you flash your eyes at me like that. You're driving me mad."

"Good." Her voice went all dark again, making him curse her.

He sighed raggedly. "We're going to be married in three months. What are we waiting for? You know I love you."

"I'll think about it," she said lightly, turning on her heel and striding away.

He caught up to her and took her hand. People smiled at them as they passed. Alex hardly saw them. He was trying to force his mind to go blank and his body to go numb. Isolde liked power, but she was careless in the way she wielded it. She was trying to break him, make him beg. He wouldn't.

"I'm so happy they finally caught the witch. I was so scared."

"It's nonsense, Isolde. *If* there is a witch at all, that poor old woman certainly wasn't her."

"You're wrong." Her voice was cold.

"No, I'm not. How can you believe—"

"What?" she demanded. "How can I believe what? You're blind if you think anything other than justice was done back there. The witch is dead, and good riddance."

Alex pursed his lips, a guilty weight settling inside his head. He'd hoped…but he couldn't even speak his mind to his fiancée. He sighed, trying to let it go. She tugged lightly on his hand. He looked down into her face. She smiled easily at him for a moment, then her eyes flashed dark and seductive again.

"Eight points, Alex," she whispered. "Bring me an eight point buck by tonight, and I'll give myself to you."

He stopped walking and faced her. "Odd price for your virtue."

"I need the antlers for my bridal jewelry. If I have them, I will best Lucinda's. No bride will be able to match me for a very long time, if ever."

"I see. This is about your pride," he said flatly, not bothering to hide his annoyance. She was making it cheap. Selling herself to him for a price, like a whore.

She moved forward and pressed her chest against him. "What does it matter? You bring it to me and we both get what we want."

"Is this how it will be after we are married? Always bargaining?"

That jerked her up short, and she frowned. "No," she said slowly. "I'm sorry… That came out wrong. I regret it. I *do* want the buck, and I thought…" Her cheeks flushed. "I thought it would excite you if I was, you know, forward, improper. I've seen older men, heard their talk, they want…"

He huffed and shook his head. "Stop *trying* to be something. You're going to be my wife. You don't have to lure me. You have me. All I want is for you to be faithful, and just…" *What?* Kind was what he really wanted to say, but he didn't. "Just be yourself."

She looked down and nodded.

"Hey." He tipped her face up. "If you want the buck, all you have to do is ask. I can get it for you. But I won't buy your body, Isolde. You give it freely or not at all."

"Okay, Alex." She was contrite for a moment, then she smiled, placing her hand on his cheek. "You know I'm happy don't you? It was destiny that our parents paired us from infancy. If you weren't mine, I'd scheme until you were."

"If it was your choice, you could have anyone."

"And I'd still choose you. All the girls envy me."

He smirked, his ego swelling. "All the men, young and old, envy me when they look at you. You're so beautiful."

She smiled. "I'm glad I please you." She glanced at the house. "My mother will be wanting me soon. Will I see you tonight?"

"I'll come when the sun sets, with your buck."

"Thank you." She framed his face with her hands. "I love you, Alex. I can't wait to be your wife."

"I can't wait for you to be my wife, too."

"I want to come and look at the house again, but Mother insists I have to be escorted, and she never has the time to go with me."

"What do you need to see it again for? You've told me many times it was to your liking."

"Yes, but I want to start making my mark on it. I made curtains for the windows. It's not fair that you get to live there before me," she pouted.

"Last night was my first time to sleep there. The roof wasn't finished until yesterday."

"Was it wonderful?"

He chuckled. "No. It was lonely and weird. I'm so used to my brother's snore I could hardly sleep without the dumb sound. The place is really bare. I was cold during the night."

"That's why I need to go over there. I can make it more comfortable for you. When you come this evening, I'll have some things for you to take back. I would prefer the first time the quilt I made was used was our wedding night, but I can't have you being cold."

Moved by her unusual show of concern, he leaned down and kissed her lips.

"Alex!" she whispered as though scandalized. "We're outside."

"Sorry." He stepped back from her. "I better get going. Apparently, I have some hunting to do."

"Eight points," she said sternly. "Absolutely no less."

"I'll do my best, Isolde. There's no knowing what the forest will yield to me on any given day. I might be unlucky."

Her temper, always so close to the surface, lit small sparks in her eyes. "A real man makes his own luck."

He sighed, turning away from her before she started nagging at him and a quarrel began. "Until this evening," he said over his shoulder.

Alex jogged home to get his gear and a bite to eat before heading out into the forest. His mother stood, stirring stew in a large pot on the stove. She looked at him over her shoulder and smiled. He kissed the side of her head.

"Hello, sweetheart. What are you doing here this time of day?"

"Do I need a reason to see my loving and beautiful mother?"

She snorted. "Save that charm for Isolde. And yes, I'm sure you do have a reason."

"I need my bow. I'm going hunting. I had hoped to grab something to eat, too."

"Sit down. This stew is ready if you want some."

He parked at the rough kitchen table. "I was hoping you'd say that."

She set a steaming bowl in front of him and ruffled his hair. Too eager, he scalded his tongue on the first bite. She brought him a cup of water before he could ask.

"Thanks, Mom."

She took a seat next to him and watched him for a moment. Then her chin trembled slightly.

"What's wrong?" He shifted immediately into protective mode.

She patted his hand. "Nothing, son. I was just thinking how much I'm going to miss you... You're a man now. You don't need me anymore."

"Sure I need you! If you hadn't made this stew, who knows what I'd be eating right now. Moldy bread and poisoned water, I'm sure. I'm totally pathetic. I'll always need you."

She chuckled as he hoped she would. "Tis a bad mother I am if you're that helpless. I should have taught you better... Oh, well. It's too late. You're completely ruined. But soon you'll be Isolde's problem, and I can focus my attention more to your brother. He's not quite the jackanapes you are."

"Brenden is a little too capable. I always knew he was your favorite child."

Her expression went totally serious. "You're right."

The next second they both laughed. She got up and kissed the top of his head and began scrubbing the counter. "You better hurry, Alex, if you're going to have enough time to hunt."

He scarfed the last of his food, grabbed his stuff, and hugged his mom goodbye.

The golden afternoon sun streamed through the tree branches in bright beams, lighting Alex as he ran through them, teasing out the red undertones of his dark brown hair. His heart lifted as his muscles sang with exertion. He pushed himself to run faster and deeper into the forest than he'd ever gone before. His bow and quiver slung across his body, and the new hatchet he'd completed yesterday hung off his belt, the handle tapping against his leg in time with his stride, as if it was impatient to cut something.

He could *almost* thank Isolde for this. In the sensual solitude of the woods, he was able to let go of the irksome irritation of his feelings, leftover from the witch burning. Guilt with touches of sorrow had been lingering in the background of his heart, but now he was totally distracted. He set his mind on his goal as he vaulted over the stream in one long leap.

Suddenly, lines of ice slid down his back, like someone with freezing hands caressed his bare skin. He skidded to a halt, alarmed by the sensation. Goosebumps lifted on his forearms. Spooked, he held still, his eyes cutting through everything around him. There was nothing to see, just the ordinary. But there was something else, beyond sight...the shivers continued. What was wrong with him? There was nothing to be scared of.

His instinct argued otherwise. He waited, not breathing, his heart galloping.

28

Bracken crunched on the ground.

He grabbed his hatchet, holding it up at the ready. Movement in his peripheral vision. He pivoted toward it, his grip tightening on the hatchet's handle. Breath gasped into his lungs and his fear was replaced by excitement and awe.

Alex had never seen a more magnificent beast. The sunlight made the fur covering the massive buck glimmer golden. Forget eight points, that was nothing compared to the fourteen on this animal's rack. Slowly, making his movements as smooth as possible, Alex lowered the hatchet and slid it back into the loop on his belt. He lifted the bow and strung it with an arrow.

The buck's eyes turned on Alex. Time stopped dead. He'd looked into the eyes of his prey before, but this was different. He shouldn't kill it. It was too special. But if he let it go, no one would believe him. He didn't listen to his conscious, his heart stinging as he let the arrow fly. It sank through the fur and flesh, embedding deep and perfectly behind the shoulder. A ripple went out all over the buck from the arrow's point of entry. It staggered once and then ran.

Alex dropped the bow and ran after the buck, snatching his hatchet back out. Again, guilt smarted in his chest, but he had to finish it now. The buck jumped a fallen tree and sprinted into a clearing. He skidded to a halt, took aim in the span of a heartbeat, and threw the hatchet. It spun through the air, blade over handle, over and over. He held his breath, waiting for the fateful moment... but he never saw it.

An invisible force hit him in the chest, lifting him off his feet and throwing him backward. The air was knocked from his lungs as he slammed to the ground. Dazed, he looked up through the trees at the sky. A spiral of dark grey smoke coiled over him like a snake and plunged straight into his chest. White sparks danced and snapped inside his eyes. The snake-thing slithered deep, winding around and around under his skin. Convulsions jerked his muscles in a full seizure.

29

The snake continued to move after he lost consciousness, moving up through his skull, exploring the folds of his brain. It moved around the base of his neck just above the collarbone, like a choker made of a wisp of grey smoke. The second it closed the circle around his neck, a tremor rushed through his whole body. His bright future went out like a candle in a storm.

Hours slipped away as the light shifted over Alex and left. As the evening began darkening the sky, cold mist crept through the shadows of trees, just above the ground, and shrouded him. The screeching of a night bird woke him suddenly in a rush of adrenaline. He sat up, freezing, weirdly sore, and unable to open his eyes. He touched his eyelids with his fingertips. They were sealed shut. The gunk gluing his eyelids together felt like a hard line of wax to the touch. Bracing himself, he pulled at it. It came loose, lightly tugging his eyelids before letting go.

The second he opened his eyes, Alex cried out in pain and fear. His pupils constricted into tiny pinpoints and then swiftly blossomed open in full dilation. He clamped his eyelids shut and rubbed them. His eyes felt flooded. Cold filled his irises like ice water pouring into a bowl up to the rim. Shivers rose aggressively over his skin.

Trying to breathe slowly, he opened his eyes again. His sight was changed, but he was too scared to acknowledge it. But it wasn't just his eyes, there was something wrong with *all* of him. He touched his neck, slowly tracing the cold line just above his collarbone. What had happened to him? His heart pulsed harsh and heavy.

Movement and a faint grey light through the trees ahead of him, had Alex jumping to his feet. He reached for his hatchet, only to find the loop empty. Then he remembered the buck. He'd hit it with an arrow, chased it, thrown his hatchet...and then? There was nothing beyond that. He focused on the apparition in the distance, defenseless. It moved toward him.

His new sight sliced through the shadows and focused on the buck as

30

it came closer. For a moment, his mind ardently refused to accept what he clearly saw. It walked slow and steady, straight at him. It was the same animal, there was no denying it. But it was no longer flesh, only the spirit approached Alex, transparent grey, and iridescent in the moonlight.

Alex couldn't move, frozen in wonder. The buck stopped ten feet in front of him, holding his gaze. He lifted his hand and took a step forward. Could he actually touch it? Was there anything to touch? The buck looked at his hand, its ghostly eyes widening. Its shape changed, rushed at him like a stream of smoke in the wind. Before he could do anything or even cry out in alarm, the spirit went straight into his outstretched hand, sucked in as though his palm was a vacuum.

Alex choked as it charged through him. Oh, the power! It crashed through every inch, filling him up in a rush that was both ecstasy and pain. The buck's spirit vibrated through his extremities and then shrank into the size of a fist and burned a mark on the right side of his chest before pushing out of him. A tendril of grey swirled before his eyes, and then disintegrated into the air, losing all shape.

He looked down at the mark the spirit left on his skin and touched it gingerly. He winced, it was indeed a burn. The blackened skin was rough like a scab and twisted in the shape of the buck's antlers. He closed his eyes tightly. *Wake up. Please, please let this be a dream.*

The screech of the night bird jolted him again, and he opened his eyes. If this was real…no, he wouldn't allow himself to think that for even one second. He was dreaming, and he would wake. Holding desperately to that thought, Alex pushed the fear down.

He turned in a circle, his sight probing the darkness as easily as if it were midday. He glanced up at the night sky, but it was no help. He knew what direction he faced in the day, but he couldn't find direction in the stars. Again he forced the fear down as it slithered and whispered behind him. It was a dream, and therefore, it made no difference that he was lost.

He contemplated. He could sit down right where he was and wait for the dawn to lead him home. Instead, he thought of the buck. Looking down, he saw the hoof prints on the ground and began following them. If he found the carcass, he'd find his hatchet. Then he wouldn't be defenseless.

As he walked, every muscle ached, but the pain was only the backdrop. Over the strange soreness was an even stranger sensation, deep inside, like metal and glass and cloud. Alex didn't feel real anymore. He didn't feel human. *I just ate something bad before bed. I'm dreaming.*

He rubbed his hands together. Buzzing hummed deep in his palms. He looked down at them. Nothing new to see there, but the pull... His hands were channels, open doors, hungry portals. He curled them into fists and kept walking.

He had the feeling that he was walking even further away from home, but he couldn't be sure. The stars, the forest, and the darkness itself, embraced and claimed him as its own. He felt a deep internal harmony with the night, as if he was made of it. The moon moved over his head as time and distance lost shape and meaning. He just walked, absentmindedly touching the cold line on his neck. What was it? Did it mean something? His heart trembled in a way it hadn't since he was a small child.

Tree shadows danced back and forth with the light of a fire ahead of him, and muttering filled his ears. He slowed down, sneaking through the dark toward the fire. Anyone this deep in the forest in the dead of night couldn't possibly be savory company. He peeked around the side of a large trunk.

"I know you're there," the woman said blandly.

She had her back to him, standing between him and the fire. The blazing light behind her turned her into little more than a silhouette.

"Show yourself now, or I'll kill you."

Not that he feared her threat, but since his presence was already known, Alex stepped out from behind the tree as she turned to face him. Her eyes reflected at him like an animal's as their gazes locked. She was curvy and tall, a smidgen taller than his six two, with a pixie-like face poking out from under a long mess of dark red curls and braids. This was the real witch. He was certain, but she was far from the hag he'd imagined. She was strangely beautiful and not at all old. A clear stone hung on a chain around her neck. It flickered white light into his eyes. He stepped back, raising one of his hands to shield his gaze from the painful brightness.

"You're the witch."

"True enough," she said jovially, smiling at him. "Who…or *what* are you?"

The light from her necklace dimmed down and he lowered his hand. "I—"

She cut him off, rushing at him and grabbing his hand. "Oh, no!" she screeched.

He tried to recoil, but her hands held fast around his wrist. "Let me go!"

"Shut up and hold still!" she ordered.

He did, but he wasn't sure why. She lifted both of his hands and touched her fingers to his palms. She jerked her hands away from his quickly, but she didn't back up. She traced one fingertip on the cold line on his neck, and then put her hands on both sides of his face. Her sequin-like eyes pushed hard on his. Last, she pulled the side of his loose collar and eyed the burn mark on his chest. He would never have stood still for this *inspection*, or let a witch touch him at all, but he was too interested in gaining answers about his physical state.

Her eyes flared, and her cheeks reddened as she took a step back. She put one hand to her head as though she had a headache and sighed loudly. "I'm so sorry," she said.

"*You* did this to me!" he accused. "Didn't you?"

She walked to the side of the fire and sat down on a stump. "I didn't mean to. I'm sorry. I've just ruined your whole life I'm afraid... What's your name?"

He didn't want to give her his name. When he didn't answer, she sighed again as though she might cry.

"My name's Maggie." She held up the clear stone that hung around her neck. "See?" she pointed at the center. A crack ran down the length of the stone. "The spell broke the stone. It was meant to be locked inside, but it rushed out and through the trees. I figured it would run itself out and fade into nothing... What were you doing so far out from the village?"

"Hunting." The word ground out from his clenched teeth. His heart had never beat so hard before. "What have you done to me? You have to fix it!"

Maggie held her hands out in defeat and shook her head. "It's been inside you too long. I can't fix it. It's settled...merged with you. It cannot be undone...I'm afraid you can't go home."

"No! I have to go home."

"They will kill you. You're a magic user now."

"I won't use it. Not ever. I'll hide it. No one will know." His voice rose frantically.

"Oh really?" she scoffed. "I assume you haven't looked at yourself."

"What? The mark on my chest? I can make up a story for that."

She shook her head, pity in her eyes. "What color are your eyes?"

"Huh?"

"Your eyes. What color are they?"

"Blue."

"Blue like what? The sky? The water?"

"Dark blue, like the ocean. Can you not see in this light?" he demanded.

"I see everything, boy. What about your hair? What color is that?"

"Brown."

She laughed darkly and shook her head. "You won't be able to hide your magic, or convince anyone. I doubt anyone you know would even recognize you now. And if they did, you'd be burning at the stake before you could blink."

Alex ran his hands through his hair and pulled out a few strands. His mouth dropped open as he held the hair up to the fire light. He couldn't exhale the breath he was holding. The hair was so blond it was almost white. He pulled out some more. Still blond. Frantically he pulled out more.

"I think it's a nice color myself," Maggie's voice was mildly amused. "But bald is a way to go, too. I guess. Your head will get cold."

"What color are my eyes?" He panicked.

35

She gave him a sad smile. "Blue."

He heaved a sigh of relief.

"*Ice* blue," she amended. "Like the color of moonlight on snow... Really beautiful, though. I'm a little jealous."

He began to shake. "What am I to do? Is there a chance it will fade? Will I go back to normal?"

"I can't be totally sure, but I highly doubt it. That spell was never meant for a human."

"What was it? What has it done to me?"

"It will take time to know the extent of your abilities. We'll have to test them, but given that you've already pulled a spirit into yourself, I can at least be sure the spell was what I intended, so—"

"How do you know I pulled a spirit into myself?" He cut her off.

"The mark on your chest could mean nothing else."

His shaking grew more violent. "What am I? What kind of magic do I have?"

Her look of pity deepened. "You're a Necromancer."

He shook his head in an attempt at denial. "No." His voice was barely a whisper.

Maggie got up, strode over to him, and grabbed him by the hand. "Come here. Sit down before you fall over." She towed him to the stump she'd been sitting on. "Stay there, I'll be right back."

She disappeared into the shadows. In a moment she was back, carrying a tankard. She thrust it into his hands. "Drink that."

"What is it?"

"Ale."

He eyed it suspiciously for a moment, then deciding he didn't give a damn if it was poisoned, began to drink. He drank it all and handed the tankard back to Maggie. The alcohol hit his blood stream quickly, and his head began to spin.

"What's your name?" she asked again.

"Alex." His eyelids drooped. "I'm a blacksmith. I..." His lungs grew heavy. "I'm about to be married. I built a house for my bride."

She pursed her lips but didn't contradict him. He was sloshed as she hoped he would be. She lifted his muscular arm and pulled it across her shoulders, hefting him to his feet. "Come on. You sleep it off. When you wake up, we'll deal with this."

He staggered and leaned on her as she took him into her house. He dropped onto her bed. Grunting, she lifted his feet up off the floor. She rolled her eyes as he let out a loud snore. Maggie shook her head in disbelief at the turn her life had just taken. She had wished, just that afternoon, that she wasn't so alone. It was the first wish to come true for her.

He snored again, making her think she might already regret the company.

Poor thing, she thought. *He's lost everything.*

She sighed, realizing the amount of work she now needed to do to protect him. It was going to be a long night. She took the scissors from her shelf and cut off one small strand of his white blonde hair before leaving him alone in her house.

Maggie tucked the hair safely in her pocket as she approached the fire. She needed energy. Firelight danced across her face as she closed her eyes, whispering words of focus and power. Her hands warmed. She placed her palms on her head as they surged the spell out. The magic absorbing inside her skull, filling her with a jittery restlessness.

"Okay," she said to herself. "I need to make blood. Lots of blood."

She retrieved her cauldron from the side of the house, waddling, grunting and cursing under the weight of the pot, taking it to the fire and hanging it above the flames. She sighed again and chewed her bottom lip in contemplation.

"Are you really going to do this?" she asked herself. "Hell of a lot of work, you know..." Her thoughts circled. "He's very fine. Not that he's for me. I'm too old for him. I'm probably the same age as his mother. Well, that doesn't change the fact he's nicely made. It would be a shame for him to die. He'll steal someone's heart... He said he was about to be married. Poor girl, a widow before she's a bride... All right, all right. I just hope he appreciates this someday. Alex." She said his name again so she wouldn't forget it.

Maggie used her strongest wand, the one carved of human bone, to fill the cauldron. The liquid bubbled as she put his hair in and turned a rust color. It needed an hour to simmer.

She rubbed her stone necklace until it illuminated her path into the darkness, re-tracing Alex's steps that led him to her. She found the dead stag. Her tears choked her momentarily. She'd seen him before from a distance. Admired his majesty, but she hadn't ever spoken to him. She was glad now. The task she'd set for herself would be unbearable if she also faced the grief of losing a friend. Alex didn't know any better, she soothed herself. She would teach him...No. She would advise, but it was the magic inside him that would teach him the real price of taking life. All too soon, he would know the weight of death, perhaps better than any other human that had ever lived.

She looked up through the tree branches into the steady golden eyes of White Owl. He turned his head to the side and hooted in question at her.

"Hello, Owl. Please, can you go tell Bear I need him?"

Owl puffed his feathers in annoyance but took flight in compliance. In five minutes, Owl returned, looking surly. Bear lumbered through the shadows toward her.

"Thank you for coming," Maggie said, scratching between his eyes. "I need a favor."

His nostrils flared, and he looked at the dead stag. He scowled and snorted out a puff of steam.

"I know. It's bad. I need to stage a human death. You'll play the killer."

A low rumble of laughter rolled in Bear's throat. *Is that so?* His thoughts came into her mind. *Why?*

"I have to protect the young man who shot the stag."

Owl hooted loudly in indignation.

Maggie held up her hands. "I know. I know. But trust me. He's worth saving. He's just a dumb human, or he was. He's something different now. Something more. Help me with this, and you shall see the elemental monster he will become. I have no doubt it will be something worth witnessing."

I'll help you. Bear said. *I'm not sorry to see the stag gone. He was so full of himself he should have been a peacock.*

Thank you, Bear. Just mess the place up a bit. Leave scratch marks on the trees and ground so the humans can't miss them. Drag that branch across the ground as though it's a body, that way," she pointed in the opposite direction of her house. "I've got some fake blood brewing. I'm going to bring it back here and splash it about."

39

Bear snorted again and began doing as she asked. It only took him a few minutes, then he lumbered away.

"Thank you," she said to his retreating backside.

Are you sure you know what you're doing? Owl asked.

Maggie laughed. "I never know what I'm doing. If I did, there wouldn't be a magically altered man snoring in my bed." She glanced up at Owl. "Do you think the humans will be convinced?"

Oh, sure. Dim creatures, those things.

She sighed, feeling the energy spell begin to fade. She needed to wrap this up before she became so sleepy she made a mistake that accidently led the humans right to her instead of away.

The blood was ready when she went back for it. She splashed it on the trees and poured it on the ground, and trailed it over the drag marks Bear made. Owl stayed, watching her complete her task. He remained silent until she was finished.

Bad idea, this. He probably won't live long anyway.

"I don't care how long he lives. I'm so lonely."

You have us, the creatures of the forest, for company. He was giving her attitude. *Are we not enough for you?*

"You're good company," she said wearily. "But it's not the same. I'm not human, but I look like one...You try being the last of your race, then you can scold me for needing someone."

Perhaps there are others. How do you know you are the last?

"Mum told me right before she died. There is no question, Owl. I am the last witch. I feel it...deep down inside my heart. Just as I feel the wizards, wherever they are. It's the truth. I am the last."

Before he opened his eyes, Alex knew he was sick. More ill than he had ever been before. Cold rushed into his eyes as he opened them. Through the grubby window, the sun washed the space in whiskey-colored light. Gasping, he sat up quickly, unsure where he was. His head hammered.

He scanned the unknown room. He sat on a lumpy, quilt-covered bed. A wooden chair occupied the corner. Dried herbs hung in bundles from the ceiling, glass bottles and a few well-worn books were crammed on a shelf. Moss and roots grew through the joints of the log walls.

Shivers and sorrow pricked under his skin as he remembered the night and the witch. His hands shook as he stood. The hair on his head touched the low ceiling. Light outlined the door. He pushed it open and stepped out into the morning.

Smoke wafted into his face. He blinked it from his eyes as he approached her. Maggie was her name, he remembered. She had her back to him, roasting something over the flames. His stomach rolled at the smell. He was starving and nauseated at the same time.

"Good morning, Alex," she said brightly, not turning to look at him. "Did you sleep well?"

"I...uh..."

He'd tried, so desperately, to convince himself that last night was nothing more than a dream, but he wasn't able to continue anymore. Maggie turned. The open smile on her face vanished. Her cheeks flushed, and her eyes filled with tears.

"This is real." His voice shook. "All of it was real..."

She came to him and grasped him in a tight hug. "I'm so sorry."

She was the cause of all this. But at that moment, his heart tore so viciously he hugged her back, accepting the comfort she offered. Slight as it was. He was reduced to the lowest possible level. The pain swallowed him whole, and all there was that let him know he was still alive were the arms of a stranger around him. The pain and his pulse were his only possessions.

"I want to go home. I can't. Can I?"

"Not unless you want to die."

He pulled away from her and dashed the tears off his cheeks. He tried to steady his breath but was only able to for a second. More tears came, burning his cold eyes. He turned away from her. "I want to say goodbye to my family...my friends...Isolde. She loves me. She will still love me, even like this."

"You think so? You don't sound so sure."

He spun on her. "What do you know?" he shouted. "You're a witch. No one has ever loved you!"

The slap she cracked on his face was surprisingly fierce. Her eyes flashed fiery autumn colors. "Damn you! How dare you say that to me? I went out of my way to save your life last night, and this is how you repay me?" She trembled in rage.

"What are you talking about? *You saved my life?* You *destroyed* my life!"

All the color drained from her flushed cheeks and she turned and walked a few paces away from him. "I'm sorry...I understand you're suffering. I won't hold your words against you...not today."

Alex exhaled and touched his stinging cheek, unsure what to do or say next.

"I did destroy your life…" Her voice was dejected. "It was an accident. I'm sorry. I've said it a few times now. I'm sorry. I would take it back if I could, but I cannot. You have to choose a new path for yourself, either that or go home and die, only to be remembered as a monster by your loved ones."

Her words rang true and poured more pain through the cracks of his broken heart. "How…what did you mean when you said you saved my life?"

"I thought perhaps they would come looking for you. I staged your death next to the stag you killed. My friend Bear helped. If anyone tracks you, they will find the gruesome scene and go home with the knowledge you were attacked and killed by a bear while hunting."

Alex envisioned it: his parents and brother looking on what she described. His stomach pitched. There would be a funeral. Isolde would be in mourning for six months, forced to wear black. Someone else would claim the house he built and make it theirs. All of his blacksmith tools would be sold or stolen. His life truly was over, but he was still alive. The ground that had always been solid under his feet fell away. He floated, adrift in a colorless, directionless, nameless reality. Was there a point in living? In finding a new path? Creating one? This wound was too new. The pain too fresh for him to answer.

He touched the burn mark on his chest with one fingertip and contemplated his morals. He'd been a good and honorable person. He did no harm. He cared. Maybe not enough to speak out when he should, but still he was a good person…or had been. *Necromancer.* That's what the witch called him. She'd made him into something evil. Given him an unnatural, immoral power that should never be used. Could he even control it?

"Alex! Alexander!" Shouts echoed through the forest. *"Where are you, Alex?"*

Maggie's eyes widened as she faced him again. His breath caught in his throat. He almost called out. Half a word came out of his mouth before he clamped his lips shut. His heart raced, and he began to shake. What should he do? He looked at her desperately. She came to him and held out her hand. He grasped it as though it was a lifeline.

The shouting of the search party moved closer.

"They're almost there," she whispered. "They'll see the blood in a second. You should go back to the house, close the door, and stop up your ears."

He nodded, but then it was too late. A woman's scream rose up through the trees. He was unmade by the sound. It was his mother. He covered his mouth with his hand. Her grief echoed through the forest, bouncing in his ears. The sound tunneled deep into him. He would never forget the sound of his mother crying as she realized he was dead. How could he not go to her? *I'm alive, Mom. I'm here.* He couldn't move at all. He just stood there, holding Maggie's hand and dying inside. Because if he did go to his mother, it wouldn't stop her pain. Just the look of him would mutate her pain into something worse. So for the love of her, he held still and let her believe he was dead.

An hour passed, and he still didn't move an inch. He listened to it all. His father and brother. His friends all came and looked on the place where they believed he died. Among the voices he knew so well, Isolde was not there. He was thankful. She didn't need to see that. She would suffer enough as it was. And yet underneath that relief was a twinge of pain. Why was she not among those searching for him?

Maggie didn't try to move him. She stood next to him the whole time and held his hand. He couldn't account for the way he felt about the witch, but all through that time... The worst of his whole life...the firm grip of her hand grounded him, and he was thankful for it.

Through pain, he was born the first time. And through pain he was reborn, as someone new. Someone with no history and no name.

CHAPTER THREE

Two days passed. Maggie took care of Alex, allowing him to occupy her one-room house. She brewed him a strong drink that kept him sleepy and numb. When he woke, she'd give him more to drink, and in a matter of minutes, he'd be out cold again. She felt sorry for him, and so guilty that she had accidently been the cause of his pain, that she was more than likely to encourage and enable him in self-destructive behaviors.

He surfaced in the late morning on the third day, looking hungover. His hair hung in his icy blue eyes that were horribly bloodshot with dark circles under them. He looked around as though he were lost and confused.

"Hey!" she called to him. "You need to eat, Alex."

"Don't call me that," he snapped. "That's not my name anymore."

"Okay," she said slowly, handing him a hunk of the bread she'd made earlier that morning. "What do you want me to call you?"

He scowled and answered her with a shrug as he tucked into the bread. "I don't give a damn what you call me."

She smiled broadly. "This will be fun. I'll call you whatever I want to in the moment. And you'll answer to it, won't you, Blondie?"

Her attempt to get a response from him felt flat. He was too dejected to care. He just shrugged again, looking at the ground. She handed him more bread. He took it, his eyes suddenly bright.

"How long was I out? How many days has it been since I died?"

"This is the third day. Why?"

He closed his eyes and exhaled raggedly. "My funeral…it will be today."

"Are you going?"

His eyes snapped open and onto hers. "I…are you going to try and stop me?"

"No. I thought you might try to go to it. I could help you go undetected. I can't make you invisible, but I can make you unrecognizable. Not that you aren't already, but just in case someone looked too closely at you and did realize it was you. This would be safer."

"A spell?"

"Yes."

"No, thank you." His words were polite, but his tone was anything but.

She pursed her lips and looked down, determined to hold her temper. "Fine. You're a total mess, though. If you don't want to draw attention to yourself I suggest you bathe, because I could smell you the second you stepped outside."

He looked down at his clothes and grimaced. "What good will that do? I could wash up, but my clothes will still reek and I've nothing else to wear."

Maggie smiled and flexed her fingers. She closed her eyes. He took a step back from her as she began whispering words. Light swirled in the air in front of her. She lifted her arms and caught the folded clothes that materialized out of thin air.

"Here. Your size, I think."

When he stepped back again she thrust them into his chest. "They're just clothes, for goodness sake! Nothing dangerous. If anything's dangerous here, it's the funk you're emitting right now."

"All right," he snapped. "You're really scary, you know that?"

"The stream is that way." She pointed over his shoulder.

He stalked toward the stream. She waited till he was out of earshot before chuckling to herself. She heard him splash into the water and then howl and curse because of how cold it was. Her smile faded as she thought about what he was about to do. He might not survive his funeral...if he was discovered. Or even if he wasn't, being there, hearing it, seeing it, might destroy him again. He'd already been destroyed; this might be too much for him to come back from.

Maggie wrung her hands together as she pondered. She would go with him. He wouldn't know she was there. She would stay in the shadows unless he needed her.

Before he came back, she decided to make him something else. A gift.

Naked, dripping wet, and frozen, Alex dressed quickly in the clothes Maggie had given him. His eyebrows shot up as his arms slid through the sleeves. The shirt was soft, warm, and the perfect size. The socks and pants, too. He put his boots back on, grateful he didn't have to put his old socks back on. Gross.

Fully dressed, he stood straight, looking at the water, his eyes sliding out of focus. What was he thinking? How could he go to his own funeral? What the hell for? Why did he want to? Morbid curiosity? Yes, that was there, he acknowledged. More than anything he wanted to say goodbye, even if it was a silent goodbye. But did he really have the strength to go and not speak to his family? To hide and not touch Isolde one last time.

He closed his eyes and looked at her beautiful face in his mind. His stomach dropped. He'd lost her. She wasn't his anymore. She would marry someone else. The pain of this loss was so strong it resonated all the way up his spine to his neck and stabbed him through the head. His whole life, she had been his. He'd protected her, cherished her, loved her, and desired her. Trying to let go was like cutting out his own heart with a small, dull blade.

Alex forced himself to exhale. *Let go. Let go.*

He wanted to cry but refused the urge. Instead, he marched back to where Maggie waited. She glanced at him as he approached and smiled. She had something leather rolled and tucked under her arm.

"Looks like everything fit just fine."

"Yeah…Thanks," he said grudgingly.

"Here." She held the leather up. "A guilt offering. I thought you might like it."

He took the black hooded riding jacket from her hands, momentarily distracted from his grief. "Damn." He slipped his arms through the sleeves. The jacket fit perfectly. The hem fell six inches below his knee. He pulled the hood up, shrouding his face in shadow.

"Like it?"

He snorted. "Yeah. I *like* it...Thank you."

"Here, you might want these, too." She handed him a pair of black, fingerless, leather gloves. "Your palms could be a danger to others right now. Be careful what you touch."

He slipped the soft leather over his hungry hands.

"Ready to go?"

He sighed. "As ready as I'll ever be, I guess...If I don't come back..."

"I'll assume you're dead or you've moved on."

"Yeah. Okay," he said awkwardly.

"I know we don't know each other. We've hardly spoken since you came here...and I know you hate me, but...you're welcome to come back here and stay with me...we could look out for each other."

He frowned at her for a moment, a number of rude retorts going through his mind, but he held them inside as he thought about the fact she didn't have to say that. She didn't have to offer it.

"Thanks...um...bye." He walked away from her.

Alex traveled toward the village, his mind blank except for the question, *What are you doing?* repeating over and over in his head. *Maybe I'm committing suicide.*

He walked at a steady pace until he reached the halfway point. Stopping short, he couldn't move. The sunlight felt stingingly uncomfortable. He closed his eyes, feeling the coldness inside them. He should go back. This was the worst idea. He shook himself, moved ahead, and stopped questioning. This was happening, no matter the danger or the outcome.

Everything around him was familiar. The woods, so close to the village, were his second home as a child. A pang vibrated through his heart as he realized he was saying goodbye to the woods as well. The outskirts of the village were silent. He couldn't see or hear anyone. He moved toward the square, where he knew his funeral was probably already happening.

The crowd was quiet, heads bowed. He kept to the back of the people, pulling his hood further down, shadowing his face. The only noise was the snapping of the bonfire in the center of the square. He looked around for Isolde. She was in the front, next to his parents. Her head was covered in a black veil. He couldn't see her face, and she didn't move at all, as if she'd been carved of stone.

Brenden clung to Mother, supporting her as she sobbed quietly. His little brother looked older to him in that moment. The circumstance was forcing him to grow up prematurely. Brenden's eyes were bloodshot, and his cheeks were flushed, but he held his tears inside and acted the man. Alex was proud of him. He wasn't the only one to look older, he noticed as his father stepped forward to the fire, his face drawn.

The hatchet Alex had used to kill the buck was clasped in his father's hands. He held it up for everyone to see.

"Alexander was so many good things. Honest, loyal, and strong. He was a fine blacksmith, as most of you know, from needing his services over the last few years. This hatchet was the last thing he forged." His father swallowed, and then dropped the hatchet into the flames of the bonfire.

Still holding tightly to Brenden's hand, his mother stepped forward. Alex closed his eyes when he saw what she held up. Her voice shook so hard it was almost impossible to understand her words.

"I made this when I first knew I was pregnant with Alex...my...my first born...my sweet son."

Her whole body shook as she threw his baby blanket into the flames. Alex leaned against the nearest tree as his heart shattered. Why had he come to see this? Why? He turned and walked away. He wouldn't watch his brother or Isolde burn something that was tied to their memories of him. He'd seen all he could stand. But he didn't get too far away before all the people at his funeral cried out his name.

It was the custom, once the family finished speaking and putting what they brought into the fire, for everyone to say the name of the dead. Some shouted, others cried, and some whispered his name. The sound echoed over the tops of the trees and sent an icy chill down his back. Alex was truly dead. So who was he? He walked through the village and back out into the wilds. The shadows of the trees wrapped around him. His eyes felt frozen. His hands burned cold. And his heart turned to ice as he accepted his own death.

He sat down, leaning back against a tree trunk and waited. He was alone for only a few moments when Maggie came up beside him and sat down.

"Hey, Blondie. What can I do for you?" Her voice was so warm and soothing.

He sighed. "Nothing."

"What are you going to do now? Have you lost your will to live?"

He closed his eyes. "What's it to you?"

When she didn't answer he looked at her. She rubbed the stone on her necklace and chewed her lip.

"What?" he asked her.

"I've seen things, in the stone… Sometimes it shows me snatches of the future. I didn't see you at first, but I do now. You're important. The way you are now. Your transformation was necessary… There's a storm coming."

He glanced up at the cloudless sky. "Obviously."

She smirked. "Not that kind of a storm. I don't know when it will arrive, but only you can calm it."

"Me?"

"You."

He rubbed his cold eyes. "I don't know anything. I don't know where I'm going, what I'm doing, or even who I am. Leave me alone. I'm not ready to leave all this behind, yet."

"Okay. I understand. You know where to find me when you're ready to learn the extent of your abilities." She stood and walked away. Her stride made absolutely no sound as she left.

Sneaky. He wouldn't have believed it possible, but what she'd said distracted him. He turned her words around in his mind a few times, before the sorrow came back, cracking him over the head sharply.

He waited for nightfall before slinking back to the outskirts of the village. He saw no one outside of their homes. Light illuminated the windows. He was detached, a ghost floating through his past life, unable to touch any of it. He went home and peeked through the window. A crack in the curtains gave him a sliver of a view of them. They sat at the table, not speaking. He should just open the door and go in. Tell them what happened…there was a chance they might still love him anyway.

He shook himself. Yes, they would love him, but that wouldn't stop them from killing him. That short future was unquestioningly worse. He would remain dead. They would remember him as he was. That was the only gift he could give them. He leaned against the back of the house and listened to them over the next hour. They talked very little before going to bed, and he couldn't understand the words, but he committed the resonance of their voices to his heart.

The darkness matured. He wasn't done stalking those he loved. He imagined Isolde would be asleep by now. He could climb through her window and kiss her one last time. As he approached her house, another shadow beat him there. Alex ducked behind the lean-to and held his breath, watching. The shadow now tapping lightly on her window was Troy. Rage boiled hot in his stomach at his best friend's actions. What the hell did he think he was doing?

Isolde cracked the window for him. Shock slapped Alex. There was no evidence of grief on her face. No traces of shed tears. Her eyes were neither puffy nor bloodshot. She looked the same as always.

"Come on," he whispered to her.

She smiled and closed the window. What was going on here? In a minute, she came out the back door. Hand and hand, they ran into the night. Alex followed them, unbelieving what he saw. They snuck to *his* house! The one he'd built for him and Isolde.

He crept up to the window and listened. Maybe there was a perfectly good excuse for this. They didn't light any candles.

"How is this going to work?" Isolde asked quietly. "You said you had a plan."

"I said I was working on a plan. Alex dying wasn't a part of my plan but now that he's dead...we can see each other more. It will be easier."

"What about Joan? I'm not going to settle for just being your mistress. I have to consider my future and my standing in the community."

Troy laughed. "No one will know about us. I'm going to work it out so this house is mine."

"You have to marry me," she demanded.

"You know I want nothing else, but how is that going to work?"

"I'm pregnant!"

"Is it mine?"

"Of course it is! Alex never touched me. I held him back."

Alex pushed his back hard into the stone wall, both of his hands pressed tight over his mouth. He never knew betrayal could feel this way, like every one of his bones broke into slivers and entered into his veins, going straight to his heart. *How could they?* She'd made him believe she loved him. And Troy, they'd been best friends since they were boys. How could he seduce Isolde right under his nose?

"Don't worry, Isolde. Just blame the baby on Alex. He's not here to contradict you. Take the guilt off yourself. Tell people he forced himself on you. Because he was my best friend, I'll make the case that I feel obligated to raise the child in his memory. We'll be allowed to marry. I'll talk to my father about releasing me from my betrothal to Joan."

"Oh, Troy..."

They quit talking, and Alex could hear the rustling and breathing of passion beginning. Sorrow took a backseat to rage in that moment. He wasn't going to listen to that, but he wasn't going to allow the backstabbing villains to enjoy their tryst either. Now he knew why men often killed when they discovered their wives in bed with someone else. Oh, he wanted to kill them. He could. Everything inside him tunneled down to unrestrained dark places. This darkness was hot like the inside of an ember.

He strode away from the house, picked up a large rock, and threw it through the bedroom window. Isolde screamed in fright, and Troy yelled in alarm.

Alex sprinted away before he gave in to the revenge he craved. "I saw you!" he yelled at the house. "Whore!"

Burning like a blade in the forging fire, he left the village, never to return.

CHAPTER FOUR

Maggie poked a stick into the fire, letting her eyes slide out of focus. Alex would be back, she was sure of it, she just didn't know when. How long would he stalk his past? Sighing, she threw the stick into the flames and rubbed her palm over the white stone on her necklace. Tears threatened as she felt the fracture through the stone. Was there any way she could mend it? She was honestly too scared to try. Her shoddy spell work was what had broken it to begin with. The magic of the stone still worked, she had to be content with that.

She had only one other stone from her homeland, and she would have crafted a new necklace out of it, if it weren't for Alex. Not sure when or how, but she felt he would need the other stone more than she.

Warmth filled the necklace and it lit up. The light streamed through her fingers. She smiled to herself as she heard him coming back. That was faster than expected. He wasn't walking leisurely, or running. He was marching, his footfalls heavy, eating up the ground he covered. She closed her eyes and searched out to catch the tenor of his emotions. He was in a murderous rage.

Maggie got up and went quickly into her house. She got her largest tankard off the shelf and filled it with ale. Placing her hand over the rim, she whispered a spell, power going into the liquid. He emerged out of the trees just as she came back out of the house.

Tears streamed over his flushed cheeks. His mouth held a hard line, and his hands glowed pale blue straight through the gloves he wore. His gorgeous, icy eyes locked onto hers, and through his burning raw emotions, she saw his plea for help.

She strode up to him and handed him the tankard. He took it without question and drank it down. Smoke poured from his nose and mouth. He closed his eyes and threw his head back, a rumble in his throat. His hands stopped glowing. He reached out and clasped her against him in a crushing hug. Surprised, she struggled to breathe and patted him on the back. His tears fell on her shoulder.

"How can anything hurt this much?" he asked.

"The measure of pain the heart can feel is infinite."

"I need it to stop."

"It will. In time. The drink will take the edge off."

"Thank you."

"No problem. You better go lay down. That stuff will knock you out fast."

He nodded and slumped off to the house. "I thought she loved me," he mumbled. "I was...deceived."

"Go to sleep. When you wake, you'll begin a new life."

He nodded again, pushed the door open, and vanished behind it.

He slept for two days. Since there was nowhere else for her to sleep, she spent the nights dozing in the chair in the corner. During the days, she snuck back and forth from the village, stealing. No, not stealing, *gathering* things she knew rightfully belonged to Alex. She hoped when he woke he would be pleased with what she'd done for him. It had been a good deal of work, but she really didn't have anything else to do, and she was happy he'd returned.

Maggie knew when the effects of the spell she'd put in the ale would wear off. Knowing he'd be hungry, she made a vegetable soup, and a large loaf of bread. Right on cue, he emerged as soon as the bread was finished.

He rubbed his eyes and ran his fingers through his messy hair. He groaned and grimaced as he came toward her. She handed him a chunk of bread before he could ask, and then ladled the soup into a bowl for him.

"Thank you," he said thickly over his mouthful.

"You're welcome. I made a lot, figured you'd finish it off without any trouble."

Misery was deep set around his eyes, but he made the effort to smile a little at her. "I do eat a lot. My mother…" He paused and closed his eyes. "My mother always used to complain about it."

"I don't care how hungry you might be, I have to warn you, I don't kill animals for food," she said sternly. "And you won't either, if you want to avoid my wrath."

He frowned, but he looked like he was thinking. He touched the burn mark on his chest. Then he nodded. "They…animals, there is more to them than I used to know. I think. Is that why?"

"Many of them are my friends. Well, the warm-blooded ones. Cold blooded animals are not the same. They have life, but they do not carry a soul. Sometimes I kill fish to eat. There's no personality there."

"So, you can speak to animals?"

"I wouldn't be able to have much of a friendship with them if I couldn't."

His eyes lit up. "Can you teach me to talk to them?"

She was happy at his response. "Perhaps. I'm willing to try and teach you. I'll have to think about how I might go about that."

When he finished his food, he looked for a long time at his hands. He rubbed them together and flexed his fingers. "I have to learn what I can do...how to control it. I feel the hunger of this power." His shoulders slumped, and he hung his head. "I don't know who I am..." His dejected demeanor shifted into sorrow and rage. "How could they have done that?"

"What are you saying?"

"My fiancée and my best friend...behind my back for I don't know how long."

"Oh...I'm sorry."

"I thought she loved me."

"Guess not."

He looked up, hooking her with his furious gaze. "How could I have not known? How could I have believed such a lie for so long? Were there signs of the truth that I never noticed or just flat out ignored?"

"Signs of their actions?" she asked.

"No. Signs that her words were false. Signs that she really felt nothing for me."

Maggie folded her hands and weighed her words before she said them. "I'm sure there were signs... Did you ever make her cry?"

"Cry? Why would I have made her cry?"

"Thoughtless words or actions. Did you ever see the evidence of hurt feelings? Did you see her grief at your funeral?"

"No," he said slowly, going over his memories in his mind.

"Well, there it is. You couldn't hurt her. She never gave you the power to hurt her."

"I don't understand you."

Maggie smiled softly. She wasn't surprised he didn't get it. "Love is surrender. She never gave you her heart, thus you never had any power over her...if you can injure a woman by just a thoughtless word, she has surrendered her love to you. That is one of the proofs of love— pain."

"I never wanted to hurt her."

"Ah, yes. That is because you loved her. If she bleeds when pricked, that is the proof of her love. How you respond to causing the pain...that will be the proof of your love, or lack thereof." Maggie blushed and shook herself. "At least that's what my mum taught me. I myself have never been in love. But she knew all about love, more than she ever wanted to, and the pain and glory of it."

"I've heard lots of things said about love, but never anything like that. And yet your words ring true to me. I won't forget what you said...because I will never be deceived again."

"You can't know that, Alex."

"That's not my name."

"Oh, right. Sorry, Blondie."

He snorted and shook his head. "No. That's not my name either. I don't know my name yet."

"Well, until you decide, it's the one you're getting."

"It's not just what Isolde did. I was deceived by my best friend, too." His eyes lit up again. "I want to always be able to see the truth in everyone, in everything. You've already changed me magically. Can you give me that power as well?"

Maggie crossed her arms and narrowed her eyes. "I think I could manage that, but I won't just yet."

"Why not?"

"Not until you've gained control over the gift you have. Master that, then I will add to your ability. In fact, now that I'm thinking about it, this is a good request. Coupled with your current power, a bullshit detector will give you a good balance. You need to know the truth of things as a necromancer."

He shuddered slightly.

"What's with you?" she asked.

"My head is all wrong. I'm angry, and I'm thinking about everything in the wrong way because I'm angry. I shouldn't learn to use magic. I should learn to repress it. But..."He flexed his hands. "I'm ashamed to admit this, it feels good. It hurts, too, at times. But since I've lost everything, I'd like to think it wasn't all in vain. Maybe I could do something good with this evil power, but how do I practice without killing people or animals?"

"Learn to use your sight first. Focus on your eyes. Look at me. Can you see where my soul is inside me?"

His eyes roamed over her, searching. He scowled, frustrated and shook his head. "No, wait...I see..."

Maggie smiled as she watched him. The pale blue of his eyes sharpened, and his hands began to glow.

"Put your hands behind your back!" she ordered.

He blinked and looked down at his hands. "Whoa! Okay, that's weird."

She sighed in relief when he clasped his hands behind his back.

"I see a light inside you. It's sort of orange in color and shapeless like a puff of smoke. It's moving!"

Maggie laughed. "You'll find most move around inside the body they inhabit. With practice you can choose to see or not see. Likewise, you can choose to take it from the body, leave it, or hold it captive."

"*What?* I can hold a soul captive?"

"Yes. Easily. You can cage it, talk to it, and use it."

"Use it how? What you're saying sounds like slavery. Like I could be a slave master of souls."

She nodded gravely. "You could be."

His expression wrinkled like he'd just swallowed something sour. "I would never do that."

Maggie pointed her finger at him. "Careful. The word *never* has terrible power to prove you a liar."

His eyes flashed brightly, and his mouth set into a thin line. "I will *never* do that," he said through clenched teeth.

"Ease up. I'm just telling you what your power will make you capable of, not what you will or should do with it. I will, however, give you this one solemn warning. Are you listening?"

"Yes."

"Pulling a soul to yourself as someone dies, whether through sickness, old age, or in battle, is different than taking a soul from someone healthy. It is a line you should never cross. If you do, your power will go from a neutral place and become dark. Taking for taking's sake, or vengeance, will push you through a door that will bolt behind you. Your power will twist your mind and turn you into a monster. There will be no redemption for you after that."

He hung his head and exhaled raggedly. "Why not just kill me? What point is there to me? Will you promise to end me if I go that way?"

"I promise."

"Will you be able to? Are you strong enough?"

Maggie half smiled. "I'm up to it, Blondie. Don't worry. I hope it doesn't come to that. I've made it sound more wild than it has to be. You make the right choices, your power will not run away with you. You will master control of it very quickly, if you set yourself to the task."

He sighed and stood, bringing his hands back around and rubbing them together. The glow faded away. "All right, seeing was easy, but as soon as I saw your soul, my hands opened up and wanted to take it. My palms feel *hungry*."

"I expect they do. Put the gloves I gave you back on. I want you to take a stroll deeper into the forest and work on seeing the soul of every living creature you come across. Don't give in to the pull in your hands. Just practice looking until you can see the soul immediately."

"Then what?"

"Then come back. I'll have a present for you when you return."

He frowned. "A present? What for?"

She flipped her hair over her shoulder and began walking away. "Just another guilt offering. See you later."

He watched her go into the house and close the door, feeling a bit lost and unsure about following her instructions. Maybe she wanted to turn him into a weapon. She was the one who'd created the spell to begin with. He decided to ask her that evening why she'd cast the spell in the first place. He thought about what he was going to do, and his hands began to buzz. He needed his gloves.

64

As if she could read his mind, the next second, Maggie opened the door and held out his coat and gloves. He walked over and took them from her hands, careful to not touch her.

"Thanks."

She nodded and closed the door again. He walked away, shrugging on the coat. As he slipped his hands into the gloves, a terrible sorrow sighed inside his heart. Would he ever be able to touch someone again? His mind raced through all the ways humans touched one another. A helping hand to a stranger, a hug to the grieving, the caress of a lover…would he ever be able to do those things?

His hands buzzed harder, distracting him. Power was his mistress now, and he would learn how to please her.

The forest grew thick around him as he walked. Things lit up before his eyes as the cold shivered into his irises. He saw life thriving all around him in ways he never knew existed. Light and color in shades and levels he couldn't name. Plants and trees held a steady illumination of color that was green, violet, and grey all at once. The few animals he saw startled and amazed him. The birds streaked through the sky, burning a trail behind them. The squirrels chasing each other blurred a vibrant reddish gold.

His heart swelled, instantly in love with this new beauty, grateful he could see it. The day slipped swiftly past him as he wandered. The sun sank beneath the treetops, but there was so much light everywhere. It was only more beautiful in the dark. The longer he looked, the better he could see the difference between types of life and spirit. The animals carried a spirit made of a brighter fabric than the plants. He could see what Maggie meant about things that had life but not soul.

He came to the edge of a small river. Pale white lights darted under the water's surface. Delighted like a child, he pulled off his boots, coat, shirt, and gloves. The centers of his palms lit up as he walked into the river up to his waist. He put his hands in the water. The white wisp of life in the fish swimming past him shot out through the gills and straight into his hand. The fish floated to the surface, dead.

It wasn't at all like when he'd pulled the stag's spirit inside himself. That had been a soul. This was like a breath, a fast flash of something unsubstantial, and then it was gone. It felt like a cool breeze in his hand, and it didn't move through his whole body the way the stag did. He touched the mark on his chest as he thought about that night and what that experience felt like.

His stomach rumbled. He gathered the fish floating on the surface and laid them out on the shore. He let himself drip for a few minutes before dressing again and hooking his fingers through the gills of the fish. He and Maggie could have them for dinner.

When he returned Maggie already had a fire burning, skewers, cut vegetables, and herbs laid out.

"How did you know?" he asked amazed as she took the fish from him.

She smiled, laying the fish out, beginning to clean and bone them. "My stone. I was watching you today. Making sure you didn't need my help or do something stupid."

"Oh..." He blushed. "I'm glad I left my pants on when I went into the river."

She snorted but didn't reply.

"Am I going to have to tell you every time I need some privacy?" he demanded.

"No. I've no interest in being a voyeur. If I did, I wouldn't have told you I watched you today. Anyway, these are ready to roast. I'm starving."

They sat on opposite sides of the fire as they ate their dinner. He watched her over the tops of the flames, trying to figure her out and slightly mesmerized by the reflective nature of her eyes, like an animal's.

"Thank you for bringing dinner home," she said. "Have you decided to stay here with me after all?"

"You're not asking for a *relationship*, right?"

"I'm asking for you to be my closest neighbor. With an understanding of mutual cooperation. As I said before, we could look out for one another. I am not asking for your affection, plutonic or otherwise. I will act as your teacher until you are secure in your powers. Perhaps, I hope, in the future we may become friends. That is all, Blondie."

He nodded. "All right. I agree." He looked over his shoulder at her small house. "I need to build my own house."

"That you do! I'm sick of giving up my bed just because you're drunk with a broken heart."

"I appreciate your forbearance. I'll sleep under the stars tonight."

She smiled, and he was struck by the sly, foxlike nature of it. He wasn't attracted to her in any way romantically, but it was impossible to deny she was beautiful. Her smile fell, and the color drained from her cheeks as the stone around her neck flashed.

Maggie gasped and held the stone up next to her eye like a monocle. He held his breath, alarmed. After a few seconds she exhaled and lowered the stone.

"What? What is it?"

"It's all right. Just the storm. It's churning, drawing closer."

"What storm?" he asked. "When will it get here?"

"Soon. You will know when you see it. You are the only one that can calm it."

"How? Do I have power over the clouds?"

She smiled again and shook her head. "I told you, it's not that kind of storm."

He sighed and scowled at her. "You're not going to elaborate, are you?"

"Nope."

He looked down at his hands, removed his gloves, and flexed his fingers.

"You feel better now?" she asked.

"Yes. Not quite so shaky. Not so worried. I saw beauty beyond description today. It lifted my heavy heart a bit."

"I'm glad." She yawned deeply. "I'm fading. Is there anything else you need to ask me right now? I want to show you your present, and then get a full night's sleep in *my* bed."

His mind ran through the pack of questions in his head, but he settled on the one he wanted to know most. "Why did you cast the spell to begin with? The one inside me?"

"Of course you would ask me that when I'm so sleepy." She complained. "The answer will only give you lots more questions. I will answer them all, but not tonight. Tonight I will tell you I created the spell, trying to trap the power in my necklace, to protect myself from my enemy. I am not human. I was not born on this world. My mother brought me here as a baby, when she fled our homeland of Mordian. What was once a vibrant world of witches and wizards is now an aberrant place of only wizards, who refuse the fate of a natural lifespan. Desperate for immortality, they steal life from other worlds. My mother taught me all about them. I am of the same race as them. They cannot be defeated, except by the dead. Their power has no effect on those already dead.

"As I told you, there is a storm coming. The wizards are on the move, seeking to conquer new worlds, to drink the sources of life, so they will never die. I had hoped, that if I ever happened to cross paths with a wizard, I could chase him away, or kill him with the help of a willing soul."

"How could a soul kill a wizard?"

She shrugged. "I don't know. I only know it's the only method of defense my mother taught me. I don't know why the spell rejected me and decided to chase you down instead. Please accept that is all I can tell you for now." She yawned again. "Come with me. I'll show you your gift."

He stood and followed her. Around the back of her house, fifty feet away, tucked in a tight circle of trees was a structure. It was nothing more than a roof on poles, but he recognized it for what it was. It was a workshop, like his old one. As he walked into it, his heart lifted. All of his blacksmithing tools were there. Everything he needed to forge again.

"I didn't consider it stealing when I took all of this stuff, because I know it was yours to begin with," Maggie said.

He picked up his favorite hammer, enjoying the familiar weight of it in his hand. "Thank you...I...this means so much to me."

"You're welcome."

With a sleepy smile, she turned and walked back to the house.

He set up the fire pit and organized his new workshop for a few hours. When he finally felt sleepy, he laid down on the ground, under the stars. His mind wandered over what Maggie had told him about wizards. He didn't want to believe her. He wouldn't have before his transformation. He'd have just thought her crazy.

All of his life, he'd been led to believe that magic was evil and magic users had done something evil to themselves to become that way. But that wasn't the truth. He had to change his thoughts. It wasn't easy, like lifting something heavy and oddly shaped for the first time, the newness making you sore. Maggie hadn't chosen to be a witch. She had been born one. If she was evil, that darkness wasn't her origins or blood.

He touched the cold line on his neck. His choices would determine his level of darkness, but how could he truly gain control? How could he be near the dying? How could he know where to be, at the right time, without being the killer himself?

His stomach squirmed a little. If there was some greater forces at work in his life, he felt they had made a mistake. Or was it the spell itself that chose him? He wasn't the right man for whatever this job would be. Wizard killer? Storm calmer?

He closed his eyes and sighed. *What's my name?* He fell asleep with that question drifting in his mind.

He'd never been much of dreamer, but while he slept he saw the flash of sparks and flame reflected on a bright blade.

Loud clanging of metal on metal woke Maggie early in the morning. She groaned and put her fingers in her ears, but the noise still came through.

"I'm an idiot!" she said angrily to herself. "Why didn't I think about the noise he would make with all those tools?"

Groggy, she stalked out of her house to order him to cease and desist, at least for another two hours. As she crossed the distance to his workplace, the morning air woke her more fully. She slowed her pace, and then stopped, fascinated by what she saw. She'd never watched a blacksmith do anything. It was like its own magic. Raw and elemental. His focus was razor sharp, and she had no desire to distract him. Instead, she hoped he would continue without noticing her, for she felt deep inside her bones, she was witnessing something important.

"Come closer, Maggie, if you like." He didn't take his eyes off his work. "Maybe you can explain this."

The heat was intense under the roof. She looked at the glowing hot metal, not getting too close.

"I dreamed about this," he said. "Along with a few other things."

"It's an axe blade, right?" she asked.

"Yes. I've never made one shaped like this before. Do you know what it is designed to cut?"

She pursed her lips and looked closer. She did know. Questions she had about him now fell into place like puzzle pieces. She was surprised she had not seen this coming. He looked at her, eyebrows raised. She nodded.

"I know my name," he said.

"Well?"

"X."

She smiled. "Short for Axe?"

"No. Short for Executioner."

CHAPTER FIVE

PARADIGM, REGIA

Kindel rubbed his head and sat on the edge of his bed, unable to sleep, again. He glanced up at the wrapped present on the shelf, feeling stupid beyond measure. A layer of dust covered the grey wrapping paper and bow. How long had it sat there? He shook his head. Why pretend he didn't know? It was almost a year old, not that it had sat there on the shelf all that time. No, he'd moved it all around his house. Every morning he swore that would be the day he would give it to her, and every day he chickened out and left it in his house.

He felt his cheeks burn even though he was alone and in the dark. Ena didn't care for him as anything other than a co-worker. She wasn't attracted to him. She never flirted or tried to tease him. He figured she probably didn't even like him as a friend. She was driving him crazy.

He'd been incredulous at himself when he first started looking at her, *really* looking at her. And even more incredulous when he noticed his feelings had changed as well. She wasn't his type. She was demure, and girlish. He'd always been attracted to strong, rebellious women, like Forest. For years he was convinced he was in love with Forest, but he let go of his fantasies instantly when she came back from her mission, mated to Syrus. And letting go of her emotionally was easy, so he guessed it hadn't really been love at all. Forest was one his best friends now and that was all, besides being his boss.

But Ena... She was precious to him. She twisted him into knots every day. Her laugh was adorable and infectious. The way she raised one eyebrow and pursed her lips when she was angry turned him on completely. She *was* strong, but it was a quiet strength. And she was intelligent and worked hard without complaint. He wanted to protect her, well, he wanted to protect her from everyone but himself. Her innocent ways made him want to teach her some things, get her a little dirty.

A rumble rolled over the sky as the blood lock shuddered. This could be the end, he thought. The wizards were trying to kick in the door. What was he waiting for? He got up and dressed carefully for the day. He didn't care that it was way early for him to go in to work; he wasn't going to get any more sleep in any case. He'd finally take Ena the small present he'd gotten for her a year ago, and try to tell her how he felt. And whatever happened, happened.

Fortress was mostly dark when he arrived. No one but security was there this time of morning. He used his key to open the office. His desk was on the side of the room, while Ena's was in the center. Taking a deep breath, he set the little wrapped box on her desk, straightening the edges of the bow and turning the little piece of parchment tied to the ribbon face up. The ink on the parchment was a little faded but still readable. *To Ena, from Kindel,* was all it said.

Knowing he had a while before she came in, he made some coffee and looked over his workload for the rest of the week. Work was a fairly ineffective distraction. The present kept drawing his attention, as if it occasionally screamed at him. He thought about taking it back. There was still time to punk out. He was going to make a fool of himself. She didn't have any feelings for him.

He leaned back in his chair and closed his eyes, remembering the day he met her, when Forest took up her position as Hailemarris. She'd sent him to the Onyx Castle to offer Ena the job as her secretary. She'd accepted the job enthusiastically before he'd even finished offering it to her, and was ready to go with him in a matter of minutes. He'd thought her very young and cute at the time, and probably a poor choice for the job, but she proved him wrong the very first day. She was a quick study, and had shown herself to be serious about her job and future.

He knew she wanted to travel. She had let it slip once, but he caught it, and remembered. If only she might give being with him a chance, he would take her anywhere she wanted to go. He never did anything, living a modest lifestyle, and had saved most of his income. Travel, even extended, exotic travel was something he could afford to give her.

As the morning wore on, the sounds of shuffling feet filled the halls, as people began arriving. His stomach squirmed as Ena came in. She looked surprised.

"You're very early this morning, Kindel," she said, taking off her jacket. Then her eyes rounded. "Oh, no, was there something we forgot to do yesterday? Is that why you're early?"

"No." His voice sounded off, too high, or something. He cleared his throat. "There's nothing. I've been having trouble sleeping. I was awake early and had nothing else to do."

She sighed, relaxing. "Oh. Okay. It's going to be busy. Forest messaged me. She won't be in today. I'm going to have to reschedule all of her appointments."

"Would you like some help with that?" he offered.

"That's sweet of you, but your work is more important than mine. I can handle it."

His chest constricted as she sat down at her desk. She picked up the box, looked at the note on the top, glanced over at him, and then put the present down on the corner of her desk, unopened. She opened her ledger and began scribbling as though nothing had happened. She didn't look at him or speak to him again, ignoring the present as if it wasn't there at all. Perturbed and confused he went about his work. Was she waiting for something like her lunch break to open it?

As she predicted, it was a very busy day, and the present just sat there on the edge of her desk the whole time. People came in and out. Ena talked with them easily, promising them Forest would honor their appointments at the next available time. When no one was in the office with them, Ena didn't speak or even look at him, and the present was the damn elephant in the room.

Kindel had never had such a bad or stressful day in his life. Of all the scenarios he'd imagined, no response at all was not even among his worst case ideas. When quitting time rolled around he closed up his desk, feeling defeated and sad. But there was a little anger as well. Ena had never been rude to him. So what if she didn't feel anything for him? They weren't enemies. They worked together, and he had brought her something. Why didn't she open it? Or acknowledge it in some way, at least? Had he done something to offend her?

"I'm going home now," he said.

She looked at him, but said nothing. Anger won out in that moment. He walked up to her desk and reached for the box, prepared to take it back. "I thought you might like this, but since you can't even be bothered to open it..."

As soon as his fingers closed over the edge, she stabbed her letter opener into the top of the box. He jumped, retracting his hand. "Whoa!" he exclaimed.

She dragged the box to the center of her desk with the letter opener handle. "What is this about, Kindel?" her voice was cold.

"What do you mean?"

She scowled beautifully and tore the wrapping open and lifted the lid of the box. Instead of delight, she raised one brow as she lifted the shimmery, grey scarf out of the tissue paper.

"I just...I know you like grey," he said apologetically. "I saw it one day, and thought of you."

She put the scarf back in the box, closed the lid, and stood up. She walked right up to him and looked hard into his face. He couldn't help the heat that flooded his cheeks. She grabbed his wrist and lifted his hand up, touching his sweaty palm with her index finger. She dropped it and took a step back.

"Are you trying to make a move on me?" she demanded.

"I...well..."

"You're really nervous. You're blushing, and your palms are sweaty."

"Maybe I'm getting sick." He paused, he wouldn't be a coward any longer. "No. You're right. I am making a move on you. I can't sleep, I can't think about anything but you. You're the only thing in my mind. When I do sleep, I dream of you. I want you to be happy. I want to protect you. I want to give you things. I know you don't feel anything like that for me...but please consider giving us a chance."

She closed her eyes and sighed. "About time."

"What?"

To his surprise she threw her head back and laughed. He'd never seen Ena laugh so hard. "Oh, you stupid man. So dense. Don't you know I'm totally into you? I've been dropping you hints forever!"

He was stunned "When?"

She just laughed again and shook her head. "Why don't you kiss me, and we'll see if there's any chemistry between us?"

He moved slowly, cupping her cheek, and running his thumb lightly

76

over her lips.

She bit down on his thumb, shocking him. "Not so easy," she said.

He kissed her roughly. The way he really wanted to. She wanted chemistry? He didn't know if she felt any, but he was swamped in it. He pulled back and looked down at her. Her eyes fluttered open and fixed on him.

"Well?" he asked.

She gave him a small smile. "Are you taking me to dinner?"

"Uh…yes. I suppose I am."

She flounced back around her desk, opened the box, pulled out the scarf and draped it over her shoulders. He offered her his arm. She linked hers through his as they left the office.

Tesla dozed, her mind half awake, waiting for her parents to finally go to sleep. As soon as they did, her eyes sprang open, and she slid out of bed. She dressed quickly, feeling antsy. She was going to find something tonight, she was sure of it. The feathery fingers of destiny tickled all around her. Merhl's words about letting her heart lead, rang in her mind again, as they had over and over since he'd said them.

She took a deep breath and exhaled on a hiss. She was about to open the strata, but her hands surged. Stabbing, shocking, and throbbing, the power pushed under her skin. She curled her hands into fists and bit down on her lip, holding in a cry of pain. Before it got worse, she tore open the atmosphere and rushed to the Everpath.

As soon as she felt the ground under her feet, she screamed. Lightning shot out of all ten fingers, flying through the air in long snakes through the hallway. The release had helped. She panted as the pain eased back to an ache and looked down both sides of the hall. Goosebumps rose on her skin, and her hair stood on end. She was alone, like always. But also, like always, cold fingers of warning and dread curled all through her. Although it seemed a neutral place, the Everpath was creepy, and there was no doubting the danger, especially when the wind blew down the hall. She closed her eyes for a second, pushing the fear away so she could listen to her instincts.

Tesla's footsteps echoed down the hall as she walked. She reached out and let her hand run lightly against the doors on her left, seeing if touch might direct her to the place she needed to be. She counted the doors as she went. Each one looked the same, but they all felt different. She knew immediately when she touched the door to a world she'd already been through. Suddenly, she stopped.

Tesla put both of her hands flat against the door. A ripple went through her hands, soothingly cool. This was a non-magical world. Basic. Plain even. So why did she want to go inside? What could it possibly offer her? Merhl said to try this kind of thing. The fact that she wanted to go inside so badly made her pause and question...almost fear.

No sound echoed down the hallway, but still Tesla jumped in alarm, her heart in her throat. Long shadows, like reaching fingers, stretched over the floor and walls toward her.

"I feel you... Come to me," a low seductive voice whispered.

Startled, Tesla ran as fast as she could, away from the shadows.

"Who are you? Don't go... I will give you everything... Anything you want, if only you would stop thwarting me. Come back, sweet thing... Come back... I need you..."

She reached the door to Regia and pushed through. She landed hard in her bedroom, her ankles burning and stinging as she hit the floor.

What was that? Was it talking to her, or was it a trap for anyone in the Everpath?

Chills rolled up her spine. That voice—it was disgusting, beautiful, rough and simultaneously soft... too soft. Tesla knew she would never forget that voice. She paced her floor. She had to go back. Was there any real danger in the reaching shadows? Was its power any match for hers? Well, she knew one thing. It wasn't going to stop her. She *had* to jump. There was no choice for her in that. And she was going back to that door, the one that called to her. She grabbed the strata and then hesitated. Not yet. She would wait, at least a little while before going back, and hopefully the thing lurking would give up. She shook out the opening in the air and went instead to the Heart.

She landed just outside the ring of crystal trees circling the flame. The fire sparked around the top in response to her arrival.

"Tesla." The Heart's guttural, male/female voice whispered inside her head.

She went down on her knees and placed her hands flat on the ground in a bow.

"It's been a few days. I've missed you." The Heart said.

I was injured while jumping. I had to seek my grandfather's assistance. He knows about the blood lock. I had to tell him. She answered in her mind.

"Have you found anything new? The attacks on the lock have become sporadic. The wizards are trying new ways to break through. Each time is different. The lock needs maintenance. There's a fracture. I'm sure the wizards are unaware of it for the moment. But a moment longer may be all we have before they discover it and focus their powers on it."

Tesla got to her feet and entered the circle. She reached into the flames and opened the tesseract. She saw the fracture immediately. *Help me.* She pleaded to the Heart.

"Of course."

She pulled her right hand out of the tesseract, letting the lightning extend out through her skin. The flames wrapped around the red currents, mixing with them, until a small tornado of lightning and fire twisted in the center of Tesla's palm. She tossed it into the air and caught it sideways before shoving it into the crack in the blood lock. The edges of the fracture fused back together, and a red tremor rolled through the sky.

"Beautiful work, Tesla. As always."

She sighed, closed the tesseract, and took a step back. *Thank you, but it's not good enough. I haven't found anything new, but I feel as though I may have found the door to something. I didn't go through because there was something...odd in the Everpath. It frightened me, and I ran away.*

"Why did you not just attack it?"

It caught me off guard. It won't a second time.

"Take care of yourself. I love you. It would cause me grief if you died."

Thank you...I love you, too.

"When are you jumping again?"

Tomorrow night. I'll come back soon.

"Stay safe, princess."

I'm not a princess.

"Your lineage would suggest otherwise."

Tesla frowned, trying to imagine what her life would be like if her parents had decided to take the thrones. She looked down at herself. Torn jeans, combat boots, and a knife on her belt. A strange, strangled giggle bubbled up her throat.

Maybe my dad is right about me. I am like my mother. Some princess I'd be.

Tesla bid the Heart goodnight and decided to go home and not back to the Everpath. She changed into her pajamas and climbed into bed. She was home earlier than usual. Closing her eyes, relaxing under the warmth of her comforter, the voice slithered back into her mind. She listened to it over and over with a kind of morbid pleasure. It was not for her. Too mature, too dirty. Repulsed and intrigued at the same time as to who or what the voice belonged to. She shook it off. Her mind drifting onto the door she hadn't gone through as she fell asleep.

Forest scowled in the darkness of her bedroom and rolled over in bed. "She's back," she whispered to Syrus.

"Good," he grunted.

He reached over and pulled her into his side. She tried to relax against him, but she was rigid.

"Did you think your parents were stupid, when you were a teen?" she asked.

"Yes," he admitted easily.

"I'm angry, Syrus."

"I know. I am, too. But what can we do? We can't go with her wherever she's going. Not even Rahaxeris can go with her."

Forest ground her teeth together. "Why are you so calm about this?"

He sighed. "I'm not. You're too preoccupied in what you're feeling to listen to my heart. I'm as torn up as you are about this. I'd ground her, except that wouldn't work. My power can't hold her."

"We've known she was sneaking out, but I wish Rahaxeris hadn't told us what she was doing." Tears choked Forest. "How can I help my baby? What can I do?"

"There's nothing, Forest. She's trying to save the world. She knows things, can see and do things that no one else in all of Regia can do or comprehend."

Frustration rippled all over Forest. She growled and climbed on top of Syrus, grabbing him roughly by the wrists and kissed him violently. She rose up at the waist and looked down at him. His eyebrows raised in question.

"I have nowhere else to alleviate what I'm feeling."

He chuckled and grabbed her hips. "Bring it. Take it all out on me, baby."

MORDIAN CASTLE

A warm fragrant breeze blew playfully through the open balcony. The wizard king, Lachlan, walked barefoot on the pale green marble floors. He carried the universe sphere in one hand. Stolen from a recent world the wizards had consumed, it was his new favorite toy, and perhaps the most powerful and deadly tool he'd ever come across. He'd gutted it immediately, since its previous owner had filled it with good. Lachlan poured his own magic into it, connecting it to Mordian and his own personal desires. And tonight, it had come through for him. The sphere began to follow the movements of the power that prevented him from conquering Regia.

Aside from the fact it was still in his way, the wall over Regia didn't interest him. He cared about the wall's creator. All he knew of the individual was they were cunning, magical, and could jump through worlds in a way that gave him a pang of jealousy. With the help of the sphere, he'd come very close to getting a glimpse of him or her tonight.

The breeze flowed in his long dark hair and billowed through his open robe as he stepped out onto the balcony. He looked out at the open night sky. Golden stars winked in the clear expanse of midnight blue, and an ocean of pink clouds stretched as far as he could see just under the balcony, obstructing his view of anything under them. Unfortunately, the opulence of his castle, the unsurpassed beauty of Mordian, along with wealth and pleasure, was losing its flavor for Lachlan. He'd grown depressed.

In the last year, Mordian had taken over many worlds. His lust for eternal power was boundless, but his desire was never satisfied. Regia was supposed to have been an easy snatch and grab. Being thwarted only intensified his hunger for the Heart of that world. Since he still didn't have it, the desire to capture and consume the person who created the wall was more seductive than the world itself. Perhaps spilling their blood would slacken his thirst for a while.

He held up the sphere and gazed into its moving, cosmic depths. The light signature of Regia's wall creator held steady at the moment. Their essence was as beautiful as a dark nebula. He knew they would taste good.

"Sire?"

Lachlan didn't turn to acknowledge Peyton. He came up behind him and ran his hands intimately up and down on his shoulders.

"Don't touch me," Lachlan snapped. "Until I've found a witch, or another female I can procreate with, I'm abstaining."

"As you wish," he backed away.

Lachlan turned then, eyeing his long-term consort. Peyton had an angry look. Lachlan returned it with a sardonic smile.

"Such a disrespectful look, Peyton." He tsked. "Speak your mind."

"All the witches are dead. You'll never find one."

"Perhaps... I still have hope. And when I find one, she will be my queen, and bear me children."

"What if you find one and she's ugly?"

"You're so narrow-minded. It's not her beauty I'm interested in, but her womb. Now leave me alone. You're too obsessed with your own beauty to be of any use to me."

"Actually, I *do* have news I know you care about."

"Well?"

"The last of our scouts have died."

"Good," Lachlan said. "About time."

"Are you planning to make any more?" Peyton was apprehensive.

Lachlan gave him a wide smile. "Scared I'd choose you? Relax. You've never displeased me that much. And no. No more scouts for now. I won't totally rule it out in the future, but I think we might have moved well beyond those methods."

Peyton let his relief show.

Lachlan rolled his eyes. "You've shown too much of your feelings on the matter, Peyton, and given me a great weapon against you. Idiot...If that is all, leave now."

Peyton curled his lip but bowed and walked away.

Once he was gone, Lachlan raised the sphere back up to his face, dragging his tongue over the cool, hard surface in one long lick. "I will own you, wall builder...whoever you are."

CHAPTER SIX

Maggie didn't pester X while he was working in his shop, which was most of the time. After two weeks, he'd made himself a hatchet, a woodcutting axe, arrowheads, a dagger, and completed his executioner's axe. When he needed a break, he took long walks alone, but he always came back by dinner time. With each passing day, she grew less and less anxious about his progression with his power. It seemed to her that he'd made peace with being a magic user. There were short bursts of time he became obviously angry, but he battled his inner demons in silence, pouring his fury into the metal he shaped.

She desired to talk to him more, but she didn't push, mostly because once he'd finished his day's work and eaten his dinner, he was exhausted. He said his sight felt natural to him now. It was time for her to direct him on the next level of his ability. She suspected he was thinking about it and putting it off out of fear, but then one morning X proved her wrong.

He woke her before the dawn, not with his usual anvil music, but a soft knock to her door. Barely coherent, she rolled out of bed and opened the door. The cool morning air breathed on her, waking her fully. X looked at her expectantly. He was clean, bright-eyed, and holding his woodcutting axe.

"I'm going to begin construction on my house today. Are there any trees in particular you don't want me to cut down?"

"Yeah, there are." She yawned and wrapped a shawl around her shoulders before heading outside with him.

Maggie pointed out the trees she wanted left alone.

"Is that it?" he asked.

"Yes. Just those. Otherwise, I don't care. Take your pick."

He smiled at her then, causing her to blink a few times. This was the first time she'd seen genuine happiness in his face.

"Ah, good. You didn't point out the one I really want."

Intrigued, Maggie smirked and crossed her arms over her chest. "Do you mind if I watch you?"

"I guess not. But it might look a bit…odd. I was going to try something before I cut it down. I'll need to concentrate, so you'll have to promise to not interrupt me."

More than a little intrigued now, she nodded. "You won't even know I'm there."

X approached a large tree and set his axe down on the ground. He removed his gloves. His hands began glowing faintly.

"You will be with me always," he whispered to the tree as he placed his hands flat on the trunk.

She couldn't see the way he could, but her eyes caught the hazy edges as the spirit of the tree retracted from the leaves and branches, sliding down to the base, and straight into his hands. He closed his eyes, his forearms trembling. She saw the shiver go through him.

X exhaled and opened his eyes. "Thank you," his voice was quiet as he held his hands together.

He looked over at her.

She walked up to him, looking intently at his hands. The glow faded into nothing. "You've got the spirit inside? You're holding it there?"

He nodded. "I'm holding it. It's not without effort. The spirit is trying to leave. If it doesn't settle in a moment, I'll let it loose. I was just hoping it would be content to remain with me."

Maggie's affection for him grew in that moment.

The next second he grimaced in pain and pulled the front of his shirt open. Smoke rose off his skin and black lines traced on his chest next to the antler mark, as if an invisible person tattooed him.

"Wait, please," he said to the spirit trying to push out of him, placing his hand over the growing marks. "Stay with me."

The smoke stopped. He pulled his hand away. The silhouette of the tree on his chest was no longer black, but a pale grey, like the ring around his neck.

"Well?" Maggie asked.

He smiled at her. "It broke into pieces and left, but one small sliver remained. It *chose* to stay with me!"

"I'm impressed, X, really."

"Do you think I'm ready to move on? Are you read to teach me more?"

"Yes, to both of your questions."

"I've been going over it in my head a lot the last few days. I thought I could go to the other village close by; I don't know anyone there. I would take my axe and see if there's a way I might be needed there as an executioner...When I say it out loud, it sounds stupid. But I have this feeling." He put his hand to his stomach. "I've dreamed about it. I think it will work."

"You're not scared?"

"Not scared, no. I know the reality of ending life, even guilty life, will probably not be like the way it is in my head. I feel unease but not fear. If I had anything to lose, I think I'd be afraid. Having nothing is miserable, but also freeing in a way."

Maggie's eyes widened in an *I just got an idea* kind of way. "When were you planning on going?"

He shrugged. "Tomorrow or the next day."

"I know I said I wouldn't give you anymore abilities before you mastered your current one, but…"

He smiled and held up his hand to silence her. "I think I know where you are going, and I've already thought of it. It's the only reason I would ever consider being an executioner. If you give me the power to see the truth in people, I will know if someone is guilty or not."

"Yes! But have thought about what do you plan to do if they aren't? If you don't kill them someone else will, you know."

He sighed and ran his hands through his hair. "I'm no hero. I don't have any illusions about that, but you said I could hold a soul. I need to learn how. If someone I executed was innocent…could I somehow give them a chance to right the wrong?"

She pursed her lips. "Hmm…that's quite an idea, X." She considered the possibilities. "Go ahead and cut that tree down. I have some work to do on this concept. We've got our work cut out for us. I'll try to get most of it done before dinner tonight. We can talk about this again then."

He picked his axe back up as she strode back to her house. She knew now what she was going to do with the other stone from Mordian.

Maggie took the stone from its hiding place in the crack in the wall and sat down on the floor with it. Her heart began pounding as she laid it down in front of her. The stone was the same cloudy white as the one

89

hanging around her neck. Her mind raced through flashes of ideas. The necromancer spell had cracked her stone in half. Inspired by that, she decided she needed to cut this stone in two as well.

Touching the tip of her bone wand to the stone, she closed her eyes and began building the spell with whispered words. A surge went out from her hand, into the wand, and filled the stone. The stone vibrated on the floor, gently at first. The tremors grew until the stone jumped. Light flashed painfully into her eyes as the stone broke into two equal pieces. Smoke rose up from the split edges.

She hummed and chanted a few Mordian words, as she ran the tip of her wand around the rough sides of each piece, over and over until both were smooth and rounded. She put her wand down and held the stones in her hands. *This will work.*

She got up from the floor, placed the stones on the bed, and spun a long strap of black leather out of thin air. Instinctively, she knew how long she needed it to be, just as she had known the right size to make X's clothes. As she tied knots around the stones her vision blurred, and her necklace flashed. Her hand trembled as she lifted the stone and looked into it. She saw X, perhaps only a day or two in the future...what she saw confirmed the truth of what he said he'd dreamed.

Maggie had finished her work by noon, and running on excited jitters, she busied herself with making bread and beginning soup for dinner. Anxious to show him what she'd done, she didn't want him wandering off to go fishing that afternoon. The constant sound of his axe allowed her to keep tabs on him without having to glance in his direction every few minutes.

He finally quit in the late afternoon. She couldn't help but be impressed with his physical stamina. She wished she could exert herself the way he did, for such long periods of time and still stay upright. He put his axe down next to the house, and then began walking away.

"Wait! Where are you going?"

He laughed as he turned back around. "I'm filthy. I'm going to wash up, so don't watch me on your little magic spy glass, because I won't be keeping my pants on this time."

She smirked and nodded. "Are you coming right back?"

"Yes. I'll be right back."

He ducked into the house and grabbed a clean set of clothes before heading off toward the river. She paced and stirred the soup while she waited. When she heard him coming back she quickly dished up food for him, anxious for him to eat so they could move on to their discussion.

"Here. Eat fast."

He sat down, his hair dripping, and smiled amusedly at her. "I don't want to burn my tongue."

"You won't. It's the perfect temperature. I swear."

He touched the surface of his soup with his fingertip. "You're right." He tucked into his food while she waited impatiently.

"I'll listen to you while I eat," he said over his mouth of bread. "You're obviously bursting to say something."

She shook her head. "No. I'll just work while I wait."

She pulled her wand from the deep pocket in her skirt. He watched intently. She squinted and moved her wrist back and forth in quick little jerks.

"What are you doing?" he asked.

"Starting your truth seeing spell. It will take a few layers to mature."

His eyes widened. "Just like that? You're going to make the spell, then what? Shove it on me?"

She laughed and turned her wrist in a circle, a wisp of red smoke rose out of nothing. "Were you expecting a bit more ceremony?"

"I don't know. I guess."

"Relax and eat. I'll not spring anything on you. It might take a few tries before the spell takes hold anyway."

She continued to turn her wrist, adding new colors of smoke to the red. He kept eating, not taking his eyes off what she was doing for a second. Every color he knew mixed into the ball until it was black as shadow. The glowing red of fire embers shone through cracks in the smoke. She pointed her wand straight at the cloud, shrinking it down into the size of a coin.

"Stand up, X."

He did, bracing himself for the unknown.

The smoke floated toward him and stopped right in front of his face.

"Swallow it."

He exhaled unevenly, his pulse hammering. *Here goes nothing*, he thought, and opened his mouth. It moved in. He closed his lips over it. For a second it hovered under the roof of his mouth then it slid under his tongue and branded him. The heat of it seared through the soft flesh in the bottom of his mouth before gliding down his throat, burning like a shot of strong whiskey. The heat pooled in his stomach and then vanished.

He looked at her questioningly. "Did it work?"

"I created the necromancer spell just for you. I picked you long ago," she said.

A rush of heat, like a warm breeze, flashed inside him and then was gone. "That's a lie! It was an accident," he said confidently.

She smiled broadly. "I guess it worked. From now on you will know when someone has told you a lie."

"Can you *really* talk to animals?"

"I can."

No heat rushed on him this time, but he couldn't say he felt nothing. There was a solid sensation inside him, like pressing against a boulder. This was truth. It was hard and immovable.

He smirked devilishly at her. "Are you attracted to me?"

She scowled. "Bastard."

"Is that a yes?"

She pursed her lips and then smiled. "No."

He felt heat again, but this time it had hard cool places. He allowed himself time to fully experience the sensation before it faded. "That's a half truth."

"You're right. I'm not attracted to you romantically, X. I'm growing to like your personality. I recognize that you're very nicely put together. I'd have to be blind to not see that, but I don't fantasize about you and me. I'm not sure what my type is, but you're not it."

"That is the whole truth," he said easily. "I'm sorry for asking that. I shouldn't have. But knowing how you feel makes me feel better, because I can honestly say that is how I feel about you. You're very beautiful, Maggie. Like you said, I'd have to be blind to not notice, but there is nothing else. I think I'm growing to like your personality as well. Thank you for this gift of truth."

He held out his hand to her. "Friends?"

She smiled and shook his hand. "Friends."

Her eyes brightened, and she jerked her hand out of his.

"What? Oh, I'm sorry!" he said. "Did I hurt you? I know I shouldn't touch anyone ever. I'm not used to having to avoid all contact yet."

"It's not that. You didn't hurt me, or pull anything of me to yourself. I could stop you if your power was doing that without your knowledge. No, I just want to give you something now. It's what I've been anxious for all day...here."

She pulled something from her pocket and held the mess of leather straps out to him. "Hold out your hands."

He did without hesitation. She unwound the leather straps that were fastened like a harness around the round white stones and placed them in his hands. They fit nicely in the centers of his palms and she fastened the straps over the backs of his hands, securing the stones in place. "These stones will act as soul cages. I have no idea how many souls will fit inside them, perhaps there is no way to overflow them."

He flexed his fingers, adjusting the leather. The power in his hands lit up and reached into the stones. The force pulled the stones flat against his palms like a vacuum seal and held them there. Amazed, X moved his hands and found having the stones there was not only comfortable, it was comforting, like having glass doors shut over the portals in his hands.

"Wow," he said quietly. But then he frowned and walked toward the house. He picked up his axe, trying to move his hands naturally on the handle with the stones over his palms.

Maggie walked over next to him.

94

"It feels awkward. I'll have to practice."

"You won't need to wear them all the time, unless you just want to."

"They feel good. I just need to get used to them...I...Thank you for this."

"It was a sacrifice, I'll admit. Those stones are priceless. But I support this vision you're contemplating for your life, strangely vigilante as it may be. And it's not without thought for myself. The more accomplished you become in your gifts, the safer I will be from the wizards. Should any decide to come here, that is."

"Why would they?"

"For me. If they discovered I'm alive, they would surely come to collect me." She shivered and rubbed her arms as though cold. "I'm the last witch."

Before dawn, X got ready to go to the village neighboring the one he grew up in. He hadn't been there since he was a child. No one would recognize him there. He put on his coat and pulled the hood up over his head. He fastened the stones on his hands, and then covered them with his fingerless gloves. Lastly, he slid his dagger into his belt and took up his bright, virgin, executioner's axe.

His hands tightened on the handle. He swung it a few times. After the second swing, he barely noticed the stones. As he continued to mimic the movements he'd need to remove someone's head, the stones began to add a strange balance to his body. They didn't hinder his accuracy or coordination, just the opposite. A surge of adrenaline went through his chest. It felt so damn good. All the magic inside him, and around him, felt good.

He turned to begin the five-mile walk, when the door on Maggie's house creaked open.

"Catch," she said, throwing him an apple. "I'll be watching you."

He smiled. "Thanks. I hope this works like it did in my dream."

She frowned.

"What?" he asked.

"Be careful...Mind your hands."

He held out his gloved hands for her to see. "I am. I will."

"I have one more gift for you." She came toward him and handed him a handful of black leather.

He held it up and smiled, bemused. An executioner's mask. "You and your gifts. I'm quite the freak now. Are you proud of the number you've done on me?"

"In a way, I must say that I am. Guilt for ruining your life notwithstanding...Good luck, X."

He walked quickly through the forest. The adrenaline pushing him on like a sweet, cool breeze at his back. Why wasn't he scared? When he thought about what he was about to do, why did it feel okay? Had the magic really changed him that much already?

The dawn broke right before he arrived. People were awake or waking, already beginning their day's work. His memories of this village were faint. He hadn't expected it to be this large. X meandered through the streets to the center, where there was a large well, and an open market.

The people he passed did double takes, or openly stared. Most of them moved aside and gave him a wide birth. He wasn't sure how he felt about that. He caught a kid running past him by the arm, and then remembering he must not touch people, quickly let go of the boy.

"Hey, where does the governor live?"

The freckled face looked up at him with wide eyes before pointing across the square. "Over there, sir. He lives in the brownstone house with the tile roof."

"Thank you."

"Did he send for you? You're our new executioner aren't you?" the kid's gaze fell and held on X's axe.

X smirked. "Perhaps."

The kid took a few backward steps, staring at him, before he turned and ran.

X headed toward the governor's house. His dream had been right; this would just fall into his lap. He paused at the door and listened. He didn't want to wake the man if he wasn't up.

Faint noises of movement came through the door. He knocked.

"Oh, bloody hell, can't they even let me finish my coffee before they start in on me? Why did I ever let the stupid people push me into this position for a second term?" someone muttered behind the door. "Who is it?"

"I'm your new executioner," X said loudly to the door.

The door swung inward. The middle aged man looked at him in surprise for a moment. He blinked, inhaled, and soothed his sleep-rumpled, salt and pepper hair back.

"Take that hood off."

X pushed his hood off his head. The man blinked a few times, and then frowned. He looked at the axe X carried, and then stepped back and ushered him inside. He shut the door behind him.

"You're the prettiest executioner I've ever seen," he muttered.

"Is that a problem?"

The man harrumphed. "What's your name?"

"Executioner."

"Your mother gave you that name at birth, did she?" he said snidely.

"Call me X. What does it matter what my mother named me? Or that I'm pretty? I'll wear a mask when I collect heads for you, if you'd prefer."

The man blew out a breath and extended his hand. "I'm Johnston. Governor of this *fine* village." He wrapped sarcasm around the word fine as he said it.

X looked at his hand and took a step back. "Forgive me, but I don't touch anyone."

Johnston shrugged and let his hand fall. "Whatever. I've got a man waiting for your axe right now. The people grow more uneasy everyday he still lives. He's a bloodthirsty monster—killed six young girls. If he escapes..." He shuddered. "We caught him by sheer luck. Most believe him to be a warlock, or some kind of demon, possessed with hellish powers. That's how we lost Monk, our last executioner, in the struggle to subdue him...You don't look like much. I can see you're strong, but I'm not sure you're up to the task, no matter how many heads you've chopped off. And you're axe looks unused."

"It's new, true enough. Why don't you give me a chance? I'll charge you nothing. Let me kill this man in private, so if you're not pleased with my abilities, I'll leave and never come back, and you won't lose any face."

Johnston shook his head. "The people need to see him die, or the hysterics will never cease…but I like your proposition. There is someone else also waiting to die, just a normal criminal. You can kill him privately first, and then I'll make my decision about you."

"Shall we go now?" X asked.

He huffed and grabbed a mug off the desk behind him, downing the contents quickly. He wiped his mouth. "All right, let's go."

X put his hood back up as he followed Johnston to the stone building they used as a jail. He felt calm and wondered that he could feel calm at all. He was about to take a human life.

The place was dark, dank, and felt disgusting. Even the air. There were three cells. One was empty.

Looking through the bars, X knew immediately which man was the one everyone feared. His eyes danced when he saw X. He didn't have a scary appearance in the way of broken teeth, or a wild unkempt beard. At first glance, he looked normal, which was one thing that made him frightening. The man gave X a chill in his heart.

The other man looked at X with placid acceptance.

"Found a new headsman, have you Governor?" the man asked in a bored tone. "I almost welcome his axe, just to get out of this shit hole and away from that devil next to me."

"Well, you won't get any fresh air before your head jumps off your shoulders. You get the privilege of being this young man's job interview."

The criminal sighed and leaned his head back against the filthy stone wall. "How insulting."

Johnston looked at the guard. "Go get me a round from the wood pile out back."

He nodded and went outside. In a minute he was back, carrying a two-foot-tall section of tree trunk. He set it down at X's feet. Axe marks grooved the top. It was a chopping block all right, but this one had only ever had wood chopped on top of it before. X stared at it, not moving as the man was brought out and forced to kneel. He didn't whimper or beg as he leaned over the block.

X's hands tightened on his axe handle. His focus sharpened as he looked at the sweat beads on the back of the man's neck. The soul hovered in his chest, a wisp of grey smoke pockmarked with black. The man's breathing and pulse hummed loudly in X's ears, mingling with his own. He inhaled and swung his axe upward and brought it down.

A shock went through his heart. A fraction of a second, a flash of light on his axe, and the edge separated the head from the body. The soul drifted up and hovered for a second in front of X. He lifted his right hand. It was effortless. The soul flew right to his hand, swirling into the depths of the stone, and there it stayed. Nothing of the man's spirit went inside X, much to his relief.

Neither of the other men could see the soul or what X had done with it. The guard picked up the head and carried it out of the jail.

Johnston eyed X appreciatively and nodded. "Excellent precision. You're hired."

"Thank you, sir. When would you like to handle the other one?"

"In about an hour. I'll spread the word around the village. Meet me at the platform in the square, with your mask on, pretty boy."

"Yes, sir. Shall we discuss my fee now or after?"

"After." The governor cast a quick glance at the man behind the bars

100

and then left the jail.

Alone with the man, X approached the bars, looking inside him. His soul was completely encased. Black oily cords of disease writhed around and around it like snakes.

"What are you staring at?" the murderer asked in a raspy voice.

"I'm looking at your soul."

"That's brave of you." His tone sounded bored.

X nodded. "Indeed. It's quite disgusting to be honest. When I kill you, I will keep it a while. Maybe it might be useful to me."

The man's eyes widened as he looked more closely at X. He shivered and curled into a ball. "I see you. Leave me alone, necromancer. The governor said an hour. I'd prefer to spend it in solitude."

X backed away and stepped out into the fresh air. He took a few deep breaths to clean out his lungs and strode away from the village into the cover of the nearest trees. Alone, he leaned against a trunk and closed his eyes. How did he feel? He'd done it. He wasn't judge or jury, victim or accuser. He was the boatman. He was the catalyst. And for the moment, at least, he was okay with that.

He raised his right hand up and pulled his glove off, so he could look at the soul inside the stone. He hadn't taken much time to really look at it before. It had a similarity to the one inside the man still waiting to die, but the darkness was less. Struck by inspiration, X removed his left glove as well and put his hands together. Focusing his power on the soul, his left hand pulled from his right. The stain on the soul went into the stone on his left hand, leaving the soul itself scrubbed clean, on his right. He smiled, energized that his idea had worked.

He put his gloves back on and the jacket's hood back up before going back into the village. He stuck to the outskirts, waiting for the hour to run itself out. He headed toward a stable, his mind moving onto the idea of possibly buying a horse after he was paid, when he caught sight of Troy, approaching the same stable from the opposite direction.

What was he doing here? It all slammed into his stomach again. The hurt and rage of his betrayal. X saw red, dropped his axe and charged at Troy. Caught off guard, Troy's eyes bugged as X grabbed him by the throat and shoved him against the outside wall of the stable. He lifted him off his feet, bearing down on his windpipe. Troy clawed at his hold, and kicked his feet.

X's hands lit up. He was going to kill him right there. He was going to pull his soul straight out of his body. Troy's soul moved up toward the pull of his hands. X's vision clouded over and a rush shot through him. His power flashed a split-second warning and a promise. He remembered Maggie's words. If he did this, his power would go dark, and there would be no redemption for him.

X let go, blowing out a breath as he realized the terrible cliff he'd almost jumped off. Troy fell to the ground, coughing. He looked up at X standing over him. There was no recognition in his eyes.

"Who are you?" he hissed roughly, holding onto his abused neck.

He didn't answer. Instead, he reared back and punched Troy as hard as he could in the face. Troy fell backward, knocked unconscious, and X spit on him before turning and walking away. He picked up his axe, experiencing a sense of closure. The past, so vivid and painful, now faded dull. He closed up his feelings about Troy and Isolde and sealed them. They were nothing now, except tutors who taught him to not trust.

The sound of the crowd in the square let him know when it was time for his second execution. He put his mask on before walking through the crowd to the platform. Everyone parted and backed away from him. They whispered fearfully as he passed. Johnston stood next to the criminal, who was bloodied and tied to the block.

The governor began speaking to the crowd, riling them up. X wasn't listening. He worked to regulate his heart rate and his breathing. All eyes were on him as he climbed the stairs and stood behind Johnston. He moved aside and gestured for X to come forward. He stood over the man, his hands tightening on the axe handle, his muscles pulling taut. He took a deep breath about to swing when something caught his attention.

A sweet smelling gust of wind seemed to come from ripple in the air in the back of the crowd. He squinted, seeing and still not seeing someone appear out of nowhere. She was insubstantial and flashed in his vison like a trick of the light. She looked him straight in the eyes. Trapped and transfixed, his pupils dilated. He caught the hint of a smile on her lips, but it was hard to be sure. He could barely see her. Then as quickly as she had appeared, she was gone.

He blinked.

Everything around him came back into focus. The crowd, the criminal, and his axe. It happened fast. Just the blink of an eye. The people cheered as the head rolled away from the chopping block. X did what he had before. He grabbed the soul as it rose out of the body, storing it in the stone.

Johnston slapped him companionably on the shoulder and handed him a leather pouch of gold coins.

"I'll come the first day of every week to see if you have need of my services," X told him.

"That will work fine," The governor agreed. "Thank goodness you showed up today."

He left the village as quickly as possible, wishing he could find the girl, and wondering if she was some kind of ghost. He wanted to see her clearly, for what he'd perceived of her, slight as it was, she was very easy to look at. Haunting and disarming.

He arrived back home in the late afternoon. Maggie was pacing back and forth agitatedly. As soon as she saw him, she bounded up to him.

"I watched some, but oh, how was it? How do you feel? Are the stones holding the souls? Do you think you'll go back? Who was that guy you choked?"

X laughed. "Calm down. I'll tell you everything. I'm starving though."

She was bouncing on the balls of her feet. "There's food. Eat fast! I have to know everything."

He had the ornery desire to eat really slowly just to torment her, but she was putting so much pressure on him to hurry up, he took pity on her and ate quickly. He told her everything. Every detail because she wouldn't settle for any less. He took off his gloves, and the harnesses that held the stones against him palms, so she could look at them closely. He explained how one side held the evil stains and how he'd managed to separate them from the souls. She stared at each one in turn, but she refused to touch the one that held the stains.

"Are you in pain?" Maggie asked.

"No."

"Emotional pain?" she pressed.

He took a deep breath and mulled it over, thinking about how he felt. "Well, being an executioner...It's weird. I know I'm going to have to center myself often on how I feel about it."

"And running into Troy?"

X shrugged it off. "It's over. It felt good to rough him up. But if Isolde presented herself to me now and proclaimed undying love for me, begged me even…" He made a sour expression. "I'd rather cozy up to a snake. She's hideous to me now."

He got up and cleared away his dinner plate. Stored his axe inside the house and changed his shirt. When he came back to where Maggie was still sitting, she gave him a funny look.

"What's with that goofy grin on your face?" she asked.

X touched his mouth, not realizing he'd been smiling. "I don't know if it was real, or just my imagination, but I saw a girl in the crowd today…she…it was like she flashed out of nowhere. She smiled at me and then disappeared…what? Maggie, what is it?"

Worry filled her eyes. "What did she look like?"

"I hardly know. She was like a ghost."

Just as he said it, the air rippled as it had earlier, and there she was, standing ten feet away. Both he and Maggie jumped, startled by the sudden appearance of another person. She wasn't ghostlike now. She looked at Maggie for a second, then her gaze settled on him. Her eyes shot an arrow right through his heart. He gaped at her, open-mouthed. She was the most beautiful creature he'd ever seen. And *creature* was the word that seemed to fit. The tops of her ears were pointed and her large almond-shaped eyes were grey, rimmed with a tiny band of red. A riot of wavy black hair tumbled over her shoulders. Her hands were covered in pulsating red light. And she wore very strange clothes. Clothes made for utility, like a man's.

She made no move forward, she just stared intensely at him. X glanced at Maggie, unsure what to do, shocked when Maggie remained silent.

He held his hands out to show her he meant her no harm. Her gaze darted to his hands, and she smiled. She was so gorgeous. He didn't even have words adequate to describe how lovely she was to him. *I'm dying*. X thought.

He swallowed hard. "Hello."

A flash of pain came into her eyes.

"What's your name?"

She didn't answer. She began walking straight at him. X couldn't move, he glanced quickly at Maggie for help, but she only backed away. He looked back as she strode aggressively into his space. He stepped sideways, and they began circling each other like enemies preparing to fight.

"What do you want?"

She held one finger up to her perfectly full lips in a shushing motion. Small lightning strikes flashed and snaked over her hands and forearms. As he looked at her, unconsciously, his hands woke up and began glowing cold and ravenous. Before he could think to step away from her, she grabbed both of his hands in hers, lacing her fingers through his, so their palms touched.

X choked on his breath as her power rushed into his hands. His eyes rolled back in his head, and he moaned. His power tangled and mixed with hers. He'd never experienced anything that felt so good. Just holding her hands was devastating, overwhelming, and nothing short of erotic.

She let go of his hands and wrapped her arms around his waist. Again he couldn't move. *I'm dreaming. There's no way this is actually happening.* He thought as her lips brushed the side of his neck. He almost stumbled sideways as her teeth sank through his skin. Pleasure exploded in his head as she pulled his blood into her mouth. He thought he might pass out, the sensation was too intense for him.

She pulled away and took a step back, blood on her lips. Her eyes

106

were wide, and she looked as shaken as he felt. She turned and ran a few feet away, grabbing at nothing in front of her.

"Wait!" he called, but she was gone.

X stared at the place she'd just been, his heart thrashing under his ribs. He turned around, looking for Maggie, adrenaline coursing all through him.

"Did you see that? Did you see her?" He scrubbed his hands over his face. "I had no idea what she was going to do. I don't even know *what* she was. *But…My gosh…Did you see her?*" He was out of breath, like he'd just run a great distance.

Maggie came close to him and looked at his neck. "She *bit* you." Her tone was incredulous.

He smiled so broadly it felt like his face would break. "She did more than that. She tore my heart straight out of my chest and took it with her."

Maggie raised one eyebrow and shook her head. He looked back at the place the girl had vanished from and stared at it for a few moments.

"Wait! Maggie! *She's* the storm you've been talking about! Isn't she? She's the storm."

"Yes, X. She's the storm."

CHAPTER SEVEN

Tesla landed in her bedroom and sank straight down to the floor, her legs out in front of her as she leaned against her bed. Shivers rolled through her over and over like waves on the sand. His blood was still in her mouth. She hadn't swallowed. She closed her eyes, looking at him in her mind. The shivers turned warm. She shook herself. First things first. She swallowed, prepared to allow her body to analyze his blood, but she couldn't ignore the taste. She disliked blood, always. But this flavor, she'd gladly sample anytime.

The next second, Tesla coughed, grabbing at her throat. It burned. All the way down, it burned like acid. She got up and rushed into the kitchen for a drink of water. A tremor vibrated down her neck as she drank, then the pain was gone. She slunk back to her room, puzzled over her physical response to the blood. Standing in front of her mirror, her cheeks flushed as her body temperature fluctuated like she had a fever. The pulsing red on her hands faded into a pale pink and the pain eased. She took a deep, shaky breath as everything inside her, all the disorder, settled.

Her pulse began to race as a small seed of hope began to bud. She swallowed, stepping closer to her mirror, so her breath fogged it as she exhaled. She licked her lips and attempted...

"Hehhloowwn," startled by her own voice, her heart raced faster. "Hello."

Tears blossomed in her eyes, and she covered her mouth with her hands. It was nothing more than a whisper, but she actually spoke!

"Ieeh aam Sestlah." She cleared her throat and tried the words again and again until they were clear. "I am Tesla."

She tried every word she could think of but in a matter of minutes, her new ability began to degenerate. The pain and wildness of her magic came back, and her voice sank back into nothing, until she couldn't hear it anymore. The cruelty of it was beyond any heartbreak she'd ever felt.

Forest awoke suddenly, unsure what had roused her, but her hair stood on end. Tesla needed her. She got up and rushed through the dark house to her daughter's room. She didn't bother knocking. Tesla was curled on the floor in the fetal positon, her shoulders trembling with silent sobs. Forest sank down and pulled her into her arms as if she were a small child. Tesla grabbed onto her desperately. They stayed like that for a few minutes. Forest smoothed her hand over and over the back of Tesla's hair.

"What is it?" Forest asked. "Are you hurting so much you need to go see your grandfather? It doesn't matter what time it is."

Tesla pulled back, shook her head, and wiped her eyes. *I spoke.* She signed. *Just now. Here in my room. I spoke. But now it's gone. My voice is gone!*

Forest frowned.

You don't believe me!

"I didn't say that."

Sure you did. It's all over your face.

"How did you do it?"

I think it was the blood. I drank… She hesitated looking fearful. *I drank human blood.*

Forest closed her eyes, trying to not be angry. "Are you addicted to it? I know you've been jumping at night. You've been going to Earth, to get human blood?" Syrus was going to lose it over this, given his own history of addiction. Forest thought.

No. Not Earth. It was somewhere else. Another human world. I'm not addicted. This was the first time I've tried it. How do you know I've been jumping?

Forest rolled her eyes. "Tesla, please. I've known you were jumping at night since you started…So you think the blood gave you your voice?"

I'm not sure. But I think so. Is that so crazy?

Forest pursed her lips, and then shook her head. "No. It's not crazy at all. A few years ago your father had a similar circumstance. When he was blind, if he drank human blood, his sight would come back for a short while. But you can't go down that road, Tesla. I don't care how it makes you feel. I won't let you become a blood junkie."

Tesla looked down and nodded. *I'm sorry, Mom. I understand your concern. I promise to be careful, but I can't promise you anything else.*

Forest sighed through clenched teeth, a tear sliding down one cheek. She opened her mouth, then closed it again shaking her head. She got up off the floor and made to leave the room. She paused at the door and looked back at her daughter, still sitting on the floor. "I love you more than anything. There's nothing I wouldn't do for you. Nothing I wouldn't give up. I'm willing to have you hate me, if that's what it takes. But you're right. I can't stop you from doing anything. You're too powerful." She closed the door behind her.

Tesla blew out a breath, feeling sad and at a loss about what her mom said. She closed her eyes and tried to refocus. The effect the blood had on her had vanished, now she needed to dissect and learn what she could about his blood and what it could mean possibly for the blood lock. Since it was in her system all she had to do was look at it in her mind. She could see everything there, down to the insides of his cells.

His magic was interesting. It was new to him, and it had wrapped around his genetic makeup. She had only ever seen this type of mutation before, and that was her own. Hers was the opposite of his. She was naturally magical, the poison that entered her in utero had been what wrapped around her genetic makeup. She looked at the shape of his DNA. It was... almost...excitement flared and then fizzled out just as fast. The missing element in the blood lock, this shape was almost a perfect match, but almost wasn't going to work. How could it be so close to right?

An idea came to her. She needed to go back. She needed more of his blood to work with. The prospect of seeing him again made her feel a nervous flush. Touching his hands had been amazing. It was such a perfect feeling. Balance and wild ecstasy, with no pain. His magic protected him from her power. She couldn't hurt him with her hands, and he couldn't hurt her. He made her feel good.

Aside from that—and it was hardly a side thing—was the way he looked. Tesla was used to seeing beauty; everyone she knew was beautiful in their own way. It wasn't that he was more beautiful, but she'd never seen someone she liked the look of as much as him. His coloring was cold. White blonde hair and ice colored eyes. When she'd wrapped her arms around his waist she felt how solid and strong he was. He was pretty without being the slightest bit feminine. She closed her eyes and imagined him standing right there in her room. She reached up and touched his face...She shook herself, the fantasy fading.

Her eyes would never be satisfied again, unless she was looking at him.

Tesla stood up and looked at herself in the mirror. She ran her fingers through her hair, feeling unsure of herself. She was used to people telling her she was beautiful, but she didn't see it. Did *he* think she was? She hoped. An odd desire hit her hard. She wanted him to long for her. She wanted to haunt his dreams and torture him with craving for her. She'd never felt such a thing before.

This was bad. Thinking about him in this way, whatever his name was. She needed his blood, possibly his cooperation, maybe his power to help save her world. Crushing on him was a bad idea. He was human, and perhaps a bad person. She'd seen him execute someone, but that was plainly his job and not an act of passion. Odd profession. But... he *was* screwed up like her, she argued with herself. And he was smoking hot, so if she could get him to work with her, looking at him was just an added bonus.

She got a piece of paper and a pen and began to write.

My name is Tesla. I wish I could just tell you that, but I am mute.

She paused. Everything she needed to say sounded insane, or it would to him. If he would let her bite him again, then she could actually talk to him. She left the note as it was and put it in her pocket. Excitement and a strange form of fear laced through her. Shivering, she shook her head before pulling the air open and going to the Everpath. The eerie, endless hallway was seemingly empty, but she was more alert since the voice and grasping shadows. She walked down to the door she wanted and pushed through, landing on her feet in his world.

It was night. She glanced up at the moon and stars. They were pale white against an all-black sky. Regia's aquamarine moon was prettier, but this was still nice. She was close to where he'd been earlier. A dying fire still burned in a circle of stones next to the small house. There were no sounds and no other lights aside from the fire. She came closer, looking at the place more carefully. A new house was under construction a little ways away. Curious, she walked over to the building site. Deep shadows pooled together all over.

She heard him before she saw him. He inhaled sharply and moved from inside the unfinished house. She held still as he came to the doorway. Fluttering filled her stomach and lungs. His hands illuminated a soft blue, dimly lighting the area around them. He looked shocked and quickly smoothed his hair back from his face and straightened his shirt. His actions reminded her of her own a few minutes ago as she looked at herself in the mirror. He smiled. She couldn't help but smile back. All the pain and chaos inside her quieted and clicked into place just being near him. How could that be? Just his presence seemed to right the wrong inside her.

"You came back. What's your name?"

She reached into her pocket, drew out the note, and held it out to him. He took it from her and looked at it for a moment. Then he folded it and slipped it into his own pocket.

"Tesla…beautiful name. So, you can't speak at all?" he asked gently.

She shook her head. Should she have tried to write more? Why hadn't she brought a pen and some more paper? Frustrated she turned away from him, trying to think of how to move forward.

He came up behind her. "Hey," he said softly.

She turned around. He held out his hands to her, hope in his eyes. "My name is X. I've never felt anything as amazing as your hands in mine, Tesla. My hands are dangerous. It looks like yours are, too. Magic has only recently changed me into what I am now, but knowing I can

113

never touch anyone without harming them has weighed heavy on my heart. I feel like you might understand that...Will you hold my hands again?"

She looked at his hands, wanting to touch him again so badly it scared her. She licked her lips and nodded, reaching for him. A small cry of pleasure came from her mouth as they touched. She pinched her eyes shut against the overwhelming sensation. It felt so good, it almost hurt. She tried to focus on her breathing and force it to slow down. Her bottom lip trembled and tears slid out from her closed eyes.

He tried to pull back from her. She gripped his hands tighter so he couldn't get away and opened her eyes. He looked worried.

"Am I hurting you?"

She shook her head.

"Then why are you crying?"

I wish I could tell you everything. She thought.

He blinked a few times and turned his head to the side like someone had just called his name. Then he looked back at her, his eyebrows pulled down curiously.

"You...you wish you could tell me everything?" he asked.

Her eyes widened. *Can you hear me?*

He looked astonished and exhaled on a half laugh. "I can. I hear a voice in my head. Am I losing my mind? You are talking to me, right? In your thoughts?"

Yes! You can hear me. This is amazing! Where have you been?

He chuckled. "I've been right here. Where have *you* been?"

Searching for you. And I didn't even know it. You unlocked my voice.

114

Can I bite you again? If you let me, I think I could actually speak aloud.

Desire filled his pale eyes. "You didn't ask my permission the first time." He leaned down and rested his forehead against hers, holding her gaze. "You can do anything you want to me."

She smirked at his words. The fluttering in her stomach coming back full force. *Are you flirting with me?*

He straightened back up. "Well, I was trying. Since you had to ask, I guess I wasn't doing a very good job."

She smiled easily. He was so cute. She decided it was best to not go for his neck this time. He didn't understand. That much was obvious. Biting him wasn't a sexual advance. So instead she lifted up their entwined hands to her mouth and sank her teeth into the fleshy side of his hand. As his blood flowed into her mouth her eyes cut to his. A whole world of unspoken knowledge seemed to go back and forth silently in their eye contact. She realized she was the one who didn't understand. Scared by the intensity she stepped back from him and let go of his hands.

He stood still, holding her captive in his eyes. It was as though he had placed her in an invisible cage.

Release me. She pleaded.

He blinked and shook himself. His look was still intense but the heat had banked.

Tesla swallowed. As it had before, a tremor went down her throat. It was easier than the first time and she knew the moment she would be able to speak. "Thank you." Her voice was quiet, but the words were clear, much to her relief.

He smiled. "You're welcome."

"You're the first person I've ever spoken to."

"I feel honored. Would you like to go and sit by the fire? Have a long conversation?"

Giddy happiness filled her at the thought and she nodded. "I would love that."

He threw a few logs on the fire and sat down on a stump a few feet away from where she sat.

"So, X? That's kind of an odd name."

He *tsked* and shook his head. "That's not nice. I picked it myself. I was going for something ruggedly masculine."

She giggled. He was teasing her. "Were you an outlaw in need of a new identity?"

His expression sobered. "No. I died. Being reborn as something different, I felt warranted a new name."

She titled her head to the side. "Magic changed you."

"Yeah. Maggie"—he inclined his head toward the little house behind her—"she's a witch. Her spell work got away from her, and it hit me while I was in the woods hunting. Alex died." He held his hands up, the glow in his palms growing brighter for a second. "And a necromancer was born...but since, as you've said, I'm the first person you've spoken to, I want to know all about you. You said you wanted to tell me everything, or you thought it, rather."

"I...I don't even know where to start."

"Why don't you tell me what you are and where you come from?" he prompted.

She took a deep breath. "Okay. You asked for it. I'm afraid I'm going to chew your ear off."

His gaze warmed and he smiled at her as though he thought she was adorable. "As you said. I asked for it."

She explained as best she could. He interrupted her often, needing more details about things he'd never seen. She feared he would lose interest, but not for one moment did his eyes glaze, or his attention wander. Tesla waited for her voice to fade away as it had before but it didn't. Being near him was enough to maintain this ability. She talked mostly of Regia and not herself, he'd asked about where she came from but it was evasion on her part. After a while he began to press her more about herself.

"I'm a human, or sort of, but you know that. Please tell me what you are."

"I'm nervous...I don't want to scare you," she admitted.

"I don't scare easily. I mean, aside from being very powerful, you seem a bit eager to sink your really sharp teeth into me, and I'm still right here. Interested for you to explain. You appear out of thin air, and the first time I saw you, you were only partly visible, like a ghost."

"My father is a vampire and a mage. I get my magic from him, along with my teeth. I can eat anything I want to, but occasionally I have to drink blood to stay alive. If I go for too long without it, my health starts to suffer. My mother is a Halfling. Half elf, half shapeshifter. Elves have the ability to become invisible. Since I'm only one-fourth elf, I cannot fully vanish. That's why I looked like a ghost. I've never been able to shift my appearance, and I have no true face. Perhaps I have some small level of ability there, but for now, it's dormant. That's what I am. A mixed-blood freak."

He frowned. "That's not all, is it?"

"Isn't that enough?" She laughed darkly.

117

"What did you mean, you have no true face?"

"Shapeshifters have a true face. A face they can show no one except their destined life mates. When a shifter meets their destined life mate, all their mate can see is their true face, no matter how they shift. My mother has a true face. She's shown me a very close resemblance of it, but that is all she can do. Only my dad can see her real face."

"That's romantic...So the face I'm looking at right now is the only face you have?" he asked.

"This is it."

"Good."

"Good? Why is that good?"

"You want the unedited, honest truth? I think you might need it, if you have to ask me why it's good," he said seriously.

Her eyes widened and she swallowed.

"You have the most gorgeous face I've ever seen. You're beautiful... like the darkness of night. There's nothing easy or soft about the way it makes me feel. Your beauty is violent in its excess. It's destructive to my heart. Completely disarming. From the moment I first saw your face, it has haunted me...I fear it always will."

She closed her eyes and hung her head. "Pain has twisted me so far. When I look at my reflection, all I see is the pain. How can you truly see such things when you look at me?"

"Tesla." His voice commanded her to look up. "It wasn't easy for me to tell you that. It was a kind of surrender to admit it that freely. Please don't discount my words as pretty lies, for they cost me greatly to speak aloud."

She held his gaze. The moment was too intense for her. She blushed and turned her face away. "So, um...you kill people for a living?"

The tension broke, and he laughed. "Yeah. My new profession for my new life. It's certainly nothing I ever aspired to. It looks worse than it is. I need to show you something, so you don't think me a monster."

He got up and walked toward the half-built house. In a moment he was back, strapping smooth, flat, white stones to his hands. Once he had them secured over his palms, the blue glow of his hands began to shine again. He held them out for her to see.

"I don't think you should touch them. I'm not sure it's safe for you, or them."

She looked intently, unsure what she was seeing. The left one swirled black. The right was the same blue as his hand.

"I don't understand."

She wanted to know everything about him. He evaded telling her anything about his life before his transformation. He explained his power to her and his desire to use it to help the wrongly accused. She wanted to ask him many questions but she could feel the length of time she had been there and decided to keep her questions for another time. She understood well enough for now. She would wait for the next time to explain to him that he didn't seem like a monster to her and that both of her parents were revered, legendary killers.

"My throat is starting to hurt," she admitted. "It's certainly not used to this."

"Do you want something to drink? Water? Hot tea?" he offered.

She looked up at the sky. She'd been there all night. "I need to go."

"Don't go."

She smiled. "Just a few more moments. I have to ask you an

119

important question."

"What's that?"

"Will you help me save my world?"

He frowned. "What could I do?"

Before she could answer, the door of the little house opened, and Maggie came out. She walked up to Tesla and touched her cheek gently. "I've been waiting for you, princess hurricane. I'm so glad you finally found us. Our fates are bound together."

Tesla examined Maggie quickly. She'd noticed her in the background the first time, but she'd been too focused on X to really take her measure. Her pupils opened and beckoned Tesla in. For a moment, Tesla couldn't breathe as she realized what was really in front of her. X had called her a witch, but she hadn't thought he used the word in its appropriate or literal sense.

"You are not adequately protected here," Tesla said severely. "If they find you..."

Maggie smiled. "I know, but I'm not *completely* unprotected. X is here with me."

"How can he protect you?"

"He's a necromancer. Only the dead can kill a wizard."

Tesla's mouth fell open. She felt like she'd just been punched in the gut. She closed her eyes and put her hands on her head. She looked at the blood lock in her mind. Her grandfather was right. He said the answer was probably not what she thought. Now she had the answer right in front of her. She knew it was the answer, but the equation still didn't figure. What was she not seeing?

"I have a favor to ask. Please, may I have one drop of your blood?"

120

"Oh...sure," Maggie said.

"Hold out your hand."

Tesla pointed her index finger at Maggie's wrist, a tiny line of lightning shot out of her finger, into Maggie's vein. The lightning wrapped around one drop and extracted it out through her skin. In her other hand, Tesla spun a marble-sized sphere and encased the drop of blood inside it. She put the sphere into her pocket and turned to X.

"May I?"

He removed the stones and lifted his hand to her without hesitation. She repeated the process on him.

"Thank you both, so much. I have to go now, but I promise I'll be back as soon as I can."

She turned to walk away, but he caught her hand. "Wait." He looked over at Maggie.

She smiled, understanding his silent request, and went back into her house and shut the door.

"I have to go, X," she insisted.

"I just need to know something, in case I misunderstood. Are you married?"

For a second she didn't understand his question. Then she remembered the word and its meaning from her cultural studies of Earth.

"Oh...no."

"Are you engaged?"

She smiled, the fluttering filling her up again. "No."

"You're not promised to anyone?"

She shook her head. "It's different in Regia."

"Is there no one who has a hold on your heart? You don't have a… destined life mate?"

"Why do you care?"

"I want to know who my competition is."

"Ah, you're flirting again."

"No. I'm deadly serious." He brought her hand to his lips.

Her heart did a little jump. "I have important work to do. I can see you're going to make it hard for me to concentrate."

"Come back soon." He smiled and released her.

Flushed, she grabbed the atmosphere and escaped him. She leaned back against the cold wall of the Everpath and closed her eyes for a second. "Oh, my…" she whispered to herself. A faint breeze slid down the hallway, slamming off her warm, tingly thoughts of X.

Any wind in the hallway meant someone else had just entered the Everpath. Her eyes darted the direction the breeze had come from. Footsteps echoed down to her. Intuition screamed, *Danger. Get out!* To get home, she had to run *toward* the danger to get to the right door. She pushed off the wall and ran, her footfalls giving her away. As soon as she began to run, so did the other person. The door was in sight but so were they. The light should have allowed her to see them clearly, but they were nothing but a silhouette. A shadow form, no eyes, just a huge mouth of long, sharp teeth and claws on the hands. It was moving too fast. She wasn't going to make it.

She skidded to a halt. As soon as she stopped, the thing slowed to a stroll.

122

"There you are." It was the same voice she'd heard before, the seductive, dirty voice. It turned its head slightly from side to side, and she knew, even though it had no eyes, it was looking at her. A low growl rumbled from it. An over long, forked tongue slithered out the mouth and licked the lips. "Now I see you, pretty thing. Come with me...let me taste you..."

Tesla held her hands straight out toward it. A blast of lightning shot from her hands and rushed at the thing. Her power pierced through it like spears. It screamed once.

"Vicious," it hissed. "So lovely... so pleasant... so *worthy*..." Then it vanished in a puff of smoke.

Disgusted and shaken she reached for the door and went home. The dawn was coloring the sky as she landed in her room. She flopped on the bed, overwhelmed for a moment. Killing that thing, if it was in fact dead, had been easy. Too easy, she suspected. Had she done the wrong thing by attacking it? She exhaled, trying to wipe it from her mind. It was going to stalk her nightmares, of that she was sure.

She heard her parents talking in the kitchen. She got up and put her ear to the door. They were arguing about her. She grimaced, sad she was a source of discord between them. She chanced cracking the door open to hear better, but then their fight was over. The anger left their voices.

"I'm sorry," he said.

"Me too."

She heard them kiss and felt relief. Nothing could really come between them for very long. Neither one of them could stand it. She'd seen her dad leave for work irritated, only to come back in an hour or so to make things right between them. She smirked and closed her door again as their make-up kiss turned into a make out session. A few minutes later, the front door opened and closed again. She looked out the window and saw her dad leave. Why hadn't he told her goodbye? Was he mad at her?

So much had happened during the night; her mind was all over the place, and there was something important she needed to do right then, before it was too late. She swallowed and cleared her throat.

"Hello," she said to herself. He voice was growing faint. The ability to speak was leaving her swiftly.

Desperate, she ran from her room, into the kitchen where her mom stood at the counter, drinking her coffee. She set her mug down as soon as she looked at her daughter.

"What is it? What's wrong, Tesla?"

She grabbed Forest by the hands. Forest winced as Tesla's power shocked her, but she didn't pull away.

"I love you, Mommy." Her voice was barely audible.

Forest gasped, tears immediately filling her eyes. "Oh, my baby." She pulled Tesla against her in a tight hug. "Please say something else. What a beautiful voice you have."

"I'm sorry, Mom. I'm so sorry for everything. I'm sorry how much I've hurt you." That was it. Her voice was gone then.

Forest sobbed against her, and shook her head. "Oh no, sweetheart. No. Don't say sorry." She pulled back and put her hands on Tesla's cheeks. Forest laughed through her tears. "I didn't think I'd ever hear your voice."

It's gone now. I can't hold it for very long. She signed.

Too happy to care about anything else, Forest pulled Tesla tightly against her chest again. "Thank you for speaking to me." Her sobs choked her again. "I don't think I've ever felt this happy before. Such a beautiful voice. More beautiful than any sound I've ever heard."

She pulled back again and grasped Tesla by the shoulders. "You know what this means? It means there's an answer! If your voice can be unlocked for even a moment, then it can be unlocked for good. There's an answer. You can solve it. No one can solve problems the way you can."

Maybe. I've got bigger problems to solve first though. I think I might be close to a breakthrough. I need to work in Kyhael today.

"Can I help you at all?"

No. Thanks though.

"Your birthday party is tomorrow. Everyone's coming. Is that still going to work? It would be a shame to cancel."

I don't want to cancel! Aunt Sabra said she'd bring the baby. I want to see Sophie. I want see everyone else, too. But I really want to see Sophie the most.

Forest leaned in and kissed Tesla's cheek. "You're sweet. You look better, by the way. Like you've been resting better, even though I know you haven't been."

Tesla thought about X and smiled. *I feel better...I should get ready and go. Questions are burning through my skull. I need answers.*

"I need to go, too. I'm going to be late for work."

Tesla felt a bit icky from her long night and decided to take a shower. By the time she got out, Forest was already gone to work. She dressed, put her hair up in a ponytail, and carefully retrieved the two small spheres from the pocket of the jeans she'd worn the previous night.

When she landed in *Rune-dy* headquarters, Merhl almost walked right into her.

"Hey, you," he said, smiling. "What mischief have you been up to?"

I think I found something! My brain is about to explode. I found these people—you have to meet them. I'm going back there tonight, if I can manage it, and I think I know a way you can go with me. But before that, I've got some lab work to do, and then I have to go to the Heart and work on the blood lock.

Merhl chuckled. "Who's the busy girl? I've never seen you sign that fast. I almost missed what you said. I'll be here all day, if you need me. Rahaxeris is in the library."

She smiled and rushed past him to the lab. She meticulously laid out her work space and positioned the spheres on two different trays. Placing both hands flat on the large work table, she lifted a red light hologram of the blood lock onto the surface and enlarged it so the strands, elements, proteins, and molecules were clearly visible.

She broke open Maggie's blood first. She didn't look up as her grandfather came into the room and looked over her shoulder.

"Where did you get that?" He was astonished, eyeing the genetic strands Tesla had visually projected into the air from the blood. "That's..."

Tesla looked up, smiled, and nodded. *Yup. I found a witch.*

He gaped at her. "Holy shit!"

Damn straight, she answered. *That's not all. Look at this.* She broke open X's blood and projected it up the same way for him to see.

He narrowed his eyes, and his brows came down in confusion. "What is that? Is it mutated?"

Magically altered human. He's a necromancer.

126

She showed her grandfather the shape she'd found in X's blood and how it almost fit the hole in the blood lock.

"You're missing something."

I know, but what?

"I see it now. It's a prism, Tesla."

She looked back at it and shook her head. *It's incomplete. There's a symbol that has to go in the center. The power of the Heart can only be refracted through the symbol I can't find. This blood is only one half of the symbol.*

He sighed and patted her shoulder. "I'll leave you alone for a while. I know you work better that way."

X's blood was one half of the symbol, and even though she knew it was important, Maggie's blood wasn't the other half and possession of her blood didn't help their defenses at all. Tesla closed her eyes, her mind wandering onto X. She lifted her hand and ran her thumb over and over against the pads of her fingertips.

What if...

Tesla grabbed a needle and jabbed her finger. She held her finger over his blood so hers dropped on top of it. A flash sparked and smoke rose into the air from the mixed blood. She held her breath as she pulled an image into the air from the drop.

Son of a bitch. There it was.

Her blood mixed with his, formed the complete symbol. She extracted the image and placed it in the hologram of the blood lock. Of course it was nothing but a model of the real thing, but she saw when placed in the real blood lock, this would cause a chain reaction. But there was still something nagging her. She waved her hand through the hologram, making it disappear. She wasn't ready to share this. Wrapping her and X's mixed blood in a sphere and slipping it into her pocket, she cleaned everything else up, leaving Maggie's blood for her grandfather to mess with if he wanted.

She scrawled him a quick note, saying she'd be back later, and opened a portal for herself to the Heart.

The flames sparked at her arrival. "Tesla," the Heart said inside her head. "The lock is holding steady. Attacks have gone down in number over the last few hours."

I have something I want to show you. She thought.

She reached into the flames and opened the blood lock. With a shaking hand, she put the blood filled sphere inside. The lock wrapped around it and absorbed it. A shiver beginning in the center, vibrated all the way out to the edges of the tesseract. The living machine took a breath. Then came the explosion. Tesla was blasted backward, struck a tree trunk, and fell to the ground, unconscious.

"Wake up. Please, wake up," the Heart pleaded to her.

A part of her heard it, but she couldn't answer. Couldn't surface.

When she came around, the afternoon had grown long. White light from the soil held her aloft, suspending her an inch off the ground.

"There you are. I tried to keep you comfortable," the Heart said as the light lowered her and faded away.

Thanks. I'm all right, or will be soon anyway. She rubbed her head, and then adrenaline hit, and she jumped to her feet and ran to the blood lock.

"Don't fear. It is not damaged."

She exhaled and blinked a few times examining the change to the lock. The symbol was there, in the center, but it hadn't changed the strength of the lock. Her heart sank. The symbol was completely integrated, but it seemed to be doing nothing.

"Why are you disappointed?" the Heart asked.

I don't understand. I thought this was the answer that would make the lock perfect.

"The lock is perfect, princess. Don't you see? I think you don't because you don't want to. You had other ideas and this does not fit into them. You must adapt."

Tesla hung her head and nodded. *You're right. I wanted to hold them out forever. But the wall will fail. War is inevitable. This is not the answer of defense. This is our offense...*she thought back to her night with X and what Maggie had said. *Only the dead can kill a wizard.* Tesla closed the blood lock and took a step back from the flames. *We will be your prism. X and I.*

"Yes. But not yet. You must bring him to me."

I care for him. His magic balances mine.

"I see everything inside you, Tesla. Do not fear the gifts destiny gives. We will continue holding the wizards back as long as we can. But now we must also prepare to fight. So work hard, but live hard too, for we might fail. Live as if this is the last of your time, because it might be. If there is joy to be had, seize it."

CHAPTER EIGHT

The wall over Regia had changed, but much to his irritation, Lachlan couldn't perceive exactly how. It was just different. This unexpected challenge was beginning to really turn him on. Especially now that, through the power of the universe sphere, he'd gotten a glimpse of the wall's creator. And oh, she was exquisite. The Darkthing he'd sent hunting her had been successful in being his eyes at least. It hadn't been able to capture her, but next time, maybe... And since she'd attacked it, he knew what kind of power she possessed.

He shivered. So long, over a thousand years, since he'd had a woman. All the worlds they'd conquered had provided various races, but none of their females were compatible, and he hadn't given them a second thought...but her...

He didn't care if she was capable of giving him children. He wanted her. And as powerful and unique as she was, perhaps offspring would be worth striving for. Any barriers of natural laws could be manipulated if necessary.

He rubbed his hand over the cool surface of the universe sphere, forcing it to show him what the Darkthing had seen again. She was against the wall, fear in her eyes. That's how he wanted her, pinned between his body and the wall. He couldn't tell her age. She was physically mature, but there was innocence around her. He hoped she was untouched so he could have the pleasure of turning this snow white rose to crimson.

Innocence couldn't hold out very long against his touch. He'd wake her up and turn her dark. Make her hunger for things she didn't know existed. She'd be his, willing or not. His queen or his slave. He didn't care either way. Both prospects were sweet enough to make his teeth ache.

He set the sphere down on the center of the bed, surrounded it with pillows, and got up. He padded naked through his bedroom to his mirror wall and looked at himself with scrutiny. What kind of man would she desire? Two thousand years old, but his appearance didn't give his age away. His body had been rebuilt long ago and maintained its youth effortlessly.

He flashed his eyes at his own appearance, seducing himself. What woman, or man, wouldn't want him? When he had her, he would overwhelm her with his physical perfection. He would charm her until she fell in love with him. He ran his hands over his hard, muscled chest. She wouldn't hold out for long.

X tried to sleep after Tesla left, but it was useless. His brain wouldn't shut off, his body wouldn't relax. He felt strung out and hyper. He'd kept quiet for a while, to let Maggie finish her sleep, but as soon as the dawn broke, he began to work on his house. As he knew she would, Maggie came stalking over to him, a cranky look on her face, as soon as he began hammering.

She didn't say anything at first. She just stood there watching him for a few minutes. "In a hurry? You're working like a man possessed."

"I'm feeling a stronger need for privacy at the moment."

She snorted. "Uh huh. Thinking you might have a girlfriend you'd like to invite in and close the door?"

He gave her a dirty look but didn't reply.

"Are you planning to pursue her?"

He stopped swinging his hammer. "Of course I am," he said, as though it was the most obvious thing in the world.

"Are you sure you're ready for that, given you're just coming off a broken engagement?"

He answered her by returning to his hammering. He hoped she'd leave him alone, but she continued to stand there.

"She's a princess. You know that, right?"

"So?" he demanded.

"Why do you think you have a chance?"

He gave her an angry look, but then his face turned smug. "Why are you messing with me? I have a chance. I'm the only one who can calm the storm, remember? *Me.*"

She smiled indulgently. "All right. I'll leave you alone."

"Thank you!" he said emphatically, rolling his eyes.

His energy crashed at midday, and he stopped working. He'd managed to finish the walls, frame the single window, and install the door. The only thing left was the roof, and that would take him two days, at least, on his own. Exhausted, he wasn't even going to start anything else until he slept.

He ate, took a bath in the river, and put on clean clothes before flopping down on his bed for a nap. He looked up at the sky through his open roof, his mind stuck on all the details he could remember from last night. It wasn't even dusk, but he wanted to be presentable in case Tesla came back that night. He fell asleep remembering her face, her hands, her body, the way she smelled, the sound of her laugh, everything... Damn, he wanted to put his hands on her.

He roused slightly in the middle of the night and turned onto his side, adjusting his pillow. His eyelids dragged open, and he blinked a few times before closing them again. Moonlight spilled into his house through the open roof. He thought he was dreaming as he felt a hand gently slide along his forearm. His eyelids dragged open again. She sat on the floor next his bed. He came fully awake in half a second.

He sat up, putting his feet on the floor. "Tesla," he said quietly.

She smiled and rested her hands on top of his. He turned his hands over and laced his fingers through hers. He watched her react to the contact of their hands. She pinched her eyes shut, her lips parting before she bit down on her lower lip, a little moan of pleasure in her throat. *I'm dying*, he thought again. He waited silently for her to open her eyes, enjoying the wonderful sensation of their hands together, but not as much as he was enjoying watching her enjoy it.

She opened her eyes and smiled at him.

"Hello."

Her perfect lips opened, but she didn't say anything. She shut her mouth and looked down. *Not yet. Almost.* Her voice came into his head.

"Do you need to bite me? I don't mind."

I want to see if I can do it without biting you. Just being near you... Sorry for waking you.

"I'm not."

She closed her eyes again and breathed easily. Time meant nothing. He might have stared at her, just like that, for seconds or hours. While her eyes were shut, he visually memorized every detail of her face, his heart breaking again. Feeling anything for her was the greatest risk he'd ever taken with his life. They had only spent a handful of hours together, but she was already too important to him. He had to find a way to slow himself down. His heart rushed toward her recklessly, and she was a cliff.

A shiver moved over her, and she opened her eyes again, smiling. She exhaled a strange sound, then cleared her throat.

"X." Her voice was little more than a whisper.

"You did it. It worked," he said happily. "You still can bite me though, seriously go ahead."

She gave a quiet chuckle. "I shouldn't. I want to, but I run the risk of becoming addicted."

"Oh? Then I really think you should bite me. A little addiction never hurt anyone."

She laughed a little louder and shook her head. "What is it about you? How are you able to quiet the pain inside me? How can you unlock my voice?"

"I don't know. What is it about *you*? What is it about your power that feels so good mixed with mine?"

She looked up at the moon, the easy smile fading from her face, and pulled her hands free of his. "I can't stay long. Just a moment really."

"Why?" he was crushed. He wanted her to stay all night.

She licked her lips, her eyes widening nervously. "I..." She shook herself. "Two things. Business first. I'll be back in the morning, with a friend of mine, Merhl. He will stay here with Maggie and protect her, while you come with me, if you're willing to."

"Come with you where?"

"To Regia. Travel might be complicated for you, but I know we can manage it together. If you were just a normal, non-magical human, it would be impossible. But I know you can survive in Regia. The Heart of our world wants to meet you. Please come, X. I need you. My whole world will die if you refuse."

He blew out a breath and ran his hands through his hair. "Wow. Um...okay. That's really persuasive."

"It's totally unfair." Her voice was aggressive. "It's not your fight. I wouldn't ask you to risk anything if I had another choice, but I'm begging you."

He stood and paced next to the wall a few times. "I can't tell if you're telling me the truth."

She stood as well. "What?"

"Maggie gave me the ability to know when someone is telling me the truth or not, but I can't get a reading on you. I couldn't last night either. I didn't realize it until right now. You are immune."

"You think I'm lying?" Hurt filled her eyes.

"No. That's not what I said...I'm sorry. I have trust issues."

She didn't say anything. She just looked at him expectantly.

"I'll go with you, Tesla."

"You don't have to answer me right now. If you need time to think about it."

He shook his head. "I don't need to think about it. Your life is in danger."

"It's not just mine."

"Yours is the one that matters to me."

She blushed and looked down. "Thank you."

He took a step toward her. She looked up, almost fearful.

"You said there were two things."

"I'm scared to do what I'm thinking of...The Heart told me to live hard...I...uh..."

She was obviously flustered. He didn't try to rescue her. He just waited, caught in hopeful anticipation.

She sighed and closed her eyes. "It's my birthday."

He groaned. "Why didn't you tell me yesterday? I have nothing to give you."

She smirked. "You might."

"What?"

"A kiss...My first kiss."

"You give *me* a gift for your birthday."

"Then don't disappoint me. Go slow. Do it well."

He crossed the small distance and took her in his arms. He would have gone slowly, even without her request. She titled her head back. He cradled the back of her head in his hands. He could feel the beating of her heart against his chest. There was so much there. So strong a pull, how was he to kiss her and let go?

Her eyelids fluttered shut. He leaned down and pressed his cheek against hers, his mouth next to her ear. "You make me feel like I'm dying," he whispered. "You ask me to have a strength I do not."

"How?" she whispered back. "What strength?"

He rubbed his cheek slowly against hers before turning his head and kissing her mouth. A rushing filled him, like he was falling. Violently soft, painfully sweet, she sighed into him. It was slow, not just because she'd asked, but because he could remain there, just like that, all night, or maybe for the rest of his life. How did he let go? He couldn't. How could he steal her heart and make it his? He wanted more. She kept her lips closed. Soft but closed. He wanted more.

No. He told himself. No more. Not yet. He had to show her more respect than that.

He pulled his lips away from hers and gazed down into her face, guilt assailing him for taking such a liberty with her, even though she had asked for it. He shouldn't have.

"Thank you."

He laughed darkly. "Don't thank me."

"Why not? You gave me what I wanted." She smiled. "I liked it."

He groaned internally, angry at himself and feeling even more guilty. "You should be careful what you ask for. I'm not a gentleman. You twist me up inside. I want to make love to you, Tesla. I've thought about it a lot. I can tell you're not ready. I'm not asking. We barely know each other. You just need to know. I'm not noble. My desires are dark where it comes to you. I want to claim you. I want you to dream about me. I want you to fall in love with me." He let go of her then and put his head in his hands. "I shouldn't have said that, but you need to know the villain I am. So you can tread carefully."

She laughed, shocking him. He looked at her in disbelief.

"You think I don't already know all of that?"

"How can you?"

She laughed again. "I think there's some cultural differences at work here. Let's just leave it at that for now. You're no villain, X. No more than I am anyway."

He absorbed her words. "Are you saying you want what I want?"

"I'm not answering that." She took a deep breath. "I made a mistake."

"What do you mean?"

"I have something to show you, but the timing is cruel. I should have showed you before we kissed...or maybe not. I don't think there's ever going to be a time this will be easy."

"What are you talking about?"

Her hands came together in front of her. Her fingers pushed the top button of her shirt open and then the next. His eyebrows shot up, his lips parted, and his brain went up in flames. She snapped her fingers in his face.

"X!"

"What?" he forced his eyes off of her chest and back onto her face.

"I'm not seducing you. I need to show you my heart. I need to know you can hear me."

"Okay. I'll do my best to...focus. No promises."

She continued unbuttoning her shirt until it hung open, giving him a clear view of the space between her breasts, her sternum, down to her navel. Nothing would have been able to keep him focused on anything other than sight of the sides of her breasts barely showing through the open fabric. Nothing except the flashing light over her heart.

"Are you listening?"

"I'm trying."

"My heart is the source of my power, not my hands. If something bad happens to me, and I'm in danger of dying, I think you could save me, if you touched my heart."

"Why do you think that?"

"Because of the way it feels when we hold hands. My power is chaotic. You give it peace. My heart usually doesn't hurt the way my hands do, *usually*. But there are times. It's like a heart attack. My pulse gets out of control. The power rages and runs wild through me. It's terrifying. Like I could destroy the whole world around me and not stop myself."

"How did you stop yourself before?"

"It's only happened twice. I sped up time. To escape the moment."

He stared at the pulsing light, mesmerized. "Lightning Flower," he murmured.

She smiled. "You're not the first to call me that."

"Show your chest to all your suitors, do you?" Irritation was sharp in his voice.

She shook her head and made to button her shirt back up. He reached forward and stilled her hands. He lifted his hand to touch the light over her heart. She pulled back, crossing her arms over her chest.

"No! Not now. You don't understand."

"I want to understand. Why can't I touch you?"

She buttoned her shirt quickly. "It's too intimate. I fear... I might be overwhelmed. It would be difficult to not go... too far."

He scowled, but after a second, he nodded in agreement. "You showed me yours. My turn."

"Huh?"

He grabbed the hem of his shirt and pulled it over his head. Her eyes dilated. He smiled obscenely wide, seeing her apparent enjoyment at gazing at his bare chest. He took a step forward and snapped in her face as she had done to him. She blinked and looked in his eyes.

"I'm not seducing you." He used her words. "I'm showing you my marks."

He touched the black mark of the antlers and the paler one of the tree next to it. She reached up and traced the shapes with her fingertip. He let her, enjoying it a little too much.

"The black one is nothing but a token of the night I changed. I used my power without realizing what I was doing. I had no control over it. The other is a small fragment of the spirit of a tree. It chose to live inside me."

She tore her eyes away, looking back up at him. Shivers rolled out onto his skin as she traced her finger along the cool grey line around his neck. Her eyes smoldered as she splayed her hands flat on his chest. The look in her eyes brought back a nasty memory of Isolde. She used to look at him like that when she wanted to string him along. He grabbed both of her hands and pushed them back toward her.

"Too much. Don't tease me, Tesla."

She arched one eyebrow in a beautiful anger. "You're as guilty as I. It feels like...being here like this..."

"What?"

"It's a rush. Like I'm pushing a boundary I'm not supposed to."

He narrowed his eyes and pulled his shirt back over his head. Anger flashed inside him that his ability to detect truth was useless on her.

"I'm sorry, X. Don't be angry with me... I confess my innocence. I don't have any experience. I don't know what I'm doing to you."

His face softened, and he touched her cheek gently. She reached up and placed her hand over his.

"I have to go. I'll be back before midday." She turned to leave. It felt off, unfinished. She stopped by the door and turned back to him. "I will not lie to you. I hope you will grow to trust me. And I've never shown another guy my heart. If you suggest that again, I'll bust your head open. My family sometimes calls me Lightning Flower."

"I'm sorry. I was..."

"Jealous."

He nodded in defeat.

"I want you jealous."

He blinked at her a few times in surprise, making her laugh.

"See? I'm as much a villain as you," she said.

"Hurry back. I'm greedy for your company."

"You'll probably change your mind on that soon enough. Pack what you need for a few days."

She tore the air open and vanished.

He groaned and flopped back onto his bed, covering his face with his hands, thinking about their kiss. He wanted it again. He would have her. If he had to fight to the death for her, he would. His mind moved back to Isolde. In all the years, since his adolescence, the way he'd wanted her, it paled in comparison to the way he wanted Tesla. All the times he had kissed Isolde, it always made him feel happy and in love. Kissing Tesla made him feel deranged. He didn't know the words to describe it.

He was hungry for her lips again. But he wouldn't let her play him.

If she was Contarren, he would be starting the process of negotiations with her father for her hand in marriage. Her father would decide with little or no input from her. But she wasn't of his world. He didn't know the rules for such things in Regia. She'd only told him things were different. He had a lot to learn. Her father might kill him the second he mentioned any such thing. Perhaps, when he went with her to her world, if he could make a difference in their troubles, become a hero, maybe, just maybe he could be considered good enough for their princess. Despair slunk into the back of his mind. He was an executioner and a necromancer. What worth or rank was that? Not enough, he was sure.

She'd come here and asked for a kiss. Aside from how gorgeous she was, he liked her. It was early still, their association new, but she was becoming his friend. He had real hope he could win her heart, but that didn't mean he would be allowed to marry her, or whatever kind of arrangement they did in Regia. She'd talked about destined life mates. He needed to know more about that.

Tesla crept through the Everpath with more stealth than she'd ever used before, hyper alert for another shadow. She was close to the door home, when she saw it. It was far down the hallway, just standing still. It made no sign that it knew she was there. She pulled from her elf blood and became as transparent as possible. She needed to take the Everpath with her this time. Eyes locked on the shadow, she put her hand flat on the grey wall, her power reaching into it, grabbing its code and pulling it back into herself. She rushed through the door, still the shadow made no move.

She landed in her darkened bedroom. She wanted to go back to X, even though she'd just left. The time in between now and when she planned to go back seemed long. She had to stifle a giggle as a rush of excitement surged through her. She'd had her first kiss, and it was good. So good. She closed her eyes, remembering what it felt like. His words came back, too.

She felt powerful in a totally new way. It wasn't power from the magic inside her. It was something else. Something primal, barbaric, and *normal.* He wanted her. The way a man wants a woman. He said she twisted him up inside. Her lips parted in a broad smile. For the time being, at least, she'd captured his attention and tormented his thoughts.

She sighed and lay down on her bed. She imagined he was lying on his bed, thinking about her while she was thinking about him.

"X," she whispered, feeling connected to him, despite the fact they were galaxies away.

Just a few more hours, then you can see him again, she soothed herself. Her cheeks heated, and she smiled, running her fingers lightly over her lips. She was learning what desire felt like. It was an insatiable madness, or so it seemed. Frustrated hunger on her skin, aching to be touched. She'd tasted something, realizing too late she'd crossed a line she couldn't return from. One kiss. Now that she'd had it, this knowledge begged to be added to. The experience wonderful and... immediately not enough.

Her soft shivery thoughts turned angry. Who else had he kissed? Who else had he put his hands on? She wanted to be the only one. Possessive and jealous already? She chided herself. She couldn't show him she felt like that. He thought she had other guys buzzing around her, and it obviously bothered him. She'd told him she wouldn't lie to him, and she wouldn't, but she didn't have to correct him. He'd figure out soon enough that he didn't have any competition.

The sky was quiet outside her window. She snuggled into her pillow, enjoying the lack of pain that remained from being with him, and dozed off.

CHAPTER NINE

X tossed and turned in his sleep, deep in the throes of a nightmare. He was back in the village he'd grown up in. Isolde clung to his arm. People moved all around them in the square. Annoyed, he tried to pull his arm free of her grasp, but she wouldn't let go. Tesla stood across the square. She looked at him expectantly, like she was waiting for him. Shadow monsters slunk up behind her. She didn't notice; she just looked at him. He had to get to her.

"Let me go!" he shouted at Isolde.

She just smiled and shook her head. "What? You think you'll ever be good enough for her? You're mine, Alex."

"That's not my name!"

"I'm your wife, Alex. I know your name."

Troy walked past, running his hand over Isolde's breasts as he went, not halting in his stride.

He looked back for Tesla. Shadows swirled around her legs, but still she only looked at him.

Isolde tugged on his arm. "I'll always tell you the truth. You can trust me. Just like you can trust her. Tesla will always tell you the truth."

X gagged and shoved her away. Finally she let go, laughing. Everyone disappeared except him and Tesla. He tried to go to her, but he couldn't move. The shadows swallowed her whole.

"No!"

145

Then his family surrounded him. His father, mother, and brother clung to him. He absorbed their affection for a moment, the warmth was better than sunlight. Then his hands opened up. He wasn't wearing his gloves. He tried to pull away from them, but again he couldn't move. Their souls rose through their bodies and rushed into his hands. They crumbled like dry clay to the ground.

X woke suddenly, his stomach pitching, covered in sweat. He put his head in his hands and pinched his eyes shut. Silent tears ran out through his closed eyelids. He swallowed and tried to ease his breathing.

Damn the past for poking at him like this, just when something had come into his life that made him happy. It was over. That life was gone. He missed his family like a hole in his chest, but he wouldn't have taken Isolde back if she begged. He wouldn't touch her again even if someone paid him. The part of his heart that used to be hers was seared.

He shoved the pain of loss down, tucked it away deep inside, where he could ignore it and deny its existence. He stood, ran his hands through his hair, and tried to shake it off. The worst part of his dream had been watching Tesla consumed by darkness and being powerless to save her. A sudden fear seized him. Did this dream mean something? Was something happening to Tesla right now?

X took a deep breath. It was just a dream, that was all. She'd said she would be back before midday. He needed to pack a few things to take to Regia. Under his disquiet that Tesla needed him was a disbelief he would be traveling to another world. He couldn't wrap his mind around it.

He heard Maggie clattering around outside and went out to see her.

"Good morning," she said brightly, stoking the fire under a pot of water.

He yawned. "You're cheerful this morning."

146

"This is going to be a good day. The stone has showed me some things that will happen very soon." Her cheeks flushed, and she smiled, bouncing on the balls of her feet.

X had never seen her this excited. She was almost giddy. She handed him a mug of hot tea.

"Thanks." He blew on it and took a careful sip.

He sat down and watched her rush around, making heaps of food like she was about to host a party.

"Entertaining guests today?" he smirked.

"Yes! Well, just one. Tesla's friend." She blushed again and turned away from him.

He snorted. "I guess you have seen in the stone that this is going to be your new favorite person. I know you don't like me that much. You've never made me cake."

"I never felt the need to show off my culinary skills to you."

He laughed at her, he couldn't help it. She smiled and shrugged helplessly. "They will be here soon. Are you ready to go?"

"Almost."

"Are you taking a gift for her mother?"

"Huh?"

"You will meet Tesla's parents, you know. You should take her mother a present."

He frowned. "How much of the future have you seen?"

"Just lots of today. Like I said. Today will be a good day."

"Okay...well, what should I take to give to her mother?"

"You should give her that new dagger you made a few days ago. The flame shaped one with the etchings."

He raised his eyebrows. "Really?"

She nodded emphatically. "Trust me. You want to win points with that woman? Forget delicate feminine things, give her a weapon."

He snorted. "Okay. Anything else? Do I need to give something to Tesla's father as well?"

Maggie pursed her lips and then sighed. "Sorry to tell you, but nothing you could give him is going to make him like you."

X nodded. "Well, I guess that's not totally unexpected. I am after his daughter."

"You are, are you?" she teased. "She came to see you last night, didn't she?"

"Oh my gosh!" he exploded. "Were you watching?"

"No! I wasn't! I swear! I told you I won't watch you like that. I was just guessing."

He eased back. "Oh. Okay. Sorry."

"So, she did come to see you?"

It was his turn to blush. "Yeah."

Her smiled turned devious. "Had a nice time?"

He groaned. "No. It's torture. And I'd take it all day."

She patted him on the arm sympathetically. "Sorry."

He shook his head. "Is there anything else I need to take with me on this trip besides clothes, and a gift for her mother?"

"Take you palm stones and your gloves. Be on guard against your power getting out of control. You'll be fine, just stay alert. You will have to adjust to the various types of magic in their world. Stay calm at all times if possible, no matter what you encounter... and take your axe."

"Why? I doubt I'll be freelancing while I'm there."

"Status. Be open about what you are. Regia is a warrior culture. Strength is respected. You have an impressive skillset making weapons. Your axe is a flashy example of what you can do. Plus, you never know. You might need it. I only know today will be good. Tomorrow might be bloody."

"What could I give Tesla for her birthday?"

"You know her better than I do. I've barely spoken to her. You monopolize her."

He smirked. "I'm not apologizing for that...I have an idea. How much time do I have before they get here?"

She held up the stone on her necklace and looked through it. "Just enough time. Hurry up. I've already started the fire for your forge."

He glanced over his shoulder at his workshop. Sure enough, smoke was billowing up from his fire pit. "So you already know what I'm going to make her?"

"No. I only knew I should start a fire."

He pointed at the stone around her neck. "That thing is inconsistent."

"Don't I know it? You're running out of time."

He shoved his breakfast in his mouth at record speed and got up.

149

The forge went fast. The thin metal flower emerged fairly easily from the plain strip of steel. But it was missing something when it came out of the water. He wanted to add color to it. He etched the edges of the petals with thin veins of lightning.

"Maggie!" he called.

She came over, dusting flour onto her skirt and looked at his work.

She nodded approvingly. "Very nice."

"Can you make the lightning red?"

"Bleed on it."

He scowled. "Really?"

"Yes. Just a little."

He shrugged and sliced his fingertip. He ran his finger along the edges of the petals, the blood going straight into his etchings. She took it from him, muttering under her breath, a flash went out from her hand over the flower. She handed it back. The lightning was bright red against the dull grey of the steel.

"There. The color will never fade."

"Thanks."

"They will be here very soon, and you're all grimy now. Go clean up."

He wiped the sweat off his brow with the back of his hand. Maggie put her hands together and closed her eyes, muttering again. Folded clothes appeared in her hands.

"Here. You'll look good in this." She handed him the clothes.

He took the clothes and kissed her cheek before sprinting off toward the river. As soon as he was out of sight, she packed for him, making him three other sets of new clothes, a new belt, a pair of new boots, and a knapsack to put everything in. She pulled out her wand and made a carved wooden box for the metal flower to go into and topped it with a red ribbon.

She took the knapsack, put the present inside it and set it on the table. Now she needed to address her appearance as well. She went into her house and took off her flour-covered dress. She made a burgundy one to go nicely with her hair color. Primping too much made her feel silly, so she stopped after tiding up her braids, chewing a clove leaf to make her breath sweet, and adding a hint of color to her lips.

Tesla woke early. Excited, nervous butterflies fluttered in her stomach. She raced from her room, past her parents eating breakfast, and went straight to the shower. She wanted to look perfect today. She wanted to look so good it made X crazy.

After an hour, Forest knocked on the door. "Tesla? Are you okay? You've been in there a long time."

She opened the door, steam wafting out. Forest looked in at her, standing at the mirror in a towel.

"Are you wearing my perfume?"

Just a little. She signed. *You don't mind, do you?*

"Uh. No I don't mind. Your hair looks amazing. Are you getting ready for the party already? It's not till this evening."

I know.

"So why are you primping?"

Grandfather told you what I've been doing, right?

"Yes." Stress pulled around Forest's eyes.

I've found something really important. I'm going to get it and bring it back today. Merhl is going with me. I'm going to meet him in Kyhael in a few minutes. It won't take too long. I'll be back long before the party.

Forest twisted her hands together and nodded resignedly. "Be careful, sweetheart."

I will be. Promise.

"Your dad left already. You took too long in the shower. He couldn't wait. He was a little disappointed he didn't get to tell you goodbye. I think he's a bit sentimental today. He's having a hard time accepting you're a young woman."

I know. He threatened to give me a dollhouse the other day.

Tesla frowned. Her mom's words brought something to mind she felt needed saying, especially now because of X. She made a mental note to tell her father as well, when she got the chance.

I know it must be hard that I've grown up so fast. I need you to know that I am really grown. I don't have the mind of a child inside this adult body. I went through all the years you never saw. I sped up time when I forced myself to age but that doesn't mean that in that breath of time that I didn't go through the years. Because I did. Do you understand?

Forest smiled sadly and shook her head. "No. I don't understand. Not really. I understand you are a woman despite how short of a time it took you to get there...It makes me sad, for myself. For the time I didn't get with you. And it makes me sad because I fear your life will be very short." Her voice broke on the last word. "I can accept you as a grown up. Your father on the other hand is having a harder time letting go of you being his little girl."

I'm sorry. I hope I never have to age myself again. I want to stop and just let time move as it is meant to.

Forest smiled again and touched the ends of Tesla's hair. "So beautiful."

Am I?

"Yes. You are."

She gave her mother a cheeky grin. *You're just saying that 'cause I look like dad.*

Forest laughed and came to stand next to Tesla. "Look."

They looked at their reflections side by side. "You look like me as well. Your eyes are the same shape as mine." She flicked the top of Tesla's ear. "Your ears, too."

I want to look my best today. Can I borrow something to wear?

Forest smirked and narrowed her eyes at Tesla in the mirror. "Like what?"

Your grey shirt with the long sleeves.

"I suppose. It's a little sexy though. The edges of your light will show." She touched the ends of the lightning flower where it reached up the highest on the top of Tesla's breast.

Do you think I should be ashamed?

"Of course not! You're beautiful. All of you. You just usually hide it."

You said you could accept me as a grown up.

"Are you trying to capture someone's attention?"

Maybe.

153

"You're being cagy. All right take the shirt. It's hanging up in my closet. Your father's going to kill me when he sees you wearing that."

Thanks, Mom. I need to hurry now. Merhl is waiting for me.

Forest crossed her arms over her chest. Who was Tesla trying to attract? She was so isolated because of her accelerated aging and her scary gifts that she didn't associate with people her age. Forest frowned. Was it Merhl? She knew they were close.

Once she was dressed, Tesla looked at herself in the mirror, scrutinizing her appearance. She felt confident. X warned her not to tease him. Was this teasing? Should she change? The cut of the shirt was lower than anything she'd ever worn, and her jeans were snug. Was it teasing to dress up something he already liked looking at? She was doing it *for* him.

She needed to hurry. She didn't have time to change anyway. She poked her head out of her room. Her mom was sitting on the couch, scowling. She looked over at Tesla.

Bye, Mom. I'll be back later.

Forest nodded and smiled, but she looked frustrated. "Tesla, wait. It's not Merhl, is it?"

What?

"You don't have a crush on Merhl, do you?"

She hesitated. *Would that be a problem?*

"No," Forest said slowly.

Really? You don't look too happy. I thought you liked Merhl.

"I love Merhl."

A strange sounding laugh bubbled up Tesla's throat. *Merhl's my*

154

friend. He's like my brother. I don't like him like that.

"I was just checking. It didn't seem like you two felt that way about each other. If I seemed weird about it, it's because I was confused. I wouldn't object if that's how it was."

Well, that's not how it is. So, stop being weird.

Forest smirked. "No dice."

Tesla rolled her eyes and opened a portal to Kyhael.

Both Merhl and Rahaxeris were waiting for her in the *Rune-dy* antechamber.

"Wow, Tesla. You look gorgeous," Merhl said when she landed in front of him.

Thanks. She looked over at her grandfather.

He gazed at her and scowled.

What?

"Merhl's right. You look gorgeous. I don't like it. Why are you so dolled up?"

She shook her head, annoyed, and refused to answer.

"I still don't see why you think this little experiment will work on Merhl and not me," he complained.

I'm in a hurry, Grandfather. Can we discuss it later? I promise to try to come up with a way to bring you to the Everpath, too. Just not right now. Merhl's father made it there; he will be able to as well. She signed.

"Plus, you didn't want the job of guarding the witch for three days," Merhl reminded him.

"All right, all right."

Merhl faced Tesla. "I'm ready."

She exhaled and closed her eyes, pulling the code she absorbed from the Everpath into her hands, pushing it down into her fingertips. She reached up to his face, placing her thumbs on his eyelids. Tiny lightning strikes shot into his eyes. He staggered backward, grimacing in pain, and swearing.

Rahaxeris caught him by the arm. "You okay?"

Merhl blinked and rubbed his eyes. "Yeah. I'm okay."

Sorry. Tesla signed. *I didn't know it would hurt that much.*

He looked at her intently then, his eyes bloodshot. "Show me. Open it up."

She grabbed the atmosphere and tore it open wide. Blackness swirled beyond the tear, a grey light in the distance.

He squinted. "I think I see it. It's just a dim light."

She nodded and held out her hand to him. He took it and followed her through the breach. They walked through the rushing, vaporous darkness toward the light. She pushed the door open and pulled Merhl through, into the Everpath. She looked at him and held her finger to her lips. He nodded. She did a quick check for the shadow thing. It wasn't there.

Relived, she led the way down to the door to Contarren. She opened it, and they went through. They landed in the woods. Merhl blinked and rubbed his eyes again before looking around.

"Is this the place?" he asked.

She nodded and pointed in the direction they needed to go.

"Is it safe here? It feels very mundane. Non-magical."

She nodded again. *It's safe.*

"I'm sorry I'm going to miss your birthday party," he said. "I got you something. I guess it will have to wait until I get back from this little covert operation."

What is it?

"Not telling. I'm doing you a favor coming here, so you have to wait for your present."

Fine. I really appreciate this, Merhl. I know this all seems odd, but I promise the answer is with these people. I know it is.

"I trust you."

There. That's where they live.

Apprehension was thick in the air as they approached and it came from both sides. X stood waiting for them to arrive, and as they did, a nervous excitement filled the air. Tesla halted as X caught her gaze. The butterflies in her chest were fierce. For a few seconds, he was all she could see. He looked amazing. Dressed all in black, the dark contrast against his white blonde hair and ice blue eyes was striking. He didn't smile at her, he just stared.

Merhl put his hand on her shoulder in a protective motion. X's eyes darted sharply onto Merhl's hand and then onto his face, then he looked at her questioningly. She rushed toward X holding out her hands. He grasped them tightly, pulling her close to him. The glory of the ecstasy of touching one another caused both of them to close their eyes and breathe unevenly.

"Tesla?" Merhl took a step forward.

X's eyes shot open and pinned Merhl with a warning look, then he glanced down at her. "Why didn't you explain this to him?"

He's always with my grandfather. I couldn't think of a way to explain that wouldn't put my grandfather on edge or possibly make him furious. She spoke in his mind.

Merhl took another more purposeful step forward. "Tesla, what's going on here?"

She looked at him over her shoulder apologetically.

"Just wait a minute, and she'll answer you," X said, not letting go of her.

"If you would let go of her hands, she could answer me now." He was getting angry. "Why are you silencing her?"

"I'm not!" X fired back.

I'm almost there... Almost... She exhaled in relief as the shiver went down her throat. She smiled at X and let go, turning to face Merhl.

"It's okay," she said aloud.

His mouth hung open in disbelief. "Tesla! You spoke to me! Didn't you?"

"I did, Merhl. You hear me."

Laughing with joy, Merhl swooped down on her, picked her up, and spun her in a circle. "How?" he asked, setting her back down and hugging her tightly.

"I can properly introduce you to my friend X now."

"X, this is Merhl, Merhl this is X. I don't know why, but he unlocks my voice. I just have to be near him, and all the pain and distortion goes away. All I have to do is touch him for a moment, and then my voice comes."

158

Merhl looked at X in a less threatening way then. "I'm sorry. I had no idea what was going on."

"I gathered that… So, you're going to stay here and protect Maggie?"

"That's the plan. Where is she?"

Right on cue, Maggie emerged from her house. She walked boldly up to Merhl, who stared at her with wide eyes. Tesla had never seen Merhl dumbfounded. He looked like he'd just suffered a severe shock. Given her height, Maggie didn't look dwarfed next to him. The top of her head came to his chin. She held out her hand to him. He took it in both of his and brought it to his lips.

Tesla and X exchanged an amused glance. He leaned over and whispered in her ear, "They're going to get along fine, looks like. She got up this morning and started cooking for him. I've never seen her that goofy. She's very excited to meet him."

Tesla surveyed Merhl as he spoke to Maggie. The she moved closer and whispered to X, "Looks like the feeling is mutual. I've known Merhl most of my life. I've never seen him look at anything or anyone quite like the way he's looking at her."

"Shall we go then, and leave them to it?"

Tesla walked over to Merhl. "We're going now."

"Okay," he said easily.

"Will you be all right?"

Maggie piped up. "Don't worry. We're going to be just fine. Merhl and I are going to be fast friends. There is no danger for me here. You're the ones heading into danger." She gripped Tesla's shoulders. "Take care, princess. Today will be good. Enjoy it. It won't last."

She frowned but nodded and walked back to where X was waiting for her. He put his palm stones on and his gloves over them before strapping his axe to his back and slinging a pack over his shoulder. "I'm ready."

"No you're not. Not yet. I can't just take you to the Everpath by towing you along by the hand. You have to drink my blood first." She feared he would argue or be grossed out. He didn't, he just nodded.

"Okay."

She put her index finger in her mouth and sliced it on her incisor. "It won't take much." She said, holding her finger next to his lips.

He opened his mouth. She touched her fingertip to his tongue. He closed his lips around it and sucked once. He never broke eye contact, speaking intimately to her without any words.

I know. She said in his head. *I know.*

She pulled her hand back, and he swallowed. "I don't think you know at all...So is that it?" he asked casually.

"I think you'll be blind to the path, but I can take you there now. Don't let go of me."

A small smile pulled into the side of his mouth. "Never."

She held out her hand to him but then retracted it. "You've got the stones on your hands."

"Yes, but they're covered by my gloves. I'm in control of it. It's okay."

She tore the air open and grabbed his hand, pulling him through. Her heart rose up her throat in fear. What if this hurt him? What if she was wrong? His hand was solid in hers as they crossed into the Everpath.

"Are you okay?" she whispered.

"I'm fine. I can barely see. Everything's in shadow. I see shapes."

160

TENAYA JAYNE

"That's more than I expected. Let's get out of here."

She pulled him along briskly.

"What's the rush? Where is this place?"

A gust of wind blew from behind them. "Hurry! There's danger."

They were almost to the door. She could feel the darkness slithering behind them. "Wall builder…" it hissed seductively. "Don't run from me…I want only to taste you…"

"What the hell is tha—"

She pushed X through the door to Regia and slammed it behind her.

"Whoa!" he exclaimed as they landed in her bedroom. "Are we safe now?" his eyes cleared, and he looked around her room.

"Yes."

"Good. I can't wait any longer." He pulled her against him and kissed her mouth.

It wasn't soft or slow like before. It was desperate. She was quickly overwhelmed. It was too good. Too much. Too intense. She was losing herself inside it. Terrified by the force pulling her to him, she pushed him away.

"Stop!" She was breathless. "You make me want so much, X."

"I doubt it comes close to how much you make me want… I'm sorry. I lost my head. I didn't mean to show you any disrespect."

She was confused. "Disrespect?"

"I have to be more…distant. I don't want you to think I assume…" He paused, groping for the words. "You're not mine."

161

She thought she understood, but she wasn't sure. She wanted clarity, but it would have to wait. Or rather she figured it *should* wait for another time.

"We are in Regia. How do you feel? Can you breathe easily? Are your senses disoriented?"

He seemed to take stock of himself then. "I feel fine. My head is a little light, but maybe it's just your lips that make me feel like that."

"This is my room in my parent's house."

He cast his eyes around again. "It looks a lot more comfortable than my house."

"It is. Your world is primitive. Please don't freak out. There's so much here you will have never seen."

"I'll try. What am I to do? How do I behave?"

"Hmm…I hadn't really thought about it. Just be yourself."

"But our cultural differences," he argued.

"I won't leave you alone. I'll help you avoid any missteps. But making friends or a good impression isn't important right now. I wish things were that easy."

"Whatever it is you've brought me here for, I can tell you, me making a good impression might not matter to you, but it's crucial to me."

"Why?"

"Without it, how am I to…" He stopped and shook his head. "Never mind."

She smiled at him. "Okay. Don't worry. Put your stuff down." She looked out her window. "Let's go outside. My mother's out there. You can meet her."

X walked to the window and looked out. "That can't be your mother."

"I can assure you she is."

"Your sister, perhaps. I'd believe that. She barely looks older than you."

"You're the only human here. We age differently, and we live longer." Tesla smiled. "She's beautiful, isn't she?"

"Stunning," he agreed. "The second most beautiful woman I've ever seen."

"Second?"

"You're the first." He winked at her.

She rolled her eyes. "You're over the top."

"*You're* over the top," he countered.

She looked at him seriously, her cheeks flushing.

"What is it?" he asked quietly.

"I'm sorry, it just really hit me again. I'm *talking* to you. *Out loud*...I love talking to you."

He leaned toward her, his lips an inch from hers. She closed her eyes, but he didn't kiss her. She opened her eyes again.

He backed away, shaking his head. "I love talking to you, too."

He set his things down on the floor, took his gloves off, removed the stones on his palms, and put them in his pack before slipping his gloves back on. "I brought a gift for your mother."

She continued to look at her mom through the window. Forest was decorating the garden for the party that evening. "What did you bring?"

He took the knife out of the pack and held it out for Tesla.

She raised her eyebrows and smiled as she took it from him. "Wow. You made this?"

He nodded. She handed it back.

"Clever choice. You're going to try and make her like you, aren't you?"

"Shamelessly."

She chuckled. "I think you'll succeed. Come on."

He followed her through the house to the front door, forcing himself to ignore everything he saw that he wanted to look at and ask questions about. He blinked in the alien sunlight, his eyes straining to adjust.

"Stay right here for a second," she said.

He hung back on the front porch while Tesla strode up to her mother.

"Mom."

Forest jumped and turned around. "Oh! You're speaking again!" She clasped Tesla against her in a tight hug. "Who's that?"

"That's my friend, X. He's going to help protect us from the wizards."

Forest looked him over thoroughly. She leaned over and whispered in Tesla's ear. "Now I see why you wanted to borrow my shirt."

Tesla felt her cheeks heat up. *"Mom! Please!"* she whispered back desperately.

"Okay. You're going to have to explain how all of this works together and how you've managed to get a human to be able to survive here. I'm dying to know what kind of ability he could possibly have to help us, but at the moment, I'm just going to tell you, nice work. He's cute."

"That word is not adequate to describe him," Tesla said.

"Well, I was trying to not embarrass you too much, but you're right. He's hot."

She nodded emphatically in agreement. "He's nice, too. Complicated, maybe a little brooding at times. He's been magically altered. He won't shake your hand. His hands are dangerous; he won't want to hurt you. That's why he's wearing gloves. He can't hurt me, just as I can't hurt him. It's *him*, Mom. He's the reason I can speak to you right now. Something about him balances me."

"Well, introduce us. Goodness knows what he'll think if we stand here whispering about him much longer."

She waved at X to come closer. He walked up to them and put his hands behind his back. Forest smiled at him.

"I'm Forest. It's nice to meet you, X."

"Thank you. It's very nice to meet you as well." He inclined his head in a little bow. "Tesla has told me all about you."

"Really? She hasn't said a thing about you. She's kept you a secret."

"I'm sorry if my presence is an untimely surprise."

Forest chuckled. "You can relax. You're welcome here."

"Thank you," he said again.

"It seems like perhaps I should be thanking you for coming here.

165

Giving Tesla her voice."

"I don't feel like I can take any credit for that. I don't understand how it works...I...um... brought you a gift." He held the knife out. "Hold out your hands flat."

She did. He laid the blade in her hands without touching her at all.

Forest held it up, pleasure plain on her face. She gripped the handle and moved it back and forth so the sunlight flashed on the blade. "Nice balance, especially for the shape. Beautiful work. Thank you. I love it."

"X made it," Tesla informed her.

Forest raised her eyebrows and looked closer at the knife. She tossed it in the air and caught it. "I'm impressed. I've been known to make blades from time to time as well."

"Really?" He smiled broadly. "That's something we have in common then. Would you show me some of your work?"

"I will later. Did you make that axe strapped to your back?"

"Oh, yeah. I meant to take it off in the house. Here." He unfastened it and handed it to Forest to look at.

She gripped it with both hands and nodded approvingly. "Pretty badass..." Her eyes narrowed. "Use it much?"

"Just for work."

She glanced over at Tesla, and then back at him, her expression turning shrewd. "How did you get to be a headsman?"

"It's a long story. I don't get any pleasure from taking life. I just..."

Forest shook her head and handed the axe back to him. "It's okay. It can wait."

166

He looked uncomfortable and slightly dejected.

"Go and put it in the house, 'cause you know what can't wait? These lights I need to hang in the trees. Could you help me, X? I'd appreciate it," Forest said.

"Of course."

When he went back into the house, Forest pinned Tesla with her eyes. "Why didn't you tell me he was an executioner?"

"Are you judging him?" Tesla fired back. "Cause the last time I checked, you sentence people to death in your line of work."

Forest smirked. "Touché. Actually, the only thing I wanted to judge was how you would respond if I criticized him...I like him, based on my first impression at least...and it's a pleasure hearing your voice tinged with a hint of indignation."

"Mom!"

Forest closed her eyes and smiled. "Ah! That's great! Just like that! I love it."

"I'm just going to quit talking now."

"Don't you dare. I need to hear you. I don't care what you say, just talk to me."

Forest couldn't remember being as happy as she was over the next two hours while Tesla and X helped her decorate the garden. Just listening to Tesla talk as easily as if she'd always been able to, her voice cheerful and flirtatious, sent waves of overwhelming happiness through Forest. X had been a surprise, but she was fast growing to like him. She liked the way he treated Tesla and the respect he showed. He was unique, but that fit with Tesla. It was obvious he had romantic intentions, but Forest found that didn't bother her as much as she would have thought.

"Looks like we're all done," Forest announced when they ran out of decorations. "Thank you for helping, X."

"You're welcome. It was fun."

"Tesla, your dad is going to be home soon. Why don't you and X go watch a movie or something? The party will start at dusk."

She watched Tesla thread her fingers through his and pull him back into the house. She had a little twinge of objection in her chest that was outweighed by her joy that her daughter could hold a boy's hand at all. She shook her head, bemused, when the door shut behind them.

Forest fussed over the details of the place settings on the tables while she waited for Syrus. He showed up a few minutes later, striding through the garden gate, a case of beer tucked under his arm. Forest laughed and took it from him.

"Where did you get that?"

"Don't ask." He rolled his eyes, before swooping down on her. He picked her up by the waist and kissed her mouth, hard.

"It looks great." He glanced around the garden. "I can't believe you got all this done by yourself."

"I had help." She smiled.

"Oh? Who?"

She put her hands on his chest bracingly. "Well...your daughter has decided to bring a date to her party."

Syrus just blinked at her for a second. *"What?"* he exploded.

"Calm down."

"No! No! Don't tell me to calm down."

"Calm down!" she said again, emphatically. "His name is X. And he's very nice. She brought him here from another world. He's human, sort of. He has magical abilities."

Her words did the opposite of calm Syrus. His eyes lit up, and lightning snaked over his hands and forearms. "Well she can take him right back where she found him! This is totally unacceptable!" he yelled.

Forest gave him a droll stare. "Why?" she said slowly.

"She's just a little girl!"

Forest sighed. "She's eighteen. She's a grown woman."

He shook his head. "No, she's not."

She put her hands gently on his cheeks and looked deeply into his angry eyes. "She is."

"I'm very, *very* unhappy, Forest."

"Yes. I see that. And I get it. It's not easy… Everything Tesla's been working on…she told me Regia needs him. I believe her. So this is bigger than your protective, shotgun feelings."

"My what?"

"Never mind." She smiled broadly, her eyes dancing. "I like him. And there is something precious you can now experience that you never could because of him."

"What's that?" he said through gritted teeth.

"Her voice. When Tesla is near him, she can speak."

The anger drained from his face, replaced by awe. "She can speak?"

"Yes."

She watched his eyes slick over with tears, feeling her own tears begin again as well.

"She's been out here helping me put all this stuff up, just talking as if it were nothing, Syrus. It's beautiful."

"Where is she?"

"They're in the house."

Panic flashed in his eyes then as he looked at the closed front door. "You left them alone in the house?"

"Yeah. So?"

"*So?*" he strode quickly toward the house. "Goodness knows what they're doing!"

Forest followed. "Ah, yes. I see where you're going with that."

Syrus burst through the front door like an old school comic book super hero. Forest had to stifle a giggle as she imagined him yelling *Ah ha!* But they didn't catch them doing anything. X stood at the counter in the kitchen while Tesla handed him a mug of coffee.

They both turned to look at Forest and Syrus. Syrus barely glanced at X before locking his gaze expectantly on Tesla. She smiled and ran to him.

"Daddy!" She caught him around the neck.

He laughed through his tears just as Forest had the first time Tesla spoke to her.

"Oh! Talk to me, sweetheart. Say anything," Syrus said hugging her tightly.

She giggled. "Wee willy winky, running through the town, upstairs, downstairs, in his nightgown."

He laughed again. "Goofball. How is this possible?"

She pulled out of his hug and directed his attention back to X, who watched apprehensively.

"Dad, this is my friend, X. When I'm with him, I don't hurt. Everything inside me clicks into place. His magic grounds mine."

X straightened his shoulders and inclined his head to Syrus. "Sir."

Syrus stared at him, trying to work through his tangled emotions connected to the presence of the young man. He took a deep breath and held out his hand in greeting. "Thank you."

X looked down at his hand and shook his head, then he held his hands out, palms up, the centers glowing blue.

"Forgive me, but I can't shake your hand."

Syrus raised an eyebrow as he looked at X's hands. "Hm. Interesting."

He pulled his gloves out of his back pocket and slid them on. "I usually keep them covered, but my hands are no danger to Tesla."

Syrus scowled. "No? Well you might be in danger of losing your hands if you don't keep them to yourself."

"Dad!" Tesla gasped.

X had no visible reaction to the threat. He merely nodded. "Understood."

Syrus waited for X to try and sell him the typical lies that he had only the noblest intentions in regards to Tesla, and he would never, blah, blah, blah. X remained silent, earning him a tiny, grudging shred of respect from Syrus. But he still didn't feel he'd made his point adequately. "This is *my* house. Tesla is *my* daughter."

X didn't flinch from his ire or break his gaze. He just nodded again. "Understood."

"But..." Forest moved to stand between them and faced X. "You are a welcome guest."

"Thank you."

Tesla moved away from her dad and stood by X, reaching for his hand. She gave Syrus a challenging stare. "Surely you won't object to us holding hands. Touch is what keeps my pain at bay and helps me maintain my ability to speak."

He grimaced like he'd just bit into a lemon. "Fine...Don't push it."

"Okay, Daddy."

Forest broke the tension again. "We don't have much time before the guests begin to arrive. Tesla, help your father with the food." She laced her arm through X's and led him away. "X, you come with me. I'll show you some of my favorite weapons."

"Sorry about that," she said quietly, once she'd pulled him into the other room.

"Please do not apologize. I understand. His reaction to me was not at all unexpected. Thank you for your hospitality and for providing me a way out of the room. They need to be alone to talk."

Forest smiled warmly and nodded. "Yes. I'm glad you get it. And I really did want to show you my favorite sword."

X gave her the reaction she wanted when she pulled her obsidian glass sword from its scabbard. He was speechless and looked slightly winded as she handed it to him.

"Careful," she warned.

"It's...phenomenal. I'll never be able to make anything like it, that's for sure." He handed it back. "Your skill far surpasses mine. Perhaps I could persuade you to teach me?"

Forest sheathed it and set it aside. "I didn't really make it. It was a group effort, and the glass chose me. I almost consider it alive."

"The lightning inside it, did Tesla do that?"

"No. Syrus did. They have some of the same power. Hers is stronger, *wild...*" Forest gave a little gasp and put her hand over her heart.

"Are you all right?"

"Oh, yes. It was just a pang of what Syrus is feeling right now. He's so happy. Having a conversation with Tesla is making him happier than he's been in a very long time."

"You feel his emotions?"

She smiled. "Yes. And he feels mine."

"Because you're destined life mates? Tesla told me a little bit about it. How does it work? How do you know you've found your mate?"

"There's no doubt when it happens. Your first eye contact, your first touch, it binds you together, body and soul. It's a singular feeling. There's nothing like it. You know, beyond doubt when it happens."

"Hmm..." He looked at the floor, his shoulders slumping. "So, there's someone like that for Tesla. She just hasn't met him yet?"

Forest understood his interest on the subject, and his dejection. She reached out and touched his shoulder for a second. "Don't despair. Not everyone has a destined life mate. She might, and she might not. But whatever the answer to that question is, it doesn't mean she can't feel for you. I see she already does."

He shook his head. "I know, deep down, there is no hope. I have no rank or fortune. She's a princess and I have nothing... "

"I think I should tell you a little about myself and my profession, X. Personally, if you had some great rank and title, I would be more hesitant about you. Tesla comes from royal blood, but there is no throne waiting for her. She's free to live her life as she pleases."

Forest explained some of her personal history, her job as Hailemarris, and how she worked to destroy the class systems and erase the racial lines in Regia. His disposition brightened the longer she talked.

"It's time for me to play hostess, now. I've enjoyed our conversation, X."

"Thank you for telling me all that. I understand your culture much better than I did before. But I'm nervous about this party. How am I to behave?" he asked.

"This will be just family and close friends. Most of them are very laid back. It will be a casual event. Just food, conversation, and whishing Tesla a happy birthday. Gifts will be given, but I wouldn't worry about—
"

"I have a gift for her."

"Okay. You'll be fine." She turned to leave the room, then stopped and looked back at him. "What kind of fighting skills do you have?"

He shrugged. "I can hold my own in a fist fight. I'm a decent shot throwing knives or hatchets."

"Weapon of choice?"

"A bow and arrow."

She smiled approvingly. "Nice. It's been a long time since I've come across an archer."

"Why do you ask?"

A mischievous light flashed in her eyes. "There will be a sparring element to this party. You can join in or sit out as you like. But the one thing Tesla asked for her birthday was combat training. Just warning you, it could get a little wild."

"Wow! What if someone gets hurt?"

"Syrus is a great healer. No worries there. That being said, I wouldn't consider it wise to go hand to hand with Netriet. She has a robotic arm that could tear your head off."

She laughed at the expression on his face and left the room.

CHAPTER TEN

X watched from the living room window as the evening sky erupted in deep jeweled colors that undulated across the horizon. His nerves grew as people began to arrive at the party. All was quiet, and then the next moment, the garden was full of people. His eyes fell onto every male, scrutinizing them, wondering when he might see another guy in line for Tesla's attention and affection. She came up beside him and looked out, too.

"What do you think?" she asked quietly.

"I'm not sure what I think."

She pointed out a tall, slender man with long golden hair and red eyes. "That's my grandfather, Rahaxeris. Tread lightly. And there is my other grandfather, Zeren. He used to be the king, before my parents decided to reject their thrones and turn the world on its head. He's easy; you don't need to worry about him. He likes everyone."

"That must be Netriet," X said, pointing at her.

"How did you know?"

"Your mom warned me not to spar with her because of her arm."

"Ah, yes. Sound advice. And that's Merick with her. They both are cool. I love hanging out with them. They have this awesome little house on a cliff overlooking the sea… Oh! Shreve and Sabra just showed up and they brought baby Sophie."

He chuckled at her. "Like babies?"

"Yes! But it makes me so sad I can't hold them. I can give Sophie a kiss though."

He pulled his gloves off and held his hands up toward her. "Do you think you could hold the baby if I help you with that?"

She grabbed his hands. A strong surge went through both of them. Inside their hands, his power reached deep and twisted around hers until the blue and red mixed purple. He pulled her closer and rested his forehead against hers. Her breathing turned hard, and she looked on the verge of tears. Her expression was a gorgeous mix of pain and pleasure.

"It's so strong, X."

"Yes." He was breathless, too.

"Kiss me again."

He smiled. "I can't. Holding hands is all we're allowed remember?"

"Screw that."

He raised his eyebrows. "Such language. You should mind your tongue."

"Why don't you get a little closer and mind it for me?"

"Oh my gosh. Look at you, bad girl."

Tesla threw her head back and laughed. The next moment her eyes flashed dark. "Please?"

He abruptly let go of her hands and stepped back from her. "Later...And I'm going to make you regret asking for it."

"Regret... Ruin... Passion... Pain... Torture... Pleasure... Denial... Rage..." She said each word very slowly, holding his gaze, never once blushing.

He swallowed, feeling like he was drowning in fire. "How do you do that? Why?"

She seemed to shake off the desire in her eyes, and the burning energy between them faded back. Laughter and music drifted in from outside. "Are you ready to go meet everyone?" she asked.

He slid his gloves back on and took a deep breath. "Yes, murderess."

"Why do you call me that?"

"Because you're going to be the death of me."

She frowned. "Hmm...I understand. I'll try harder to not treat you like this, but its pull is so seductive...And you're wrong. I will bring you life."

"Sure," he said disbelievingly. "Then, whatever that means, your father will kill me. Either way, I feel sure I'm going to end up dead."

A flash of lightning surged angrily over her hands. "I won't hurt you, and I won't let anyone else hurt you either."

His eyes only reflected sorrow and mistrust. She absorbed the pain his distrust caused in her.

"Are you retreating from me, X? Have your feelings reversed?" She looked as though she was about to cry.

"No." His voice was passionate.

He reached out and took her in his arms. She held herself rigid for a moment, then she exhaled. He felt her surrender. She put her head on his shoulder and he rested his head against hers.

"I don't think we're communicating very well," he said gently.

"I'm sorry. It's my fault. I want reassurance. I'm insecure. I behave badly because of it. I'm too wild."

178

"Insecure how? Reassurance of what?"

"Reassurance of you. That you really feel something for me."

"I followed you blindly to another world. What more do you want?"

She laughed lightly. "You're right. Sorry."

"Do you feel better now? I think it's time for you to join your party."

She took a deep breath. "Yes." She pulled away from him. "Are you ready?"

He shrugged. "I guess so."

They stepped out the front door, and all eyes fell on them. She seemed to swell up with excitement.

"Thank you all for coming to my birthday party!" she said loudly.

Everyone gasped. For a second X was confused at their response, then he remembered none of them had ever heard her speak aloud. She pulled him into the crowd now surging around her. Everyone bombarded her with the same question. *How was it possible she could talk?*

She explained vaguely and introduced him to everyone in turn as they came to hug her and wish her a happy birthday. He felt like he was walking through a strange dream. There really weren't that many people but it seemed like an ocean of eyes on him. All surprised and suspicious at his presence.

Tesla was as good as her word and didn't leave his side.

Forest stood off to the side with Netriet, Journey, and Sabra, looking on at Tesla sitting beside X, their heads were close together, seemingly oblivious to the world.

Netriet poked Forest in the side. "So, our little Tesla has a boyfriend. That's very interesting."

"They're so cute together," Sabra added, bouncing baby Sophie on her hip.

"He's *fine*," Journey said boldly. They all looked at her and laughed. "What? You don't think so?"

"No, I agree," Netriet said. "I'd be all over that, if I was Tesla."

"Oh, stop it," Forest complained lightly.

"Is this really getting under your skin?" Sabra asked.

Forest took a sip of her beer. "Not that much actually. He's been here a few hours and he's already growing on me. Now, Syrus on the other hand..."

Across the garden, Syrus stood scowling with Shreve, Merick, and Redge.

"She's just so young," Syrus complained. "He's sitting too close to her."

"How can he even survive here?" Redge asked.

"He was cursed by a witch," Syrus said distastefully, as though X had some communicable disease.

"Did you see that?" Merick said urgently. "He just put his hand on her knee under the table!"

"Oh, hell no," Shreve piped up angrily. "Let's go show that punk his place."

Syrus and Shreve stormed toward where Tesla and X sat.

Redge chuckled and moved closer to Merick, holding up his beer in a casual toast. "You really like starting shit, don't you?"

"Yes," Merick said dryly. "Yes, I do."

"Did you really see him put his hand on her knee?"

"Nope."

Redge chuckled a little harder. "You're a sucker."

Merick shrugged, looking at the disruption he'd created. "Oh, shoot. The women have swooped in and come to lover boy's rescue."

"It's probably a good thing. His life was just about over…In all seriousness, I don't envy Syrus one bit right now," Redge said. "To have a daughter that beautiful and he's got to cope with the fact that she grew up so damn fast. Gotta be tough."

"Yeah. It's still fun to mess with him."

"I'll remember that when your turn comes around."

"What do you mean?" Merick demanded, narrowing his eyes.

"Come on. Our women talk. Netriet's gone clucky. I know she wants a baby."

Merick scowled and gave a little grunt in the back of his throat. "Yeah, she's after me all the time. Turned into a freakin' nymphomaniac."

"Oh, poor you," Redge said sarcastically. "Journey and I can't even have children. I know it makes her sad. At least it's possible for you."

The music playing in the background abruptly grew louder and changed to a higher tempo. Everyone looked over to where the speakers were connected to Forest's iPhone.

"Dad, really?" Forest said to Rahaxeris as he set the phone down.

"What? You don't like *Caribou Lou*? Is this a party or not?"

"All right, should we give gifts now?" Forest asked everyone.

"*I* think so!" Tesla said loudly, making everyone laugh.

She began opening her presents. Everyone gave her weapons, except Rahaxeris. His gift to her was a large, leather-bound book. *The Book of Worlds* was embossed in gold on the spine. When she opened it, the pages were all empty. She looked quizzically at her grandfather.

"I have a Book of Worlds, but I didn't know, until recently, how limited it was. It's for you to fill. More of a traveler's journal than anything else...I hope you'll let me read it one day."

A deep flush of emotion filled her eyes, and she nodded. "Of course. Thank you."

After she had opened everything, Syrus came forward and set a wrapped box in front of her. "From your mother and me."

She tore it open, lifted the lid, and gasped. "Oh...wow!" She turned to X, sitting beside her. "Look."

Inside the box were two butterfly swords made of black glass, filled with red lightning. Smaller versions of Forest's sword. The only difference besides size, was these blades had no handles, just bare glass tangs.

"We weren't sure what you would want for hilts, so we left them for you to choose," Forest said.

She got up and embraced both of her parents. "Thank you so much! I love them! Now you'll have to train me, Dad."

"That was my plan."

"So." Forest put her hands together. "Who's ready for a little friendly tournament?"

X stepped back as all the tables were moved to the sides and decided to just watch, fascinated that this was their idea of fun, and anxious to see who in the group would be the victor. The baby was handed off to Zeren as Sabra and Netriet went first. The ex-king walked over and stood beside X. The baby flailed her little fists in the air and squawked.

"You look a little discombobulated," Zeren said amusedly.

"Yes sir," X responded. He winced as Sabra landed a right hook to Netriet's jaw. "Sheesh! They're so vicious. Women in my culture don't fight."

"Really? That's very odd."

"I never thought about it, but I guess you're right. Forest warned me to avoid fighting with Netriet. Not that I would have anyway."

"Sabra has no fear of anything or anyone. Ohh! See that? You know that's got to hurt."

Netriet punched Sabra in the stomach with her black arm. She doubled over. X could feel his eyes bug as Sabra's hands elongated and turned monstrous. Netriet moved again, but Sabra caught her robotic arm in those hideous claws and twisted it around behind her, kicking the back of her knee at the same time. Netriet went down. A whistle sounded, and Sabra let go.

Netriet got to her feet, huffing and rolling her eyes. "How did you beat me?"

Sabra laughed. "You've been drinking too much. You're slower than usual."

She gave Sabra an affectionate little shove. "Whatever, bitch. I guess there's a first time for everything."

"So, they fight each other a lot I take it?" X asked Zeren.

"Those two are close friends. They're very competitive."

"What about the rest of them?"

Tesla's eyes captured his from across the garden. His heart stilled. All the movement and noise, all the oddity and questions about what he was really doing here vanished in that moment. It was just a chance, that was all. A slight, insubstantial chance he could reach out and claim her as his own. But as she walked to him, not flinching or blushing, connecting to him in a way beyond words, he knew he would never want anything as much as he wanted a life with her. And knowing it terrified him.

Tesla leaned down and rubbed her cheek against Sophie's head before coming to stand next to X.

"What do you think?" she asked him.

"You all are a bunch of freaks." He smiled and poked her in the ribs.

"Then you should fit right in."

"Do the men fight the women?" he asked.

"Sometimes."

"So, in this group, who's your money on?"

"My mom. Hands down."

"Oh yeah?" he looked over at Zeren. "Would you agree with that?"

"Yes," he said without hesitation.

"She can beat your dad?"

"Well, that's arguable. They fight all the time, but it's more like play for them. If they were both really trying, I have no idea who would win. It would probably be a toss-up because they know each other's moves so well."

She stared at his profile as he watched the fighting and moved closer so their sides touched.

"Do you think you'd like to fight me?" she whispered in his ear.

He looked down at her, his expression serious. "No. Never. Not like this. I couldn't strike you. It would break my heart."

"Does this seem barbaric to you?"

"I'm not judging it. It's different. They are having fun. That much is obvious. Maggie told me this was a warrior culture. She surely wasn't wrong on that."

"You don't consider yourself a warrior?"

"No."

"Well, what do you think of yourself as?" she asked quietly enough Zeren couldn't hear.

He smirked and leaned a little closer to her. "Yours."

She smiled broadly. "You're flirting again."

"*Again?* Did I stop?"

She shook her head, took his hand, and turned her attention back to the fighting. He glanced at it on and off, but mostly he just looked at her in his peripheral vison. The men were at it now. X couldn't remember their names. They were sword fighting. When one forced the other to drop their sword, he pulled a knife from his belt and threw it. They deflected, the knife hitting the sword and ricocheting right toward the baby in Zeren's arms.

X jumped, turning as he did, using himself as a shield, and caught the knife under his left shoulder. Confusion and panic ensued as X fell to his knees, blood streaming down his back from the wound. Sabra screamed, realizing her baby had almost been hit. Everyone rushed around them.

"Dad! Help him!" Tesla cried.

"Step back," Syrus ordered everyone. He leaned over X, putting one hand bracingly on his shoulder and grasped the knife handle with the other. "Hold still."

X swore in pain as the knife was pulled out. Then he swore again in alarm as Syrus put his hand over the bleeding wound and zapped it. Buzzing and snapping filled his torn flesh, fusing it closed. Syrus offered him his hand. X hesitated a second, but then because he had his gloves on, he grabbed it and was pulled to his feet.

Syrus nodded approvingly at him. "Well done," he said quietly. "Truly."

The next second he was enveloped in the gaggle of women. Sabra about choked the life out of him, she hugged him so hard.

"Thank you! Thank you!" she sobbed. "You saved my baby's life."

X couldn't say anything. He was being suffocated by everyone thanking him and hugging him. Tesla grabbed his hand and pulled him through the group. He followed her back into the house. She shut the front door and leaned against it, pulling him to her. *Closer.* She said in his mind.

He kissed her then, he had to. She was trapped between him and the door because she'd put herself there. She held tight around his waist.

He put his hands on either side of her neck, his thumbs moving slowly back and forth in the soft hollows under her ears.

This kiss wasn't slow and soft like the first time and it wasn't desperate like the second time. It was both. Soft and desperate. Fast and tantric at the same time. The moment shifted the gravity. *I'm lost,* he thought. *Right here. Right now... Just her... I'm lost.* He pulled back, his eyes searching hers.

"You're wonderful," she whispered. "What you did out there."

"I just reacted."

"I know. That's what makes it wonderful. You're good, X. Very good."

"I don't see what the big deal is. Even if the baby was hit, your father..."

Tesla shook her head. "Not everything can be fixed. Sometimes death comes too fast to reverse. You saved Sophie's life."

"I just reacted," he repeated. His eyes fixed intently on her lips. "I want more."

"Take it."

He closed his eyes and kissed her again. For a moment there was nothing else in the world. Just them. She yielded in his arms, soft and giving. She fit perfectly against him as though the stars had fashioned her to be his from the very beginning. He pulled back, cursing himself for thinking that way.

"Can I give you your present now?"

"You already gave me what I asked for last night."

He shook his head, a small smile in the side of his mouth. "Doesn't count."

"If you say so."

He led her back to her bedroom, pulled the wooden box from inside his knapsack, and handed it to her.

"So pretty," she said, running her fingers on the carved designs on the box.

"Maggie made that. I made what's inside."

"More weapons?"

"Not quite."

She opened the lid, her face going blank. He was confused by her response. He thought for sure the flower would please her.

"Don't you like it?"

She lifted the metal flower out and twisted the stem between her thumb and index finger, her expression still blank.

"Was I wrong? I thought you—"

"Shhh..." she whispered. "Watch."

Tesla sliced her fingertip on her incisor and rubbed her blood on the petals. Tendrils of smoke rose off the flower when her blood ran over his. The flower shivered, the petals stretching out.

"See? Our blood, mixed together... It can make things happen," she said.

X stared at the metal flower. It continued to move like it was real. The petals trembled as if in a breeze.

"That's...fascinating...but do you like it?"

She laughed lightly, put the flower on top of her dresser, and grabbed him around the back on the neck, pulling his mouth back down to hers. Her kiss made him drunk. She opened her mouth and let him in. Again, he felt like he was dying. There was no hope for him anymore. The force pulling him to her was growing stronger every second. His body began to rage for more, for everything, but his heart ground to a halt. She was a cliff, and he didn't feel secure jumping just yet. He feared what he was feeling, and he feared she wasn't going in the same direction.

The sounds of voices calling from outside gave him the power to let go of her, and he was relieved.

"I hear your mother calling you."

She sighed. "I need to go out and say goodbye to everyone. Stay here, otherwise you'll be swarmed again. I have somewhere to take you when I get back."

"Will we be alone in this somewhere you're taking me to?"

She smirked and shook her head. "In a way, but not completely."

He caressed the side of her face gently with his fingertips. "Probably a good thing. Being alone could be dangerous."

"For whom?" she asked mischievously.

"Me."

She stretched up and pressed her lips to his again quickly before going back outside. Alone, X exhaled and ran his hands through his hair. It was such a strange day. Regia was an odd place. He shook his head, bemused. He'd just been stabbed at a birthday party. He reached around and touched his back where his shirt was torn. There was no pain, no ridge of a scar, nothing. The ability to heal...how awesome was that? He made a mental note to ask Maggie if she could give him that power as well.

He thought about everyone he'd met and talked to. One thing that really impressed him was how honest everyone was. His power to know truth worked on everyone, everyone except Tesla. He watched her from the window as she hugged everyone, carefully keeping her hands from touching them.

He could hear what was being said through the window.

"I need to thank him again!" Sabra insisted to Tesla. "Can you bring him to the Lair tomorrow?"

"I don't know if we will have time. He and I have a lot of work to do."

"Please?"

Shreve came up behind her. "Yes. Please bring him tomorrow. Let us thank him formally."

X smirked to himself. Shreve had been hostile toward him at the beginning of the party. His tune had changed completely.

"I'll try."

The party began to thin, but some still remained, talking. Tesla came back inside, carrying a handful of gift boxes. She set them down on the floor of her bedroom. He watched her shift through them until she pulled out the short swords her parents gave her.

"I hadn't even dreamed they would give me something so awesome."

X nodded in agreement. "They are amazing."

"I can't wait until I can begin practicing with them." She put them back in the box. "So, are you ready to see my work?"

"Your work?"

"Yes. I need to show you the blood lock and what I've discovered."

190

"Do I need to bring anything?" he asked.

"Put your palm stones back on. I think the Heart might need to see them."

"The Heart?"

"I'm about to take you to the most beautiful place in all of Regia. You've done amazingly well not freaking out so far, but I'm afraid I'm about to put a bit more pressure on you there."

He smiled. "I'm impressed with myself as well… Seriously, in all honesty, I would think I'd completely lost my mind with everything I've seen, but I don't question anything anymore. Not since I accepted my transformation. Magic exists in many forms. It lives inside me, is a part of me. And…I'm starting to feel glad of that."

She looked thoughtfully at him, as if she had something to say but remained silent. Her eyes focused on his chest, her pupils opening wide. "Hold still," she whispered.

"What are you doing?"

"Looking inside you."

"Oh? Do you see your name written across my heart?"

She smirked but didn't move her gaze off his chest. "Shut up, smooth operator. Let me finish… All right. Let's go"

He strapped the stones to his hands, and she grabbed the air and tore it open.

CHAPTER ELEVEN

She opened a portal to the Wolf's Wood and pulled X through it. His eyes bugged as they landed on the beach near the waterfall.

"That's crazy! You travel like that all the time?"

"Yes. This is the Wolf's Wood. The Heart of our world lives in this forest."

He stared at the water. She came up beside him and laced her fingers through his, letting him look as long as he liked.

"Oh, I should warn you about the shadow sand. It's on the ground, not right here, under the trees. It has hallucinogenic powers. I've gone through your genetic makeup a few times, and I don't think you'll be susceptible to it, but just in case, don't walk on the black or grey areas of the ground."

"What do you mean, my genetic makeup? What's that?"

She smiled and lifted their entwined hands up. Pulling her hand free, she touched the fingertip of her index finger to his, rubbing it in a circle. "This."

A red light hologram lifted off her palm showing the helix of his DNA. "This is you. All that is inside. Blood, bones, tissue, and going deeper, the smaller, invisible to the eye... Well most eyes. There's a universe inside you. I can see it."

He looked at the projection in her hand, and then back in her eyes, a satisfied expression on his face. "It's like what I can see. Different but

192

same. You're taking about my body?"

"Yes."

"You see a universe in the physical. I see a universe in the spiritual."

"What do you see?"

"I can't show you the way you've shown me."

"Then just tell me," she prompted.

"I see your soul, Tesla. When I choose to."

"What does it look like?"

"Hmm...it's like the night sky. Shooting stars, constellations, and fluid brush strokes of deep color, almost too dark to see."

She smiled, feeling like she'd just received the complement of her life, but the warm feeling faded quickly, leaving a cold dread instead.

"What? Why are you looking at me like that?" he asked.

"You want it, don't you? You want to capture my soul."

He narrowed his eyes, a small flash of anger there. Then he blinked, and his expression relaxed again. "The only thing I want to capture is your heart. I like your soul exactly where it is."

She grinned, dismissing her fear. "Slick."

He snorted and looked back at the water.

"We can come back here, you know."

"Let's."

"There is more to see, X."

193

She led him through the ribcage, to the Heart. He walked at a steady pace, but his expression moved over his amazement as they walked.

"Stay right here," she ordered when the Heart was in sight.

Tesla approached the Heart, stopped at the crystal trees, got down on her knees and put her hands flat on the ground.

You brought him. The Heart said.

"I did."

The flames danced a little higher. *It pleases me to hear your voice aloud. Tell him to come closer.*

Tesla got up and turned to X. She gestured for him to come. Even a distance away, she could see him swallow before he began walking toward her. She took his hand again as he came up beside her.

"It's okay," she said. "Don't be afraid."

The music chiming through the crystal leaves was hesitantly hopeful.

"This is the power the wizards want?" he asked.

"Yes. And they will kill us all to get it."

"What can be done to stop them?"

She reached into the flames to the tesseract suspended in the air and opened it. Red light images of the equation and biological makeup filled the air. X looked but he didn't comprehend any of it.

"This is the blood lock. A metaphysical wall that holds the wizards out. The Heart powers it. So far it has held against their attacks, but time is running out. Eventually they will break through."

"How much time?"

"I don't know."

"We should ask Maggie," he said. "She can see the future, sometimes."

Tesla's expression changed.

"What?" he asked.

A cracking like thunder came from overhead. A red wave of sparks rolled through the sky.

"What was that?!"

Tesla watched the sky for a moment, then she put her hands into the box she'd opened and moved things around inside it. "It's the wizards. That was an attack. They keep changing their methods."

She was collected, but he could feel the tension radiating off of her.

"Did they—"

"No. They didn't get through. But they did some damage." She huffed as she worked. "I know!" she said aggressively.

"What?"

"I wasn't talking to you... Damnit. Give me a boost in the eastern corner. More. Flood it... There. It's patched." She pulled her hands out and turned to face him. "Sorry. I was talking to the Heart. We needed to work together quickly."

"Is it okay now?"

"Yes," she said easily. "Relax. I just get upset when the wall takes a hit. It wasn't that close of a call. There are many levels of fail safes. See this?" She pointed at a triangle in the center of the red light images hanging in the air. "This is us. When you let me take some of your blood, it didn't work the way I thought it would until I mixed it with my own.

Together, with the Heart, we can defend Regia. You and I."

"How?"

"I'll show you, if you're ready."

I don't want to scare him, Tesla. The Heart said in her mind. *Tell him to take off his gloves and put his hands in the flames.*

"The Heart wants to talk to you, X. Take off your gloves and put your hands in the flames. It won't burn you. You'll hear a voice in your head."

"Oh...okay," he said slowly.

He removed his gloves and palm stones and stepped up to the flames. Taking a deep breath, he slowly pushed his hands into the manifestation. The flames licked at his hands, exploring the power in his palms.

Light rushed into X's eyes, and he couldn't see anything anymore. Comfortable heat moved through him from his hands.

I've been waiting for you, Enforcer. A guttural voice said in his head that was both male and female. *You must make a choice.*

"What choice?"

To protect Tesla.

"I've already made that choice."

You are not yet the weapon you must become. Not quite. Will you let me bless you? Will you let me tie your power to Tesla's?

He felt her run her hand down his arm until she rested her hand on top of his. His heart began thundering under his ribs. Something important was happening, and he wasn't sure how he felt about it.

"Will you merge with me, X?" Tesla asked.

196

"Yes…I will do whatever it takes to protect you."

The flames wrapped around both of their hands, and then moved straight through their palms. It burned for a second, and then turned cool like a rushing breeze. Like two strings tied together, the Heart tied his power to hers. It was tenuous, brittle, and temporary. Then Tesla let go and stepped away from him, but the Heart had not yet released him. A surge went into his fingers. Warm light moved up through his wrists, arms, all the way up to his chest, where it burrowed into his heart.

There, the Heart said. *Now you must collect the dead of Regia. You must continue to separate the stains from the souls, as you already have learned to do. Closely guard the stain, for it is a weapon only to be used in the most desperate of times. I have fortified your heart and your powers. You are stronger than ever. I have added layers to your power and given you total control over them. You are not quite human anymore. You will be very hard to kill now. Thank you, for your brave choice, Enforcer.*

The Heart released him, and he stepped back, his vision returning. He looked down. A burned looking triangle now marked the back of his hand. He touched it gently with his fingertip. It glowed a pale purple under his touch. He looked over at Tesla. She held her hand up for him to see. Her hand bore an identical mark. Emotion threatened to choke him as she smiled. They were tied together. However long it lasted, they shared a bind. He felt like they had just undergone some kind of strange marriage ceremony. The only thing lacking was the kiss.

He reached out, pulled her to him, and kissed her.

She looked up at him, her eyes lightly teasing. "You think this really means something, don't you?"

"Don't *you*?"

"I think it means a great deal, I just wonder what you think it means."

He wouldn't tell her what he was really thinking. He held his marked hand up. "This means I have an edge over your other suitors. The Heart tied us together."

She rested her head against his chest. "You have no competition, X. There is no one else pursuing me. And even if there were...there still wouldn't be any competition."

He took a deep breath and let it out on a shudder. "Please don't say these things unless they are true."

She looked back up at him again, her eyes serious. "Believe me."

He placed both of his hands on her face and kissed her again. The ground under her feet fell away. His mouth claimed hers in a new way. His kiss was possessive. She gave in to it. She yielded.

"I have work to do." His voice was quiet and resigned. "Can you leave me here for a while?"

"You need to be alone? I can't help in some way?"

He shook his head. "There's a lot for me to learn about what the Heart just did to me and what I'm capable of... You distract me."

"How long?"

"I don't know, a few hours perhaps." He looked up at the darkened sky. "It's early still. Come back for me when you're too tired to stay awake any longer."

"But what if you're in danger?"

"You'll know, right?" He held up his marked hand again. "You'll feel it, I bet. We're tied together, like destined life mates."

She smirked. "I don't think it's quite the same."

198

"It might be the same." He argued.

"No. If we were destined life mates, we'd have already...well...you know..." Her voice trailed off at the look on his face.

"Oh my gosh!" he exclaimed. "How am I to concentrate on work now? Go away."

She laughed. "Sorry. But don't act like you don't think about it without any encouragement."

His eyebrows shot up, and he turned his face to the side. "Wow. Please, *please* get out of here before I do something that will result in your father killing me."

She smiled broadly and opened a portal for herself. As soon as she was gone, he threw his hands up and huffed in exasperation.

"She's going to be the death of me," he said to himself.

He sighed, trying to shake off his desire for her and focus on what he needed to do. X fastened the stones over his palms and approached the cloudy crystal tree in the circle around the flames. There were two souls in there. He could see them as easily as a beacon in the night.

Be careful, the Heart said. *They belong to me. I will allow you to access them, but you cannot cage them, you must leave them in the forest.*

"I promise," X said, placing his hands on the trunk. The force in his palms woke up and began pulling.

Trapped in stasis, Leramiun awoke. Shi was asleep in his arms. Worry moved through him. Why was he awake? A pull began tugging on his back, instantly sending him into a panic. He wouldn't leave her. He wouldn't let go. The pull grew stronger.

"Shi! Wake up."

She opened her eyes slowly. Tiredness hung heavy in her gaze as though she didn't really see him.

"Wake up!" he said more forcefully. "Something's happening! There's a force pulling me."

She blinked, her eyes clearing. Her arms clung tighter around him. "No, Ler! Fight it. Don't leave me!"

The next second the pull won, jerking him out of her arms and out of the tree. Ler's ghost landed on his transparent feet on the ground, screaming in rage and sorrow. "Shi!"

He pounded his fists against the tree. She was still inside. He could see her, her hands beating on the crystal separating them. "Shi!" he yelled trying to get back in.

Hands touched his back, and a wave of calm and grounding went through him. He turned to see who touched him.

"It's all right," the young man said. "You haven't lost her. I'm going to bring her out now."

"No! You must put me back! Death will take me if you don't."

He smiled. "No it won't. Not if I say it won't. You're not going anywhere."

He placed his hands back on the tree and pulled Shi out next to Ler. Terrified sobs came from her as she landed on the ground next to Ler. Ler picked her up and clung to her, looking intently and suspiciously at the one who had drawn them out.

"Who are you?" Ler demanded.

"My name is X...There is a war coming to Regia. War that can only be won with the dead. I need your help."

Shi looked at him, temper in her eyes. "You scared me. Pulling us out like that...*What* are you?"

"I'm a human, cursed by a witch. A necromancer and a truth-seeker."

Shi drifted toward him. X frowned at her, and then gasped as she passed right through him. She drifted back to Ler's side, a contemplative expression on her face.

"You speak the truth," she said. "What do you want from us?"

"Please tell me about yourselves. Why were you inside that tree? Why are you the only souls in this forest?"

They talked for a long time. Shi and Ler took turns telling X about themselves. X told them what he knew about the wizards and the plan he was making to combat them.

"You need the guardians," Ler said. "Hybrid entities. Every forest in Regia has them, except this one, obviously. Control the guardians, and you'll have your army."

"Thank you."

"What happens now?" Shi asked.

X shrugged. "Nothing for the moment, I guess. I assume you two will remain here? With the Heart?"

"Is it safe? What if death comes while you are away and takes Ler?"

X shook his head. "I grounded him. There is no danger of that for now. I'm not sure when I'll be back, but I will be."

The air rippled next to X, and Tesla stepped out. Shi's eyes widened, and she gasped as she looked at Tesla. Then she drifted to her and touched her hair.

"You're her! Forest's daughter. Oh my goodness! I never thought I'd get to see you with my own eyes! Look, Ler. She's ours."

Ler came closer to Tesla. "How is she ours, Shi?"

"Forest is my adopted daughter, Syrus is your grandson. This is their child. It's like she's our granddaughter. Almost. What's your name?"

"Tesla."

Shi drifted in a circle around her. "Oh, just look at her. Isn't she gorgeous? And so strong. Such magical abilities. You look like your mother...well, sort of. I see lots of Syrus in you, too."

"Who are you?" Tesla asked.

"Shi...your mother never told you about me?"

Tesla smiled and bounced excitedly on the balls of her feet. "She did! She's told me all about you, but she said I would never get to meet you, 'cause you were gone, or frozen."

Shi reached out again and combed her ghostly fingers through the ends of Tesla's hair. "Will you bring your mother back to see me? I've missed her so."

"Of course. She was getting ready for bed when I left the house."

"It can wait. I'm not going anywhere."

"I'll come back tomorrow. I promise." Tesla looked at X. "Are you ready to go back now? My parents are getting antsy. They want to know exactly where you are before they go to sleep." She rolled her eyes. "They're nervous about the sleeping arrangements. My dad wants a hundred foot wall between us."

"I'm ready when you are."

She looked at the ghosts again and smiled. "It was wonderful to meet you."

She opened a portal and pulled X through. They landed in the living room. Syrus sat reading in the corner, and Forest was putting a pillow and blanket on the couch. Both of them looked up as they came through the portal.

"Oh, good," Forest said on a yawn. "I'm exhausted. X, you'll sleep here, okay?"

"Okay," he said easily. "Thank you again for your hospitality."

Syrus grunted from the corner, put his book down, and stood. He strode up to X and gave him a menacing glare. "You were brave today, taking that knife in the back. It showed character. I respect that...still doesn't mean I like you."

X nodded. "Understood. And I understand why you're uncomfortable sharing your roof with me. I give you my word, I'll stay away from Tesla during the night."

Syrus narrowed his eyes at X. "Good," he said shortly.

His demeanor changed as he looked at Tesla. He caught her up in a hug and kissed the top of her head. "Did you have a good birthday?"

"It was wonderful."

"I was thinking about going in late to work tomorrow and spending a little time training with you in the morning, if you want."

"Yes! Of course! Thank you, Dad."

"All right. It's late. Go to bed."

"Yes, sir," she said obediently.

Forest shocked X by giving him a little hug. "Help yourself to anything in the kitchen if you're hungry. Is there anything else you think you need?"

"No. I'm good. Thank you."

Forest and Syrus went to their room and closed the door. Tesla gave X a sleepy smile.

"Well, I guess this is good night."

"I guess so."

She placed her hand on his cheek and stretched up to kiss him lightly. He barely responded. When she moved back, a questioning look in her eyes, he smiled and took her hand. "You're going to get me in trouble with your dad. I gave him my word."

She returned his smile with a look caught between amusement and annoyance. "All right. Good night then."

He watched her turn and retreat to her room, sighing in relief when the door clicked shut behind her. It was going to be hard enough to sleep so close to her anyway, he couldn't let her make it worse for him. X took off his gloves, stones, and boots before stretching out on the couch. He closed his eyes, his mind turning over the events of the strangest, and in some ways the best, day of his life.

Enforcer. That's what the Heart called him. He'd named himself Executioner. Not even a real name, a thing, a dark profession. *Enforcer,* he liked that. In this warrior culture, perhaps being the enforcer might grant him a higher level of status.

Forest chuckled lightly at Syrus, standing with his ear pressed against the door.

"Just crack the door open and come to bed."

He opened the door two inches before crossing the room and climbing into bed next to Forest.

She tried to snuggle with him, but he was stiff.

"Relax," she whispered. "It's fine. They're sleeping in different spaces."

"Yeah, well, it's not the sleeping it's the creeping."

Forest snorted a laugh. "You're so funny."

He gave her a scowl. "I'm serious. Would you have trusted us in this situation?"

She pursed her lips then shook her head smiling. "No. Not for a second."

"See? This is a stupid arrangement. Why didn't we think to send him to stay at the Onyx Castle?"

"Let it go," she said. "You have no control over their relationship."

"Is that right?" he said challengingly.

"Yes, my love, that's right. If they wanted to mess around, why would they do it here? Under our noses? She can take him anywhere she likes."

He let out a sigh that was half growl. "He promised me."

"He promised you he would leave her alone during the night, that's all. What if she decides to seduce him? Would you expect him to say no, regardless of what he promised?"

"Yes."

"If it were us in this situation, and I came on strong to you, would you shove me away?"

His scowl vanished, and he snorted. "Hell no. As if."

He relaxed a bit then and gathered her against him. She fell asleep almost instantly. He lay awake for a long time listening to nothing at all.

CHAPTER TWELVE

Shi pulled her lips away from Ler's. He gave her a split second to breathe, not that she needed to breathe, before he captured her lips again. They were ghosts, but that didn't mean anything to them. When he touched her, she felt him just as she had when they had been alive. Likewise, she felt like she *was* alive, solid, and tangible. The agony of their past faded from their minds. They were together. Forgiveness was complete, his and hers.

Shi clung to him, luminescent tears streamed down her cheeks. She was happy. Happiness frightened her. Hope blossomed in her ghostly heart. Hope choked her with terror. They were together. But for how long? When the war was over, would death finally come back and claim him, leaving her alone for all eternity?

Were they free, or only caught in a cruel repeat of their tragic romance? Just a few days to love each other, and then torn away?

"I'm very happy to be awake."

"I know. You've told me that more than a few times, Ler." She smiled. "I'm happy, too. It scares me."

"So, it's not just me. I'm terrified. I hope this can be another chance for us. A new beginning."

Shi shivered in his arms. "Oh, Ler. Don't say any more. I can't stop thinking the same thing, but maybe we should just expect the worst."

"What would that be?"

"A repeat. A few days of bliss followed by the annihilation of our world. It would be just like before, only with even more death this time."

He combed his fingers through her long hair and pulled her closer. "I wish I could promise you I won't let that happen. But I'm too old to say such a thing. Unfortunately, I know better... But I can tell you I have loved you for thousands of years, and no matter what, I will continue to love you. I will love you forever, Shi. That's the only real promise I can make you."

She smiled and buried her face in his neck. "I'll take that."

"We'll do everything we can to help X... What did you think of him?"

"He's different. I don't think there's ever been anyone like him in Regia. He has no idea how strong his power is. I hope he can handle it when he learns. The Heart tied him to Tesla. Did you get a sense of her?"

"No. Not at all," he admitted. "It was like I was looking at something I couldn't quite comprehend."

Shi nodded. "She's kind of scary. Sweet and beautiful, but the things she can do... I looked inside her. She's a lot like her mother. But she has a stronger self-destructive nature than Forest ever had, and hers was bad enough."

"Hmm...If that's the case, she needs to feel loved and secure. Perhaps X will give her that."

"Yes. I hope he will. He wants to, but he's insecure, too," Shi said.

The flames of the Heart surged higher. *Come to me, both of you.* It said. *Come inside.*

Shi and Ler obeyed, drifting into the flames.

I love you...so much...my wayward children. You have paid enough for your crime against me. Now you must heal me. You must restore me.

The flames around them burned a light grey with only slight tinges of purple and yellow, like a fading bruise. They felt the hope inside the Heart, but it was still tainted with grief. Like a broken heart ready to move on, not having taken the first step, but finally ready.

Journey awoke in the quiet dark of the predawn. She sat up in bed, the hair on the back of her neck standing on end. Redge roused next to her and touched her arm.

"What is it?" he asked sleepily.

"I don't know...I...I need to go." She got out of bed and began to dress.

"Go where?"

"To the Heart. I think it needs me."

Redge groaned and pulled himself upright, rubbing his eyes. "All right. I'll go with you."

Journey opened her mouth, about to argue, but decided not to. It wouldn't do any good anyway. He'd come, no matter what she said.

"Thank you."

He shrugged as he pulled his boots on. "You're my woman," he said, as though that simple statement was the answer to everything regarding him and her.

She smiled. "Yes."

He grabbed an End of the Bridge and put it in his pocket before grabbing a second and smashing it between his palms.

They landed close enough to the Heart Journey could see it in the distance. "Stay here," she told him. "Don't get any closer."

He nodded and yawned before kissing her lightly.

Journey's hair continued to stand on end as she approached the manifestation. Her eyes darted around. Something was happening. The crystal tree that was always cloudy was now clear like the others. The blood lock cube still hovered in the center of the flames, but that wasn't the only thing in the flames. She squinted. Pale, translucent figures clung together in the grey flames.

Her heart began heating fast. Journey sat down and placed her hands flat on the ground. Light streamed along the ground toward her. It reached up and wrapped around her hands.

Hello, Alien. It's been a while since you've come to see me.

"I came because I felt you needed me. What has happened?"

My children have been released to me.

"Is there something I can do to help?" Journey asked.

Sparks snapped around the top of the flames. *Can you help me commune with them? Can you form a bridge between me and them so there is no more misunderstanding? We must come to the same place before I absorb them and move them to the next life.*

"I'll try. I've never read the hearts of the dead before." She closed her eyes and began to hum.

Her power reached out to Shi and Ler. The rush of feeling that came back to her from them caused Journey's breath to catch in her lungs. They were so old. The depth of emotion over that long of a period of time was unlike anything she'd ever encountered. She took a steadying breath and began to sing, weaving a story for the Heart and the ghosts.

Redge stopped pacing as soon as he heard Journey begin to sing. Her voice could never be commonplace even though he could say he was used to it by now. But this song... He'd never heard anything like it from her. He didn't move. He scarcely breathed, not wanting to miss a single note.

It was a full bodied experience of loss and passion. Warm shivers rolled all down his spine. Her voice was seduction incarnate, but that was only the beginning. She turned darkness and pain into pure healing. The story wove for a long time, and finally...finally ended with a promise.

He waited. Journey walked back to him very slowly. He ran to her and caught her just as she stumbled. She coughed once, and was like a dead weight in his arms.

"What have you done?"

"Look," she said feebly, pointing back at the Heart. "So close. There's still something holding it back."

He glanced at the Heart. The tops of the flames were a shimmery pearl white, only the base was grey and purple.

"I'm exhausted, Redge. Take me home. This is going to take me a while to recover from."

"Will you be okay?"

She gave him a weak smile. "I'll be fine. I just need to rest."

After they left the wood, light streamed over the ground again from the Heart. It raced along the roots under the soil, all the way to the outer boundary. Burning heat flashed through the light, scorching the ground. The light retracted, leaving death behind. The ground dried up, turning brittle and cracked. The light of dawn caressed the tops of the trees of the Wolf's Wood. What was vibrant and green the day before was now brown.

"What's happening?" Shi asked the Heart.

The time for rebirth is coming. The two of you, as you are now, has to end.

Before they could protest or question, the Heart pulled them down inside its depths underground where they were turned over, broken, and dissolved.

Faint voices woke X. Morning light streamed through the windows. He sat up and stretched, looking around. Forest was clattering around the kitchen. He caught her eye, and she smiled.

"Good morning," she said brightly. "Would you like some coffee?"

He stood up, running his hands through his hair, and stalked to the counter. "Thank you."

She set a steaming mug in front of him. "Did you sleep all right?"

He blinked a few times, trying to force his eyes to hold themselves fully open. "Like the dead."

"Hungry?"

"Always," he chuckled.

He watched the strange machines in the kitchen Tesla showed him yesterday. Warm bread jumped out of the shiny one on the counter.

Forest smeared butter on the bread and set it in front of him. It didn't matter how young she was, or how young she *looked*, or the sharp edge to her, Forest was warm and maternal. His heart ached at her kindness.

"You make me miss my mother," he admitted sadly.

She stopped in her tracks and gave him her full attention. "Did you lose her?"

"Yes. Recently."

Sympathy filled her deep emerald eyes. "I'm so sorry."

"Thanks." His voice was quiet.

"Do you want to talk about it?"

He shook his head. "No. But I appreciate the offer."

"The offer stands, if you change your mind."

They looked at each other for a second. He picked up his toast and bit into it.

"Would you like some eggs to go with that?"

He nodded emphatically. "Please."

She smiled and pulled a skillet from the cupboard. When he finished eating, the voices that woke him sounded again. He looked for their source.

"In the garden," Forest said, refilling his coffee.

He hooked his finger through the mug's handle and walked to the front room window. X blinked in the sunlight. "Wow," he said under his breath.

He leaned against the window frame, took a sip of coffee, and watched.

Tesla had her new glass short swords, and Syrus was coaching her on her fighting stance. X's eyes devoured the details as his heart pulled. He took his time, memorizing the way the sunlight caught in Tesla's loosely braided hair. The excited glint in her grey eyes as she began to spar with her father. The pulsing red designs on her hands. She didn't move gracefully like Syrus did. She fought with fast, vicious, whipping movements. She could strike out and coil back so fast, it was like the attack of a snake.

He sighed, losing himself in his feelings. How odd. This beautiful creature had captured him in a way he had never been captured before. Whatever love he'd felt for Isolde…no, it wasn't like comparing two of the same emotions to see which was stronger. What he felt for Tesla was not a stronger version, it was a completely different emotion. He tried to dissect it. He never questioned with Isolde. She was his, always. He was confident in that. And he'd been dead wrong.

A ragged pain clung to his feelings for Tesla. He couldn't allow himself to feel what he felt. A dark agony laced tendrils like black smoke through his heart. She needed him to help save her world. He took away her physical pain and opened up her voice. She might think she felt something for him, but she was using him. She *needed* him. He didn't want her to need him. He wanted her to love him. *Him.* Not just what he could do for her.

X pushed the pain down where he could ignore it. He compartmentalized as only males can. His eyes remained glued to her. She jumped back from Syrus' attempt to disarm her and laughed. Her lips turned up in the sweetest smile. His mind roved slowly over every kiss they'd shared as he stared at her mouth. He glanced at the mark on the back of his hand for a second before looking back out at her. He scolded himself for doubting her. He should trust her. She was pure.

Forest came up beside him and looked out the window, too. "She's learning very quickly."

X didn't say anything.

"I have a gift for you."

He turned his head to look at her. "Why?"

She smirked. "Why not?"

He watched her leave the room. In a minute she was back, holding the strangest looking bow and quiver he'd ever seen. She held it out to him. He took it, running his fingers along the smooth black surface, unsure what it was made of. The arrows, likewise, were alien to him. Not made of wood and rough arrowheads. They, too, were black, smooth, and tipped with bright metal spiked on the sides of the arrowheads.

"I can't accept this," he said.

"Don't you like it?"

"It's amazing. It's just too much."

She waved her hand dismissively. "I don't have a use for it. Like I told you yesterday, there aren't many archers around here. I want you to have it."

"Thank you... Why are you so nice to me?" he asked.

She looked back out the window, her face contemplative. "I like you, and I think...maybe... you might become a permanent fixture in my family."

His smile was bittersweet. "I'm trying to not let my hope run away with me...and I have trust issues."

Forest sighed. "You and she are caught in a strange and dangerous situation. It can be hard to trust in others and yourself in times like that.

The closeness of death heightens emotions beyond what they might have been in a peaceful setting. Even when I knew Syrus was my destined life mate, I still hung on to my fear and distrust."

"Why?"

She gave a little half laugh. "I had...what did you call it? Trust issues? I almost ruined my whole life with one bad decision."

"But Tesla isn't my destined life mate."

She patted him on the shoulder. "Hang in there. I'm running out of time. I have to get to work. Why don't you join them outside and try out that bow?"

"Thanks, Forest. For everything."

She smiled warmly at him. "Thank *you* for everything."

X finished his coffee next to the window, and Forest left for work. He put his boots on and strode outside with his new bow, hoping he might be able to show off his skill a bit. He wanted to impress Tesla, but more importantly, he hoped he might gain a little more respect from Syrus. But Syrus was gone.

"Where's your dad?" he asked her.

"He left a moment ago, with my mom." She gave him a devious smile. "Well, you kept your word. You left me alone all night."

He returned her devious smile with one of his own. "Are you implying something?"

"I missed you... And I lost sleep, waiting to see what you would do, if anything."

"I did something."

"Yeah. You proved your word is worth something when you give it. I

216

guess that qualifies as *something*."

"Oh, thanks," he said sarcastically.

She walked up to him and reached for his free hand. Their power entwined ecstatically, and the marks on their hands glowed purple.

He closed his eyes. "That feels so good," he said under his breath.

She leaned her forehead against his collarbone. "Seriously, I did miss you last night, even though you were just feet away."

"I miss you right now."

"How can you miss me, when I'm right here?" she asked. "You're touching me."

"I'm greedy. I don't think I'll ever have enough of you."

She looked up into his eyes. They stared at each other. After a moment, pain creased her features, and tears filled her eyes. "How can you look at me like that?"

"Like what?"

"Like I'm not a sick freak?"

He dropped the bow and pulled her against him. "Because you're not."

"I *am* a freak," she insisted.

"You're exotic," he countered.

"Gosh, X...I never thought anyone would ever look at me the way you do. Everyone tells me I'm beautiful, but then I see the pity they have for me, and the fear...it's in the background, but I see it."

"Can you blame those who care about you to feel sorry for you?

They know you're in pain. They wish you weren't."

"But the fear. Even my parents fear me. You're the only one who doesn't."

He chuckled. "You're wrong about that. I'm terrified of you."

"Why?"

"I..." He hesitated, wishing he hadn't just said that. "You're twisting me all up inside, and I fear when I'm too far gone, you'll just walk away from me... You'll find the man you're really supposed to be with, your destined life mate."

She sighed and pulled back from him. "Why is it like this? Why do we do this to each other? There is no time for us."

He smiled, catching her off guard.

"What?" she asked.

"You want to be an *us*?"

"Umm...I thought we already were. But it's true, you didn't ask me."

"How do I ask? Is there some special way I'm supposed to say it here in Regia?"

She laughed and shrugged. "I have no idea. How would you do it in your world?"

"There really isn't a way to be casually connected in my world. But if we were there, I'd ask your father for his terms to allow me to marry you. If he didn't turn me away, and I met his terms, we'd be engaged. Exclusive to each other, able to have a few liberties of affection before the wedding."

"And after?" she asked.

"After the wedding you'd be mine completely, and I'd be yours. For life."

"That's nice...if you were Regian, I'd put a lover's mark on you. Only vampires can do that. The mark I put on you would strengthen our feelings and lend to a stronger *aspiration* for monogamy."

"So what if I'm not Regian? I'm open to experimenting. You could try to mark me."

She smiled and shook her head. "Very brave. But I have a sneaky suspicion my father would object to me doing that. It would indicate an *intimate* relationship."

"If you marked me, would that negate the claim your destined life mate would have?"

She shook her head sadly. "No. Nothing but my rejection of them could negate it."

"That's all? You could just reject them?" His face brightened.

"I wouldn't. Rejecting one's life mate comes with terrible agony. And I see my parents...how they are with each other. Who wouldn't want that kind of love and security?"

"What if I killed him?"

"X!"

"*What?* It's just a question."

"I'm done with this conversation. I don't need to define our relationship, but if you do, call it whatever you want. I have no life mate, at least not yet. I might never have. So you can grouse about it or you can accept you have my feelings and come here and kiss me."

He pulled her close again. "Murderess," he murmured against her lips before kissing her in earnest.

They were getting better at it, familiar now with the shape and taste of one another. She melted against him, but he knew this had to be short. They were alone, and he already wanted to take her back inside. He wanted to pretend she was his wife. He couldn't, so it couldn't go any further. He held her gently and rested his cheek on the top of her head, sighing. *I love you.* He thought. His thought jerked him up short and sent a chill through his blood. Did he? Had his heart jumped over that cliff already? Surely not.

"We have work to do," he said. "Right?"

"Yeah. You have Guardians to gather... This will be *interesting*, to say the least."

He leaned down and picked up the bow from the ground. "I was going to show off for you, but I guess that will have to wait. I wanted to impress you."

She smiled into his eyes. "I'm impressed already."

"Stop being so sweet. You're breaking my heart."

She quirked an eyebrow. "Should I be mean to you instead?"

"It might make things easier on me."

Her smile turned wicked, and she walked her fingers up his chest and caressed the grey line on his neck. "I'm your woman. It feels only natural to me to want to torture you."

He narrowed his eyes at her. "Don't say things like that to me. You find yourself in danger of making me lose control. No, stop that saucy look. I mean it. Stop playing with me. I want you so much. You have no idea."

She pulled her hand back, her eyes round. "I'm sorry...That was teasing, right?"

"Yes."

She looked down. "Sorry." She said again. "I'll try to be better, it's just...I want you, too."

He closed his eyes and groaned. "We have to get out of here. Do something else."

"Okay. You're right. Get your stuff. We'll get to work."

He pulled an arrow out and strung it. "Just one. Give me a mark."

She looked at the far end of the garden. "The knot the on the last tree."

It was a great distance and a very small target. He exhaled and loosed the arrow. X turned and walked to the front door, not even waiting to see if he'd hit the mark. She raised one eyebrow as the arrow sank directly into the knot. Yeah, she was impressed. That was gangster.

She waited for him, thinking about where she should take them first. He came out a few minutes later, stones and gloves on, with his axe on his back and a set expression on his face. She smiled unconsciously. X was cool. As she gazed at him she realized nothing had changed in her since the first time she'd laid eyes on him. She'd never seen anyone else she liked looking at as much as him. And he wanted *her*. The butterflies came back and partied in her chest at that thought. For the first time in her life, there was something she really wanted and she could have it. So they had to save the world... That didn't mean she couldn't fall in love with him in the process.

Tesla thought about her history lessons with Zeren before deciding where they should go first. Battles fought in or around forests where she knew the body count was high was the goal. She tore open the air and took them to the wilds near Halussis.

As soon as they landed, X's eyes widened, and he seemed to freeze. His gaze darted around, and he reached for Tesla, pulling her protectively behind him before taking his gloves off. His hands lit up through the stones. She wanted to ask him what he saw, but the tension in his stance stopped her.

"I can see you," he said aggressively, raising his hand up. "Come here!"

Tesla gasped as a Guardian appeared out of nowhere in front of them. The monstrous deformed entity growled. It was a sickly green hybrid mess of two enemies who'd fought and died in the same battle, damned to live as one. Their bodies grossly entwined. It looked down at them, at least four feet taller than X. He didn't even flinch. He lifted his chin and looked up at the thing with authority.

"Are you the leader?" X asked nonchalantly.

"Yes!" It hissed. "Of all in this forest."

"You serve me now," X said.

It laughed loudly, a wet, snarling sound. "Why would I, or any of us serve you? The dead don't fear anything."

X relaxed a bit. "I could enslave you, but I won't. You will serve me not out of fear, but hope. A war is coming, and you will fight. All of you. If you protect the living from the enemy and help deliver victory, I will separate you."

Its many eyes looked at X's hands for a second. "Prove you can! Separate me now, and we will fight for you."

X stepped closer to it and reached for its gnarled hand. He grabbed ahold and pulled one arm free of the other wrapped around it, then he let go and stepped back. The Guardian whimpered like a child.

"No! Finish it! Separate us!"

"You are treacherous. I can feel your lies. Now you know I have the power to free you. You serve me."

It roared in rage and frustration. Tesla cringed away from the sound, but X gazed at it placidly, unmoved by its anger. More guardians appeared until a hoard crowded around the first, touching and examining the arm X separated.

"All right!" the leader bellowed, looking at the other guardians who all nodded and murmured their agreement. "We'll fight, Necromancer. But not just because you offer us freedom, because, though we are long since dead, Regia is still our world."

"Line up," X ordered. "You are all diseased. Your souls stained with the hate you died in. I am going to take that from you."

Tesla hung back, watching amazed as the guardians formed a line. X walked down the row, his hand passing through each one, blackness pulled from them and ran into the stone. When he reached the end, he turned and came back. His other hand now passed through each of them, trapping a small part of them in the other stone, chaining them to him.

He held his hand up to all of them when he'd finished. "When the enemy breaks through, I will send you where you are needed. You will protect Regians and kill the wizards. You need have no fear of them. Their power cannot harm you. Stay here. You will know when I have summoned you."

X turned to Tesla and gave her a meaningful look. She straightened and opened a portal, taking them back to her house. They landed in the garden. X blew his breath out and leaned against the rock wall.

"You were incredible! How did you just know what to do?" she asked.

He scrubbed his hands over his face. "I didn't. That was insane!" He looked at the stone now holding the first platoon of guardians. "The Heart strengthened my power. It was just instinct that led me."

He leaned his head back and closed his eyes for a moment. Then he took a deep breath and stood up straight again. "All right, let's keep going. We need to gather them all."

Tesla opened a new portal, taking them to another forest and then another. Each place they met the same kind of resistance. And each time, they caved to X quickly. She stopped being nervous, now she knew the guardians couldn't hurt X. They jumped all day, gathering the unusual army. She'd counted loosely as they went. The stone now held a part of more than two thousand guardians.

Her mind began working on something new. She imagined the battle, seeing X's place in it, but where was her place? What could she do when the moment came? Could her lightning cause damage to a wizard at all? Could she become a storm when she needed to? She thought about when she'd sped up time to escape the destruction she was creating and unable to stop. If she could storm at the right time, would it cost her life to just let it run its course? Could X pull her back from the edge at the last moment?

She looked over at him. She wanted to live. He made her want to live.

"I'm starving," he said as they landed back in the house after eight runs, gathering guardians.

The sun was going to set soon. Her parents would be home. She wasn't ready to have her dad separate them.

"I can fix something for us to eat. There's leftovers from the party. I want to shower and change my clothes before we go see my grandfather for a few minutes, then we can do something fun."

"Whatever you say, just feed me!"

He took off his stones and washed his hands in the sink, messing with the faucet a few times. "This thing is handy."

"I take things like that for granted," she confessed, pulling food from the fridge. "I shouldn't."

"What can I do to help?" he asked.

"Nothing really. I'll show you how to work the microwave."

She hadn't realized how hungry she really was until that moment, and once the food was warm, she ate almost as fast as he did. When she was finished, she began to feel thirsty. At first she didn't realize it was blood thirst. She glanced at the fridge where she knew there was blood, then she glanced at X. Nope. She'd ignore her thirst for now.

They cleaned up the kitchen quickly. She went to her closet to try and find something sort of nice to wear. He followed her into her room and got his pack of clothes from her bedroom floor and headed to the bathroom.

"Tesla, how do you make this thing work?" he called from across the house.

She walked to the bathroom where he held the door open, bare chested, staring at the shower confusedly.

She allowed herself a split second to look at his muscles before slipping past him and turning on the water. "There. Just twist the knob to adjust the temperature. And don't take too long. I want to get out of here before my folks get home."

Unthinking, she touched his shoulder and let her hand gently slide down his arm to his hand before looking in his eyes. A dangerous level of heat surged behind the icy color.

"Don't," he whispered.

"You're beautiful, X. I like looking at you." She backed up and closed the door, feeling feverish and like she was ready to jump out of her skin.

He scowled at the door after she closed it and twisted the water to full cold.

Tesla pinned her hair on top of her head and went to shower in her parent's bathroom. She tried to be fast, but when she came through the house only wrapped in a towel, he was already dressed and sitting on the couch waiting for her. He didn't move or speak, but his eyes followed her to her room. She felt his gaze like a physical touch. She cursed herself for being stupid as she shut her door. She could feel the desire between them was getting impatient.

Tesla dressed quickly in a pretty, wine-colored blouse, jeans, pumps, and long dangly earrings. He stood up when she came out.

"Wow. You look...I don't even know."

She chuckled. "Ready?"

"I've been ready. You took so long." He looked her up and down and smiled. "It was worth waiting for."

"Hold on. I just remembered something." She went to the kitchen, grabbed a sticky note, and scrawled a few words to her parents.

"What was that?" he asked.

"I just left my mom a note saying we'd be back later."

"So which grandfather are we going to see?" he asked as she grabbed at the air.

"Rahaxeris. Don't try to joke with him."

He snorted. "Not my plan."

226

"I really have no idea how he feels about you being in Regia. He probably won't act like my dad has, but I never know with him. He surprises me at times."

"Okay. I won't touch you. What are we going to do anyway?"

"More work. I focus better in the lab."

She opened the portal all the way and pulled him through. She watched him from the side of her eye as they landed in the antechamber of *Rune-dy* headquarters. She was starting to worry he'd begin to freak out, that all the new things and places she'd showed him would begin to overwhelm him. He blinked and looked around, his face showing his amazement.

"This is where the *Rune-dy* used to meet and conduct business. They are all dead now, except my grandfather. He could have filled the open places with new priests, but he feels it was time to let the organization go. They were evil."

"Evil?"

"Oh, yes. Morality never entered into anything they did. Science, torture, and fear were the currencies they worked in. Part of what's wrong with me was born right here. They created a monster, banished him, and when he returned, he captured my mother and poisoned her, while she was pregnant with me. The monster was created here and so was the poison."

"Tesla, how…"

Her eyes had gone flat. She shook herself. "Sorry. That's a long story. One for another time. Anyway, Rahaxeris is not so bad…"

He strode into the room at that moment. "Yes, I am." He said with a smirk on his sharp mouth.

Rahaxeris walked straight up to X and looked him in the eye. X returned his scrutiny easily. Tesla was impressed X didn't flinch. She would have.

"I didn't get a real chance to talk to you at the party, or take your measure. Then there was all the nonsense with the baby and you being stabbed and that was it."

X didn't say anything. Rahaxeris looked him over with the critical eye of a doctor. He pointed at one of his hands.

"May I?" Rahaxeris asked.

X lifted his hand up and held it out to him. Rahaxeris didn't touch him, he just looked closely. Then his eyes lifted to the grey ring around X's neck.

"That was a powerful spell. It's a wonder it didn't kill you. You're strong." His gaze eased, and he took a step back. "Thank you for coming. I owe you a great debt. All of Regia does."

"Tesla asked." He shrugged as if that was an adequate reason to risk your life for strangers.

Rahaxeris looked at her then, his eyes betraying the love he had for her. "She usually gets what she wants. If not through temper, by cunning."

Tesla blushed. "I need to work."

"Go on then. Everything is where you left it. I didn't mess with it...much."

X followed her down a hallway and through a door into a cold white space. As soon as they were inside, he could almost see her focus sharpen. She walked to a large table and gestured for him to join her. She put her hands flat and a burst of red light shot over the surface. X stepped back as an image rose off the table.

"That's the Heart, right?" he asked pointing at it.

"Yes, and the blood lock. Can I have your palm stones?"

He took them off and handed them to her. She set them on the top of the red light image, where they hovered.

"What are you doing?"

"I'm trying to figure out how I can make the guardians stronger…I really want to bring Maggie here, but I don't want to endanger her in that way. The wizards are already looking at us." Tesla sighed and pulled at the image, manipulating it with her hands.

"Why are you frustrated?" he asked.

"I have no way of testing our plans. I feel…I think it will work, but I have no way of knowing for sure until it happens. I'm gambling with everyone's life."

"Am I distracting you? Should I leave?"

"No." She leaned closer to the image and pulled on it some more. "Everything's here. The equation is complete. I just…I want to add to it. Create a new layer. Hedge our bets."

"So do it."

She looked at him sharply for a second, and then nodded.

Tesla gave him back the stones and moved her hands through the image, wiping it from the air. He backed up some more as her energy heightened and she started doing something different. New images lifted off the table in quick succession. He didn't know what she was looking at, but he saw no use in asking. Rahaxeris came into the room, but he hung back next to the door and just watched.

Tesla took the drop of Maggie's blood and held it in the palm of her hand. Lightning from her hand lifted it up, slid through it, and wound around it. She spun a new sphere, the size of a marble, and filled it with the drop of blood. Ball lightning covered both of her hands. The power caressed the sphere for a second. She sent a shock into the blood. Sparks flew into the air.

"Tesla, no!" Rahaxeris yelled, moving forward.

Fear gripped X. He didn't know what was happening, but he was sure it wasn't good if it made Rahaxeris yell like that.

She pushed the sphere into her skin, right over her heart. The lightning flower swallowed the blood. A surge went over her skin. She turned to face her grandfather a defiant light in her eyes. He just gaped at her.

"The risk…"

"It doesn't matter!" she shot back. "Now I don't have to endanger Maggie."

"The blood lock will kill you! You've got their DNA inside you!"

"You think I didn't work that out before I decided? I tweaked the equation. I'll be fine."

He shook his head, disbelief mixed with anger on his face. "You're impossible. You always have been. I wish I could stop loving you. You're so reckless! You only bring me pain. I try to protect you, but I've never figured out how to protect you from yourself."

X wisely kept his mouth shut, slightly embarrassed to be witnessing this level of family drama.

The hurt was plain in Tesla's eyes, but she covered it quickly with contempt. "Well, what goes around comes around. Come on, X, we're leaving."

He followed her into the portal, expecting to land somewhere, but nothing happened. They remained in the darkness.

"Where are we?" he asked.

"Nowhere." Her shoulders fell, and she collapsed into tears.

He picked her up and held her. "What did you do? Why was he so upset?"

"I absorbed Maggie's DNA. There is witch in my blood now… My body is grafting it in right now. It's only because of the poison in me that I can do that. It will stop my body from rejecting it. "

"So, now you're a witch?"

"In a way…" Her breath came in and out in little jerks. "I see…" Her eyes rolled back in her head. "My eyes are changing. I see more." She moaned in pain.

"What can I do? Will you be all right?"

She shivered again, sweat beading on her skin.

"Are you sick?" He was starting to panic.

"It will pass in a second. Just don't let go, please."

He held her tighter. She continued to shiver.

"Your grandfather's pretty harsh."

"Yeah. But he loves me, despite how he is. It's like I told you, I scare everyone."

I love you, he thought again, for the second time that day. "You don't scare me. Not *you*. I only fear you'll break my heart."

"I won't," she whispered. "That would be foolish of me."

Her choice of words stuck in his head in a nasty way. *Foolish? What did that mean?* He drew a wrong conclusion. He was about to question her about it, so he knew he understood, but then she cried out.

"Sorry," she hissed. "It's almost over. I'll be fine in a second."

A flash came from her heart, red light sliding over her whole body and then vanishing. The shivering stopped.

"I'm okay now. You can put me down."

He set her feet on the black nothing ground. She straightened her shoulders and took a deep breath. A subtle shimmer that wasn't there before tinged the edges of the light pulsing on her hands. He looked in her eyes. The shimmer was there too, just around the edge of her irises.

"My gosh, you're killing me. Stop getting more beautiful. I can't handle it."

"It doesn't bother you I'm part witch now?"

"No. Why should it? I'm used to Maggie. But why did you choose to do that?"

"To know my enemy. So I can be sure of our plans. So I can see more…"

"You just put yourself in danger though, right? You said you didn't want to bring Maggie here because it would endanger her. Did you just put a target on yourself?"

She reached out and placed her hand on his cheek. "You'll protect me, won't you?"

"Yes. But—"

"I feel fine now. It's getting late. We've worked hard today. I still

232

would like to take you somewhere. Have some fun for a little while before we're too tired. Want to?"

"Fun? Sure."

"We have to go to the Everpath to get where I want to take you. So you'll have to drink my blood again."

"Okay," he said easily.

She did as she had before and cut her finger on her incisor. She offered it to him, but he just looked at it.

"Does that hurt?"

"Not really. I heal fast."

He moved closer and wrapped his hands around her waist. "Cut your tongue instead. I'd rather suck on that."

Her pulse instantly sped up, lightly scandalized, but mostly excited by his boldness. She licked her lips before running her tongue along one of her teeth. He leaned down and captured her mouth. His lips forced hers open before he drew her tongue into his mouth. She gasped, and a yummy sensation hummed through her. Her own blood thirst came back hard. Heat exploded through her core, and her brain went missing.

The next second she was clawing at him and clinging to him. He pulled his mouth away from hers, a stunned look in his eyes.

"Tesla...I...I'm sorry..." He shook his head.

"Shut up," she said breathlessly, pulling his collar open and sinking her fangs into the side of his neck while lacing her fingers through the back of his hair.

He hissed through his teeth, his arms trembling as he held her against him. "Stop." he begged. "I'm sorry. That was a bad idea. It's my fault. I shouldn't have..."

She didn't stop.

Shivers covered his skin, and he moaned as she pulled hard with her mouth. "If you don't stop now, this will go too far. I will ruin you. I swear, Tesla. I'll claim your body."

His words fell lightly on her fogged brain. She realized he was talking about sex. Half of her brain shrugged and thought, *bring it on*. The other half was scared of the finality of it and losing her virginity.

She let go and forced herself to take a step back from him. Her cheeks burned and she looked down. "I don't know what to say. I'm ashamed. I just want to be with you. I just want to be free. Your culture says what you want from me is forbidden, or disrespectful. That by desiring me you have to walk some gauntlet to get me, or something like that. I don't understand."

"No." He sighed. "It's about commitment. I've made you no promises. Taken no vows. You shouldn't give yourself to me without that. It's a risk for you."

She frowned, trying to sort it out. "Cause you might change your mind and leave me?"

"Yes, I mean no. Yes, that's the idea, but I wouldn't change my mind."

She smirked. "I bet that's what they all say."

A smile broke through his serious expression, then he laughed. "You're right. Men will say just about anything."

"Not you. You play the edge then you slam on the breaks."

"Well, you make me off balance. You mess with my head." His expression sobered completely. "I shouldn't touch you at all. I shouldn't kiss you, and I shouldn't think about you the way I do."

"Why?"

"You're sacred, Tesla... And you're not mine."

She crossed her arms over her chest. She was touched and annoyed at the same time. "Okay, fine." Her voice was flippant. "Are you ready to fly?"

"Fly?"

She gave him a devious smile. "Not scared of heights, are you?"

"I don't know."

She grabbed at the darkness and tore it open. "Take my hand. We'll move quickly through the Everpath, just in case we're not alone."

"Huh?"

She tugged on him, and he followed. He blinked, his vision going opaque. All he could see was grey and faint outlines.

"It's clear." Her voice was relieved. "Come on."

They walked down a ways then she stopped. "This is the door. Don't be afraid, just jump."

"Jump?"

She opened the door. X was enveloped in warm fragrant air, and he could see clouds. She jumped off the threshold and fell. He jumped after her. His vision fully returned. They were falling through the air. She whooped loudly, her hair streaming straight up. He reached out and grabbed a hold of her foot. There was no ground under them, just endless sky and fluffy clouds.

"There's hardly any gravity!" she yelled to him.

Rushing filled his stomach, and he laughed. "Now what?"

"Nothing at all. See what you can do."

He let go of her foot, stretched his arms out over his head, and began to spiral. She tucked her feet into her chest and somersaulted through a thick clutch of pink clouds.

"We're going down, try to stop and go up," she called.

"How?"

She swooped down toward him as if she really was flying. He turned over and looked up at her as though he was just lying on his back in bed. She brought herself parallel and wrapped her arms around him. He held her back, and they began to spin together.

"Is this fun?" she asked.

"Lots!"

He pulled her closer and pressed his lips to hers. She smiled against his mouth. He felt her muscles tighten, and the speed they were falling slowed. She let go of his waist and grabbed his hand.

"Come on, pull."

She was holding them up.

"How?"

"Just imagine the air is solid, push off from it."

He tried, it didn't work. She rolled her eyes.

"Here, use that." She shot a bolt of lightning into the air. It hung there and didn't vanish.

He hooked his boot on the lightning. It held his weight like a rung on a ladder. He looked up and pushed off. It was slower than falling but he was rising.

"What is this place? What else is here?"

"Nothing!" she laughed. "It's pointless, except as my playground. I've scoured the place. There's nothing else here."

They stayed there until he got really good at making himself go in the direction he chose. It felt wonderful, but it was also physically taxing. The sky land began to darken, and stars began poking out. She made another lightning step for them to stand on. She leaned her head against his shoulder, and they watched the stars shoot across the sky.

He yawned, the weight of the whole day crashing on him at once.

"Let's go home."

"Sounds good. Thank you for this. It was fun. Maybe we can do it again sometime?"

"Absolutely. I've always liked it here, but it's way better to share it with someone," she said.

He glanced up. He knew the door was up there somewhere, but he couldn't see it. They pushed off together and floated upward.

"We're almost there," she said. "Maybe you should kiss me goodnight right now. Once we get home, it's back to holding hands and nothing more."

"I'm content holding your hand."

"Is that a rejection?"

"No."

"You don't really like kissing me?"

"Are you insecure again?" he asked.

"Always."

"Seriously?"

"Are you going to make me beg?"

He tried to read her eyes. She looked earnest. "That's an interesting idea."

"Please?" she whispered.

The look on her face and the sound of her request slew him. He pulled her closer and crushed her mouth with his. "Okay, don't do that again," he said.

"Do what? Say please?"

"Yes! Don't do that. Murderess."

"Well, then, don't make me."

He kissed her again, slower, softer.

"That's better," she murmured. "Like that."

I love you.

It went through his head again. Damnit. He had to figure out a way to make her his. He had to make her love him, and not just any kind of love. A love so strong she'd reject her destined life mate when she met him. She *was* his. Now she just needed to learn it. If only he could tell if she was honest or not. What if she wasn't? Isolde had broken his heart. Tesla had the power to crush his soul.

CHAPTER THIRTEEN

It had been a long day, but Tesla was happy. Happier than she could remember ever being in her life. X was falling in love with her. She knew it. She could see it in his eyes. She opened the door to the Everpath and took his hand so she could lead him back to Regia.

A gust of wind stopped her in her tracks. The dark thing slithered up in front of them. It panted obscenely and flicked its forked tongue at her. X couldn't see. She'd have to protect him.

"I have you, wall builder...come with me," it hissed.

It was her turn to pull him protectively behind her. He was tense and squinting his eyes, trying to see the thing in front of them. She lifted her hands, ball lightning engulfing her palms.

"Get back!" she ordered.

It laughed. "You can't kill me. You've tried before. Leave him...come with me...I'll give you your dreams."

"What do you want? Who do you serve?"

"I want to love you. I serve you, my lady."

"If you serve me, then obey me. Go away."

X moved forward, pressing against her back, and grabbed her hand. He lifted their hands straight out at the dark thing. The marks on their hands burned as one.

"You're a stain, and I will cage you," X said.

It slunk to the side, ducked down, and jumped at them. Tesla and X were knocked backward. It flew over them, scratching her on the chest with its claws, then it vanished.

A sting like acid eating her skin burned on the gashes it gave her. She cried out in pain, never having felt anything like it. X picked her up and began rushing down the hall.

"Where, Tesla? Tell me where."

"Keep going," she gasped. "Three more... Stop."

She reached out and grasped the door to Regia. She was jostled in his arms as his feet landed on the ground. His vision cleared, and he looked at her, terror in his eyes. Blood was spreading over her torn blouse.

"What do I do?"

"Set me down," she wheezed.

He knelt and laid her on the ground.

"Let me bite you."

He didn't hesitate. He lifted her head up to his neck. She took one drink and sank back down, smoke hissing on the gashes. She panted for a moment, then her breathing began to ease, and she touched her chest gingerly.

"I need to get home. My dad can fix this all the way. Help me up."

He lifted her to her feet and supported her as she slumped against him. Weakly, she opened a portal for them. They landed in her bedroom. He laid her down on the bed and rushed out into the living room.

"Syrus!" he shouted.

Forest and Syrus both jumped when X burst into the living room.

"Tesla's hurt."

Syrus was beside Tesla the next second. He tore her shirt open, looking at her wounds. He sucked in a breath. "What did this?"

"Shadow thing," she said feebly.

Syrus' hand hovered over the gashes, small strikes of lightning hitting her flesh. The wounds sealed up, leaving long red stripes on her skin instead. Forest pulled on X. He turned and looked at her.

"Come on. She'll be all right. Come."

It killed him to leave her side, but he went with Forest. She shut the door behind them.

"Sit down, you look really shaken. I'll get you some water."

"Do you have something stronger?"

She nodded. "Wine?"

"Whiskey?"

She gave a little snort and then shrugged. "All right."

Forest poured two fingers of whiskey in a snifter and brought it to him. He knocked it back in one shot.

"Thanks. I understand I shouldn't see her undressed like that. Please, go back in there and check on her so you can tell me how she is. Please."

Forest turned and went back to Tesla's room. He grimaced when she opened the door. Tesla was crying in pain.

"I need him!" she cried. "I need X!"

241

"Tesla, calm down," Syrus said.

X was on his feet without realizing he'd stood up. She screamed in agony. He was almost to her door when Forest blocked him.

"No. It's all right," Forest said. "Just relax."

She continued to cry.

"Okay, Tesla. Let me help you get a new shirt on. Then you can see him," Syrus said. "Here. Sit up a bit. This shirt is soft. Just lay back, sweetheart. I'll get him."

Syrus came to the door behind Forest. She moved to unblock his way, when Tesla screamed. The whole house shook. The floor jumped under their feet, the windows rattled in their frames, and the lights flickered on and off. Huge lightning bolts came snaking out of Tesla's room.

"Shit," Forest said to Syrus. "She's losing it."

Syrus reached into the tangle of electricity and began to tear at it, but then he retracted his hands, smoke rising off his skin.

"I can't get through it!"

"Syrus!" Forest cried. "We have to do something! She'll die!"

"*X!*" Tesla screamed.

He shoved past them, remembering what she'd told him about her heart. He slid right through the lightning as though it was nothing. The room was filled with a storm, and her whole body was covered with electricity. He pulled his gloves and stones off as fast as he could. Her limbs jerked with tremors. Taking a deep breath, he shoved both of his hands up her shirt and covered her heart.

She inhaled on a gasp. The power in her heart grabbed onto his hands and held them there. Her heart trip hammered against his palms. The whole storm fizzled into nothing, and her body went limp. X was vaguely aware of Forest and Syrus behind him, but he paid them no mind.

Her breathing began to ease, and her eyelids fluttered open. Her eyes were glassy as she looked up at him. Then she looked at her parents.

"It's okay now," she whispered, then her eyes rolled back, and she fell unconscious.

Her heart let go of his hands. He slid them back and stood up, facing Forest and Syrus.

"She told me what to do, if that ever happened," he explained. "And Maggie, the witch who cursed me, saw the future. She told me I was the only one who could calm the storm. She was talking about Tesla before I ever met her."

Syrus looked severely at him and then down at Tesla. He sat on the edge of her bed and put his hand on her forehead. "She's very sick. Whatever attacked her infected her with something. I don't know what this is. I've never seen these kinds of wounds before. I...I don't know what to do. I'm afraid to try and her magic responds badly again." He stood up, left the room, and then came back with X's knapsack in his hand. He dropped it on the floor. "You'll sleep in here tonight," he ordered X. "You will stay by her side all night and make her better."

Surprised, X nodded. "Yes, sir."

"You'll inform us during the night if something changes with her, or if she gets worse."

"Of course."

"Good. She needs to rest." He looked back down at Tesla, still

243

unconscious. "Keep her comfortable and her magic steady. Hold it back if another wave comes."

"I'll do my best. I promise."

Syrus nodded curtly, took Forest by the arm, and left the room, closing the door behind them. X blinked at the closed door a few times, amazed.

Forest pulled her arm free from Syrus' grasp. "I can't believe you just did that. You trust him that much?"

Syrus sank onto the couch, his head in his hands. "I was powerless against it, Forest." Emotion choked him. "I couldn't get through. I'm the most powerful mage in Regia, and she blocked me. If he wasn't here..." His shoulders trembled. "I accept there is something between them that is...I don't know. You saw what I saw. I understand that I don't understand what's between them. And I...I'm so grateful for him...I see he cares for her. She's not just a notch for him. He won't use her and move on. Even if he did, at this moment I could hardly care, so long as he saves her life."

CHAPTER FOURTEEN

For three hours, X sat on the floor next to Tesla's bed and held her hand. She tossed in her sleep, her temperature going up and down in swift spikes and drops. He held himself still inside. The sensation there was too great for him to really feel it. He could barely comprehend the periphery of his emotions, so his subconscious locked his heart down tight in self-preservation. What was wrong with her? What more could he do? The fact that her father had ordered him to stay the night in her room, alone with her, let him know Syrus must believe she was in danger.

X yawned and got up, his back hurting from the position he'd been sitting in. He stretched and decided to get more comfortable. He glanced down at her. She was asleep, but he thought it best to turn off the lights before he changed his clothes. Once he was dressed for sleeping, he sat back down on the floor and took her hand again.

She moaned and gave his hand a little squeeze. "X?" she whispered.

"I'm here."

She opened her eyes. His ability to see perfectly in the dark kicked in.

"What's going on?" she asked quietly. "Did you sneak into my room?"

"No. I was given permission. Ordered, actually, to stay in here with you tonight. Don't you remember what happened?"

"I remember coming home, my dad tried to heal me. It was terrible, it felt like he actually made it worse. I...that's all. I don't remember anything else."

"You made a storm inside the house."

Even in the dark, he could see her cheeks blush. "Oh, great. That's embarrassing. Sorry you had to see that... Wait, did you touch my heart?"

"Yes."

She let go of his hand and set it on her chest, frowning. "Hmm... So that worked?"

"Yes. As soon as I touched you, your heart grabbed my hands and held them fast. The storm stopped, and you fell unconscious. How are you feeling now?"

She groaned and shifted. "Cold."

"You've been feverish for the last few hours."

She shivered and rubbed her arms. "Will you hold me?"

He moved to a kneeling position and reached for her somewhat awkwardly. She put her hands on his shoulders and pulled on him. "Come here. Lay down with me."

"Are you sure?"

She moved over to make room for him. "Yes."

He climbed under the blanket beside her. She turned her face to the wall, moaning again lightly. She pressed her back against his chest. He didn't move much. He waited to see what would make her comfortable. She grabbed his hand and pulled his arm across her body.

"I'm so sorry," she whispered.

"Why?"

"I'm a lot of trouble for you."

"You're worth it. Are you getting warmer?"

She sighed and nestled down closer to him. "Yes. I still feel so...off."

"Is it more than just that thing that attacked you? Is the witch stuff causing you a problem, too?"

"Maybe a little."

"Your dad says you need to rest. Try to sleep."

She laced her fingers through his and brought his hand under her shirt and back to her heart. He held totally still. The power in her heart reached up and caressed his hand. He pressed his palm flat against her skin. It was like when they held hands, only stronger. His power mixed with hers in a dance of sensation. Her whole body tensed for a second and then relaxed. He exhaled and tried to focus just on the feeling of their power connected, and not the fact that half of her breast was in his hand. She needed this connection because she was sick. It was nothing more than that. *Nothing. Nothing. Nothing. Don't move.* He told himself firmly. His fingers began to ache with the desire to roam over her skin.

"Did my parents see you put your hands on my heart?" she asked.

"Yes."

"I bet that was awkward."

"No. I was doing the only thing I knew to do to save you. I was terrified."

"Did you see my boobs?"

"I *wasn't* looking."

Her back shook lightly with a quiet chuckle. "Are you regretting you

247

missed that opportunity now?"

"If you weren't facing away from me, I'd kiss you, just to shut you up. Go to sleep, Tesla."

He tried to pull his hand away from her heart. She whimpered. "No. Stay here. I'll be quiet. Keep touching me. It's making me feel better."

He was exhausted, and holding her felt like bliss, but he couldn't sleep. He laid there, his heart in a tangle, imagining there was nothing wrong with her and they were in bed together just because they wanted to be. He felt her relax deeper until he was sure she had fallen back asleep. He began to doze when he heard his name. He opened his eyes and lifted his head up an inch.

X... it was Tesla. She was asleep, but she was talking to him in his mind. She hadn't really been doing that since she brought him to Regia. He laid his head back down. He wished he could answer her. Her breathing changed. She was partially awake.

*X...*she said again in his head. *I love you.*

His heart stalled. He swallowed hard. She wasn't really awake. *You're mine,* he thought. *I will have you. One day... I love you, too, Tesla. One day, you'll be my wife.*

Her breathing slowed as she slipped into a deep sleep. He leaned closer to her and pressed his lips against the side of her neck. His heart raced to the edge of the cliff and dove off. But the fall wasn't glorious, it was terrifying. He would crash at the bottom, irrevocably broken.

I'm holding everything I'll ever want in my arms right now. What if I lose my grip on her? One day, she'll met the man destiny has chosen for her, and she'll leave me. Losing her is inevitable. It could be tomorrow or a hundred years from now. The pain will be the same. No. The pain will be worse the longer I have her...it's not real. She doesn't love me. She loves what I do for her. I'm her doctor.

248

All that should have been beautiful, knowing he felt love, swirled with anger. He wouldn't be deceived again. He was finished with flirtation. A line must be drawn. A hard, precise line. Confusion brought agony to his heart. He couldn't get his head clear.

Falling asleep in X's arms felt perfect to Tesla. She became well under his touch. Her whole life, her body hurt. But now, she slept as she never had before, wrapped in warmth and comfort. She woke when it began to leave her. She woke up alone in bed. Tesla blinked in the darkness. The dawn was an hour away, the edge of the sky turning from black to a midnight blue.

She sat up, coming fully awake. She felt good, physically and magically. Tesla looked for X. He was sitting in her desk chair, looking at her. She frowned. Something was wrong behind his eyes. He was fully dressed like he was about to step out the door. He even had his gloves on.

"Hey," she said quietly. "What's wrong?"

"Nothing." His voice was flat.

She got out of bed and came toward him. The way he looked at her made her heart flinch. He was hurting and trying to cover it. She hesitated for a second, and then climbed onto his lap. He inhaled sharply, his muscles tensing. She placed her hands on his cheeks.

"What's wrong?" she asked again.

He frowned, different emotions interweaving through his eyes. He opened his mouth, then shut it, shaking his head.

"Let me in," she pleaded.

"That's the problem. I already have."

"I don't understand."

"You talked in your sleep. You said you loved me."

She leaned a little closer, her eyes tunneling into his. "I wasn't asleep. I know what I said."

He shook his head and stood up, forcing her to stand as well.

She looked at him desperately. "I love you, X."

He sighed. "This is unnecessary, Tesla. You don't have to do this. I said I would help you. I will. You don't have to say things you don't mean to try and make me feel more invested."

She choked on her breath. His words shot an arrow straight through her heart. "I love you," she repeated.

"No, you don't." His voice was firm. "You love the way I make you feel. You love being able to talk. You love you've found an answer to your equation. You don't love me."

Tears welled in her eyes, and she shook her head. "Are you sure of that?"

"Think about it, please. Really think about it. You know I'm right. You're manipulating me, consciously or not."

She looked down, thinking. Was he right? Was it just the relief of her pain she was in love with? Was it the sound of her own voice? Everything inside her pulled against the very idea. Her eyes sought his again, and she shook her head.

"I could cut off my hands and tear out my tongue. I could pull my heart out so I could never feel you touch me there again. And I'd still love you...I see what you're afraid of. Let it go. Trust me. It's not a lie...I want you. I want us."

Panic filled his eyes, and he took a step back from her. He was pushing her away. He wasn't going to accept her love. A cold rage closed like a glass lid over her heart. She turned herself off and looked at him with sharp analysis. She *would* get him to answer her.

"You said you were still willing to help me. Why? Why would you be willing to help me at all if you don't care?"

He swallowed, his eyes going flat. "You're a beautiful woman. I wanted your body."

"Is that all?"

"That's all." His voice didn't even sound like him.

"Okay." She was blasé.

She ran her fingers through her hair before grabbing the hem of her shirt and pulling it over her head. His eyes rounded as she dropped the shirt on the floor and began to unfasten her pants.

"What are you doing?"

"My body is your price. That's fine. Take it. I need your help. If I have to whore myself to get it, I will."

He exhaled a sound like she'd just punched him in the gut. He stepped forward and stilled her hands, shaking his head. "No."

This time it was his eyes that filled with tears. The glass covering her heart shattered, and she felt the pain of what he'd done to her. He picked up her shirt and handed it to her. She grabbed it roughly and pulled it back on. Then she shoved him in the chest.

"What's the matter? Not in the mood now?" Hurt mixed with contempt in her voice.

He turned away from her and hung his head.

"Look at me, coward."

He turned back, wiping the tears from his eyes. She stepped into his space, grabbing his gaze hard with hers, her lip curling in a sneer.

"The truth seeker, who lies. You're the liar, X. Not me... Tell me it wasn't real! Make me believe it! Tell me!"

"Tesla..."

"Tell me it wasn't real! Tell me you don't love me!"

He was shaking. "I can't."

She didn't try to hide any of the pain he caused her. She showed him. All the color drained from his face.

"Why would you hurt me like this? What for? When it's a lie."

"I..."

"No! I don't want to hear anything else," she cried.

She shook her head slowly and reached up, wrapping her arms around his neck. He grabbed on to her tightly, his breathing uneven. The truth throbbed in the space between them despite any words. She pulled on him, bringing his lips down to hers. It was the sweetest bitterness he'd ever tasted. He was at a loss, then her blood ran into his mouth. His eyes shot open.

"No, Tesla. Please. I'm sorry."

She grabbed his axe and pack and slung it over her shoulder before reaching behind him, tearing open a portal and shoving him through it. His sight blurred in the Everpath. She pushed him from behind with both hands. He tried to turn to face her, then he was falling. He landed hard on the ground back in Contarren in front of Maggie's house.

She threw his stuff on the ground at his feet. "Forget it!" she yelled. "I'll figure out how to stop the wizards on my own. I don't need you."

"Tesla, wait!"

She strode away from him "No!"

"Please." He was running after her.

She stopped and turned back to him, her eyes streaming. "*I* didn't lie! You did!"

He tried to reach for her. She punched him square in the mouth, splitting his lips. Then she was gone.

Maggie and Merhl came up behind him.

"What *in the hell* did you do?" Maggie demanded.

He fell to his knees and put his head in his hands. "I panicked. She offered me the world. She offered me everything I could ever want, and I panicked...I hurt her. I wasn't thinking clearly..." He laughed bitterly. "She saw right through me. She called my bluff. What do I do now?" He looked up at Merhl. "How do I get back to Regia? I have to fix this."

Merhl looked furious. "Why would you hurt her? Can't you see how special she is?"

X got to his feet. "Of course I can see it. She's everything to me."

Her eyes came back into his mind, all the pain he put there. *He* caused the pain. Realizing what he'd done to her, his chest tore open and gutted out.

"Damn fool!" Merhl yelled. "Tesla does things, reckless things, especially when she's hurting."

Maggie came up to him, an expression of sorrow on her face. "Remember what I told you about pain?"

His eyes widened. "Yes."

"You hurt her. So, there's your proof. Congratulations, dumbass."

He picked up his axe, strapped it to his back, and walked up to Merhl. "Take me back to Regia. Please. I'm begging you."

Maggie's necklace flared. She held it up to her eye and gasped. "Oh, no..." Her voice filled him with ice. "You're already too late, X."

CHAPTER FIFTEEN

Tesla leaned against the grey wall and sobbed. She was feeling so much, she was flooded with sorrow, anger, and pain. She hadn't realized before then the level of power he held over her. She ground her teeth together, rage taking over. It was all up to her. Screw her connection to X. Screw the blood lock. She pushed off the wall and stalked down the endless hallway. She'd end this shit right now.

"Where are you?" she yelled, her voice echoing. "I know you're here, shadow. Come out and play with me."

"Oh, yes…" the voice hissed sensually.

Darkness slithered along the floor toward her. She stopped. It pooled, and the dark thing rose up out of it.

"Are you ready to let me taste you, wall builder?"

She sneered. "Perhaps. After you tell me what you are."

"Nothing. I am merely a probe. My only purpose is to find you."

"Who do you work for?"

"Lachlan. The wizard king. His eyes are on you right now. He desires you." The forked tongue flicked out and licked slowly over the pointed teeth. "As do I. Just one taste, please…"

A deep shiver of revulsion went down her spine, but she kept it from showing. She held her hand out to it, as though it were an animal. It slunk closer and grabbed her hand. It was like touching cold fog, insubstantial, and unstable. The tongue slithered out and caressed her skin. All the rage she was holding inside exploded. Her voice was fading. She would lose it soon.

As it licked her, preoccupied, she leaned down toward it and sank her fangs through the top of its head. Smoke filled her mouth and it laughed. She let its disease into her lungs, her eyes opening to its origins. She knew the door she needed to take.

She shook its hold on her. It backed away smiling. "Yes… Yes, you see the way now, lovely. Take it. You won't be sorry."

"No, but *he* will be. Now skulk off and die."

It gave her a little bow and vanished. She wiped the back of her hand on her pants. Disgusting.

The door to Mordian lit up like a glow stick far down the hall. She ran to it. A storm was building inside her. She skidded to a halt, hesitating, her hands flat on the door. This was probably a one-way ticket. She'd bring the wizards death in a hurricane of her own making. She'd give herself over to its senseless rage and let it bleed her out. The faces of her parents loomed in her mind. She hadn't said goodbye.

Then again, heroes didn't always get the luxury of goodbye.

She kicked the door in and stalked through.

Silence and opulence met her. She blinked and looked around, slightly surprised, not sure what she was expecting, only certain it was not this. The pale green marble floor was pleasantly warm under her bare feet. She turned in a circle. It was a palace. Perfect. She could start at the top and work her way down.

Her rage shifted to neutral without her consent. The light, the fragrance on the air, the temperature, it all tickled the pleasure centers of her brain. The witch inside her roused and took a deep breath of her native land. Tesla blinked and shook herself, realizing the danger of this place hiding under the beauty.

She brought the raw pain in her heart back to the front and let herself drink it down. She glutted on the pain, her hands lighting up, her heart igniting the storm. She looked down, a circular mosaic medallion was right under her feet.

The power rose up and pushed out through her skin.

"It ends here." She would have screamed it, but it came out like a hoarse whisper.

She put her hands together, the lightning gathering and building on itself. She brought her fist down on the center of the medallion. The floor cracked. Lightning rushing along the breaks, spreading them open.

Clouds filled the vast empty room. Thunder roared through the halls. Ecstasy filled her as she let her magic take over. No thoughts, just feeling. Only vengeance.

Over the sound of the thunder claps came a laugh. The laugh grew louder as a shimmering lit the air around her. It shrank down over her like a glass bubble. She hit it with a bolt from her hands. It shattered. The laugh echoed around her. She turned, looking for him.

A blast of wind shot through the room, blowing the storm clouds away.

"Show yourself," she whispered.

"Gladly." It was the same voice. The seductive, dirty voice.

A man strode into the room. Tesla blinked. He wasn't the old man she'd expected. He was young and beautiful. A thin robe hung open on his bare, muscled chest. His hair was a rich dark brown and hung long over his shoulders. The color matched his eyes, a few shades darker than the olive color of his skin.

She shot a blast of electricity at him. It hit his skin and bounced off in sparks.

He laughed again. "That was impressive, but not impressive enough. I know you can do better. You can do all kinds of things, can't you, wall builder?"

"I will kill you with—" Her throat seized. Oh, well. Talk was cheap.

"With?" he prompted, his demeanor completely relaxed.

She took a step toward him. He smiled, his eyes flashing hotly. Her brain was racing. He'd sent that dark thing looking for her because he couldn't go himself. He wasn't a world jumper. She just had to get close enough. His smile broadened as she took another step toward him.

"That's right. Come here, pretty baby. I'll hold still. You can try whatever you're contemplating. I can promise you I'll retaliate, but I'll give you first strike."

She stopped just barely out of his reach. His eyes devoured her slowly. A faint scent came off his skin, intoxicating the pleasure centers in her brain again. She shivered. Why was she moving so slowly? Why was she just staring at him? He was her enemy. She was close enough.

"Do it," he whispered, licking his lips. "Do it. Do it. Do it... *DO IT!*"

She flinched, grabbing desperately at her rage. The ball of lightning hit him in the face as she spun behind him, tearing the air open in an endless loop portal. He faced her, his eyes blackened around the edges, burned by her power. She grabbed the front of his robe and fell backward, pulling him with her into the portal.

She had to get out and close it behind her to trap him. His hands locked around her wrists. The next second, the portal she'd made fizzled into nothing, and they were still in the marble room. It felt like he'd cut off her hands. She looked down, disoriented. It wasn't his hands locked around her wrists at all, it was two metal cuffs.

"That was fast," he said lazily. "I thought it would be harder to cage you. Oh, well. It was still a good move. You almost pulled it off. Now we can move on to other things... Tell me your name."

The cuffs around her wrists felt heavy, like they were magnetically drawn to the floor. She couldn't lift her arms, but more than the weight was the negative pulse. The metal sent waves into her, neutralizing her power.

He frowned when she didn't answer and walked a circle around her. "Hmm... This isn't enough. You might still get away."

Tesla tried to move. She couldn't. He knelt in front of her and locked cuffs around both of her ankles. His hands gripped the backs of her legs. He rose up slowly, his body skimming intimately against hers.

"There. That should hold you. At least for a little while. I know you'll be able to get out of those soon enough. I look forward to when you do. We can play another game at that time. But for now, I know you're not very comfortable. I can make that better."

Her voice was gone, and her magic was locked. He bent down and picked her up. She was powerless against him. Strangely, she wasn't really scared. She'd made a colossal mistake, but he didn't seem anxious to kill her. She might be able to turn the tables.

He carried her through hallways made of the same pale green marble and took her through a door into an ornate bedroom. Her stomach twisted into a knot. What was he going to do to her? The huge bed was covered with a shimmery gold fabric. He set her down and propped her up on the pillows. Her heart beat so hard it bruised against her ribs. His face was very close to hers, and he smiled. Then he stood and backed away a step.

"What do you think? Do you like it?" He waved his hand around the room. "I confess it can be lonely. I like the look of you there on my bed."

He frowned again when she didn't speak. The next second he was snarling in her face. "Answer me."

She shook her head, her eyes wide. He took a deep breath and backed away from her. "I'm sorry about that. It's just...I'm so happy you're finally here with me. I've wanted it so badly. I just want to talk. I want to get to know you."

She shook her head again and tried to raise one of her hands. She lifted it three inches when the cuff dragged it back down. He narrowed his eyes at her then he grabbed her hand and unlocked the cuff. She touched her throat and shook her head. She looked at the fabric on the bed, struck by an idea. She dragged her fingernail on it, writing the word *mute* in the soft texture.

"You spoke to me."

Ability is gone now. She wrote.

He locked the cuff back on her wrist. "Hmm...I don't like that. It could be fun on one level, but I think I'd rather talk to you naturally."

He climbed on top of her. She turned her head as he tried to kiss her. He grabbed her head roughly and forced her face forward. "Relax. I'm just going to loose your voice."

But that wasn't all. He kissed her obscenely. His tongue was long. It filled her mouth and probed halfway down her throat till she gagged. Heat rushed down her neck painfully. He pulled away and got off of her.

"There. Now tell me your name," he ordered.

She coughed three times. "Tesla."

"Tesla," he repeated, his voice caressing it. "It suits you."

She glared at him. "I'm sure it was unnecessary to kiss me."

He laughed. "Oh, sweetness. That wasn't a kiss. When I kiss you, you'll know it."

"Something to look forward to," she said acidly.

He laughed again. "Perfect."

"What's perfect?"

"You. You're not afraid of me. I'm all about changing that."

He grabbed her ankles and pulled her down toward the end of the bed. He climbed on top of her again, propping himself on his arms and gazing down at her. He was wrong. She was afraid.

"What are you going to do to me?"

A small smile pulled into one side of his mouth. He really was beautiful, and totally disgusting. Debauchery oozed from his pores. He hooked his finger in the collar of her shirt and pulled it down an inch.

"Everything... Every, single, little, thing I can think of."

He kissed both of her cheeks, her forehead, and her chin. His hands ran over her body. She held her breath and clenched her eyes tight. She couldn't help the trembling that began in her core. He pressed his thigh between her legs.

"Yes," he whispered against her ear. "Now you're afraid." He rolled off her, lying beside her instead.

He pressed his hand flat against her lower abdomen. Power surged out of his palm. His eyes cut to hers, and he smiled broadly. "I'd hoped you were a virgin... Thank you."

"Why are you thanking me?" she demanded, her spine filling with steel. "You think I saved myself for *you*?"

Lachlan threw his head back and laughed. He shook his head but didn't answer. His eyes moved slowly over her. "I don't like your clothes."

He held his hand up and muttered a few words. A pair of long slender scissors flew into the room. He caught them.

"Seriously?" she demanded. "You want to rape me, just get it over with."

His expression smoothed out and he gazed at her evenly. "Rape...hmm... Not right now. Maybe later. Right now, I just want to do away with your drab clothes. They don't please me. They don't enhance your beauty. From now on, you will only wear things that are fitting for a queen."

Tesla ground her teeth, furious that she couldn't move. He slid the cold metal of the scissors into her shirt and cut it open. His mouth opened slightly as he looked at her heart. His breathing picked up a little. He looked back into her eyes, showing her how pleased he was with her. She closed her eyelids and turned her head away.

Lachlan chuckled as he moved to her pants and cut them off her. He wadded up the shreds of her clothes and tossed them to the floor. She held her breath, turning her mind to the cuffs. He'd said they wouldn't hold her for long. All she needed to do was learn their molecular structure, then she could break them off.

He moved off the bed and just stood staring at her for a few minutes. No man had seen her fully naked before then. Her stomach knotted harder.

"What colors do you like?" he asked.

"I'm not playing," she said flatly.

"Neither am I. Tell me what you want. I'll give you whatever you ask, except your freedom."

"Yeah? Go kill yourself."

"I'm immortal. I can't die."

"Bullshit."

"Maybe I should take your voice away. I don't have to be nice to you. You're not very grateful," he said.

"Get used to it. Gratitude is nothing you'll ever get from me."

He sighed and sat down on the edge of the bed. "You don't understand, Tesla. This isn't what you think. I'm never going to let you go. Settle with that...I never expected you to come to me the way you did. I've been tracking you since your wall thwarted my plans. When I learned more about you, I changed my plans. Sure, I still want Regia, but I want you more. Destiny has brought us together. You will be my queen. You will give me children. And you will give me your heart."

"My heart already belongs to another."

"If that is so, why did he spurn you?"

"What do mean?" she demanded, rankled as he hit a nerve.

"Forget him. He can't love you, not like I can."

"You can say you love me all you want, sicko. I will *never* love you."

He smiled. "We'll see."

He stood, walked across the room and opened a door. He pulled a tall metal frame through the door and brought it close to the bed. It looked like a rack to hang things on. He picked her up. The cuffs dragged her arms and feet down toward the floor. He placed her on the rack, pegs holding her up under the arms. She grimaced.

"Does that hurt?" he asked.

"Yes," she admitted.

"Good. The pain will grow in this stress position. I'll come back for you when you've had all you can take." He turned and made to leave the room. He stopped at the door and looked back at her. "I am everything to you now. Everything you will experience will come from me. Pain and pleasure. I will anger you, and I will make you happy. You will be cold, and you will starve. I will warm you and feed you. I want to learn you. Only when I know who you really are will I know exactly how to love you. Be patient. This will take some time. When you show me everything, then I can become the man of your dreams. You will love me, Tesla. You have no choice."

She looked at him contemptuously. "I see. So, Stockholm syndrome is the ultimate goal here."

He took his time looking her over again. "You are exquisite, Tesla. Your body is almost as perfect as mine. You're intensely beautiful. I look forward to copulating with you. You will look like a goddess when your stomach swells with my child." He left the room then.

Bile rose up her throat. Her mistake was bigger than she originally guessed. It might take her some time to get another opportunity to kill him, and what would she endure before that moment came? Her head fell down, her chin pressing against her chest and her hair hanging down over her breasts.

Regret poisoned her. X had said he was sorry. He'd asked her to wait. If only she had. Now she'd probably never see him again. And even if she did, he wouldn't want her. Lachlan was going to damage and use her in vile ways. X wouldn't want her after that. A tear slid from her eye. She tucked X away deep in her heart. No matter what happened to her. She would hold on to her love for him and keep it in a place Lachlan couldn't touch.

Lachlan touched the wall. It shimmered and gave him a perfect view of Tesla. He could see her, but she couldn't see him. He crossed his arms over his chest. For a long time, he stood still, staring at her and thinking how he wanted to proceed.

Peyton came into the room and gave Lachlan a little bow. "You sent for me, sire?"

He nodded. "Look what I caught."

Peyton came up beside him and frowned. "Who is that?"

"That is the future queen."

"What is she? She's not a witch. She can't be."

"She's a hybrid, but there is something... It's as if she has some witch in her. I've touched her. I already know I will be successful in impregnating her."

Peyton scowled. "Did you summon me here to gloat?"

"Yes," he said simply. "And to show you she's not ugly."

"You're cruel to me. You know I love you."

Lachlan snorted. "I know. And because of your emotional inclinations toward me, I had a feeling you might hate her on principle. That could be useful to me."

"How?"

"She already has me. I will be in love with her very quickly. It might make torturing her hard on me. You will design elements of pain for her."

A sexual glint lit Peyton's eyes. "You want *me* to administer pain to her?"

"Calm down. Not necessarily. Possibly. If I cannot come up with adequate levels on my own because of my feelings for her, you will help me. And when the time comes, I will stop hurting her altogether, and that will become solely your job."

"Why?"

"So I can become the savior. Her hate will transfer to you, and she will only feel love and trust then for me."

Peyton gazed at her hungrily. "Why go through the charade? Just let me hurt her now."

Lachlan cut him with an outraged look. "She is mine. I will not be denied anything where it comes to her. Especially her pain. She must be kept off balance at all times to begin with."

Peyton shrugged. "Fine. So when can I start?"

"Tomorrow. I am her whole world today. She can't meet you yet. And when she does, she must never know about you and me. If you tell her, or even hint that we've been lovers, I will kill you."

"All right," he conceded angrily.

"You'll stay here. Take your old room back, if you like."

He shuddered. "So I'd be forced to hear you make love to her? No thank you. I'll find another room, far away from yours."

"Oh, I think you'll hear it anyway, when it happens."

"*When?* You haven't touched her yet?"

Lachlan smiled. "Off balance, remember. She thinks I'm going to rape her."

"Well, aren't you?"

His smiled vanished, rage burning in his eyes. "I told you, she's going to be my queen. I want her to cry with pleasure in my bed, not terror. She won't forgive me if I rape her."

"Shall I do the honors then? It will make her hate me more."

"No one is to touch her like that, except me. Understand?"

Peyton nodded. "Can I go now?"

"No. You will stay right here and observe her. Look for weaknesses, beyond the obvious."

Many hours later, Lachlan lifted Tesla off the rack. Tremors shook her body. Her skin was clammy. She cried out in pain as he moved her. He laid her gently back onto the bed. She wasn't unconscious, but she wasn't lucid either.

"There now," he whispered soothingly. "You're weak."

He unclasped all the cuffs on her. As soon as the weight was removed, she pulled into the fetal position and passed out. He covered her up and forced the light to dim down. He would let her rest for a little while. Not long. But still, weakened as she was, he couldn't just leave her free like that. He backed up, holding his hands out over her, and encased her in a bubble. Even if she woke suddenly and was strong enough to open a portal, the bubble would trick her eyes and disorient her too much to get anywhere.

After she'd slept a half an hour, just long enough to fall into restorative sleep, he came back, made the lights shine overly bright, and pulled the cover off her. Her body jerked as she woke abruptly. Her eyes fixed on him. The bolt of lightning she shot at him hit the bubble and ricocheted back on her. She fell back, gasping, smoke rising off her skin.

"Poor thing," he mocked. "You hurt yourself... Don't do that. It does give me an idea, though. I didn't realize you could hurt yourself with your power." He dimmed the lights again. "You need to rest. You'll never have enough strength to stand up to me, if you don't."

He left the room. Tears threatened. She tried to ease her breathing. Her heart hurt as it beat erratically and her head swam. She was powerless against him this exhausted, and she couldn't think. Delirious, she pulled the blanket over her and fell back asleep.

Air filled X's lungs, but he still felt like he couldn't breathe. "Where is she?"

Maggie was still looking through the stone. The light shining from it flickered and died. She thumped it with her finger. It didn't light again. She let go of it.

"Where is she?" he asked again.

Maggie pinched her eyes shut and wrapped her arms around herself. "Mordian. The king has her. She tried to take him out on her own."

"She's..." He choked on the words. "She's still alive?"

"She's alive, but you have no hope, X. Even if you could get to her, she won't come with you."

He stopped listening, his mind burning as it made plans. He took off his gloves and touched the mark the Heart put on the back of his hand. *Hold on, Tesla. I'm coming for you.*

He picked up his axe, considering. Then he put it back down and slung the bow and quiver Forest gave him across his chest.

"What are you doing?" Maggie demanded.

He looked up at her. She flinched.

"I'm going to get my woman."

"I've told you there's no hope. It's impossible."

He smirked. "The Heart of Regia blessed me and it tied me to Tesla."

"But—"

He held his hand up to silence her. "You don't get it. I'm *human*. Save your logic. I can't hear it. I'm irrational. I will get her back with adrenaline and sheer stupidity."

Maggie shook her head sadly and turned away from him. She went to Merhl.

"I think I could get to Mordian." Merhl said. "I should go back to Regia first and get Rahaxeris. I don't want to leave you here like this, but Tesla is my family."

X could hear them talking, but the words meant nothing to him. The traces of Tesla's blood were still under his tongue. He put his finger in his mouth and brought her blood out. He traced the triangle with the blood on his finger. Smoke rose off his skin. He closed his eyes forcing his power to reach higher and harder. His hands lit up, and he felt the extent of what the Heart had actually done to him. *Merged*. That's what Tesla had said. Their power was merged. His eyes burned cold. He touched one of his palm stones. They were from Mordian. They would be his map.

Tesla's power was in him. He just hadn't accessed it before then. His eyes burned brighter. He could see the fabric of the atmosphere. He grabbed it and tore it open. X stepped into the rushing darkness. The dim grey light of the Everpath shone in the distance.

He was gone before Merhl, and Maggie had noticed what had happened.

X swore as his feet hit the grey floor. He'd gotten there on his own, but he still could barely see. His vision was blurry as though he were underwater. He looked down one way and then the other. Everything was identical. Every door was the same, and the hall was endless. He didn't know which direction to go. His heart thundered in his chest and pulsed in his ears. This could take forever and he was already out of time. How did Tesla know where to go when she was here?

"Help me out, baby." He touched the mark on his hand. "How do I find you?"

Lachlan sat on the bed, gazing down at her while she slept. Strands of hair stuck to her face where her sweat had dried. When he woke her again, she'd have some reprieve in the next round, he decided. The cuffs were too heavy to use on her again so soon. He twisted a collar around and around in his fingers, deciding exactly how he should order her. It couldn't be typical. Even if she disobeyed, he couldn't allow the collar to really harm her. Since he wanted to use a collar, he had to do it now, before things went further. A few more days, and she might become suicidal. A collar was a foolish choice for someone wishing for death. She still had hope.

She gave a little whimper in her sleep. He liked the sound. Damn, he wanted her. It had been so long. He hadn't cared, or hadn't realized he cared how long it had been until her. She wasn't going to get away.

Happiness that had been so elusive to him no matter what he conquered now came back violently. He didn't care about plundering her world anymore. She was his sole focus. Together, they would create a family. He would be the first wizard to become a father in thousands of years.

But first, he would court her. He would make her want to be the mother of his child. He shivered with pleasure. Their love would be forever. Closing his eyes, he gave the collar an order. The stone in the gold ring turned blue. He slipped it on her index finger and kissed the top of her hand as the spikes inside the band stabbed into her finger, all the way to the bone. It was then he noticed the mark on the back of her hand. He touched it curiously. He hissed in pain and pulled his hand back. The mark had burned him.

The deep smooth bass of ambient music woke Tesla. The opulent room she'd fallen asleep in had changed. The ceiling over the bed glittered with gold stars in an illusion of the night sky. It tricked her for a moment, making her believe she was actually outside. Everything hurt. Everything. Inside and out, physical and spiritual. Her throat burned. She wished she could drink X's blood right then.

X... Another pain smarted in her heart at the thought of him. She lifted her heavy hand up and kissed the mark. *I love you, X.*

X stopped short and turned around. "Tesla? I heard you!" he shouted, his voice echoing down the Everpath. "How do I find the door? Tell me! I'm coming for you."

Nothing. She didn't answer. She couldn't hear him the way he could hear her. He took a deep breath and focused. There was nothing else he could think of... He'd have to open every door.

CHAPTER SIXTEEN

Tesla held still, listening. It seemed like she was alone, but she knew he was watching her. The pain was acute but she was no stranger to pain. Much of her strength had returned. Why would he allow her to regain her strength? It made no sense. Did he underestimate her that much? She doubted it.

Tesla remained on the bed, covered up, and looked at the ring on her finger. It was attached to her. The spikes in her flesh made it easier for her to analyze it. She took it apart in her mind. It had many layers. The witch in her recognized the magic of it. Lachlan had tied it to her senses. There was something she must do, or must not do, she couldn't tell. And if she violated whatever the order was, he would take her senses away. All of them. Hearing, sight, smell, taste, and touch.

She sighed. She needed to know what the order was and if the punishment for disobedience was permanent or temporary.

"Hey," she called out.

Lachlan strode into the room, a garment of grey silk in his hand. He was wearing different clothes but in the same fashion as before. He was barefoot, in loose trousers, and a thin robe hung open over his bare chest. His long brown hair hung over his shoulders. She frowned. He must be terribly old, but he looked so young. His beauty didn't hide the vise in him. He wore cruelty as easily as his robe.

He sat down on the bed next to her. "I brought you something to wear. It's nothing really. Just a wrap. You need to clean up before I show you your real clothes."

"Don't you have anything better to do?"

He chuckled. "No. Come on, Tesla. I know you're a fighter. I know being powerless is killing you right now, but try and put that aside, if you can. I hope you can. I don't want to hurt you today. I did enough yesterday to hold back my appetite for your pain for a while. I want today to be easy for you...and possibly pleasurable."

She held up her hand. "What's the order on this?"

"No opening portals. No attacks. That's all. If you do—"

"I know. I'll lose my senses. I picked it apart already. If I disobey, will I be senseless permanently?"

He smiled devilishly. "What do you think?"

She gazed at him as though bored. "I think you're not going to show me anymore of your hand right now."

"You're right. Come on. Stand up and put this on. I'll show you around. Then I'll leave you alone for a while, of you want me to."

"Why would I want that?" she said sarcastically. "Your company is so delightful."

"You're making me angry."

A few nasty retorts were dying to come out, but she could see that he wasn't only becoming angry, he was becoming aroused. She swallowed her bitchy responses. He hadn't raped her yet. She didn't want to provoke him into it. She took the grey silk from his hand.

"Turn around."

His lips curved up. "Not a chance."

Tesla feigned indifference as she stood and pulled the wrap around herself and belted at the waist. She managed to keep from wincing, sore as she was. He stood and put his hands on her shoulders, his eyes searching hers.

"I want to pretend, Tesla. Will you play along?"

Fear pricked like ice. "Depends... Pretend what?"

"I want to pretend you're here because you want to be. That you're not scared."

She frowned. "You wanted to scare me yesterday. You said so."

"I didn't say I didn't want you scared, I said I want you to pretend you aren't... Just for now. Pretend you like me. I want to ask you for more, but I'll wait."

She thought about it. She needed time to figure something out. If she played along...perhaps.

"Okay. I'll try. This isn't a game I'm used to."

"I only have one more request. Don't interrupt me."

Tesla blinked and nodded in agreement, resigning herself to biting her tongue. He reached for her hand. Gah! She hated this game already. She exhaled once and gave him what he wanted.

"So much power in your hands. They hurt you, don't they?"

"Sometimes."

He led her out of the bedroom. She looked around at everything. There was no denying it was a gorgeous place; she tried to look impressed for his benefit, but she was really looking for an escape.

"Can I ask you questions?"

He smiled. "Yes. Please."

"How old are you?"

"Two thousand two hundred and six. How old are you?"

"Two. Or eighteen, depending how you count."

"So fresh and new. I love that."

"How long have you been king?"

"Hmm...about fifteen hundred years." He led her to a massive balcony. In spite of herself, Tesla gasped as she looked out.

An ocean of pink clouds rolled slowly under the rails. Rich, velvety blue sky sprinkled with glittering gold stars filled her vision.

"How high are we?"

"This castle is built on the highest mountain peak in all of Mordian. Most of the time the clouds are here like this, but sometimes the breeze blows them away, and you can see almost the end of the world from here... Do you like the view?"

"I wish I could say no. But I do. It's beautiful."

"Does it make you happy to know it's yours now?"

Tesla faltered. "Mine?"

"I told you, I'm never letting you go. This is your view. This castle is your home."

Her heart wailed within her. What if he was right? What if she never escaped? She exhaled raggedly. "Okay...It makes me happy." The words came out disjointed.

He frowned. "Try harder. We're pretending remember?"

"Sorry." The word was acid set on fire in her mouth. *I'll kill you. You*

275

sick, twisted, greedy bastard. You're going to die. You'll never have me.

Because she couldn't say the words, because she couldn't attack, frustrated tears began pooling in her eyes.

He looked at her from the side of his eye for a moment before facing her. His eyebrows rose slowly. "Oh, look at the hate in your eyes." He smiled indulgently. "All right. You're no good at this yet. I'll forgive you. You can go where you like in the castle. I'll leave you alone for a while, but I'm watching you. Don't forget that. I see you wherever you are. Wander. I'll put your dress on the bed."

He let go of her hand and backed away from her a few steps. She held still. Was it a trick?

"Don't be alarmed if you run into Peyton. He's here to serve you. Whatever you want or need, just let him know. Tell me if he's rude to you. He can be...bad tempered. There is no one else in the castle, except Iva."

"Iva?"

He smiled. "Yes. You'll like Iva. It's hard not to."

She watched him walk all the way to the end of the hall and turn a corner. Her heartbeat ratcheted up a notch, and her gaze darted around. All was quiet.

Wander. He said to wander. He was watching her. She must never forget that for a second. Her face must become a mask. Her eyes must flatten. She couldn't afford to hand him any more power over her. He must not know who she really was, or how she really felt.

The marble under her feet was warm, the pale color comforting. She walked slowly past broad, open windows. Sheer floor-to-ceiling curtains danced in the sweet breeze blowing in. What time was it? The sky was dark, but perhaps it was always like that here. She passed columns and

276

under arches. Her throat burned with thirst, and her stomach twisted with hunger. She still felt rather weak.

There were doors, but she didn't try any of them. She walked slowly, her power picking at the collar as though it were a scab. She tried to force her will on it and make it retract its spikes. It was difficult to work at it without appearing to work at it.

A swishing of fabric slithered behind her. She turned. This must be Peyton. He smiled at her as though she were something to eat. He immediately gave her the chills. He was just as wrong as Lachlan, but he had a different flavor. He wanted things from her, not the same things Lachlan wanted, but just as dark. His hair was short and a light caramel brown. His eyes matched his hair. He was young and beautiful like Lachlan, but with a smaller build. He reminded her of a venomous snake.

"Are you Peyton?"

His smile widened. "Yes, Tesla."

She stood still as he circled her once. His expression was passive, then he grabbed her roughly and shoved her against the wall, pinning her there with his body. Her muscles locked down. He pressed his fingers against the veins in her neck for a second then he backed up, letting her go.

"You really are part witch. A *small* part. But enough I guess. I'm sure we'll be cloning you soon. After Lachlan's had his fill of you first."

She lifted her head defiantly. Unless he surprised her, she doubted Peyton was ever going to be her ally.

"Lachlan said you were to serve me."

Peyton snorted. "He's besotted with you. He'll say anything right now."

"He said to tell him if you're rude to me. So, I guess your ass is in trouble."

He laughed. She could tell he was genuinely amused.

"I'd worry about my own ass, if I were you. Play nicely, Witch, or it will be the worse for you."

She smirked. "You don't know whose daughter I am. I never play nice, especially not with slimy *things* like you."

He raised his thin eyebrows, his face masking passive again. "Lachlan is king. He said today was to be easy for you. Tomorrow is another story... You look horrible from your time on the rack, and that won't do. So here's my great *service* to you today." He turned on his heel and strode away. He looked back at her over his shoulder. "Follow."

She hesitated a moment and then followed him at a distance. He stopped at a white door. The door arched at the top and was carved with beautiful designs.

"As much as it pains me to let you in this sacred place, Lachlan wants you clean and refreshed."

He opened the door, and then walked briskly away. The sweet smell of rain greeted her. Moist heat came through the door and caressed her skin. She walked slowly into the room, only it wasn't a room at all. Not really. The marble of the floors and walls were a rich cream color. She was in a short hallway. Steam billowed at the end. She turned the corner and stopped short, amazed.

The room was circular. The ceiling rose thirty feet and domed upward in the same creamy marble. Light filtered through it as though the sun shone just over it, like a dim overcast day. Rain fell through the ceiling. There were no pipes. The water dropped straight through the stone. The floor plunged down in a bowl shape under the domed ceiling. What looked like thick brown fur covered the floor, absorbing the water. The fur shivered and moved lazily like an ocean plant swaying in the current.

Fascinated, Tesla knelt down and touched the fur with her index finger. The tendril wrapped gently around her finger. It felt like the softest velvet. A ripple moved over the floor from her touch.

"Hello."

Tesla started at the voice and stood straight up.

"Don't be afraid." It was like the voice of the Heart, a strange, soothing mix, neither male nor female. This voice was softer and deeper than the Heart. A calm, murmur, but she couldn't tell where it had come from.

"Umm…Hello," Tesla said. "Where are you?"

"Here." The floor rippled again.

She was surprised. The floor was obviously alive, but she assumed it was like a plant, not a conscious entity.

"My name is Iva. What is your name?"

Her breath came out in a whoosh. "Oh, you're Iva. Lachlan mentioned you. My name is Tesla."

"It's a pleasure to meet you. I've not met anyone new for such a long time."

"What are you?"

A chuckle vibrated through the misty air. "I doubt I could explain. What are you?"

"Lachlan's prisoner."

The fur bristled, and the air turned cold. Iva seemed to be displaying anger. "Poor thing. I, too, am his prisoner. He stole me from my world before he destroyed it, long, long time ago. I can only assume I am the last of my race."

Her heart broke for the creature. She could only imagine how horrible that must be.

"I wish I had better words than 'I'm sorry'... Is it okay if I touch you again?"

"Yes."

She laid her whole hand on the fur this time. Again, tendrils reached up in a soft, wet, pseudo handshake.

"Would you like to stand in the rain? It will make you feel better." Iva offered. "I can ease pain."

The raindrops falling on the back of her hand were the perfect temperature to be tempting. She stripped off the silk wrap and stepped carefully onto the fur and under the falling water. The fur was warm and shivered under her feet as she walked down the slope to the bottom. She closed her eyes and exhaled. The raindrops massaged her shoulders and back. She felt relaxed and invigorated at the same time. A faint warning sparked in the back of her head. Perhaps this was a mistake. The water was fragrant, and she feared might be addictive.

Iva massaged her feet, sending her thoughts skittering away. It was the most peaceful and sensual experience she'd ever had, not to mention unique.

"Lay down. Let me love you better, my captive friend."

She hesitated a second before shrugging and sinking down. The rain eased to a soft sprinkle as she laid face up under it. The rain mixed with the tears on her face. Iva touched her gently, coaxing out the heartache. It absorbed her sobs.

"I'm so sorry," Iva said. "I would give you your freedom if I could. Sadly, this is all I can do for you."

"Thank you. It's not a small thing. I don't feel so alone now."

Iva purred. "Of course, I could kill you, if you would like." The fur seemed to lengthen. It wrapped around her waist, wrists and ankles. It wasn't painful.

"Not yet, please," Tesla said evenly.

Iva let go. "The offer stands if you lose all hope and prefer death to your life here."

"That's oddly comforting, Iva."

"Would you like to swim now?"

"Um...sure. How?"

The rain turned into a deluge and filled the bowl-shaped floor in a minute. She floated on the surface.

"That's nice. Thank you."

"Shall I change the light?"

"What?"

The ceiling and walls darkened to a deep black, the veins in the marble glowed green. Green sparkles lit up in the water around her. Ambient music drifted in the air. The notes were soft and benign, but her heart clenched. *X.*

She sobbed once and let it go, shutting her heart off. Tesla swam a few laps around the sides. "Thank you, Iva. I think I should get out now. I can't let my guard down anymore."

The water began to drain. "Good luck then. Please come back soon."

"I'll try. If I'm allowed."

Fluffy towels hung on hooks on the wall. She took one and dried off before combing her fingers through the length of her hair. The rain continued to fall, and the room lightened back to the cream color. She put the towel back and wrapped the silk around herself again. She shivered as she gazed at Iva. Everything she'd seen and experienced in Lachlan's castle was a sensual nightmare.

Pleasure did not equate to happiness. Old as he was, it seemed to her that was something Lachlan didn't know or understand. He said she could have anything she wanted, except her freedom. She knew he would lie to her, but on that point she believed him. He would and could give her anything she asked for. A gorgeous palace, clothes, jewelry, power, status, anything and everything in such abundance. Her memories of the metal flower X made her, shivered in her mind. It was nothing, a trinket, with no intrinsic value, and yet it was worth more than everything Lachlan had to offer.

"I'll come back…" she whispered to Iva as she left.

The hall was empty as she stepped out the carved ivory door. The breeze blew in around her, flattening the thin fabric against her body. It was horrible. Her skin responded the sliding touch of the silk regardless of her thoughts or feelings. He was going to do more of this, she assumed. Everything he gave her, everything about this place was designed to seduce. She needed real clothes. Turning around, Tesla walked back the way she came, looking for Lachlan's bedroom. Hoping desperately he wasn't in there. After two wrong doors, she found the room again.

She exhaled the breath she'd been holding. The room was empty. A black river of silk lay on the bed for her. She scowled at the dress, not that she was surprised it was something like this. She grabbed it and slipped it on as quickly as possible. It fit perfectly. The back dragged along the floor in a short train. She'd have been freezing if it wasn't so warm in the castle. Spaghetti straps held the low scooping front up and crossed once over her back. The collar hung so low and v'd between her breasts, making the lightning flower over her heart totally exposed.

Sighing, she moved to the huge, gold-framed mirror on the far wall. Tears began pushing behind her eyes. She didn't want Lachlan seeing her like this. She acknowledged, without ego, that she rocked this dress. She looked like sex on a stick, which, of course, had been his goal.

Tesla turned from her reflection and left the room.

Lachlan watched her from behind the wall again, his arms crossed. Peyton leaned against the wall, not even attempting to hide his irritation.

"What do you think?"

"I'm ready to hurt her," Peyton said.

Lachlan smirked. "Of course you are. The first time has to be the worst. Then the anticipation she'll have for her time with you will be heightened after that. Do you have a plan?"

"Yes. I just need to construct the apparatus. It will be ready tonight."

"Perfect. I want to see it when you're finished. Tomorrow morning, she's all yours. At least for a while."

"Are you sure you don't want me to rape her?"

Lachlan smiled broadly. "She's got your blood heated now, does she?" he mocked.

Peyton blushed a little and looked away. "I hate her. I want to make her scream and watch her eyes fill with terror."

"Nothing has changed since yesterday." Lachlan's tone went cold. "She's mine. Don't touch her sexually."

He shrugged. "Whatever."

"Go work on your torture device. Get her screams that way. I'll find you later."

He gave him a little bow and left. Lachlan hesitated a moment. Tesla was probably hungry. Food was next. Music, dinner, and soft promises. He'd begin her seduction. He licked his lips and reminded himself to be patient. A small smile lifted his lips as he considered what angles he'd start with... His smile grew larger. He'd push her so skillfully until she was the one asking for it.

CHAPTER SEVENTEEN

Time was an oily, trippy dubstep in the Everpath. The longer he was there, the less X felt time. He pushed through his exhaustion, adrenaline fueling him onward. He just kept going. Opening doors, glancing in for a second, waiting for the stones to speak that yes, he'd found the right place. Tesla hadn't spoken to him again. He knew she was alive. He could feel her in the mark on his hand.

After his first few hours, the new levels of power the Heart gave him, began to wake up in small degrees. The first thing he noticed was his vision. It was still not clear, but it was improving. His eyes burned so cold, he no longer felt it.

X pushed the next door open. Black smoke curled out. His hands lit up like explosives without his consent. Twenty hands reached out, grabbed him, and hauled him into the blackness. The hands on him were half rotted, insubstantial and vanished as soon as the door slammed shut behind him. He landed in a barren wasteland. Jagged grey rocks jutted out of the ground like broken tombstones. Grey rocks and black smoke completed the dreary landscape. Ghosts of a strange race drifted in the smoke. A demonic rumble vibrated out of the haze in front of him. Red glowing eyes looked at him as a monster rose up from the smoke. Over ten feet tall, it looked down at X with a delighted glint in its eyes and laughed. The laughter was the resonance of the dregs of hell. Excited, hungry, and pure evil.

For one second X was bemused, then he threw his head back and laughed. His laughter silenced the monster and it blinked at him confusedly.

"Insane mortal," the monster rumbled.

X wiped a tear of mirth from his eye. "Oh, goodness. What's your name?"

"You ask *my* name?!" It roared, outraged. "None can know my name! No lips can speak it."

X laughed again. "So, you don't remember your name. That's fine. I'll call you Fluffy. And by the way, you're coming with me."

The monster blinked at him again a few times and cocked its head to the side. "I am damned to this place eternally. As are all of us. You as well. There is no escape."

"Not me. I'm leaving now. I have to save my woman. You're coming with me. Obey me, when I call you. Attack my enemies, when I order you, and you'll have the chance at another future."

"Lies!" It hissed.

"You've got nothing to lose. Pledge your fealty now." X held up his left hand, where he kept the stains. "Say it! I'll give you a chance when I'm finished with you. You're coming with me, like it or not. Disobey me when I give you an order and I'll set your black soul to the wind."

It heaved a great sigh then went down on one knee in front of X. "I swear."

X pulled the monster into the stone. "Good boy, Fluffy." He looked at the group of hovering ghosts. All their eyes were on him. "Anyone else want to come?"

Three quarters of them moved forward. They were not the stains the monster had been, just old trapped souls. He pulled them into his right hand with the other souls he kept. X turned around and easily saw the door out. He was back in the Everpath in a blink, feeling quite good about that little detour. He'd added nicely to his arsenal. Fluffy was quite the intimidating addition.

Maggie clung to Merhl. "I don't want you to go."

"I don't *want* to, but I have to. I wish I could take you with me."

"Well, why not? I can wait for you in Regia as easily as I can here. I'm not afraid of the wizards. I'm only afraid of being apart from you."

Merhl rubbed his head. "I don't know what to do, but I have to do something. I have to get back and tell Rahaxeris what's happened to Tesla."

Maggie pushed up on her tip toes and pressed her lips against his. "Please take me with you. Please."

He groaned and held her tightly, shaking his head. "I can't risk it. Nothing can happen to you, Maggie. I wouldn't live through losing you. I'll go and be back very quickly. I promise."

She let go, nodding her head, resigned. "Hurry back to me."

He hauled her up in his arms and kissed her mouth. He couldn't hold on, but it felt impossible to let go. "I'll be right back...Is there anything else to see in your stone?"

She held it up to her eye, then let it drop, shaking her head. "Nothing."

Tesla wandered the halls, her stomach rumbling, but thankful to be alone. She knew her solitude was coming to a quick end. Lachlan would be back to torment her some more. Music drifted in the air again, making her scowl. The notes were soft, fluid, and deeply sexual. She tried to shut out the sound. She turned a corner and stepped on something soft. A trail of deep red petals covered the floor. Tesla stopped. He obviously wanted her to follow them; he may as well have put arrows. It was far from a subtle move. She rolled her eyes and continued walking on the petals.

They led to the throne room. She stopped short, her mouth falling open. "Damn."

Lachlan stepped out from the side of the massive hall and walked toward her, smiling. "Thank you. That was a genuine reaction."

She clamped her mouth shut. "Um… it's big."

He circled around her, running his finger lightly across her shoulder. "Beautiful. I knew you would look amazing in this dress. Do you like it?"

"No." Her voice was stoic.

He chuckled. "No more ugly, men's clothes for you. I want you to always look your best from now on."

So many nasty retorts were going through her mind. She kept them inside and tried to hold her expression in a bored indifference. "So what now? What's the game?"

He faced her, crowded her. She took a step back, he moved forward. He lifted his hands and held them a breath from her shoulders but didn't make contact. Smiling he leaned down and put his mouth next to her ear, but again, he didn't actually touch her.

"Anxious to play?" he whispered.

"I just want the rules, so I can figure out how to break them."

"Careful, sweetness. Breaking the rules *is* the next game."

"Sounds good to me."

"You don't know what you're talking about, but you will find it good, once you learn."

"Oh?" She really wanted to back up, but she held still.

He pulled his face back from her ear, his gaze pushing hard on hers. "Hide and seek. The game is played in the darkest part of your mind. Where I will find everything. I will touch it all. Tease out the darkness in you and show you how to use it for the ultimate pleasure. You don't know these things yet, my pretty baby. It's time to taste new flavors. Try new things. Push the taboo. Break the rules. There should be no boundaries between you and me."

She sneered. "Sounds disgusting."

His smile grew bigger, and his eyes burned. "Oh, it is," he whispered intimately.

"You can't have me. You know that, right?"

"Have you forgotten who you are talking to? There is nothing I cannot have. And I want everything."

"Yes. Your appetite has killed countless people. You are—"

He held up his hand to silence her. "I'm not interested in your incriminations. I know you're unhappy being here with me... at this moment. But this is your life now. I want you to enjoy yourself. Don't you like my castle?"

Tesla swallowed. "It's beautiful. Amazing. But it's a prison."

He smiled again. "Yes. For you, it is. And it always will be. I could throw you in a pit if I wanted to. Be thankful you have my love."

"Love?"

"I want you for my queen, Tesla. I've been alone so long."

"By choice," she argued.

"Naturally, by choice. I haven't felt desire like this before. I could have anyone...I want you."

Sorrow filled her whole body, heavy and solid. She sighed and looked down. It didn't matter what she said to him. He had the control. The collar kept her from attacking him. The only hope she had was he would eventually fall asleep and she could dismantle the collar and take it off. Until then, there was nothing she could do.

"I'm hungry," she said quietly.

He took her hand and brought it to his lips. "Then come have dinner with me."

He led her through a side door and into an intimate dinning space. A table was laid with food and beautiful linens and crystal. Her stomach turned over at the aroma. She didn't recognize any of the types of food, or the smells, but she was totally enticed, nevertheless. He pulled out one of the ornate chairs for her. Her hands ached with the desire to clench them around his throat, but she sat down.

He served her. It was a freaking nightmare. Like she was having an out of body experience. Smile when you want to scream. Hold still when you want to kill. Be surrounded by beauty and romance while filled with hate. Visually she was in a fairy tale. A princess in a beautiful gown, having dinner with the king. But it was all veneer. Pseudo. She narrowed her eyes at him, curious. Did he care it was fake? Yes, she figured he did care. He wanted to pretend until the lie became real. He wanted reality. Is that how she could take him down? Hmm...perhaps. She needed time to think on that one. She needed to understand him better.

Tesla took her first bite. Warmth and pleasure sparkled in her mouth, then filled her whole body. She absorbed the impossibly wonderful taste and sensation it brought. She almost gasped for air, it was so good.

He smiled knowingly at her. "I told you it was time to try new things. And that's just your first taste."

She wanted all of it. She wanted to gorge herself. Fear spiked a warning in her, and she pushed the plate away. "I'm full."

He leaned back in his chair, scrutinizing her. She feared he was about to explode in rage. Instead, he smiled again. "You're right to not trust. Shrewd. But I'm not poisoning you."

"No. You're addicting me. Making me dependent."

"It's only fair. I need you...in so many ways. Balance must be achieved. I want us to hold equal power over one another. Come now, I know you're still hungry. It won't hurt. I promise."

"No. I don't like this. Holding food over me to make me behave is too basic a move for you. It's beneath you."

He laughed and nodded appreciatively. "Perhaps you're right. But I've been honest about it, so it's hardly a calculated move against you."

She snorted. "You're delusional."

"You're sexy," he countered.

Her cheeks flushed, making him laugh again.

"So innocent. It's time to shed that."

She scowled. "I'm not that innocent. You think I don't know what desire is? You think I've never felt lust? I told you my heart belongs to another."

"He obviously didn't know what to do with you. Not like I do."

She looked away from him, a rogue tear sliding from her eye. She waited for him to continue tormenting her. Instead, he was quiet. She exhaled and looked back at him, more collected. His face was contemplative.

"I could change my appearance. I could look like him, if you want."

The thought made her want to gag. "No!" She looked down and schooled her violent reaction. "I mean, no thank you. That's thoughtful of you, but I need to let him go. As you've already seen, I'm not good at pretending."

"I offered you a gift, and you gave me one instead. Thank you." He stood and took her plate away, placing his in front of her instead. "There. The taste will be the same, but you won't feel the same kind of *reaction* to it."

She decided to try something to test her theory. "Thank you, Lachlan." She kept her voice soft.

He looked at her in a new way, and she knew she was right; he did want something real between them.

"That's the first time you've said my name."

"Is that agreeable?"

"Very. We've obviously moved past a barrier. That pleases me."

She took another bite. Instead of feeling less, she felt more. More warmth, more pleasure. He'd lied. Before she came back to her senses, she taken three more bites. Her head rolled back on her shoulders, and she slumped back in the chair, too high to sit upright anymore. She tried to focus on him, her eyes heavy.

"Nice move," she conceded. "You got me."

"You tried to maneuver around me, but I won that round." He came to her and scooped her up in his arms. Her head swam as he carried her through the halls. "It won't feel like this next time. The next time you eat, everything will feel normal."

"I don't want to play anymore games."

"That's fine. Just give in to me, then. Surrender now, Tesla. You will in the end anyway, we both know it. Let's just forego the rest and move onto the pleasure. Otherwise, we have to play."

"I thought the struggle was part of the pleasure for you."

He chuckled as he brought her into the bedroom and laid her on the bed. "I'm so far gone over you already. I love your smart little answers. Would you like to keep the dress on?"

"What do you mean?" she asked sleepily.

"I could get you something else to sleep in."

"Yeah right, liar. You'd take the dress away and then leave me naked."

He smirked and lay down next to her. The light went out, and the ceiling lit up with stars again. He propped himself on one elbow and stared down at her.

"What?" she asked as aggressively as she was able to in her drugged state.

"I think I'm going to kiss you now."

"I think I'm going to vomit in my mouth. That will make it really hot, right?"

He grabbed her chin and tilted her head toward him. "Stop talking."

Her eyes closed involuntarily as his lips came down on hers. He'd been right when he told her she'd know it when he kissed her. If her mind and heart were detached from her body, it would have been ecstasy. His kiss could hardly be considered just a kiss. It was like the food. Shocking. Full bodied sensuality. Warmth and pleasure. Skill and magic combined. So good and so wrong. It wasn't for her. This flavor. It was too much. Too mature. Too dirty, and still it was good. Her heart cried out in protest, while her body cried out in craving. A low growl vibrated in his lungs, and he moved closer, pressing his chest against hers. She braced her hands on his shoulders and pushed.

"Stop."

He smiled down at her, heat and knowledge in his eyes. "Good girl. Say no to me. Deny what your body wants because it's the right thing to do."

She winced and clamped her eyes shut. "Ugh. Get off me, you beast. I don't want you. You drugged me. So get over yourself. If you can make me want you legitimately, then you can feel all good about your skill and desirability. Until then, it's nothing but forcing me and taking advantage."

"Whoa. You've got guts. Just makes me hotter for you... All right, maybe you have a point. Still...I know you enjoyed that, despite what you might say. I felt you respond."

"I can't stop you. Not collared. But you can't make my heart betray my love."

His voice lowered and turned to silk. "Yes, I can. You will betray him, then you will forget him, and all that will be in your heart and your body is me."

She rolled away from him. "Leave me alone."

"I love you."

"I think you really believe that."

He sighed, and she felt his weight leave the bed. She listened, but she didn't hear his footsteps leaving the room. She refused to look. She held perfectly still and could hear his breathing. Then the cover slid up over her. She was grateful for the barrier it created between them. But that turned out to be folly. The rustling of fabric got the better of her curiosity, and she rolled over to see what he was doing. He smiled at her as he finished taking his clothes off.

She groaned in disgust and pinched her eyes shut in defense against his nakedness. "Seriously?" she demanded.

He didn't answer but sild under the cover next to her. She shifted away, her head pitching with the movement. He crowded her, his bare chest pressing against her side. Leaning down, he pressed his lips to her shoulder. "Relax." He said. "If I felt like forcing you, I'd have done it already. But this is *my* bed."

She rolled away from him. "I didn't choose to be here. You're the one who put me here. I'll gladly sleep somewhere else. The floor even."

"Shhh…Just be quiet." He ran his hand over and over down her arm. Then he moved to her back and traced circles and designs on her skin. "I know you're curious. You want to know what it's like."

"Not with you."

"Lies," he breathed against her ear. "Just think, if the simple act of eating can be what I made it for you, imagine what I can do to you in bed."

Head hammering and vision spinning, she dragged herself into a sitting position before scooting to the edge of the bed and onto the floor. "You will never have my consent."

She curled into a ball on the marble floor, disoriented before she passed out. She didn't sleep long. Her eyes fluttered open, and she stared at the ceiling. Had she been dreaming? She was sure she had moved to the floor. Well, she wasn't there now. Groaning, she was on the bed, Lachlan asleep right beside her. Had he dragged her back after she lost consciousness?

Her blood felt clear of the junk he'd given her. Her head no longer felt swimmy. She exhaled slowly and moved a fraction of an inch away from him. He didn't stir, not that she trusted he was actually asleep at all. Silently, Tesla sild out of the bed. She hesitated for a second, her eyes still trained on him. Nothing. She slunk from the room and out into the hallway, moving through the shadows behind the columns lining the walls.

This was her chance to break the collar. She sat on the floor, her back against the wall and held her collared hand with the other one. Taking a deep breath and closing her eyes, she rubbed the pad of her fingertip around and around on the stone. She saw it the way she saw many things, like an equation. But the math was off on this one. The symbols like ancient glyphs. She looked for patterns. This was going to take longer than she hoped.

Slowly, she began to deteriorate the outer layers. She moved her power closer and closer to the center, to the magic inside the ring.

"Tesla..." Her name drifted down the hall like a whispered breeze.

No. She was so close. She pushed harder toward the center. Almost there. Hands reached out from the darkness and grabbed her by the shoulders. The collar fell off her finger just as a cuff clamped around her neck. Peyton smiled cruelly at her in the shadows. She grabbed at the thing around her neck. It burned her hands. He slid the collar back onto her finger and it bit down into her bones again.

"So nice to come across you like this. And just at the right time looks like. You are powerful."

"Look, I know you don't want me here. I can see it in your eyes. Just let me go. Lachlan will never know. He's asleep."

"Asleep? Perfect. He wants you all to himself. It's my turn now."

He grabbed her wrist and pulled her forward and through a door. Dim light came from the ceiling in the all grey room. There was nothing in this room, just a square black hole in the floor. She stepped back from it, afraid. It was like the open mouth of a monster.

Peyton lifted the hem of her dress and cut it with a small knife. She turned to face him, but he pulled the fabric in both hands, tearing the garment into two pieces. The dress fell to the floor. She tried to cover herself with her arms. He shoved her hard with both hands. Tesla stumbled backward and fell into the pit.

Her ankles burned as her feet hit the floor. The space was confining around her, like a coffin. Cold water filled the bottom, covering her feet. She reached up, then she jumped, but the top was just beyond her reach. She tried to brace her hands and feet on the walls, but they were too slick. Peyton looked down at her and smiled.

"I made this little space just for you. The cuff around your neck will begin to *stimulate* you, well your magic. This is going to hurt, a lot. I'm really going to enjoy watching you injure yourself."

She looked down at the black water. She couldn't focus if she was listening to him. She could get the collar off again. Now that she'd done it once, it would go fast. Tesla only made it through the very first layer of the magic in the collar before the cuff woke up. The pain was beyond anything she'd ever experienced. Her magic surged and overflowed inside her. She clawed at the cuff. It burned her hands again, only this time her hands were lit with crossing, wild currents.

Her scream echoed in the tiny space as lightning shot from her hands. The lightning bounced off the walls and back into her, scorching her body as it hit her. Electricity snaked through the space over and over. She couldn't stop. She couldn't think or calm down. It filled the water in the bottom, lighting her up that way too. The lightning in the water entered her legs like someone cutting her open from her ankles to her knees with a broken, acid-covered blade. The cuff pulsed, edging her overflow higher.

Her heart began to burn and snap. She could kill herself now. Just put her wild hands on her heart and she'd age to the point of death in a matter of seconds. Death. Such a good idea, the deep recesses of her brain thought as another bolt went straight through her stomach. The electrical storm filled the hole. Over and over she was impaled with her own power. She raised her hands to her heart and stopped just before making the connection. She felt it. There in her hand. Her tie to X.

X...

Insanity brought on by pain scattered her mind. Flashes of X. His smile. His eyes. The sound of his voice. She found the will to live. He gave her that. She crouched down and pushed her hands under the water, keeping her mind trained on him. Her memories soothed her. Her magic eased back even though the cuff continued to push and pull on her power. The storm ended, and she crumpled unconscious against the black wall, burned all over and all the way through.

The sounds of arguing and shouting woke her. She'd never been so hurt in her life. She tried to move and stopped immediately, her muscles screaming at her. Her vision hazed and wavered as she blinked.

"How dare you hurt her like that? I should kill you," Lachlan yelled.

She cried out in agony as a hand reached down and grabbed her, hauling her out of the hole. Tesla hung like a dead body in Lachlan's arms and fell unconscious again as they passed a satisfied-looking Peyton. Water running over her burns woke her with a start. Light rain fell on her face. She moaned and blinked her blurry eyes. She was with

Iva.

The soft wet fur rubbed the back of her body. Steam hissed from her burned skin as the water fell on it.

"Poor thing," Iva said softly.

"Silence, Iva!" Lachlan ordered.

Tesla blinked and looked up into Lachlan's face. He smoothed the hair off her forehead. "Sorry," he murmured. "Peyton will be punished for what he did to you."

Bullshit. She thought but she tried to give him a weak, grateful smile. She swallowed. The cuff was gone.

"Fill up, Iva," he said.

The rain poured hard and heavy, filling the bowl-shaped floor. Too messed up to even move, Tesla floated on the surface, supported in Lachlan's arms. After a few minutes, he pulled her closer to him and cradled her against his chest. Her head lolled on his shoulder. He was as naked as she was. He was pushing intimacy not sex. So much of their bodies touched. Just water and skin. Something registered in her mind she hadn't noticed about him before. She pushed the pain back and tried to focus on him.

He wasn't real. His body held a signature she couldn't believe she'd missed before. He was a machine. An organic machine. Built, not born. Not that he wasn't alive, he was. That's how he maintained his youth. This body didn't age. She pressed her hand against his chest. No pulse. No heart. He didn't need one. Just a soul. He had that, and it lived in this body, but not naturally.

She blinked, unsure of what she was seeing. Unsure if she was seeing or if her eyes were just messed up from the torture. Touching Lachlan, she looked at his body structure, but she didn't see the way she usually

299

did. It wasn't DNA strands she saw. What was that? Caged inside him? His soul? No way could she see that. Could she?

The mark on her hand constricted. Maybe she could. Her mouth lifted slightly in a side smile. X could kill him.

"Why are you smiling?"

"I'll tell you later," she said feebly.

"You're healing fast. Your skin is almost fully restored."

"I'm still burned inside. I need to sleep."

"Whatever you need."

He wrapped her in a towel and carried her back to the bedroom. He laid her down and covered her up.

"You can rest easy. I'll lock the door. Peyton can't get to you."

She closed her eyes and fell asleep instantly with the pleasant thought of X destroying Lachlan in her mind.

"So good," Lachlan whispered, holding Peyton's face in his hands. "Such a good idea."

Peyton smiled broadly, soaking up Lachlan's praise. "You said the first time had to be the worst."

He moved closer and licked Peyton's bottom lip. "That *was* bad. She almost killed herself. I think it's going to be so easy to control her now."

Peyton looked at her through the wall. "She got the collar off, not a second before I put the cuff around her neck. She'll get it off again. You need to put something different on her."

"I have something. You're not the only one who can create devices of pain. It will go on her as soon as she wakes up. She's going to look so sexy in it, too. I can't wait to see it on her."

"How long are you going to keep her to yourself? I want to taste her, too. Since you've made it clear I can't have you anymore."

Lachlan sighed and stepped back from him. "I don't know how long. Maybe I'll get bored with her after she gives me a child. I don't want her cloned until I have an heir. Then you can have your own Tesla."

"Sure," Peyton said, his tone making it clear he didn't believe him.

"Just focus on your job. Or have you already tired of hurting her?"

"Oh, no. Not even close. I have many more ideas in mind for her."

"Good."

"Can I see what you have for her?" Peyton asked.

Lachlan smiled, pulled a small box from his pocket, and handed it to him. Peyton lifted the lid, his eyebrows rising appreciatively. "It will grow?"

"Oh yes. Until it covers her whole body. She'll beg me then. She'll do anything I want, just to get me to remove it."

"Tired of breaking her down slowly?"

"My lust for her is about to choke me. I want to speed this up. I'm not going to wait much longer. Even if she resists initially, after she experiences the pleasure I will give to her, she won't fight anymore."

CHAPTER EIGHTEEN

Forest paced the floor of Tesla's room, her hands pressed to her head as tears streamed down her cheeks.

"Where is my daughter?" she cried.

Syrus pulled her against him, but he had no answer. Rahaxeris stood like a statue in the corner, looking down. The three of them had been like that for a while. Forest thought she knew hell, but now she realized she'd been wrong. The fear. The unknown possibilities that she had lost her daughter forever and would never know what had befallen her, was worse than anything she'd ever experienced.

There was nothing they could do and that made it worse. Tesla could be anywhere and was most definitely beyond the reach of any search party. X was gone, too. Was that comforting? Forest didn't know. There were moments she felt hope in the fact the X was gone as well. He would protect Tesla. She was sure of that. But what if he couldn't? What if? What if? What if...

Being helpless crashed against Forest's most basic, fundamental nature. She would go mad like this.

A thud in the living room had all of them jumping and running.

"Merhl!"

He'd landed in a crouch, and his skin was greyish. He looked up at them and stood upright, his color blanching worse. He swallowed hard.

"The wizard king has Tesla."

Forest cried out. Syrus caught her as her knees gave.

"She's alive. He wants to keep her that way. X has gone after her, but I have no idea the odds he might succeed. He managed to world jump. I don't know how he was able to do that, but he did...I..." Merhl's face crumpled. "He loves her. He will not stop. I know that. I would go after her, too. I *will*," he amended. "It was hard enough for me to get back here without her help. I felt I needed your guidance, Rahaxeris, before I did anything. I can't think."

Rahaxeris turned and faced the window, his shoulders stiff. "There's nothing to be done, I fear. I have no solutions or guidance for you, Merhl, since I've never been to the Everpath. How can I direct you? I fear Tesla's fate is in her own hands."

"I can try to take you there with me," Merhl said.

"No." he shook his head.

"What?" Forest demanded. "You won't even try?"

He turned to face her. "Tesla told me about the Everpath. I don't have the ability to see it."

Forest's face went stony. She shoved out of Syrus' arms and stalked to her bedroom. The next minute she was back, pulling her hair into a ponytail, her lightning sword strapped around her waist. "Merhl take me. I'm going to find my daughter."

Rahaxeris held up his hands. "You'll die. You're not built for jumping."

"You think I'd hesitate to die for my child?! Tesla is my blood. Why can't I do what she can do?"

Syrus moved to Forest's side. "She has a fair point. Tesla came from us. We should be able to handle what she can handle."

"That sounds good, but you're wrong." Rahaxeris said. "You can't do a fraction of what she's capable of, powerful as you are, mage. She's hidden things from you since the very beginning, because she loves you and didn't want to scare you."

"I can't stand here and do nothing, Father," Forest said.

"Okay," he nodded. "Let's go to Kyhael. Even *if* we can get to the wizard's world, we won't be able to get her from the king with nothing but passion. We need a plan, and all the wizard artifacts the *Rune-dy* collected through the years."

He struck the air, opening a portal to Kyhael. Merhl and Rahaxeris went through first. Syrus held Forest back. She faced him, confused.

"One of us should stay here, in case they come back."

"Oh." She blinked a few times quickly. "Yeah. You go. You're more powerful than I am."

He shook his head. "Not in this situation. You're more dangerous than I am right now. You're her mother. That connection is more powerful than anything. I don't want to stay, but I can heal. What if X can bring her back but they're injured?"

Forest gritted her teeth. "Damnit, Syrus." She kissed him hard and fast. "I love you!"

"I love you."

"I'll get her."

"I know. I'll let you know through our connection if they come back. I'll make you feel it."

She looked at him, knowing it might be the last time she ever saw him. She placed her hand over his heart, telling him everything she didn't have the words for, before rushing into the waiting portal.

Lips against her skin woke Tesla. She didn't have to open her eyes to know who was kissing her. Lachlan's skillfully dirty lips pressed on her neck, along her collarbone, and dipped lower to the top of her breast. That was enough right there. She opened her eyes and shoved him back from her.

He seemed unperturbed by her rebuttal and smiled lazily down at her. "You've rested long enough. You're healed now. It's time for a new game."

"Super," she said sarcastically. "I love mind games before I've had my coffee."

He chuckled. "I love you."

She scowled but said nothing. "Peyton killed my dress last night. What are you going to dress me up in today?"

His smile broadened and his eyes glinted. "So glad you asked." He held a small box over her and opened the lid. "You'll wear this today."

She tried to sit up when a black metal spider crawled out of the box and jumped down to her neck. Scrambling, she clawed at it to get it off, but it scurried too fast over her skin and under the blanket. She rolled to try and get away from it, then it was crawling on her again. Lachlan grabbed her arms and pinned her down. The spider crawled up her, its sharp legs leaving pin pricks of blood on her skin. She looked down as it settled over her heart.

"No. Please!"

"Begging already? Perfect."

The spider's front two legs reared up and stabbed deep. The legs pushed down through her flesh and wrapped loops around her ribs. Tesla's breath hitched in a gasp of pain. The other legs lengthened, growing across her body, turning into a metal web. The body of the spider twisted and transformed into a round gear with locking parts.

Lachlan pulled her to her feet by her hands. "Stand still."

Terrified, she complied. The web continued to grow, until it made a dress. More gears formed down the mesh sleeves, along the scooping neckline, over her back, and down the skirt over her legs.

He stepped back and leered at her, a shiver moving over him. "Oh, that is so hot. Come over here and look at yourself in the mirror."

"I...I don't want to move."

"Oh, come on. Nothing bad will happen to you so long as you do what I say. I'll keep the gears disengaged."

"And if they are engaged?"

"Such a curious little thing. Let's just say, you won't like it at all. Now come here."

Shaking slightly, she moved one of her arms an inch. The whole dress adjusted. Blood was running down her torso from where the spider stabbed and hooked its legs through her. She walked slowly and awkwardly to the mirror. He stood behind her, gazing at the reflection.

"This look suits you, Tesla. Brutal and yet, still submissive."

"This isn't a dress, it's a machine. A torture device."

"Quite."

"What do I have to do to get you to take it off?" she asked angrily.

"First of all..." He twisted a gear on the neckline. A spike thrust out of it and impaled her. She gasped in pain and surprise. "Change your tone of voice. I'd appreciate more respect."

Shuddering, she looked down, counting all the gears she could see. Thirty on the front. This dress was an iron maiden. Too much more disobedience on her part, and she'd bleed out, full of holes. He put his index finger under her chin and titled her face up.

"Be my queen. Stand by my side in life. Give me children."

"You didn't answer my question. How do I get out of this?"

He looked over at the bed suggestively. "Give me your consent. Ask me to make love to you, and I'll remove it, and you will never see it again."

Tears flushed her skin, and she looked up at the ceiling. "No."

At her words, three more gears stabbed her. One in each arm and one directly over her navel. Blood ran hot under the metal dress.

"You want to die?" he asked.

"No." Her tears ran as freely as her blood.

"Shall I hand you over to Peyton again?"

Fear filled her eyes, and she shook her head. "No, but it can't be that easy, Lachlan. Give me something else in exchange for my body."

"Your body belongs to me. Kneel."

"How?! I'm bleeding! I'm scared to move anymore."

"Kneel!" he shouted then he walked behind her and twisted part of her dress. It clicked and turned, then it forced her to her knees, moving her like a posable doll. It forced her hands behind her back and her head down. The spikes through her arms and stomach burned and bit harder.

"Please," she cried, her voice cracking.

"What was that?" His tone was smug.

"Please!" she managed louder.

"Hmm…" He narrowed his eyes at her then turned his back. She lifted her head a fraction. His hands flexed behind him as he paced a few feet in front of her. An emotion she couldn't recognize crossed his features as he turned back to her. If she didn't know better she would have thought it was love.

"I've been cruel," he conceded. "It's my nature. I'm so old, I've forgotten how scary the first time can be. I'm sorry… Let's try this another way."

He twisted the back of her dress again and it softened, allowing movement again. He picked her up under the arms and lifted her back to her feet. Blood was pooling on the floor under her. He smoothed her hair back from her face.

"I'm sorry. I'm so impatient. You have to learn I am your master. Then things can be good…How about this? I promise to back off Regia."

Her eyes widened. "What?"

"Ask me to make love to you. Willingly surrender, and I promise I will leave Regia alone for good. Everyone you love there will be safe."

"Prove it."

He crossed the room and came back with a sphere in his hands. "See this? This is how I tracked you. It's how I planned to finally get through your wall. His hand rubbed a circle on the top. She saw Regia in the inside of it. She saw the way the blood lock looked from the outside. The object was alien, and she had never seen anything that held so much power. He could get through the blood lock with that, if he used it right.

"See? I can annihilate your world, but I've held back. Waiting for you. I didn't want to risk killing you in the process. You mean more to me than anything I've taken, conquered, or killed. I love you. I will give up Regia if you submit to me."

She closed her eyes and swallowed, nodding her head slowly. "All right, Lachlan. You win."

"I always do. Now say it."

Her heart hammered as it broke, but she looked him in the eyes. This was her life. Here with him. He would always outmaneuver her. Her breath shuddered, and her lips trembled. "Make love to me."

He exhaled, his eyes burning. He took the sphere back across the room and set it gently inside a small trunk. He came back, hauled her up to her toes, and kissed her roughly as he walked her backward until she fell on the bed. The dress dug into her back as he climbed on top of her. She winced.

"I'll take it off when I'm done."

His tongue pushed into her mouth, and he pressed down on her, her wounds going deeper.

"Ahem." A voice came from the doorway.

Lachlan turned, shock covering his face. X stood there, an arrow trained on him, a shadow monster behind him.

"If anyone is going to de-flower Tesla, it's going to be me." X's voice was matter-of-fact.

Lachlan snarled, stood up, and threw a ball of energy at X. The monster behind him jumped in front of him, and the spell hit it in the chest. The energy fizzled into nothing in the air. The shadowy monster smiled and slunk to X's side. Taken aback, Lachlan's eyes darted from the arrow, to the monster, to the glow in X's hands. He took a slow step forward, his eyes narrowed. *"What are you?"*

X smirked. "What? You don't know?"

Lachlan raised one hand, spinning white light accumulated over his palm. "You think you can kill me with an arrow?"

"Oh, I'm not going to kill you. I'm going to enslave you."

The sound of running footsteps echoed down the hallway coming toward them. "There's another one coming," the monster thing said.

X didn't take his eyes off Lachlan. "Handle that for me, will you, Fluffy? Thanks."

The monster growled and charged from the room. There was a roar, a blast, and then the sound of Peyton screaming. Tesla struggled to get up off the bed. Lachlan's eyes widened as though he just realized what X was and he took a step back, his lip curling. "Necromancer."

"Release Tesla."

Lachlan grabbed her and held her in front of him like a human shield. "You want her? See if you can save her." He grabbed the gear over her heart and turned it. The whole dress came alive. Every gear stabbed her.

She cried out. "Shoot him."

X loosed the arrow. It went straight into Lachlan's eye. He fell to the floor.

X caught her as she fell and turned her face up. His hands shook above the metal now turning red. *"What do I do?"*

She gasped, her lungs and mouth filling with blood. She couldn't speak. Her consciousness teetered on the edge. He grabbed her hand, entwined their fingers, and moved their hands together over the main gear. A purple blast shot out from their hands, breaking the gear. The dress retracted, the spikes pulling in and the web shrinking back in on itself until it turned back into a spider and crawled away.

She gazed up at him, everything going strangely white around the edges. She was so cold. He put both of his hands over her heart. It jolted her.

"Come on, baby." He said. "Come back."

"Why? Too...Tired."

"I need you, Tesla."

Her eyes fluttered, some of her wounds began to close, but it wasn't enough. "Dying," she whispered and lost consciousness.

X had no time. The threat wasn't squelched. He didn't have Lachlan's soul. But if he didn't get her back to somewhere she could heal, he would lose her. He stripped off his shirt and put it on her. "Come, Fluffy!" he yelled as he picked her up.

The monster came around the corner and flew back into his palm stone like a wisp of smoke. He tore open the air and landed in the Everpath. X ran faster than he ever had in his life. Her blood covered his chest as he held her. The tie he had to her in his hand began to unravel. Her heart faltered.

X kicked the door open to Regia and jumped. His feet hit the floor in her bedroom. "Help!" he shouted.

Syrus took her from his arms and laid her down on the floor. "Put your hands on her heart," he ordered.

X obeyed. Her power was so faint, he could barely feel it beneath his hands. Syrus covered her in lightning. Her wounds closed.

"She's all but bled out," Syrus said.

X took one of his hands from her and thrust it toward Syrus' face. "Bite me."

Syrus bit the side of his hand. X held the bleeding spot to her mouth. "Come on, Tesla," he coaxed. "Wake up a little."

His blood ran down her throat. Still unconscious, the vampire in her awoke and she clamped her lips on his hand and sucked. X and Syrus both exhaled in relief simultaneously. They both exchanged a *that was a close one* look. Feet thudded in the living room and came charging. Forest barged into the room with Merhl and Rahaxeris in tow behind her.

She fell on her knees by Tesla's head. "Oh, my baby." She cried, kissing her forehead. "What's wrong with her?"

"Severe blood loss," X said.

"What happened?" Rahaxeris asked, also kneeling beside Tesla and putting his hands on her.

"I—Ouch!" X yelped, looking down at Tesla. She wasn't just drinking anymore. She'd sank her fangs hard into his hand. Her eyes broke open a slit, and he laughed in release of tension.

"She's going to be all right now. Just some more time," Syrus said, slapping X affectionately on the shoulder.

"She needs elf blood to heal faster," Rahaxeris said. "Let her drink from me now."

CHAPTER NINETEEN

Spellcast words woke Lachlan a second before the arrow was ripped from his head. He pressed his hands over the now-empty eye socket and looked up with his remaining eye at Peyton leaning over him.

"You need a new eye."

"No shit," Lachlan spat. "She's gone?"

Peyton nodded. Lachlan got to his feet, flying into a rage that ended with him collapsing on his bed in tears. He sobbed loudly, heartbroken over Tesla.

"What happened?" Peyton asked.

Lachlan shuddered. "You didn't see him?"

"No. I was chased by some demon. My spells did nothing to it at all. Who else was here?"

"Tesla's boyfriend, I'm assuming. She never mentioned he was a necromancer."

"Whoa. Are you serious?"

Lachlan gave him a droll, one-eyed stare. "That's how that demon thing got in here in the first place, idiot. He brought it with him."

Peyton blew out a breath. "I guess we're both lucky to have survived then."

"Yeah. I was out of it when they left, but I'm sure he had to high tail it out of here if he wanted to save her life..." He put his head in his hands, crying again. "Oh, I hope she's okay. I hope I didn't kill her. She has to live. She must know how much I love her."

Peyton frowned and crossed his arms. "So what now?"

Lachlan stood and collected himself. "First, I'm going to get my eye rebuilt. Then we attack Regia. Send out the word. We prepare for war. I will kill every living creature there and bring my queen back. Tesla must not be harmed."

Darkness and ice. That's what she felt. Cold metal everywhere, separating muscles, tissue, blood and bones. Too weak to wake with a start, Tesla slowly opened her eyes in the darkness. What was the dream? Was she having one now? She wasn't cold, or hurt, or surrounded by silk. She blinked once. Her body felt flattened. It was her bed underneath her. It was X slumped against the side of her bed, holding her hand as he dozed. She was home. He'd come for her. He'd made it, when it should have been impossible.

He'd saved her.

"X," she rasped.

He lifted his head and looked at her, his ice blue eyes bright in the darkness.

"Tesla..." His eyes filled with tears, and he pressed his lips to the hand he held. "I'm sorry."

She reached up and touched his cheek, memorizing his face. It seemed she hadn't seen him in an eternity. She thought she'd never see him again.

"Sorry for what?"

"Lying. Being a coward. Rejecting what I wanted most because I didn't trust it to be real. I didn't trust you. I was scared of the magnitude of what I felt for you...can you forgive me?"

"Yes...I should have waited when you asked me to. I can't believe you came for me."

"No matter where you go, I will always come for you."

"Why?"

A small smile pulled into the side of his mouth. "Insecure again?"

She nodded, her heart flooding with joy. She hadn't lost him. They were still the same together.

"I go through the impossible to rescue you from a fate worse than death, and you're still insecure." He huffed in mock exasperation. "Oh, Tesla, I'm sorry!" he said quickly, when she started crying.

"No." She shook her head. "I'm crying because I'm happy. You're teasing me. I missed you so much. I didn't even realize how much until right now." She shivered, thinking of Lachlan. "So cold and dark without you."

Tragedy filled his eyes. He rose up on his knees, leaning closer to her, and slid his hand inside her shirt until it rested over her heart. She closed her eyes and sighed contentedly.

"I need to tell you about Alex," he said quietly.

"I'm listening," she whispered.

X sighed, steeling himself to pour his guts out and tell her everything so she could understand who he was. But the words wouldn't come out. Not because he couldn't tell her, but it wasn't him anymore. What did it matter? He frowned. No, he owed her the knowledge. Determined to say it all, and yet still he struggled to speak.

"That's okay," she said. "Can you give me the gist of it?"

"Yeah, I can do that...I lost everything. My future. My community. My status. My fiancée. My friends. Even my family. The whole of what my life was, given and earned alike, was taken from me in one second...and yet, if that was the price I had to pay to have you, then I would gladly pay it again."

He stole her breath. Overwhelmed, she cried again.

"I lied, such a terrible lie," he continued. "And I hurt you because I feared being hurt."

"Say it, X. Please. Tell me."

"I love you."

She wiped the tears from her eyes and smiled up at him. "I know. I always knew."

He leaned down and kissed her lips. It was soft, as though he feared she would break. Just as she sighed into the kiss he pulled back.

"Are you okay? I mean, I know you're healing, but are you *okay*? The things he did to you..."

She groaned and rolled away from him, curling into the fetal position. "No. I fear I am not okay. He tortured me. Played with me. Screwed with my head. I don't want you to know what he did to me. I can't talk to you about it. You saw enough for yourself."

He was quiet for a few minutes. "What can I do for you?"

She sniffled. "Hold me."

He climbed on the bed next to her and wrapped his arms around her.

She nestled down into his embrace, her heart unclenching.

"It doesn't matter to me, Tesla. Whatever it was he did. It won't make me stop loving you. You don't have to tell me. I don't need to know."

She relaxed more. "Thank you," she murmured as she drifted back to sleep.

He lay awake for a while, his fingers slowly tracing up and down on her arm. He hardly believed the events of the last three days were real. He'd failed her so badly. True or not, he blamed himself that she'd been tortured. A monstrous hate germinated inside his heart as he remembered the machine dress that had all but killed her. His hands gripped her tighter. Never again would she be hurt because of something he did. *Never*. He swore it to himself.

His only thought had been to get Tesla back...But it wasn't over.

Knowing she was deeply asleep, he got out of bed and left the room. He strode out into the garden and looked up at the night sky. Intuition sniffed the air. X realized he'd kicked the hornet's nest. Not that he regretted it. He crossed his arms and sighed.

The front door opened behind him.

"What are you doing?" Syrus asked, coming to stand beside him.

"Wondering if I messed up. Wondering what I should have done differently when I got Tesla back."

"What does it matter? You got her."

"Hmm...Lachlan's not dead. I don't know how I know, but I know he's not going to retreat. By taking her back, I set things in motion."

Syrus nodded gravely. "You're probably right. War is upon us."

"I have a plan. The dead will protect the living. They are ready... Lachlan is the only wizard I've seen, but he's not alive. Not naturally anyway. His soul is caged inside some sort of object in his body. I have to collect it."

"I've killed a wizard before."

X faced him, his eyebrows raised. "How?"

"The same way I'd kill anyone else in the circumstance. I shot lightning into his eye and fried his brain straight out of his skull, but he was old. I watched him age as I grew up. He never got younger, he wasn't *reconstructed* as you put it when you explained earlier. Perhaps what we will face is different than the one I killed, but still, they *can* be killed. Anything can be killed." Syrus cleared his throat. "I, um, I'm sorry for the way I treated you before."

X chuckled. "Don't. You're the only thing that has played out as I expected."

Syrus raised one eyebrow in question, making X chuckle harder.

"I knew you would be hostile toward me before I came here. I understood."

"Thank you, X. For everything."

"I love Tesla."

"I know that."

"You..." X hesitated unsure how to say it. "You don't object?"

Syrus smirked. "Not anymore. You've proven yourself to me. If she wants to be with you, I won't stand in the way."

Thunder rumbled, and red rolled over the sky. They both looked up, then at each other.

"Here they come."

All of Regia's leaders gathered in Forest and Syrus' garden. The council members of Fortress, Zeren, Rahaxeris, Sabra and Shreve, Merick and Netriet, Merhl, Redge and Journey, Ithiel and the masters of the Blood Kata. X stood off to the side with his new pet, Fluffy, pacing behind him like an anxious dog, while Tesla slept, she was still too weak to stand.

"I will send the guardians everywhere," X said. "Along with the ghosts I've collected."

"We have no idea how this will really play out," Rahaxeris said. "The wizards X and Tesla have described are unlike the ones that infiltrated Regia as spies. All we know is they want us all dead, and they are near impossible to kill."

Forest's eyes lit up. "Wait! Instead of everyone fighting to protect their territories and people, what if we all mixed?"

"What do you mean?" Sabra asked.

"Each race has a particular strength. If we confronted them as a mixed army, all the races together, all our gifts together, and now with the protection of the dead as well, we might be able to tip the scales."

"Yeah. Let's do that," Syrus said.

Rahaxeris gazed at Forest with unabashed pride. "Brilliant… Are we all in agreement?"

Everyone nodded.

Zeren stepped forward. "I will lead Paradigm from Fortress castle."

"All the ogres will open portals in every city and town so the people can mix," Merhl said.

"Where will you be, Necromancer?" Shreve asked X.

"Tesla and I will be with the Heart."

All eyes moved from X on to Journey. "What about you, Journey? Where can your gifts be applied?"

She bit down on her bottom lip for a moment. "I don't know. If I can survive, I will travel through the fighting. I will be everywhere."

"The children need to be put into sanctuaries," Netriet said.

Merick pulled her into his side. "We'll handle that. Where should they go?"

Ithiel looked at Syrus, silent communication going between them. Syrus nodded.

"The Obsidian Mountain can hold the children," Ithiel said. "Well, lots of them anyway."

"We can put children in the underground of the Lair as well," Shreve said.

Thunder cracked over the sky again. Red fracture lines lit up through the blood lock.

"Let's get moving. We're out of time," Forest said.

Instead of dispersing, the weight of the moment held everyone still, looking at one another. Shreve moved first. Eyes bright, he strode to Forest and clasped her in a tight hug.

"I love you, Sister. Thank you for everything. I hope we meet again."

Following his example, everyone began to embrace and say their goodbyes.

"They won't defeat us! Not when we stand together. This is our world. It will stay that way!" Forest shouted.

Everyone raised their voices in a roar of agreement. Merhl opened portals for all of them, and they scattered, leaving Forest, Syrus, X, and Rahaxeris in the garden.

Lachlan held the universe sphere with both hands, resting his forehead against the cool, smooth exterior, watching it break Tesla's wall. In spite of himself, he smiled, proud of her handiwork. He made a mental note to tell her how proud he was when she was back.

Every wizard stood at the ready, prepared to go to Regia as soon as the wall gave. Every wizard except himself and Peyton. They would remain in the castle and watch the battle in the sphere.

"You sent word to everyone about Tesla?"

"Yes," Peyton said. "Although, I don't see that being adequate. She could easily be killed in the chaos."

"True. Here, hold the sphere for a moment."

Tesla's blood was still on the floor of the bedroom. Lachlan put his hands flat in it and came back to the throne room.

"Hold it out," he ordered Peyton.

He put his blood-covered hands on the sphere and closed his eyes, forcing it to take her into itself, along with his will that she wouldn't be hurt. The sphere vibrated and turned hot to the touch for a second. Her face swam into view inside the sphere. She was asleep. He was seeing her in real time. He grabbed the sphere from Peyton and sat down cross-legged with it, running his fingers over and over it in a sensual caress. Light sparked from his fingertips and rushed inside. He put his mouth right next to the surface and exhaled. Her hair blew back from her face. He smiled and pressed his head back against it.

"Tesla..." he whispered.

She frowned in her sleep and whimpered.

"You hear me, don't you, sweetness? I'm going to get you back. You're mine. You know it."

CHAPTER TWENTY

All of Regia prepared for war as fire began snaking through the fractures in the blood lock. This was everyone's fight. Not just the soldiers, but the merchants and farmers, the wealthy and poor alike had the same amount to lose. Thunder continued to rumble across the sky without ceasing.

Forest looked out her bedroom window at the burning clouds. This was the battle of her life, and yet there was a calm inside her, a place that refused to give an inch, like a vault door in her heart. Steel coated her spine and ran molten in her veins.

She looked over at Syrus; he was methodically laying weapons on the bed, carefully considering each one.

"Hey," she said quietly.

He glanced up, meeting her gaze.

"I want one moment, Syrus. Just one."

He crossed to her and pulled her against him. It wasn't desperate, or harsh, but it was solid, something else that refused to give an inch. Their bond connected them tightly, hands, lungs, eyes, hearts, and souls. She exhaled and leaned her head against him. Everything existed in that one moment. Everything that was real. Everything that mattered.

"Kiss me one last time."

He placed his hands gently on her cheeks and tilted her face up. His heart flooded hers as he kissed her mouth.

"That was not the last time, Forest," he said sternly, tapping her on the nose with his fingertip. "Now get your boots on, baby. You've got some ass to kick."

She smiled and nodded. Forest dressed for the fight and armed herself with multiple blades, tucked her one nine-millimeter in the back of her pants, and finally strapped on her lightning sword.

"No matter what, we stay with Tesla," Forest said.

"Absolutely," he agreed.

Only then did her eyes feel hot with emotion. "Our daughter's going to save the world."

He smirked. "I think you're right... Ready?"

She closed her eyes for one second and exhaled. When she opened them again, she was gone. Forest wasn't there anymore. She was a machine of death with cold, surgical edges.

Syrus blinked a few times at her, reading her eyes and body language. "I guess you're ready. Let's go."

X held Tesla in an intimate embrace as she sank her fangs into his neck. He shuddered and pulled her tighter, his eyes rolling back into his head at the amazing sensation. She still felt unsteady to him. She needed more rest to recover, but there was no time left. This was the only strength he could give her.

She pulled her mouth away and rested her head on his shoulder, sighing. "Thank you."

"We've got to go now."

Just as he said it, a new sound broke through the constant rumbling in the sky, a high-pitched shattering, like glass breaking. She jumped at the sound, her eyes rounding. She shoved away from him and quickly pulled on her combat boots and strapped her two, short, lightning swords on her hips. X took off his gloves so his palm stones were exposed. He slung his bow and quiver across his body and picked up his axe.

She reached to open her bedroom door, but he pulled her back and kissed her quickly.

"I love you, Tesla."

"I love you, too."

Forest banged on the door. "Tesla! We have to go now!"

They came out. Rahaxeris was still there. He looked at her intensely for a moment. There was so much he wanted to say plain in his eyes. Instead, he just bowed his head in a quick jerking motion.

"Finish this," he spoke only to Tesla. Then he opened a portal and left.

She glanced at her parents and pulled the air open to the Heart. The four of them went through it together.

The flames of the Heart were surging, stretching high over the tops of the crystal trees. As soon as their feet landed on the ground, the Heart spoke.

Tesla and X, come to me. Don't be afraid, come stand in the flames, the three of us will make the triangle. Hurry. Come be my prism.

X took her hand, and they walked into the manifestation. Both of them gasped and held on to each other as the flames engulfed them. The ground was solid under their feet, but it felt like they were falling in the down-rush of a waterfall. The blood lock crumbled to pieces in front of their eyes. The tesseract breaking and turning black.

Tesla's vision blurred white around X. The tie in their hands glowed bright and hot.

Send out the guardians and ghosts, the Heart ordered X.

The flames wrapped around his hands, and they lit up blue. A shockwave went out from his hands, the dead called and spread out evenly among all the people. They all left him, except Fluffy. Fluffy stood close to the flames, beside Forest and Syrus.

Time to make a lightning storm, Princess. The Heart said. *Let it loose, and I'll enhance it tenfold.*

All she had to do was think about the fire in the sky and the bastard who was behind it, and the pressure rose in her. The flames swirled around her whole body like a coiling snake, pressing on her. She didn't understand or have the time to contemplate what was happening in her. It was glory and it was terror. She opened up, and then she broke apart all the way down to her cells. She couldn't feel the confines of her body anymore, except in her hand, in her tie to X.

Don't be afraid, Tesla. Just hold on to X. I'm going to take the stain he's been carrying and mix it with your power, then I will send it out, the Heart said.

She couldn't answer. She couldn't move. She was hardly there, no longer a person, but a hurricane.

X's hands were her anchor and they were solid. He would never let go.

Forest and Syrus stood outside the circle of crystal trees, their weapons at the ready, protecting their child. They glanced at one another apprehensively from time to time. The shockwave of the dead had been startling, but it had passed them, and only X's pet monster thing remained with them. It paced, breathing heavily, as though impatient to kill something. Forest stared at it; she couldn't help herself. The core of it looked solid, but its edges blurred like black smoke. She felt sorry for it. At one time, it had been a person.

"Thank you for your help," Forest said.

The monster stopped pacing and turned its glowing red eyes on her. "Are you speaking to me?"

"Yes."

It blinked a few times and looked awkward. "Umm...I serve X. He's promised me a new future."

"I understand. Thank you anyway."

It looked nonplused for a second. "You're welcome. Whatever is going on here is more interesting than the place I came from at least."

More shattering filled their ears, and the veins of fire spread into a wave. A blanket of fire covered the whole sky, moving down, with the wizards behind it. The enemy had arrived.

Forest and Syrus moved closer to each other as three wizards approached them. Fluffy slunk in front of them as the wizards began to throw spells. The light and energy absorbed into his smoky chest. One wizard struck the ground; fire ran toward them like a group of snakes. They spread out, and split into more, coming at them from all directions. There were too many for Fluffy to take out on his own.

One fire snake ran up Forest's leg. It felt like being stabbed over and over fast, like a sewing machine needle, covered in poison. She cut it in half with her sword, but that only split it into two. She looked for Syrus to help, but he had his hands full as two of the three wizards were trying to tag team him.

The snakes slithered up her body. Then Fluffy grabbed her, his black clawed hands ran over her, fizzling the snakes into nothing.

"Thanks," she managed.

She tried to help Syrus, but the third wizard was suddenly right in her space. Fluffy was shielding Syrus.

The wizard, young and handsome, smiled at her, his hands burning. "Surrender."

She went invisible, rolled to the side, and came up behind him, stabbing him straight through with her sword. His power grabbed the blade, impaling him, and began to pull it from her hand. Growling, she kicked him in the back of the knee and jerked her sword back out of him. He staggered and made to turn around. He didn't quite make it as Forest's sword cut his head clean off his body. Hissing and sparks rose off his body and head. She kicked his head like a soccer ball as hard as she could before turning his body over and cutting his heart out of his chest. Only it wasn't a heart at all. It was a smooth hard weight, the color of steel.

She looked over at Syrus and Fluffy. They were both fine. One of the two wizards was down, and the last one was effectively evading Syrus' strikes and attempts to grab him. That was until Fluffy came up behind him and passed right through the wizard. He screamed, his eyes going flat, his skin turning grey, and he fell.

Fluffy looked over at Forest and rushed to her, taking the wizard's heart from her hand. "Not good for you to touch like that. His soul is in here."

"So what do we do with it?" Syrus asked.

"Get the other two," Forest said. "We'll give them to the Heart."

Syrus collected the other wizard's souls and handed them to Fluffy. As he approached the Heart, the flames were suddenly covered in lightning. He stopped and turned back to Forest and Syrus.

"I'm not getting any closer to that power. It's transforming." He put the souls into his black chest. "I'll just hold on to them for now."

CHAPTER TWENTY-ONE

Both armies were unprepared for the other. The wizards were thin in numbers comparatively. There were heavy casualties for Regia in the beginning. Then the races found a rhythm for working together, and the tide began to turn. The presence of the guardians caused initial fear. Every werewolf was in beast form. Every elf was invisible, sliding through the fighting, stabbing the enemy in the back. The shifters changed shape constantly, causing confusion. The vampires were direct offense, using their speed and brutality, tearing out throats when they could get close enough. And the ogres moved behind the fighting, opening endless loop portals, grabbing wizards and throwing them in. It was total chaos, but Regia was holding its ground.

Journey drifted near the fighting, just close enough, while Redge guarded her. Reading the wizards was difficult, and at first she couldn't do it. They didn't have hearts. They were strange and cold inside. They were driven by an insatiable hunger for life and power. They absorbed the life of others, twisting it into their own. Each one was a beautiful shell, containing an aberrant soul, perverted by thousands of years of pure selfishness.

Journey hoped to draw from some faint goodness inside them, but she could find none. She sang, trying to hypnotize them with images of the only thing they all feared...their own deaths. As soon as she broke through their consciousness, they stopped fighting and were killed quickly. Or so it seemed. No one took the time Forest had to cut out their *hearts*. They left the fallen wizards on the ground and moved on.

Rahaxeris led Kyhael in battle. He called on all of his years of stretching his abilities beyond what they ever should have been and confronted the wizards approaching the city, the dead as a shield in front, and the people behind him. He took a deep breath as their spells hit the bellis stone walls. So what if they were wizards? He was a sorcerer in his own right, and he would show them something they had never seen before.

He held the bomb cube Tesla had brought from Polyhedron in one hand. She'd turned it into a weapon ten times more powerful than it had been originally. And now he thought, if she were here, what would she do? A black stone hung around his neck. It was the most powerful stone he'd ever created. It held a thread of his essence inside it, a fragment of everything he knew and everything he was.

Rahaxeris took it off and fed it to the cube through its fluid exterior skin. The cube shivered and changed color from red to black. He reached down and opened a portal in the ground, sending the cube through it. The juggernaut bomb settled outside the city walls.

The sound of the explosion broke the eardrums of everyone in the vicinity. The ground was blasted open, a deep crack ran around the outside of Kyhael like an empty mote. The wizards that fell into it were torn to tiny pieces up by the grinding gears of magic deep inside the ground. Half of those attacking Kyhael died in its teeth. The other half quickly used their own magic to make bridges to cross safely.

The beautiful walls of Kyhael broke to rubble under the onslaught as the remaining force flooded into the city. Everyone fought valiantly, but as soon as they breached the walls, Rahaxeris could see many Regians were about to die.

The creamy colored bellis stone streets ran red with blood.

At the base of the Obsidian Mountain, Netriet faced the largest guardian there. "You!" she pointed at it. "Walk directly in front of me."

It nodded and took its place. She marched fearlessly up to the closest wizard, his spells bouncing off the guardian. She reached right through the dead thing and choked the wizard with her robotic arm. His head hung half off his neck when she let go. She turned her attention to the next one.

Merick had his own guardian in tow, but he used a different technique than Netriet's. Armed with a cache of throwing stars, he dipped each one in the dead before throwing them. The dead's essence, wrapped around the stars, sank into the bodies of the wizards Merick stabbed.

Along with the masters and a smattering of others from every race, Netriet and Merick held the line at the mountain, where most of the children were hidden.

Sabra led the people at the Lair with a frightening example of a beast mother's fury protecting her young. Shreve had her back at all times, and as skilled and knowledgeable as he was about the wizards, having spent his childhood with them, it was Sabra's savagery that invoked fear in the attacking force. And those she led adopted her example. Some of the wizards actually ran from the Lair.

It looked like an easy victory at the Lair, especially when Journey arrived.

All over Regia, the wizards were falling fast...but just when it seemed as though victory was in sight, those who had fallen began to rise again, their bodies rebuilding themselves, and now they knew what Regia's forces had to offer and how to get around it.

The flames of the Heart pushed out over the crystal trees. Forest and Syrus had to move out farther, but it didn't stop. The manifestation was no longer confined. It began to spread through the wood like a real fire. Lightning laced through every lick of flame. In moments, the whole wood was engulfed in flames.

"We've got to get out of here!" Syrus yelled.

"I'm not leaving my daughter!"

Burning branches began falling around them.

"Come here," he said.

Forest ran to him. He held up his hands, and a dome of electricity formed over them, holding out the flames. Fluffy paced outside the dome.

"Are you all right?" Forest asked him.

The monster nodded.

Tesla's storm was complete. It filled the Heart. The stain turned her lightning black. X held her around the waist, keeping her from flying apart. His vison was blurry, but he could see that Tesla was no longer conscious. She was awake, but the girl he loved was not there. He held onto a weapon.

It's ready, the Heart said.

Under the ground, the Heart of the world inhaled, holding its power.

Then it exhaled. The storm covered the entire world. In the air, and underground. Clouds walled over the sky, shutting out the sun. It was a perfect storm, and Tesla was both the eye and the epicenter. It was the beginning of the end of the battle. Regians were immune from the storm. Lightning strikes, filled with the power and malice of the evil stain, struck the wizards from overhead and reached up from the ground and wrapped around their feet.

The wizards stopped attacking and tried to shield themselves from the storm, but it was no use. In a few minutes, every wizard fell.

Your turn again, X, the Heart said.

Tesla was limp in his arms, now fully unconscious.

It's all right, lay her down. I need your hands.

X was reluctant to let go, but he laid her down gently. The white flames held her up off the ground.

"What must I do?" he asked.

Call the dead to you. Not one wizard soul must be left in its body. I will do to you as I did to Tesla. I will enhance your ability. Together, we'll get it done.

X closed his eyes, his hands waking up.

Good. Now place your hands flat on the ground.

He did. The Heart grabbed hold of him and held his hands fast. The power rammed through his palms and shot out again under the ground like a shockwave. Blue light snaked up from the ground under the bodies of the wizards. It reached inside and pulled their souls out. X braced himself and gritted his teeth as they came rushing to him. It felt like trying to holding back the ocean.

All the young, beautiful bodies of the wizards turned white and crumbled in on themselves, leaving a sick smell behind.

X knew the second the last soul came to him. The Heart let go of his hands, and he stood up.

"I don't want to keep them. How do I get rid of all of them?"

The flames wrapped like ribbons around his hands again. *I'll take them. I always meant to. I will burn them up. Nothing will remain of them. The race of wizards is no more. I will take the guardians as well. You don't need to be burdened with them.*

"But I made them a promise."

Have no fear. I will separate them and send them on to the next place. I'll leave the ghosts you brought from that other world for you to deal with.

Another rushing went through his hands, and when he looked back down at the stones, they were almost empty.

Take Tesla out of here. It's going to get really hot as I kill the wizard's souls.

He picked her up, but before he could step out of the manifestation, the Heart said, *Thank you, X. I am in your debt. Whatever you want, if it is in my power, I will give it to you.*

He looked down at Tesla. She was still unconscious. He knew what he wanted, but he wouldn't ask without her consent.

"Can I have some time to decide?"

Of course.

X stepped out of the flames.

Forest and Syrus rushed toward them with Fluffy behind them.

"She's all right," he said quickly, seeing the worry on their faces. "She's just unconscious."

Syrus took her from his arms. He didn't want to let go, but he wasn't going to argue. X looked up and around at the fire-ravaged woods. The three of them exchanged hopeful glances.

"Is it over?" Forest asked.

"The Heart has taken their souls and is burning them up."

"What about the ones you held?" Forest asked Fluffy.

"Gone. They were sucked out of me a moment ago."

"If it's not over, then it's almost over," Syrus said, smiling. "And guess what? We won." He shifted Tesla in his arms. "Let's take her home."

CHAPTER TWENTY-TWO

Tesla…Tesla…

She woke with a start in the dark of her bedroom, Lachlan's voice in her head. Her head swam as she sat up. X was passed out in the chair in the corner, his head slumped against his chest. She slid silently out of bed and crept toward him. His weapons, stones, and gloves were lying on the floor next to his feet. One of the stones was clear but the other swirled with black. She picked up the black one and strapped it to her left hand.

"It's not over," she whispered to X, too quiet for him to hear. "I have to go…I love you."

Quietly, she put her boots back on and strapped her lightning swords around her waist. This was the last time, she told herself, that she would sneak out in the middle of the night. Taking a deep breath, she tore the air open.

She'd never felt so alert as she landed in the Everpath. She'd never felt so strong, so alive, and in control of her power. Far down the hall, her eyes settled on the door to Mordian. She lifted her hand and touched the stone. The darkness inside rose up to meet her fingertip, then blackness rushed into the space next to her.

X's monster looked down at her, surprise in its demonic red eyes. "I don't serve you," it rasped. "I only serve X."

"Yes, I know. But I'm X's girl, and he wouldn't want anything bad to happen to me, so I hoped you might be willing to come with me. There's two wizards left in desperate need of killing. Will you help me?"

"Why did you not ask X to come with you?"

She blushed. "He must not see any more of me in Lachlan's company. I fear he might not love me anymore if he sees what I have to do."

"I don't understand, but I will come with you. Are we going to the castle you were rescued from?"

"Yes."

It growled, kind of like a purr of pleasure. "Good. I want to finish that one who ran from me like a little girl."

"He's all yours. The other one is my target."

Her steps were sure as she swaggered to the darkest place she'd ever been. Diamond edge focus crystalized in her mind. In that moment, she embodied the best of both her parents, but she wore it with her own style.

She didn't kick the door in, though she thought about it. Instead, she opened it quietly and moved into the same marble room where she'd first fought Lachlan. She walked to the hall that led to Lachlan's bedroom, Fluffy following close behind.

The door was open. The room was torn up, and Lachlan was sprawled on the bed, seemingly asleep, the sphere he'd shown her on the pillow next to him.

"Go find the other one," she whispered to Fluffy.

He smiled and charged off down the hall.

She approached the bed. He didn't stir. She blew out a breath and climbed on the bed next to him. She smoothed his hair off his beautiful face.

"Lachlan...I've come back." Her voice was quiet.

He opened his eyes and looked at her. "I'm dreaming."

"Yes. And this is going to be the very best dream of your long life, after you take my voice back."

He blinked and reached for her. She didn't pull away.

"Everyone is dead. Peyton and I are the only wizards left."

"So? What did they mean to you anyway? So long as *you* live forever, that's all that matters. I'm here. I'll give you everything you want, but you must take my voice back first."

He shook his head, his eyes clearing. He smiled and rolled her under him. "I'm not dreaming. You came back. Why?"

"You understood me. I'm built for submission. I want it."

"You're lying."

"Okay fine, I want the power you offered me. And I want you. No other man could measure up to you. You're a god."

His smiled broadened. "Why should I take your voice away when you say such sweet things?"

"I want to rely on my own power to speak. But I won't know if I've pushed my limits unless you let me test them."

He looked dubiously at her. "You're playing a game."

"I thought you liked those."

Doubt continued to grow in his eyes. She grabbed his wrist and placed his hand on her breast. His eyes immediately smoldered.

"Don't you want me?"

"Yes."

"You promised me pleasure beyond anything I could imagine. I want you to fulfill that. Take my voice first. Then rock me until this mute girl screams."

He laughed darkly. "Okay, my queen. I accept the challenge."

He kissed her mouth, his tongue going down her throat. Burning vibrated down her neck as he swallowed her voice. Then he pulled back a little, his eyebrows raised.

She opened her mouth to speak. Nothing. Her voice was gone.

He moved his hands over her and kissed her mouth. She kissed him back. Her hands rested on his shoulders for a second before she wrapped them around his neck. He yelled as she lit him up, lightning covering his head, snaking into his mouth, ears, and eyes.

Roaring, he rose up and threw her across the room.

"The game just changed, but it will still end the same way!"

She shook her head and drew her swords. He laughed and took a step toward her, his hands erupting in flames.

The lightning in her hands connected to the lightning in her swords. The blades lifted off her hands, hovering inches over her skin. They flew at him like harpoons, dragging a rope of red electricity. He would have been able to dodge them, except at the last second, the lightning broke both swords into three sections, the glass reshaping into six spiraled drills.

The glass bore into his body, one in each knee, both arms, one through the chest and the last between the eyes. With the electricity, she pulled the drills back to her, her power healing the swords back into two blades as she caught them.

He fell back on the bed. She jumped up on his chest, slit his throat

340

for good measure, and cut his *heart* out. Unsure how to collect his soul from the hard, metallic lump in her hand she put it in her back pocket. She picked up the sphere and threw it against the wall, shattering it.

She jumped down from the bed and left the room. She stopped at the door and looked back. His torn up body turned white and began to crumble. Tesla spit on the ground, shut the door behind her, and went to find Fluffy.

He was licking his blood-covered teeth, sitting next to Peyton's body. He held up Peyton's heart for her.

"There you go. That was most satisfying, I must say," he said.

She smiled and put Peyton's heart in her other back pocket.

"All finished? Shall we go now?"

She shook her head and touched her throat. When he looked confused, she opened her mouth in a silent scream and pointed, shaking her head again.

"You lost your voice?"

She nodded.

"Okay, um... Should we go?" he asked again.

She held one finger up and then gestured for him to follow her. There was just one last thing...Iva.

Tesla opened the carved white door; the smell of rain greeted her.

"Tesla..." Iva said as she came into the domed room and placed her hand on the soft fur. It moved and wrapped gently around the tips of her fingers.

I can't speak, she thought.

"I can hear you," Iva said. "So long as you are touching me."

I've killed Lachlan. I came to say goodbye.

A ripple moved over the floor. "I'm glad you were able to escape his grasp...I would ask a boon of you before you go home."

What?

"Kill me."

Oh, Iva, no.

"Please. It would be mercy. I've been here so long. My world is dead. My race is dead. Please help me move on from this slavery?"

Tears filled her eyes. *All right. If you're sure.*

"I'm sure."

You brought me comfort, Iva. I'll never forget you.

Another ripple crossed the floor, and the rain stopped falling through the ceiling. "Goodbye," Iva whispered.

Closing her eyes, Tesla put both of her hands flat in the fur and sent out a powerful shock. She gave it everything she had, not wanting to draw it out painfully. Iva turned a charred black. Every hair shriveled down and smoke rose up.

Iva? Iva?

There was no reply. Wiping the tears from her cheeks, Tesla stood and left the once amazingly beautiful room, with its unique inhabitant. Fluffy followed her silently as she went back to the main room and opened the door to the Everpath.

X was still asleep in the chair as she landed in her room. She held the stone up and Fluffy flew back inside it. She set the stone, and the two souls on the floor next to his pile of stuff. He roused a little as she took off her swords and put them under her bed. She watched him from her bed as she unlaced her boots.

He yawned and opened his eyes.

"What are you doing?"

She came to him and reached for his hands. He frowned at her, lacing his fingers through hers.

"Tesla?"

She shook her head.

"Your voice is gone?"

She nodded.

"How did that happen? Was it the battle?"

She exhaled, feeling her throat open up again in response to X.

"No. It wasn't the battle... You're going to be mad at me."

"I doubt that."

"Here, look." She pointed to Lachlan's and Peyton's hearts. "I didn't know how to put them into the stone so I just brought them back for you to take care of."

He looked down and then back at her. "Where did those come from?"

"Mordian."

His eyes widened. "Don't tell me you—"

"I took Fluffy with me. It wasn't over, X. I had to kill Lachlan... You're angry."

343

He exploded, jumping to his feet. "Why did you go alone? Why didn't you wake me?"

She shrank back from him, trembling. Tears pooled in her eyes and began to run down her cheeks. Everything fell in on her at that moment, and she could no longer stand. Her muscles jerked with tremors as the adrenaline she'd been running on ran out. Physically and mentally she was fragile, and his anger broke the last vestige of strength she had.

"Get out!" she shouted before curling into herself on the bed sobbing.

Furious and now confused, too, he just stood there for a second. "I don't believe you." His voice was empty. He grabbed his stuff from the floor and left, slamming her door behind him.

With shaking hands she reached up and pinched the first layer of the atmosphere and pulled it around her bed like curtain. She was visible to others. They would be able to see and speak to her, but no one would be able to touch her. Her lungs struggled to fill when she breathed, her chest shaking too violently. Everything she suffered in Lachlan's castle, everything she'd experienced during the battle, killing Lachlan, killing Iva. It all crashed over her like a black wave made of nightmares.

Sobs wracked her as post-traumatic stress set in.

CHAPTER TWENTY-THREE

X left the house and attempted to walk off his mad before tearing open the air and taking himself to the Heart. The burned forest made his heart heavy.

X. You're back so quickly. Have you decided what favor you would like? The Heart asked.

"No," he huffed. "I have two more souls for you to burn up."

Just toss them in... Something vexes you.

"Tesla makes me crazy."

The Heart laughed. *Yes. Love will do that to you. Let it go, whatever it is she did. It's not worth hanging on to.*

"You love her, too. Don't you?"

Oh, yes. Very much.

He sat down and picked at the ground, thinking. "I'm still just human."

Not so. You're much more than that.

"Even if she chooses me, compared to her, I will grow old and die very quickly."

True. But why do you say if?

"She could change her mind. I had thought to ask you to make me her destined life mate as my gift, but now...I think... Can you give me a

345

lifespan to match hers?"

Good choice. Yes I can. But since you're somewhat emotional at the moment, I'll not grant your wish right now. Get rid of your vexation and then decide.

X sighed and stood. "Okay. Thanks. Hey, whatever happened to those ghosts I pulled from the tree? I never saw them again."

Glad you asked. Come back tomorrow and you will see. Make sure Forest comes, too.

"Until tomorrow then."

When he got back to the house, Forest and Syrus were in Tesla's room, and she was still crying. He hated the sound of her sorrow. Why had she shrunk back from him like that? So what if he was mad? So he yelled? Did she think he would hurt her?

He stood in the doorway and looked in. Both Forest and Syrus were begging her to let them in. He could see the shield she'd put around herself. Forest looked at him desperately.

"Can I talk to her alone?"

They left the room and closed the door. He knelt beside the bed. She faced the wall, her whole body shaking with tears

"Tesla?"

She quieted, her body going rigid.

"What's going on? Why did you pull away from me? I wasn't going to hurt you. You know that, don't you?"

"You yelling at me was just the straw that broke me. I know you wouldn't hurt me. You should leave, X. I don't want you to see me like this. I've got to process some shit."

"You don't have to do it alone."

"I do. Just like I had to kill Lachlan alone. It just had to be that way, and I can't tell you why...or, I don't want to rather. You said you didn't need to know. You said you wouldn't stop loving me." Her tone turned accusatory.

"Okay. I meant what I said. I just...how would you feel if it was me?"

"I know. I'm sorry."

He was silent for a minute. "Hey," he said in a louder happier voice. "We won, you know. It's actually over. Everything you've been working so hard to protect, Tesla. You did it."

She rolled over and faced him, her eyes bloodshot and puffy. Then she smiled, reached through the barrier she made and touched his hand. "Yes. I haven't had time to feel that yet. I will. Thank you for everything. I know it was terrible. I can never repay you."

A devious smile pulled up the side of his mouth. "Sure you can. You can repay me today, tomorrow, and every day forever after that, just by being mine."

"Oh, X." She smiled, but the next second, she was crying again. "Please leave. I'm sorry. I will be myself again...I'm just not her right now. I love you. But the way I am right now, if you stay, I'll hurt you. I won't mean to. Please..."

He hung his head and nodded. "Okay. If that's what you really need. I guess I'll go home. I'll wait for you... When you're ready, you know where to find me." He kissed her hand, still on top of his. His lips lingered over her hand, then he abruptly got to his feet and left.

She stared at the door he'd just walked out of, a new misery piling on top of the others. It hurt to send him away, but she had to. She curled in on herself again, missing him already, and feeling her ability to speak aloud begin to ebb away.

X set his stuff down and bid Forest and Syrus goodbye.

"Thank y—"

"No," Syrus cut him off. "Don't thank us. *We* thank you. You have our eternal gratitude. No matter what happens between you and Tesla, you're always welcome and wanted here."

Syrus shocked him by giving him a brief hug. Forest hugged him tightly and seemed reluctant to let go.

"I don't have the words, X," she said.

He smiled warmly at her. "I don't need them. Oh, but I do have to tell you, the Heart wants you at the wood tomorrow. Requested you."

"Oh." She looked surprised. "All right...are you sure you won't stay? There's going to be some amazing parties."

"No, thank you. I'm not keen to take any more knives in the back."

They all chuckled.

X sobered as he picked up his axe, bow, and knapsack. "I know I will see you again. Hopefully sooner rather than later."

He could have lingered. It was tempting. Instead, he nodded to them and tore the air open and left.

His eyes adjusted in the Everpath. He couldn't go home just yet. He had a promise to fulfill. In his searching for Tesla, opening every door along the way, he'd found the perfect place to free the ghosts he still carried. X opened the door and stepped through.

The landscape was the exact opposite of the barren hell he'd originally found these souls in. It was quiet and empty, but beautiful. The air was soft and fragrant. He touched the stone on his right hand, summoning them out. None of them spoke or even looked back as they flew away. Some laughed. Some sang. Fluffy was last out.

He looked down at X and then at the world around them. "This pleases the others. But it's not for me," he said in his gravelly monstrous voice.

"What? You want to go back to the hole I found you in?"

Fluffy laughed. "No. I'd like to stay with you, if you don't mind. I hope you will help me remember who I was before I became this. Inside the stone is comfortable, and I've enjoyed the adventures you've made me a part of."

X was touched, not that he'd say so. It was weird to have such a freakish friend, but that was what Fluffy had become. "All right, don't get soft on me. It's incongruent with your looks."

He barked out a terrifying laugh and flew back into the palm stone. X opened the door and left.

It was hard for Forest to leave Tesla alone, but that was what she insisted she wanted. The sounds of celebration traveled faintly through the windows from far away. Forest leaned against the window frame and listened to it. It was more beautiful than a symphony.

Syrus brought her a glass of wine and wrapped his arm around her shoulders. "I can't get my head around it."

"I know. Me neither," she said. "I feel exhausted and strung out and high all at once."

"Well, drink too much, and you can add drunk to that list."

She chuckled. "Not sure if that's a good idea or not."

He clinked his glass against hers. "The wizards are dead. If that's not the best reason to get hammered, I don't know what is."

She took a sip and nodded thoughtfully. "Hmm...I think we should break out something stronger. Wanna bet who can last longer?"

"Oh, I can drink you under the table."

She smiled. "Prove it."

Two hours later, they barely managed to stumble into bed before passing out.

In the middle of the night, Forest woke suddenly. She got up, her head pulsing. She ignored the pain and went to Tesla's room. She knew her child needed her.

She knocked and opened the door a little, poking her head in. Tesla was still on the bed in the fetal position. She looked over her shoulder at her mother and pulled the barrier she'd made aside, reaching for her. Forest held her tightly, absorbing the shocks through her body as Tesla cried.

"I love you so much, baby. Everything will be all right. You're strong."

She pulled away from her mother and began signing. *I tricked Lachlan to taking my voice back. I wanted nothing of him to linger on me like that. I'd rather be mute the rest of my life than remember him every time I spoke. X got mad at me, because I snuck off and killed him on my own. I get it. I would have been mad, too.*

She began sobbing again.

Oh, Mom, it's so ugly. So wrong what he did to me. X wanted to

350

help, but I can't tell him. But I have to get it out. But I feel bad asking that of you. It will be hard for you to hear.

"Tell me, sweetheart. Tell me everything you need to."

She did. It was terrible for Forest, but she held it together and listened. Finally, finally, Tesla seemed to be finished telling her awful story, and she collapsed into sleep. Only when she was sure Tesla was deeply asleep did Forest allow herself to cry over what her daughter had suffered. She sat there on the floor, next to her bed, smoothing her hair over and over as she slept, just as she had done when Tesla was a baby.

Knowing what had happened to Tesla and what would have happened to her, Forest's gratitude to X grew into love and a hope he would always be in Tesla's life.

She stayed with her until she could feel the dawn coming. Forest crept from her room and went to wake Syrus. He groaned and gave her a dirty look as she woke him.

"I have to go to the Wood. Tesla confided in me last night. She's taken the barrier down. I don't want her to wake up alone."

His nasty expression vanished and he got up. "Of course. I'll go sit with her... She told you what happened to her?"

"Yes," Forest whispered. "It was ugly, but it could have been worse. She was right to send X away. She needs some time to work through it. But even so, it's a weight she will carry her whole life. She will move on. I know she will."

He sighed and rubbed his face. "I want to know, and I'm terrified to know."

"I won't tell you the details. She was tortured, but she wasn't raped."

Even in the dark, Forest could see the pressure of tears pushing in his temples. He swallowed and nodded his head gravely. "She'll be okay," he agreed. "She's tough like her mother."

"Yeah, but she's tenderhearted like her father."

He gave her a look of mock outrage. "Watch your mouth, woman. I am no such thing."

She kissed him briefly. "Okay, tough guy. I have to go now."

Forest left the house with a heavy spirit, but more than a little curious that the Heart had requested her presence.

Maggie let go of Merhl's hand, stepping ahead of him, her eyes beholding Mordian for the first time. They stood on a precipice, looking down on a shimmering, pale gold city. She swallowed, her body waking to her native land. Her power surged through her in a way she had never felt before. This place should have been her home, now it was empty, devoid of life. Her heart filled with bitterness and sorrow. She was the last of her kind. All the witches were dead, and now so were the wizards. She shook her head in disgust. Such a foolish waste. Such poor decisions.

She turned away from the city and walked past Merhl. "I just need a few minutes."

"Take all the time you need. There's no rush. You could live here, if you wanted."

She shook her head firmly. "Alone? No."

"Not alone. With me."

"No," she said again.

Maggie touched the trunk of a tree, a flower, the ground. She breathed deeply, committing all of it to memory. The feel of it, the look, and the smell.

She turned back to Merhl and reached for his hand. "I'm ready for something new. I've been alone so long in a foreign world. I want to be where I'm not afraid. I'm ready to see Regia."

He gathered her into his arms. "It makes me happy to hear you say that. I know Forest will grant you citizenship. You won't have to hide who you are. I know my friends will love you, as I do."

She smiled and raised her eyebrows. "As you do?"

"Well, not quite like I do." He leaned down and kissed her mouth.

She sank into him, happy.

"Do you need to go back to Contarren first? Get your things?" he asked.

She thought about it for a second then shook her head. "No. I left nothing behind I care about, or that will hurt anyone who might stumble across it... There's just this."

She took off her stone necklace, kissed the smooth surface briefly, and threw it over the edge of the precipice. "I'm ready to go now."

CHAPTER TWENTY-FOUR

Forest crossed into the wood just as the sun came up. Mist covered the ground, pooled at the roots of the charred trees. The burned ground crunched under her feet. All the shadow sand was gone, burned up with everything else. So much of her life, she had been right where she was now. Her heart broke roughly. She never thought it would die. The wood was a part of her. Shi was a part of her. Forest rubbed her hand over her aching chest. How could those pieces of her be gone? How did she go on without them?

Her eyes tunneled as she walked. There were no paths to take anymore. She didn't have to snake around the edges to get to the interior; she walked a straight line through the wood, to the Heart. Why did it want her? She'd never had any connection to it. It had always been too painful for her to get close to.

The thick growth of the ribcage was burned to nothing. There was nothing left alive. The crystal trees stood the same as always, their leaves chiming the music the Heart bid. She stopped, her breath catching. The flames were white and it didn't hurt to be so close to the manifestation. The music was hope, no that wasn't it...she listened closer. It was life. Life beginning.

The flames sparked around the edges. *Forest.*

She gasped again as she heard the voice of the Heart for the first time. It was so beautiful. She knew something was about to happen. Her hair stood on end.

"Why me?"

Of course you. And you're just in time. Do not fear. Stand still where you are. Watch.

Shimmering white light ran out from the base of the flames in snaking lines, like roots in every direction. The ground broke open, a sapling tree pushed up to her right, stretching toward the sky. Then another one sprouted up to her left. The two trees grew to full maturity in seconds. Their branches filled to bursting with bright green leaves and white flowers. The trees were gorgeous, vibrant, and huge.

Another wave of light came out from the Heart, wrapping around the new tree's roots, up their trunks, out through every leaf and flower petal. Iridescent sparkles winked inside and all over the trees. Then light went out from the new trees. It raced along the dead ground, life surging in its wake. Grass, flowers, and vines all broke through the ground.

The ground opened up and swallowed every dead tree, a new sapling sprouting in every empty place.

Do you see, Forest? They have been sleeping so long. Dormant, under the poisoned ground. Trapped. Those who died are gone, but their children are not.

"Seeds?" she whispered.

Indeed.

Bittersweet tears filled Forest's eyes. "All who died?"

Well...all but two. Turn around.

Forest turned, her knees going weak. "Oh!"

Shi caught her as she stumbled. *Real* arms held her. Forest looked into Shi's gorgeous face. She was alive! Really alive. No longer twisted with branchy arms and legs. She looked exactly as she had in the memory she'd showed Forest. They clung to one another and cried.

"Mother."

"Daughter," Shi breathed.

Forest let go and took a step back. Out of the trunk of the second tree that had first sprung up came Ler. Young, alive, and looking a little confused. He looked at the tree he'd just stepped out of, then over at Shi and Forest. He flexed his hands, and then touched the trunk. He looked back at Shi; amazed joy lit up his smile.

"I'm a dryad!" he shouted. "I'm alive, and I'm a dryad!"

"Yes, Ler," Shi said.

He ran at her, scooped her up and spun her in a circle. "We got our second chance!"

"That's not all," Forest said. "Look."

They looked around, beyond each other. Shi's eyes rounded, and she looked fearful. "Do I dare hope?"

Hope. The Heart said. *Your race is reborn.*

"Shea?"

No. Your sister is gone. But her child now grows in her place. The seed of your nephew's life survived, deep underground. It is for you to raise him, along with the children you yourselves will have.

Shi put her hands on her abdomen. "But my womb was removed."

You have a new body, Shi. Just as Ler is no longer a vampire. You are fertile, free to have the family you were denied before.

Shi and Ler clung to each other again, their tears of joy flowing freely.

Forest cried, too, overwhelmed and sure she must be dreaming.

She followed Shi as she ran to her sister's old place. She reached into the trunk of the sapling and pulled out a baby boy.

"Oh, my," Shi breathed, looking down at the child in her arms.

He opened his new eyes and blinked at her before wailing. She laughed and cuddled him close. He quieted as she started rocking him.

"What will you name him?" Forest asked.

"Hmm...X, I think."

Ler nodded. "Yes. I think so, too."

Forest lingered, thrilled, and her heart overflowing that Shi was alive, but she knew it was time for her to leave them alone. She would come back very soon. Before she went home, Forest approached the Heart again.

"I don't have the words to properly tell you the depth of my thanks, for allowing me to witness this miracle."

I have known you for so long. Since you were a child. I always loved you. I always wanted to talk to you, but you never could come close enough. I long to spend more time with you. Come back often.

"That will be no hardship."

She glanced over at Shi and Ler and the baby X. All around the wood, other young dryads awoke and stepped out of their trunks. Forest went home and told Tesla and Syrus all about the resurrection of the Dryad race. The happy news brightened Tesla up a bit, and she seemed anxious to go there and see for herself, but she was still despondent as the day matured.

She closed the door to Tesla's room, leaving her alone when she asked for solitude again.

"I should go in to Fortress. I'm feeling desperate to track down our family and friends. I hope they all survived."

"Sure. I'll stay here with her. If you talk to Journey, and she's up for it, you should ask her to come here and help Tesla through this."

"I will, if I see her."

Forest went to her office. The foyer of Fortress was crowded with people, looking for loved ones, or seeking confirmation that the threat was truly gone. Not wanting to be snagged, she turned invisible and snaked her way through the people to her office. She closed the door and sighed, thinking she would probably be alone in there but she was wrong. Kindel had Ena against the far wall and was kissing her passionately.

"Well, well," Forest said loudly, dropping her invisibility. "I think you two are in direct violation of co-worker fraternization rules."

Ena's cheeks turned pink, but she giggled.

Kindel raised one eyebrow. "What are you going to do? Fire us?"

Forest walked toward them, smirking. "I'll let you off with a verbal warning this time." She embraced both of them and laughed. "How long has this been going on?"

"A while," he said. "You've been out of the office for a long time. And since you're here, and everyone's so happy the wizards are defeated and all, I'm going to ask for some time off. Ena, too. We'd like to travel."

Kindel pulled Ena into his side.

They looked perfect together, Forest thought. "Take your time off. Be gone a long time. Just promise you'll come back."

Ena hugged her tightly. "Of course, we'll come back. I love my job. I love you, Forest."

Forest kissed her cheek, thankful for her friends.

"Make her happy, Kindel," she said sternly.

Before he could respond, Ena said, "Oh, he does."

Forest jerked her head toward the door. "Get out of here, lovebirds. Go enjoy each other."

The rest of the day, Forest traveled all over Regia, tracking people down. She found them all. Netriet and Merick, Shreve, Sabra and baby Sophie, Redge and Journey, Zeren and Merhl, who introduced her to Maggie.

Finally, Forest went to Kyhael. Rahaxeris was deep underground in the *Rune-dy* headquarters. He embraced her as she walked in. He'd always been so stiff when touching her, but now he held tight, and for a long time, he didn't let go.

"You didn't look for me," she accused.

"I knew you were safe. You're my child. I always know. If you hadn't come here, I was going to come to you tonight."

"I smell smoke."

"Yeah, it's controlled. Come see."

She followed him down the hall to Menjel's old operating theater. The whole room was on fire, the flames contained by a clear force field over the doorway. Instruments and books were in the fire as well. She looked at her father quizzically.

He shrugged. "Thought I'd purge the darkness from this place. The *Rune-dy* is no more. It's a good thing. I'm moving on to something else.

Not sure what yet. Something... *noble*, for a change. My granddaughter needs a clean space to work. She'll have it here, from now on."

"I need to go home, now, Dad. Come see us soon. Tesla is fragile right now."

"I've been hard on her. I won't be anymore. Or, I'll try. She exasperates me, but she knows I love her."

Forest nodded. "Yeah. She knows."

She left and made her way home.

Regia had suffered heavy casualties, but those she loved most were safe. Many times during the day, she pinched herself, too happy to believe she wasn't dreaming.

When she got home, Journey was there. She went into to Tesla's room and shut the door. The sounds of her Storyteller's voice drifted faintly under the door. Forest and Syrus waited silently on the couch in the living room.

After an hour, Journey came out and sat down across from them. She sighed heavily. She looked so tired. "You were right to ask me to come. I've healed most of her heartbreak and uncoiled the places in her mind Lachlan twisted. The rest is up to her. But she's strong, as I'm sure you know. She'll be fine."

"Thank you so much, Journey. You've done so much for us. If there is anything we can ever do for you, just ask," Syrus said.

She looked pointedly at Forest. "There is something. Perhaps it is not in your job description as Hailemarris, I don't know. But I'm sure you could pull some strings for me."

"What do you want?"

"There are children orphaned by this war. Redge and I want to

360

adopt. Can you make that happen?"

Forest smiled warmly. "Of course. That's perfect."

In the days that followed, there was as much celebration as there was mourning. Tesla acted more like herself, but she would leave the house a few times a day and take long walks alone. When she did cry at night, it was only because she missed X.

CHAPTER TWENTY-FIVE

Contarren wasn't home anymore. Maggie was gone. Since he'd left Regia, the days grew painfully long. X felt like he was walking through an endless graveyard. He thought about lighting his fire and beginning a forge, but he could think of nothing to make. He could take up his job as an executioner again. When he considered it, it didn't feel right for him anymore, like wearing someone else's clothes.

But all that was external.

Not for one second could he get his head clear of Tesla. Not going back to Regia, waiting as he said he would, was the hardest thing he'd ever done. He could hardly sleep. He listened all night. Every breath of wind, every creaking tree branch, had his heart racing with hope it was her.

She was hurting, but she shut him out. She was ashamed of what had happened to her. She wanted to hide it from him. Maybe she was right. His memories of rescuing her plagued him as it was. That metal dress kept creeping into his nightmares when he was able to doze off.

He paced, not knowing how long, thinking about her. Fantasizing about her. Touching her. Imagining her saying things to him he'd kill to really hear her say aloud. Memories of all the details of her soothed him as much as tortured him. She *was* his, he kept telling himself, attempting to reassure his aching heart.

How long would it take her to come to him? How long could he hold still and just wait? As long as he had to. His resolve was firm, but that didn't mean it wasn't bitter.

The longer he was alone, the more his old insecurities came back. What if she never came? What if she changed her mind? What if she found her destined life mate right as she was planning to come to him? Why hadn't he just asked the Heart for what he wanted the moment it offered him a favor?

Then her voice would come back into his mind. *I love you, X.* He had to keep trusting her.

The afternoon was cold, and needing something to do, X picked up his wood axe and decided to chop firewood. He walked away from his house, knowing the exact tree he was going to cut down.

A breeze, a fragrant, otherworldly breeze slid around him. He turned, his heart in his throat. He threw his axe down and ripped off his gloves as she ran at him, tears streaming down her cheeks. She slammed into him, staggering him back a step.

X…X…X… She said in his mind. *I'm sorry.*

"It's all right," he said breathlessly, holding her to him. "I missed you so much."

I never want to be a part from you again. Never.

"That works for me."

He strained her against him and kissed her mouth, trying to absorb her. Something had changed between them, grown stronger. He had to ask her something, but he couldn't stop kissing her yet.

More, X. More. She demanded.

He moved his mouth to her ear. "Oh, I'll give you more. But there's something else first."

She looked up into his eyes, expectant, maybe a little apprehensive.

"Will you marry me?"

She gave him a cute little smile and held up one finger, closing her eyes. Then she cleared her throat. "Yes," her voice was weak. She cleared her throat again. "Yes!" she said loudly. "But you have to let me mark you."

"Do it now."

She laughed.

"I mean it. Do it now. Right now."

Her expression turned totally serious. She wrapped her arms around his waist and moved her mouth to his neck. She kissed his neck once. "I love you," she breathed against his skin, then she bit him.

For the first moment it was the same as any other time she'd bitten him. She pulled back for a second and then bit him again in the same place. Her blood flowed over the small wound and then in. She let go. He put his hand to his neck and looked at her. The spot was hot like a sunburn, scars raising on his skin in a crescent. The heat eased back to a subtle warmth.

She was inside him, a part of him now.

He put his hand over his heart. She watched wide-eyed as he pulled a strand of blue light straight out of his chest. It was ghostly transparent. He wound it in a small circle and the two ends fused together.

"Here," he reached for her hand. "This ring is made of a piece of my soul."

It slid onto her finger where it shrank down to a perfect fit. She looked down at it, open-mouthed.

"I..."

He waited for her to finish. She didn't. She just stared at the ring on her hand. He was about become worried it somehow displeased her.

"Tesla?" he whispered.

She looked up, tears streaming from her eyes again. "I don't know what to say."

"Just say yes again."

She wiped the tears away and smiled. "Yes."

"You're mine now."

"Yes. And you're mine."

He picked her up and carried her into his house, booting the door shut behind them. He set her on her feet and ran his hands through her hair.

"Are you thinking of being disrespectful?" she teased.

"Absolutely not. You have a total commitment from me. There's no disrespect here."

She took a small step back from him and unbuttoned the top buttons of her shirt. The heat in his eyes shifted into concern.

"Are you all right?" he asked. "Is there something wrong with your heart?"

She laughed and snapped her fingers in his face. "Nothing wrong with my heart. I'm seducing you."

The worry left his eyes, and he smiled, looking down at her chest. "Okay then...Don't stop now."

They learned together the insanity, the heat, the wild sweetness they could give each other physically. Ecstasy broke through her pain.

Her body rushed into the stars that turned into incendiary explosions all through her.

He buried his face in her neck, trembling.

"I love you. I love you so much, Tesla. I can't stand it."

I love you, too, X. She said inside his head.

She fell asleep in his arms. Peaceful, painless, and finally satisfied.

After a while she woke in the dark. Her head rested on his chest. A small smile curved her lips. Her mind replayed everything. Now she knew what all the fuss was about between people in love. This was the only thing that could quench the frustration and the desire. And X was the only man she ever wanted to do this with.

She wanted to take him home to Regia, but maybe not just yet. She kissed him awake.

"Again," she demanded.

He answered her, just not with words.

The morning was foggy and cold. X packed everything he wanted to take, not that it was much.

"I'm starving," he complained. "Let's get out of here."

She carried his bow and quiver, and he hefted the rest of his stuff as they went to the Everpath and then home to Regia. They landed in her room and put everything down.

"Is this going to be awkward?" he asked.

"I don't know. Maybe. Let's get it over with."

They came out into the living room. Forest and Syrus were in the kitchen.

"Oh, X!" Forest said. "So glad you're back."

"We need to tell you both something," Tesla said.

X looked at Syrus. He pursed his lips and gave a little grunt in the back of his throat. They already knew what was coming. It was obvious.

Tesla held up her hand so they could see her ring. Forest got up and hugged her. Syrus got to his feet as well and stalked toward them.

Syrus sighed. "All right." he grumbled lightly. "What does this mean?"

"We're engaged," Tesla said, then she looked at X. "I said that right? Engaged?"

He nodded.

"Sure. Marriage is not a Regian custom, but we understand." Forest said. "I see she's marked you, too."

Syrus shot X a look.

"You said you wouldn't get in the way if she chose me," X reminded him.

He held his hands up. "All right. All right. I did say that. Sorry. Doesn't make it any easier on me though."

"You plan to stay here, right? In Regia?" Forest asked desperately.

"Regia is home," X said.

"So you want to have a wedding?"

Tesla nodded emphatically.

"It will be the first one ever in Regia," Forest said. "That will be fun."

"Fun?" Syrus groused. "When is this to happen? And what are you going to do, X? Where are you going to live?"

X smiled. "We're not rushing this. I will find my place in Regia, and I will build our home first...There's been so much happening. We want to take some time to be together without stress and danger pushing on everything."

"Not immediately, and not too long," Tesla said.

Later that day, a message came for X from Maggie, asking him to come to the Onyx castle.

"Don't you want to come with me?" he asked Tesla.

"No. It's all right. She just asked for you."

Traveling the way Tesla did was easy for X now. He pulled the atmosphere open and went to Halussis. Maggie waited for him in the entrance hall of the castle.

"Hey you," he said companionably, giving her an easy hug. "I was wondering what happened to you when I went back to Contarren and you weren't there."

She smiled warmly. "Looks like everything worked out for you."

"Yes. And what about you?"

"I'd say everything worked out for me, as well."

"Of course, you always know don't you? Have you seen anything else in the future?"

She shook her head. "No. I've given that up. I left the stone behind."

"So...you live here now?" he asked.

"Yes. This is where Merhl lives, so that's that. I like it here."

"Me too."

Her expression sobered, and she frowned. "I know I'll always feel guilty for what I did to you…"

"Don't, Maggie."

She shook her head. "Please tell me you're happy."

He grabbed her by the shoulders. "Happy is not an adequate word for what I am. Let it go. Stop feeling guilty."

She seemed to struggle with her emotions for a moment, then her expression smoothed, and she smiled again. "Okay." She held out her hand to him. "Friends?"

He smirked and shook her hand. "Friends…I guess we'll see a bit of each other from time to time."

"Yes, without the added bonus of you waking me up early in the morning with you darn metal work."

He laughed lightly. "I'm glad you asked me to come here. It's good to see you. Are *you* happy?"

"Oh, yes. So happy."

In the middle of the night, Forest lay staring at the ceiling, unable to sleep. She listened to Syrus' peaceful breathing next to her. She placed her hand gently on his forearm, and everything inside her relaxed. They had come through the most amazing and terrible fire, and yet remained intact. She had lost no one, when she'd been sure she would lose everyone. Regia was safe. Her family was safe. But something stirred inside her. Life was precious because tomorrow was not promised. Safety was never guaranteed. Love was an amazing gift, not given to everyone.

A small smile curved her lips as she slipped out of bed. She opened her top dresser drawer and pulled out a black silk sheath of a nightgown. It was a garment she hadn't worn since the very beginning of her mated time with Syrus. She pulled off her frumpy pajamas and let the silk glide over her body. She sighed and shivered. It felt so good, and it would feel better yet, as soon as Syrus touched it.

She picked up her portal ring and slid it onto her finger. Her lips woke him softly. He responded to her in a half-awake state, and that wasn't going to do for her. He tried to pull her against him, but his eyes were still closed. She drew away.

"Wake up, my love."

"I am awake." His voice held a hint of sleepy annoyance.

She took a step back so the moonlight coming through the gap in the curtains fell across her. "Look at me," she whispered.

She saw his eyes barely crack open. The next second he was inhaling sharply and sitting up. "Forest." He said her name with reverence.

"Follow me," she commanded as she opened a portal and stepped through it.

He did. His bare feet landed on the soft sand. The violet, silvery light emanating from the water shimmered in his eyes. In the early days of their relationship, they had often come to these waterfalls to make love, but that seemed like so long ago to him. He smiled, now fully awake. Where was Forest?

He looked around near the beach, but she wasn't there. He looked out at the water, and his heart stopped. She was standing under the falls. Her long hair clung against her skin as well as the black slip she wore. The water sluiced down her body, glistening on her skin as it went.

Her eyes taunted and teased him, daring him to come to her. Her beauty created a kind of madness inside him. Despite the fact the water was cool, as he plunged into it, Syrus felt nothing but fire in his veins. He swam the whole way under the surface, breaking through right next to her.

He put his feet down on the rock shelf and gazed at her. He wanted to grab her and ease the passion she'd created in him, but because he wanted it so badly, he hesitated. She lifted her chin defiantly in a silent dare when he didn't touch her.

He had no desire to deny himself or her, but since she was in the mood for playing...

"What's gotten into you, minx?" he asked.

"I'm happy." She said it with such ferocity she almost sounded angry. "Aren't you?"

"Hmmm..." A low rumble came from deep in his chest. He stared at her, slowly. His eyes roaming over every inch of her. "I am happy for many reasons, but right now, I'm happiest I regained my sight. You are perfect, Forest. A goddess. And you're all mine."

She reached for his hand and pulled him through the falls into the cave hidden behind the water. She pulled his soaked shirt over his head. He lifted her up, her heart next to his own, and kissed her mouth. "Baby..." he whispered as he moved his mouth to her throat.

"Yes. Exactly that." Her tone was matter-of-fact.

"What?"

"*Baby*. I want another baby. I thought this was a good time and place to make one."

He set her back down, blinked at her a few times, and then raised her hand to his lips and kissed it. "Are you sure?"

"It wasn't an easy thing to decide but I'm sure. I want to try this again."

His face remained relaxed, but his happiness shone through his eyes. He lifted her back up again, kissing her slowly. "You're phenomenal. So brave. I can't tell you how much I love you, Forest."

She smiled. "Then don't tell me. Just show me."

He did, better than he ever had before. And she conceived their son.

EPILOGUE

One year later...

Forest put Maddox down for his nap in the afternoon and went to help Tesla finish braiding her hair. Tesla was sitting at the kitchen table in her dressing robe, absentmindedly twirling a white rose between her fingers, her eyes out of focus. Forest smiled to herself, looking at her daughter. She wasn't in pain all the time now. Her magic was settled, and she was in control of it, so she no longer accidently hurt people with her hands. And she could speak easily, as if she'd never been mute at all.

"Penny for your thoughts," Forest said, picking up the comb and parting her hair.

Tesla shook herself and set the rose down. "Just daydreaming about tonight."

"There's not much time left. I bet people are starting to arrive, the over-eager ones anyway."

"Have you talked to X? I haven't seen him since last night," Tesla said sadly. "I miss him."

Forest snorted. "It *is* your wedding. You'll see him in an hour."

"I know. It's just been hours and hours."

"Still as much in love as ever?"

"More."

Forest leaned over and kissed the top of Tesla's head. "Your dad snatched X first thing this morning to keep him away from you."

She *tsked*. "Figures."

"Aww. He loves X. You know that. I promise your father will not scowl even once today."

She giggled and picked up the hand mirror, looking at the back of her hair. "That's perfect, Mom. Just like the picture on Pinterest."

"Oh, good. I was afraid I was going to mess it up. Hair is not my thing, you know."

Tesla stood. "I'm going to get my dress on. Help me?"

"Like you need to ask."

Tesla's dress was a flowy, white bohemian thing, that cut low in the front so her heart was visible, taking away the need for her to wear any jewelry. It was a relaxed, natural look that didn't distract from Tesla's unique beauty.

"You look amazing. Perfect."

"Thanks, Mom."

She looked at herself in the mirror. "I'm ready."

The dark of the warm, summer night flowed over Regia. Light shimmered through every flower on the ground and in the trees. The white flames of the manifestation burned bright and iridescent, reflected on the crystal trees. All the guests were gathered and waiting. All of their family and friends, old and new, with young dryads dispersed throughout the crowd as well. X stood next to the Heart, Syrus and Ler at his side, waiting for Tesla. Forest stood on the other side of the Heart, Shi next to her.

Everyone turned as Tesla stepped onto the grassy path the Heart grew just for her. The crystal trees began to chime music as she walked slowly forward. Her eyes fixed on X, then she looked down, blushing, overwhelmed. She looked back up again and continued forward.

He took her hand, and everything else seemed to blur in the background. Light went out along the ground from the flames, stretching under the feet of everyone there.

The world is safe because of these two. The Heart said, speaking inside everyone's minds. *They are both unique beings, and they love each other without restraint. Ever since X met Tesla, he's feared he would lose her to her destined life mate. Before the war, I merged their power together, but even then there was something else binding them. And neither of them knew it. I knew it, but I didn't tell them. I will tell them now, as I will tell all of you. Perhaps for the first time in Regia's history, there are a pair of lovers that are truly soul mates.*

Tesla's eyes widened in shock. "Did you know?" she whispered to X.

"No." He shook his head.

As is the custom in human weddings, I will now ask you if you commit yourselves fully to each other, forsaking all others, and will live for one another, forever, until death?

"I will."

"As will I," Tesla breathed.

Then step forward and place your linked hands in the flames, and I will bind you together in a new way.

The flames twisted like ribbons around their hands, slid through them, and tied a new invisible knot.

As you wanted and requested of me, X's lifespan will now match Tesla's. You may go through your lives, secure in a knowledge granted to none. That neither one of you will outlive the other... It is done. Kiss your bride, X.

Applause erupted through the wood as X kissed Tesla.

Go now. Celebrate. Make your future extraordinary. Be an example of true love, worthy of Regia's history.

The reception was held by the coast at Netriet and Merick's property. A pavilion had been built for the party. White silk tents were filled with food, and tables were placed all over outside, under the stars. Lively music played and people danced.

Maddox squirmed in Forest's arms and drooled on her shoulder. She lifted him up and blew a raspberry on his tummy. She walked on the outside of the crowd and just watched. Kids seemed to be everywhere. Sophie toddled around, into everything and causing Shreve grief as he tried to keep up with her. Sabra was pregnant again, and close to bursting. Netriet carried her baby daughter in the crook of her robotic arm. Melina was only two months and slept like a champ. She had her mother's blonde hair and her father's dark brown eyes. Redge and Journey's three adopted children ran around the place like maniacs, up past their bedtimes and high on sugar. Maggie and Merhl hung close together, laid back, and always seeming to have more contentment than anyone else. And Ena looked like the wedding was giving her ideas. She and Kindel were happily settled together, and Forest wouldn't be surprised if Ena was the next to have a baby bump.

Zeren and Rahaxeris walked over to her at the same time. They both made faces at Maddox in turn, trying to make him laugh.

"You must be so proud, Forest," Zeren said. "Tesla settled and now considered the most skilled scientist in Regia."

"Well, she is," Rahaxeris said sternly. "She deserves her acclaim."

"She's easy to be proud of," Forest said.

"How is X settling into his new job at Fortress?"

"Easy as pie. He's the best interrogator I've ever seen. He always knows when someone's lying. And when someone refuses to talk, he just brings in Fluffy. That always seems to loosen their tongues… He's getting quite the reputation. The necromancer with a pet demon. Yeah, no one wants to be questioned by him."

Tesla rushed up then and reached for Maddox. "Give me my brother. I want to spin him around the dance floor."

Forest handed him over.

"Oh, yes, big boy," she said in that silly voice only reserved for when she talked to him. "You're such a chunk, aren't you?"

As she watched Tesla take Maddox to the dance floor, she suddenly felt choked.

"Are you all right?" Rahaxeris asked.

"Fine, I just need a minute…" Forest walked away from the party, out to the edge of the cliffs, where she stopped and turned back. She took a deep breath, trying to get her heart to stop racing. The ocean breeze cooled the tears on her cheeks.

Syrus came up silently behind her and wrapped his arms around her. She sighed and leaned back against him. For a few minutes, they just stood there, silently watching the party.

"You know, I've never felt from you what I'm feeling right now," he said quietly. "What is this feeling?"

"Joy… Wild, unabashed joy."

"Ah, yes. That's it."

"Look at all this, Syrus."

"I am. It's amazing."

She turned in his arms and looked up at him. "We're safe. There's peace and oh, so much life. Children everywhere."

"And Dryads," he offered.

"Totally. How awesome is that?"

"Pretty awesome, my love."

She put her hand flat on his chest and felt his heart beat. "Thank you."

"For?"

"Saving me."

"You are my heart, my soul, the breath I breathe."

"You were the catalyst of so much of this here, now, when you came into my life."

He shook his head. "No. It wasn't me, Forest, and it wasn't you either. It was *us*."

The eternal bond that lived inside them lit up and pulled them together.

They kissed, silhouetted against the backdrop of the sea. A symbol of strength, honor, and love to all who knew them... They were legends.

THE END

ACKNOWLEDGMENTS

When the idea for Forbidden Forest first came to me, I had no idea it would become a seven book series. I have to thank a few people for sticking with me on this writing journey. First of all Amanda. You have been with me on this from the very beginning and you've helped me so much when I would hit a wall. You've listened when I was hyper with ideas and advised me through it all. You truly are my book's midwife. They are my babies, but you tell me when to breathe, when to relax, and when to push. Thank you.

Thank you to my husband, my real life alpha male. My children for being sweet turkeys. My writer's group, I love you all so much! You're such good friends. A special thanks to my editors and beta readers, Val, Ally, and Kristy. A huge shout out to my FB group for all the encouragement and support, especially Jessica C.

And a heartfelt thank you to you, my reader. I hope you will stay with me and come on many more adventures in the future.

www.ingramcontent.com/pod-product-compliance
Lightning Source LLC
Chambersburg PA
CBHW070621260626
47161CB00007B/2528